ISLAMERICA:

Isa, Y'shua, Jesus

Alexander Wilbur Fredrickson

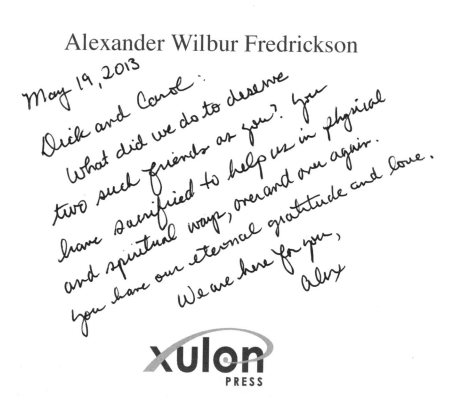

May 19, 2013

Dick and Carol:

What did we do to deserve two such friends as you? You have sacrificed to help us in physical and spiritual ways, over and over again. You have our eternal gratitude and love.

We are here for you,

Alex

xulon
PRESS

TABLE OF CONTENTS

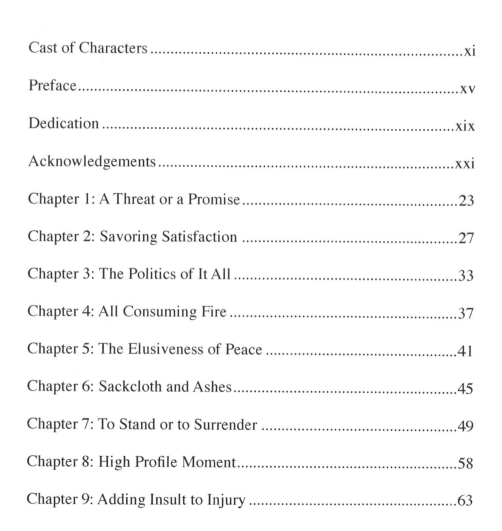

CAST OF CHARACTERS
(in order of reference or appearance)

Mark R. Basel, Pastor of the Church of the Transformed

Ariel Basel, Wife of Pastor Basel

Tim Basel, Son of Mark and Ariel Basel

Tom Basel, Son of Mark and Ariel Basel

Grace Basel, Daughter of Mark and Ariel Basel

Shlomo "Sol" Malachi Ben Y'sra'el, Orthodox Rabbi

Samson "Sam" Tuvya Ben Baruch, Prime Minister of Israel

Mundhir Kanaan, President of the Democratic Republic of Palestine

Sanaullah bin Laden, Caliph of Babylon

Addar Mansur Zaahir, Imam in Democratic Republic of Palestine

Ahava BenY'sra'el, Wife of Rabbi Sol Ben Y'sra'el

James Jacob Paulson, President of the United States

Hope Paulson, Wife of President Paulson and First Lady of the United States

Abdul-ghafoor Asim Abdullah, Vice President of the United States

Eddie Murdock, White House Chief of Staff

Naomi Levine, Messianic Friend of Vice President Abdullah

Rachel Meir, Foreign Minister of Israel

The General of the Babylonian Brotherhood

Zebulun Bartimaeus, Member of the Church of the Transformed

Hannah Fiedler, Secretary of State of the United States

Aaron Fielder, Husband of Secretary of State Fielder

Ratib Shadid, Vice President of the Democratic Republic of Palestine

Eric Battista, Atlanta Police Officer

Frank Noel, Atlanta Police Officer

Bruce Booth, Atlanta Police Sergeant

Joe Peterson, Atlanta Police Officer

Phillip Gabriel, Atlanta Police Officer

Salah Udeen Waleed, Brotherhood Army Officer

Zeev Tzion, Defense Minister of Israel

Shimon Ben Yehudah, Internal Security Minister of Israel

Abigail Wilenski, Deputy Foreign Affairs Minister of Israel

Yitzhak Gid'on, Science and Technology Minister of Israel

Ruth Keren, Justice Minister of Israel

Yaakov Nessa, Religious Services Minster of Israel

Muzaynah Afham, Muslim Mother

Charlie Lloyd, Director of the Federal Bureau of Investigation

Harold Erdmann, United States Secret Service Director

Hajar Dizhwar, Mother of Haziqah Dizhwar

Hajib Dizhwar, Father of Haziqah Dizhwar

Noah Ben Eleazar, Homefront Defense Minister of Israel

Ibrahim Shajee, Father of Jahm Shajee

Tahera Shajee, Daughter of Ibrahim and Mufiah Shajee

Mufiah Shajee, Wife of Ibrahim Shajee

Jahm Shajee, Son of Ibrahim and Mufiah Shajee

General Pierce Ellis, Chairman of the Joint Chiefs of Staff of the United States

David Rothschild, Defense Secretary of the United States

Matthew Davidson, Homeland Security Secretary of the United States

Lt. General Gideon Sharon, Military Chief of Staff of Israel

Robert "Bob" Steer, White House Press Secretary

Moshe Levine, Deputy Defense Minister of Israel

Joel Goldberg, Surgeon at Shaare Zedek Medical Center

Hadassah Weinstein, Nurse at Shaare Zedek Medical Center

Michael Rosenberg, Ambassador to Israel from the United States

Esther Ben Baruch, Wife of Prime Minster Ben Baruch

Reggie Paulson, Son of President and First Lady Paulson

Vic Paulson, Son of President and First Lady Paulson

Howard Longreen, Secretary of the Treasury of the United States

Kaashif Shajee, Muslim Reporter

Mordecai Levinson, Surgeon at Shaare Zedek Medical Center

Alex Tower, Weapons Transport Driver

Ethan Battles, Weapons Transport Driver

Mansur "Manny" Farris, Train Engineer

Emil Suarez, Train Station Controller

Lucius Black, Executive Office, USS Jimmy Carter

Samara Pall, Division Officer, USS Jimmy Carter

Lemuel Begin, Israeli Police Officer

Palti Goldbloom, Israeli Police Officer

PREFACE

❖

Faith.

This first volume of *Islamerica* sets in motion a journey of faith through the most difficult circumstances imaginable. The fight of faith bobs and weaves through ghastly political intrigue, barbaric displays of hatred, and the very incarnation of evil. Though tested, tempted, and tried, faith stands firm.

During a planning trip to Israel in the fall of 2010, I felt our Lord Jesus urging me to write a novel—what would turn out to be a trilogy. As my wife and I walked through the Muslim Quarter in Jerusalem, I knew the stage would be the last days, and the drama played out on it would be the islamization of America.

At that time, I had already preached on the islamization of Europe. Even so, the leaders of the European nations were only beginning to admit what could no longer be denied. Europe would be forever changed by Islam.

On September 22, 2010, German Chancellor Angela Merkel put it mildly when she said, "For years we've been deceiving ourselves about this. Mosques, for example, are going to be a more prominent part of our cities than they were before." In fact, Muslims plan to add another 200 mosques in Germany by 2015—more than double the current number. This goal may prove to be understated, as ground has already been broken for another 125 mosques and as Muslims want to convert hundreds of closed churches into mosques.

In 2012, about five million of Germany's 82 million people declared themselves to be Muslim—an increase of at least 9,000 percent in the last 30 years. While some experts predict the current Muslim population to double by 2020, other demographers disregard such small estimates as wishful thinking, based on the past growth rate alone.

With the dramatic increase in the Muslim populace, homegrown terrorism is on the upswing in Germany. In the summer of 2012, German Intelligence Chief Gerhard Schindler warned all of Europe to be on guard against the threat of terrorists that receive training within their borders or who leave Europe to be trained in places like Afghanistan, Pakistan, North Somalia, or Yemen.

Surveys of German citizens in 2012 show they worry over their government's policies of political correctness and multiculturalism, which have yielded a bountiful crop of Muslim immigrants who refuse to assimilate into German culture. Instead, the followers of Allah want to be accommodated by Germany to the point of having their own separate society, government, and legal system, all based on Sharia Law—which allows no criticism of Islam, Allah, Muhammad, or the Qur'an. In fact, under Sharia Law, such insults can carry a sentence of death!

Other surveys show that 80 percent of Germans believe Muslims deny women's rights, while two thirds feel Islam promotes violence. 60 percent say the followers of Allah are motivated by revenge and retaliation, and a similar percentage say Muslims want to convert Germany to Islam. As such, Muslims distributed 25 million copies of the Qur'an translated into German in 2012—enough for almost every household to have a free copy.

In the fall of 2012, two German cities signed treaties with Muslims, allowing Islam to be taught in the public schools. Hamburg, Germany's second largest city, and Bremen will allow Muslims to develop the Islamic curriculum for their students, further demonstrating how Muslims refuse to integrate into German society.

Indeed, Germany does not stand alone in the process of islamization. In fact, France has the largest Islamic population in the European Union. A third of the French population under the age of twenty worships Allah. In the larger cities like Paris, almost half of the babies are born into Islamic families. Incredibly, Islam may soon surpass Catholicism as the main religion of France.

Likewise, in Belgium, Islam now challenges Christianity as the nation's largest religious bloc. Muslims make up one quarter of Belgium's population, while one out of every two newborns has Muslim parents.

In England, where the Muslim population doubled in the last decade and should double yet again by 2030, Muhammad is the number one name for baby boys. Great Britain now hosts more than 1,000 mosques—most of them former churches—and approximately 90 Sharia based courts that dole out the brutal and barbaric law of Islam.

By most estimates, the islamization process in the United States falls about twenty years behind where the European Union stands today. Thus, considering the European model and current U.S. trends, the Islamic population here should double within two decades.

Already, Sharia courts operate on U.S. soil, even as the Organization of Islamic Cooperation (OIC), the association of 56 Islamic states for international Muslim solidarity, claims legal jurisdiction over Muslims in America. While the number of mosques across the country has jumped by 74% since 2000, United States' taxpayers fund the construction of mosques around the world. Worse yet, as jihad training camps teach American Muslims the ways of terror, the American President solicits political advice from the Muslim Brotherhood—the world's original Muslim terrorist organization.

The Brotherhood's plan for the islamization of the United States—for the entire world—began long ago. Can what has been set in motion be undone or have we ignored and denied the reality around us for too long? Furthermore, what can Jesus' followers do in a world rapidly falling into the dark shadow of the false god of Islam?

Though Europe may lead in the race, America does not trail far behind in the dash to islamization. Based on the foundation being laid by Muslims today, will Islam establish a worldwide Caliphate in this century? How will the one Body of Christ on this earth rise to face that challenge?

Indeed, while the world of tomorrow overflows with uncertainty and fear, it also abounds in hope and faith. While wars and rumors of wars rage, as destruction and chaos abound, the Light still shines for all who choose to see it!

In chapter fifteen of *Islamerica*, Pastor Mark Basel says of the growing number of Muslims throughout the world, "They are all around us, and we cannot defeat them, but we can win their souls to Jesus the Messiah!" Even now, across the Arab and African nations, untold numbers of Allah's disciples leave Islam each day to follow Jesus!

The path of death and destruction as well as the road of mercy and grace are traveled by the various characters who live in the coming pages. I pray their experiences, both the evil and the good, will point living souls to the one Saviour and Lord of this world.

As unrestrained hatred and limitless violence collide with unadulterated love and selfless sacrifice, who will be left standing? Consider such stark contrasts in the framework of the end times, and you will be ready to fast forward into the frantic but faith-filled future of *Islamerica: Isa, Y'shua, Jesus.*

December 28, 2012
Alexander Wilbur Fredrickson

DEDICATION

To my wife, God's gift to me, and our daughters, His gifts to us both. A special thanks to my bride who was the first person to read this book and encourage me to write the next two.

ACKNOWLEDGEMENTS

*I*n order to protect ministries and friends from the possible repercussions of this book, I will not name any organization or anyone
that helped me with research and information—that assisted me in
completing this assignment given to me by Jesus. If I could list and
thank my sources, several pages of this novel could be devoted to
them.

I can say that our ministry partners have given their unconditional
support and unending prayers at every stage of the process which led
to the publication of this book and those that will follow. Likewise, our
church family has steadfastly stood with us at every step of the way,
celebrating each little milestone with us, and encouraging us to move
forward.

Truly, without the team at Xulon Press, *Islamerica* would not be
in your hands. From day one, everyone associated with Xulon has
offered their expertise and kindness to a first time novelist. Xulon
shines as a first class operation and all who serve with it stand as dedicated followers of Jesus.

Thank you for purchasing volume one of this trilogy. Our prayer
is that it will not only open your eyes to the rise of Islam in America
and the world, but that it will also open your heart to the amazing
and boundless love of Isa, Y'shua, Jesus, the Forgiver of all sins, the
Righter of all wrongs, the Lover of all souls!

*"Remember thy Lord inspired the angels (with the message):
'I am with you: give firmness to the Believers: I will instill
terror into the hearts of the Unbelievers: smite ye above their
necks and smite all their finger-tips off them.'"*
Qur'an 8:12

CHAPTER 1

A THREAT OR A PROMISE...

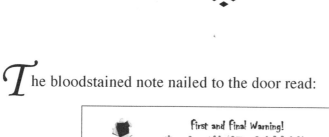

$\mathcal{T}$he bloodstained note nailed to the door read:

With sweat dripping off his brow, Pastor Mark R. Basel peered over his shoulder to his right and then his left, yet he saw no one on the hot and humid morning. Of course, Mark knew these odious men would not give him the satisfaction of truly showing themselves—at least not until they were ready to act.

Nonetheless, he slowly turned around and thoroughly scanned the landscape in front of the church. Early on that sticky Sunday morning, he could see no faces in the windows, yards, and cars on the quiet street. If indeed the terrorists could see him—and the pastor knew they could—their camouflage worked perfectly.

As he attempted to bring his racing heart beat and rapid breathing under control, Mark remembered witnessing and experiencing this mixture of fear and anger before, but not here, not in the United States (U.S.), not in Atlanta, Georgia!

He thought, *"I see one of the Brotherhood Army's symbols at the bottom of the page. I see the swords and the Qur'an. I read their warning, 'Be prepared!' This mantra means they are ever ready to face the enemies of Allah. Regrettably, the Brotherhood considers our congregation to be the sworn enemies of Islam."*

A thousand other thoughts rushed through the minister's suddenly inundated brain. *"Should I take this bloody threat at face value? Should I do what the terrorists demand? What would happen if we did close the church and did not return to it—ever? Should we run and hide or should the congregation and I meet and challenge this threat as it has been presented? Should we stand firm without fear and trepidation? Has the time come to enact the plan we have rehearsed for so long?"*

The dark bloodstains on the paper prevented Mark from reading all the words. Those drops of crimson were not dry but fresh. In fact, a couple of drops of blood ran off the page into the minister's large right hand. Troubled, Mark wondered, *"Is this human blood? If so, is it the blood of one of the terrorists or someone tortured or killed by the Brotherhood? How could this blood still be wet? Did the cringing cowards nail this ultimatum to the church door just moments ago?"*

The steamy shepherd tightly closed his eyes. *"Why today, Jesus, why today? Why is this blood-spattered warning posted on the door of Your church, the Church of the Transformed, today?"*

In the darkness behind his moist eyelids, the preacher wondered. *"Perhaps this threat comes in retaliation for my role in the peace accord that was signed four months ago today. Maybe this crimson missive promises vengeance because I influenced the Palestinians to choose self governance rather than Sharia Law. Then again, the Caliph could want my life because I guide followers of Islam to eternal freedom through Isa. Then again, these foreboding words might have nothing at all to do with me. Maybe the jihadists have come randomly to our congregation for the opening salvo of the inevitable attacks that the churches of America will face.*"

"No," Mark said to his Lord. "The terrorists have not come here by accident or coincidence, have they? Our congregation has been chosen. I have been chosen by the terrorists."

At six feet and five inches tall, with square, broad shoulders, Mark typically intimidated people by his sheer presence alone. Even so, at this moment, he felt like his back was pushed up against the wall. This man of faith viscerally sensed the overarching threat of the gory note. As he inhaled deeply, he opened his eyes to read the menacing message once more.

"We will hunt down your sons like wild animals and kill them!" God had blessed Mark and his adoring wife Ariel with two boys. At eight years old, more than blood tied Tim and Tom together. They chose to be best friends. Mark could not imagine anyone "hunting them down," and the very thought of some conscienceless terrorist killing his twin sons sent an icy shiver up his spine, despite the thick heat of the summer morning.

The loving father cringed when he read the next line for the second time. *"We will take your daughters as wives and they will bear children for Allah's Holy Jihad!"* Mark knew Muslim war possessed no holy qualities whatsoever. Instead, all the savage violence thrived on absolute evil!

The Lord had entrusted one precious female soul to Mark and his beautiful bride: thirteen year old Grace. From the moment he first held his lovely gift from Heaven in his strong arms, Grace had wrapped her 240 pound dad around her little finger! Now, vile henchmen threatened to snatch Grace away from her loving parents! The very possibility of losing Grace to such a fearsome fate forced the big man to tremble.

However, the threat loomed even larger. Mark said to himself, *"These programmed terror producing machines promise to kidnap or kill all the children of the church! Actually, they swear to kill everyone if I fail to comply with their devilish demands."*

The more Mark read, the more his fear waned, and the more his anger increased—accompanied by a likewise rising tide of hatred. From experience, Mark knew this potion of powerful emotions often proved to be deadly! Old and far away feelings remained closer than he prayed for them to be. This father of three recalled the last time he had allowed such anger and hatred to be expressed. He flinched at the dark remembrance and shook his head. "Not again!" Mark whispered in prayer. "Never again will I allow such poison to flow out of me! Help me Lord to keep that promise I made long ago to both You and me!"

Firmly resolved, the minister turned back to the entrance of the Church of the Transformed. With his handkerchief, he wiped the blood off the door, unlocked and opened it, entered the fellowship hall, and then glanced at his watch. His family and the congregation would not be arriving for another hour and a half. He had time.

Despite the chaos of the moment, the pastor began to rest in the peace of His Saviour and Lord. Accordingly, Mark knew what he must do!

"Peace I leave with you; My peace I give you. I do not give to you as the world gives. Do not let your hearts be troubled and do not be afraid.
John 14:27

CHAPTER 2

SAVORING SATIFACTION. . .

Sol had not witnessed a more beautiful afternoon since the afternoon of the day before! Though painfully hot and dry, Israel's lovely summer days always boasted a perfectly blue and cloudless sky.

Even so, this particular Sunday seemed quite special and unique for Sol—Rabbi Shlomo Malichi BenY'sra'el. *"Four months to the day!"* he said to the blue sky as his long white beard rose and fell in the searing breeze.

Eighteen weeks prior, Rabbi BenY'sra'el, an Orthodox Jew, had witnessed the signing of the historic peace treaty between the time-worn enemies of Israel and Palestine. Moreover, he had played a key role in brokering that long sought agreement that set up a Palestinian republic within the borders of the Jewish state.

Sol felt that God Himself had appointed him to the task of working out the details of the ambitious accord. The Israeli Prime Minister, Samson, Sam, Tuvya Ben Baruch, and the new President of the Democratic Republic of Palestine (DROP), Mundhir Kanaan, had signed the peace treaty in Sol's very presence. In fact, in that extraordinary moment, the portly rabbi had stood with the Prime Minister and his Foreign Affairs Minister, the American President, his Secretary of State, and his religious advisor for the talks, as well as the President of the DROP, Islam's most respected and educated imam, and, of course, the Caliph of Babylon, Sanaullah bin Laden.

Save for the Caliph, Sol now considered each of these leaders to be his friends. Although bin Laden had not participated in the negotiations, he had asked to be a witness at the signing of the agreement in Washington DC. Sol was amazed that the U.S. Government allowed a terrorist like bin Laden to even enter the states, much less come to the White House! The new American President said, "This visit is an olive branch that I extend to the Muslim world.

"How strange," Sol thought, *"the Caliph never said a word before, during, or after the signing ceremony. Instead, he stood there, motionless, stone faced, throughout the entire celebration."*

So many Israelis, Arabs, Americans, and Europeans before Sol and his team had failed—miserably so—to broker peace between the Jews and the Palestinians! In 2012, Palestinian President Mahmoud Abbas of the Fatah Party asked the United Nations (UN) to recognize a Palestinian state. Although the UN General Assembly overwhelming voted to approve nonmember observer state status, the Palestinian petition clearly violated the Oslo Accords of 1993. After those tenuous and meticulous negotiations, Israeli Prime Minister Yitzhak Rabin and Palestine Liberation Organization leader Yasser Arafat had agreed to pursue no unilateral actions in regard to a Palestinian state in the West Bank. Instead, the accords specifically called for a negotiated solution of the status of the hotly disputed territory.

Nineteen years later, the West Bank Palestinians joyfully celebrated their political coup d'état in the UN, although the decision made no mention of the Hamas-ruled Palestinians in Gaza.

Israel, then under the leadership of Prime Minister Benjamin Netanyahu, refused to recognize the UN declared state of Palestine, as the non-enforceable vote effectively endorsed a divided Jerusalem and would leave Israel without defensible borders. Netanyahu also noted that the Palestinians yet refused to recognize Israel as a Jewish state.

U.S. leaders fell in line behind the Israelis, saying the Palestinians' provocative action would stymie, if not sabotage the peace process. That assessment proved prophetic as the on again, off again war between the Jews and Palestinians continued unabated.

Be that as it may, under this day's tranquil blue sky, the rabbi asked his Creator, "With a century of failure upon failure to bring peace to Israelis and Palestinians, how did we finally succeed?"

Often the broken negotiations led to violence against the Lord's Promised Land and chosen people. Until the last decade, Yasser Arafat's second intifada, from 2000 to 2005, had been the worst of all the Palestinian uprisings. Sol was only a teen during those dark days. He had no personal recollection of the carnage but had seen the pictures and video of the wretched violence many times.

However, Sol vividly recalled the bloodcurdling violence of the most recent ten years, which made the second intifada appear almost serene in comparison. During that dark decade, the Muslims of Palestine were neither an independent nation nor a state in the Caliphate. Consequently, with the help of the faceless, merciless General of the Brotherhood Army, the Palestinians launched an unprecedented wave of terror! The "Grand Jihad," as the Palestinians called it, claimed thousands upon thousands of Jewish lives. Sol could not recall how many funerals he had officiated during those horrible years. Even so, he well remembered that the butchery did not stop until the American President threatened nuclear force against the Caliphate!

As he rubbed his bald head, Sol thought, "Why didn't the Israeli Prime Minister take that decisive step to protect his own people? Why did the United States have to finally intervene?" Sol knew the answer to his own questions. *"The Prime Minister was too weak-kneed to act!*

"After the Grand Jihad, that coward lost the confidence of his coalition government, his own party, as well as the citizens of Israel! A new, stronger Prime Minister was chosen, and he, Samson Tuvya Ben Baruch, was the bold and brave Israeli leader who negotiated peace and signed the treaty with the Palestinians just four months ago in the White House Rose Garden!"

Sol smiled as he thought, *"At last we have someone leading this country with as much chutzpa as I have!"* Over the years, the raucous rabbi had acquired a reputation of being arrogant and brusque. Even so, when someone brought those character traits to his attention, he humorously insisted, as he came nose to nose with the challenger, "I am neither arrogant nor brusque. Instead, I am both humble and wise, and my humility and wisdom intimidate you!"

As he chuckled at himself, Sol realized that finally, after more than a century of unrest, terror, and war which culminated in ten years of the worst violence of all, the Lord had truly blessed His people with peace. Though four months had passed since the celebrated signing of the treaty and the establishment of the DROP, on this bright Sunday afternoon, Sol continued to soak up the sun and the adulation as though no time had passed at all! Then, humbly, he thanked his merciful God for using him in such a time as this.

Peace was such a foreign concept to Israel! Even Sol himself found it difficult to believe that the age of terror had finally ceased, despite the sweat and years he had invested in the negotiation process. Of course, Israel had made large concessions.

The contemplative rabbi attempted to justify those compromises in his own mind. *"Sure, East Jerusalem is now the Palestinian capitol. But the Palestinians were going to govern from somewhere, and East Jerusalem was a wreck after the Grand Jihad, anyway. In no uncertain terms, I told the Prime Minister and the President, 'Let the Palestinians have East Jerusalem! At least we won't have to clean up their mess!'"*

Be that as it may, the real sticking point with Sol was that the Jews had disobeyed God by giving away more of His Land. The remorseful rabbi had sought to justify the exchange of land for peace as an absolute necessity. Though he fought to deny it, he knew deep in his heart of hearts that trading away God's land, even for desperately needed peace, only provoked the Lord of Heaven and earth.

Sol recalled the prophecy in the book of Joel concerning God's anger and judgment that He will unleash on the nations for dividing His land. *"Will Israel also suffer for willingly giving away Your Land?"* the recoiling rabbi asked his Lord. "Will Your people suffer Your wrath for divvying up Your Land?"

Other concessions Israel granted to form a Palestinian state also continued to upset Sol. He had great difficulty coming to terms with ceding the entire Temple Mount, *Har ha-Báyit*, to Palestinian control. Indeed, 126 days after the negotiations ended, this issue remained unresolved for Sol.

The seasoned teacher of his people looked through the deep blue sky and proclaimed, "Never in my life, never have I endured more than a few days without praying at *HaKotel HaMa'aravi*. Talking with You while standing before You there at the Western Wall has been part of my daily life as far back as I can remember! My heart grieves, as I have not stood before those marvelous stones for months now. I feel weaker in spirit because of it. A gnawing, empty space is growing in my heart!"

Sol stared into the sparkling blue heavens for several more moments. Then, to assuage himself, he said, *"At least we still have control over the rest of the Jewish Quarter of the Old City!"* But no amount of self-consolation would ever fill the void Sol felt over losing the *Kotel.* The Western Wall was holy ground for Sol.

Shaking his head, Sol turned his thoughts to a concession which he had fought to curtail and won. He told himself and *HaShem,* the Name, "Refusing the right of return has proven to be a wise decision! The Palestinians' ancestors fled Israel more than a century ago. If we had opened our borders to all their descendants, the Jewish State of Israel would have instantly ceased to exist! Israel would be a Muslim state today—maybe even part of the Caliphate by now! Yes, we were indeed men of discernment, choosing to offer financial compensation instead of the right of return—even if the outflow of cash has virtually drained our government coffers! Without our oil and gas reserves, we would never have been able to pay for the right to keep the Jewish state Jewish."

Despite all his reasoning and praying, Sol's original question remained unanswered. He stroked his long white beard as he spoke with His God. "Why did we succeed where so many others had failed? Certainly, we made a generous and conciliatory offer to the Palestinians. But generations of Jews have made many similar proposals, and the Palestinians always refused such overtures. "

Sol shouted toward the heavens, *"Adonai!"* Translated as Lord, *Adonai* was the Hebrew name for God that the Hassidic rabbi only used in his prayers. "Oh, *Adonai,* come to think of it, how did we exactly manage to convince the Palestinians that Israel had a right to exist? And why did the Palestinians suddenly promise to never terrorize Israel again? And I still do not understand why the Palestinians agreed to form an independent, demilitarized democracy called the Democratic Republic of Palestine, instead of finally taking our land by force and choosing to become another Islamic state of the Caliphate."

His white shirt now wet with perspiration, the Orthodox Rabbi remembered how he, the Prime Minister, and the American facilitators were stunned when the DROP President suddenly accepted the proposed treaty. Sol's Palestinian counterpart, the always engaging Imam

Addar Mansur Zaahir, an honors graduate of MIT, with both master's and doctoral degrees in Computer Science from Princeton, had adamantly fought against the sudden change of course. Sol recalled the dark, tall, and thin imam saying, "We cannot accept this package offered by the Jews! It calls on us to make far too many compromises—and these concessions also cut far too deep! Our people must be able to reclaim their generational homeland!"

Likewise, Sol recalled how the U.S. President's religious advisor for the talks, Pastor Mark Basel, said he was stupefied! The often quoted and much respected professor of Muslim evangelism had asked, "Why did the Palestinians suddenly reverse course and agree to everything that the Israelis had offered and demanded for decades?" He and his Messianic wife Ariel—an intercultural counselor—were suspicious of the Palestinian President's dramatic turnabout. Mark had asked two questions Sol could not forget: "What has changed and brought about this sudden surge of acceptance and desire for peace? What will be the ultimate, as yet unseen, repercussions of this treaty?"

In the midst of his concern and confusion, Sol suddenly smiled once more. The aged Hasidic Jew lifted his hands high and said, "Maybe, You, *Adonai*, convinced the Palestinians they would never defeat us! Yes indeed, You, *Adonai*, You miraculously intervened and brought the negotiations to a wonderful end, both for the DROP and for Israel! Just yesterday, at the end of my sermon, the people in the synagogue continued to praise You and thank me for the blessed, priceless gift of peace!" Again, Sol's soul felt full of light and happiness! "Thank You, *Adonai*, thank You!" Sol concluded his conversation with his Lord with a hearty, "Amen!"

Then, with his face glowing like the sizzling sun, Sol turned to reenter his hillside home outside the city of Jerusalem. Coming down the stairs was his ever-beautiful bride, Ahava. Sol laughed to himself as he remembered, "People think she is my daughter because she looks like she is half my age!"

Suddenly, the sirens jolted him out of his euphoria. By instinct, he and his cherished partner in life ran for the bomb shelter. The elderly couple had a mere ten seconds to get there!

"Seest thou not that We have set the Evil Ones on against the Unbelievers, to incite them with fury?"
Qur'an 19:83

CHAPTER 3

THE POLITICS OF IT ALL. . .

*T*he American President suddenly sat straight up in bed with the jarring realization that he had overslept. However, when he cleared his clouded thoughts, he remembered that this was Sunday—and he, for once, did not have any appointments or interviews or appearances to make throughout day.

President James Jacob Paulson, Double J to family, friends, and staff, considered himself a political charmer who loved to work a crowd. His full head of stylish white hair plus his rugged, youthful good looks gave him both a discerning and winsome appearance, which he exploited fully.

When people first met the President, they consistently told him he was shorter than they expected. Though he could not extend his five foot eight inch frame in person, anytime the Commander in Chief sat or stood before a camera, he always did so atop some kind of booster so that he would be the tallest man in the room.

On this easy Sunday morning, Double J was alone in bed, as his wife, Hope, had taken their two sons to church. He had considered joining them each week, if for no other reason than good PR with Christian voters. However, he did not want to add hypocrisy to his lengthy list of sins.

Besides, the Christian voting bloc was not nearly what it used to be. In fact, Islam had recently passed Christianity as the number one religion in the states, and Muslims were now the largest voting bloc in

America. Actually, more voters identified themselves as atheists and agnostics than those who identified themselves as Christians.

Furthermore, even within the minority Christian population, liberalism reigned. Thus, nothing truly distinguished Christian voters from secular voters anymore. In fact, American Christianity was so ambivalent that most of the self-proclaimed followers of Jesus did not know, much less follow, the most basic tenets of their faith.

As the President again laid his white head on his blue down pillow, his mind moved through the events of late. Though only six months into his presidency, Double J calculated that he would be remembered for three profoundly historic events.

First, capitalizing on the politics of the moment, Double J had chosen a follower of Islam as his running mate. The shrewd Democrat was the first nominee from any party to share the Presidential ticket with a Muslim. Facing a well loved and admired Republican incumbent, Double J, as the consummate political gambler, wagered that his only way to win the White House would be with a Muslim by his side.

Second, as Double J saw it, he had also made history on the very day of his inauguration. He was sworn into office with Abdul-ghafoor Asim Abdullah, Triple A as the President dubbed him, much to the Vice President's dismay. Triple A was, at least so far, the only Muslim to serve just a heartbeat away from the Presidency.

Third, a mere two months after moving to 1600 Pennsylvania Avenue, Double J had made history yet again with the landmark peace accord between the Jews and Palestinians! True, Double J had not brokered the deal himself, but had inherited it from the previous administration. Nonetheless, the treaty was signed under his watch, and that was all that mattered to the crackerjack chieftain. After all, Double J had demonstrated the presence of mind to keep the Republican administration's Secretary of State in his Cabinet so she could place the finishing touches on the pact.

Double J sighed with satisfaction as he sat up. He was a do-whatever-it-takes-to-win, no-matter-the-cost, or consequences-of-the-compromise politician. When he had first floated the idea of a Muslim running mate, his party as well as his campaign staff balked. Hence, in response, Double J had crooned, "A vote is a vote is a vote! Who cares if the majority of the ballots for our ticket come from Muslims or any other religious or people group, as long as we win? If I can secure the

Muslim voting bloc, I will be unstoppable, despite the high popularity of the sitting Republican President. I will happily ride an Islamic wave into the White House!" Double J's words had proven to be prophetic.

Not only were the followers of Islam the largest religious body and voting bloc in the states, Muslims had also become the largest minority group, long ago outpacing the Hispanic and the African American populations combined. In reality, American worshipers of Allah, who were a cross section of the world's races, tribes, and ethnicities, were the only religious body to ever become a multiracial demographic group. According to the latest analyses, Muslims would be the majority population group in the states within a few years.

While Islamic voting patterns in national elections were extremely unpredictable, Double J had convinced his party and advisors that all followers of Allah would vote for one of their own to become the first man in line for the Oval Office.

"Anyway," Double J had noted, "Many Muslims are already serving in city, county, and state, and a few federal offices, as well as judgeships. So what if a few of those Muslim judges not only consult the U.S. Constitution and our laws to determine their decisions but also consider Sharia Law—the law of Islam? Today's Americans yawn at such practices."

Truly, Double J himself belonged to the yawners. He gave no thought to the consequences of electing more and more Muslims to higher and higher offices which brought greater and greater Islamic influence to bear on every aspect of American life.

He told his political handlers, "So what if the Holocaust isn't taught in the public schools anymore? Tragic as they may be, those events are ancient history! So what if the all the kids in the public schools can no longer eat ham in the school cafeterias because Allah prohibits the eating of pork? Jews don't eat pork either—though they never bellyached when it was served in the schools! So what if some schools enforce a Muslim dress code for all students? Multiculturalism is good for our kids! So what if Muslims can pray in public schools but Christians cannot? Silent prayer cannot be stopped. So what if there are more mosques in America than churches? Times change! So what if some radical group of Islamists tried to get their representatives to declare Arabic the official language of the United States? Did anyone really think that would fly in the USA? So what if more American voters sided with the Palestinians rather than with the Israelis during the peace treaty negotiations? The agreement still brought peace, didn't it?"

One of President Paulson's great talents was his ability to ignore, even purposefully overlook, anything that he did not want to see. When faced with facts he could not avoid, he always found a way to minimize or trivialize their importance as well as their consequences.

After winning the election, Double J told his closest advisers, "The people of the Qur'an have been good to me, and in exchange, I think I have been pretty good to them—at least those who forsake terrorism!" Then, he told the Chair of the Democratic Party, "I had three aces up my sleeve: Abdul-ghafoor Asim Abdullah! Those three aces gave me the winning hand in presidential poker!" For a while, Double J had called his Vice President, Triple Aces, though the nickname soon became Triple A.

Staring as the ceiling above his bed on this sunny Sunday morning, the President mused to himself, *"So far, Triple A has proven to be faithful and virtually invisible in terms of the role he plays in my administration. He is more of a counselor on Muslim issues than he is a Vice President. After all, he has no political aspirations whatsoever, and that fact is exactly why I chose him over all the other possible Muslim running mates I considered."*

With a cagey grin on his face, the President drifted off to sleep once more.

Less than an hour later, when Double J reawakened, he wondered if he should get to know his Vice President on a more personal basis. He asked himself, *"Should not the person who made my political aspirations a reality have my thanks and friendship?"* Since the day was open, Double J decided to invite Triple A to the White House for lunch.

However, at that same moment, the President's diligent Chief of Staff, Eddie Murdock—with eyes hollow and face pasty white—burst through the bedroom door unannounced.

"As for what you see here, the time will come when not one stone will be left on another; every one of them will be thrown down."
Luke 21:6

CHAPTER 4

ALL CONSUMING FIRE. . .

*N*o matter what they were watching on their Satellite Omnicolor Holovision 3D SenseSurround Systems (HV3D), no matter what they were doing on their Satellite 3D SenseSurround Holophones (3DHP), in the same moment, everyone, everywhere was instantly drawn into the same scene!

From the center of the action, their disbelieving eyes beheld four hypersonic short range missiles bearing down on their targets. Designed and engineered through a joint project of the U.S. and Israel, the SkyShark I (SSI) missiles packed a powerfully precise payload.

Israel's legendary, topnotch missile defense shield did not pick up these locked and loaded titans before they entered the Jewish state's airspace. Until now, that shield had a perfect record, striking down thousands of rockets and missiles while saving tens of thousands of Israeli lives. However, on this sun swept day, the Iron Dome II Missile Defense Shield (ID2MDS) did absolutely nothing to stop these fiery arrows of annihilation. By the time the rockets appeared on antiquated radar systems, Israeli Air Force (IAF) XK-23's—the fastest jets in the Middle East—could not be scrambled in time to prevent the four synchronized missiles from reaching their doomed destinations.

Thus, the only warning in Jerusalem came from primitive air raid sirens. Unfortunately, with the modern day speed of hypersonic rockets, the wailing alarms gave people a mere ten seconds to flee to the nearest bomb shelters.

The missiles flashed across the cloudless sky, as Sol and Ahava as well as all the Jews and Palestinians in the hills of Jerusalem and in the city itself, ran for safety!

Muslim visitors from around the world stood atop the Temple Mount—*al-Haram esh-Sharif*, the Noble Sanctuary, to them. With special permission from the DROP authorities, Israeli Foreign Affairs Minister Rachel Meir led the group of dignitaries from Central and South America on a tour of the site regarded as sacred by Islam, Judaism, and Christianity. As the air raid warnings sounded, Rachel, her group, and all the Islamic tourists on the Temple Mount began to run in circles, not knowing where to go or what to do.

In contrast, local Muslims atop the Noble Sanctuary made a desperate run for the underground Al Marawani Mosque, but most of the panicked men, women, and children had insufficient time to reach it. Tragically, even those who managed to enter the underground mosque would fare no better than those outside it.

In the capitol of the DROP in Eastern Jerusalem, *Al Quds* to the Muslims, Israel's air raid sirens also bellowed. All the officials and employees in the DROP's temporary government building made a mad dash for the stairwells that led to the reinforced basement. Likewise, in the nearby, hastily converted office building that housed the Joint Front for Palestine (JFP) political offices, the leaders and volunteers desperately scrambled for the protection of the subterranean shelters.

Rapidly, the staircases overflowed with panic-stricken souls. Through the glass walls of the packed stairways, the horrified and helpless humans saw their fate swooping down like fiery red chariots against the vividly blue sky!

The cacophony of anticipatory screams on both sides of Jerusalem almost drowned out the howling air raid sirens.

Then, in the same instant, the four missiles zeroed in on their targets: the Al Aqsa Mosque, the Dome of the Rock, the DROP capitol building, and the JFP office building. Instantly, one massive fireball engulfed all four structures. The simultaneous explosions rocked the whole of the Israeli and Palestinian capitols, while the sound and tremors from the blasts could be heard and felt as far away as Ashdod on the Mediterranean and Amman in the Caliphate's state of Jordan.

In that one instant, all the screams ceased, as no one survived the all consuming gluttony of the missiles. No one would be rescued. No wounds or injuries would be treated. No discernable remains would be found.

Instead, as the crematoriums of the Holocaust spewed blackened clouds of ashes from their smokestacks, the Temple Mount heaved billows of dark soot from its charred ruins. Burnt bits of the searing sacrifice of human flesh and bone were strewn all over the Temple complex. The dark gloom of death blotted out the sun.

The Western Wall—*Al-Buraq al-Haan'nat*, the Lightning Wall, to Muslims—collapsed under the force of the explosions. Likewise, the above and below ground mosques, as well as the Dome of the Rock, vanished the moment the missiles hit. While the blasts momentarily reopened the Eastern Gate, the white-hot flames then vaporized the passageway of the Messiah. The entire Jewish and Muslim Quarters became heaps of burning stones and cinders. In similar fashion, flame and rubble consumed most of the Christian and Armenian Quarters. The missiles eliminated the archeological sites in the Old City of Jerusalem and Mount Zion, as well as the graves and churches on the Mount of Olives.

In Eastern Jerusalem, the mighty missiles instantly swallowed up the DROP capitol building and the JFP office complex, as well as all surrounding structures. The ensuing, blistering blazes even engulfed buildings on the extreme edges of the epicenter of the attack. In the windows of those offices and businesses, terrified Palestinians wildly screamed for help. Many of them and other Muslims became human torches, jumping from great heights, plunging to their horrid deaths.

Molten and pretzel-twisted metal covered the unrecognizable streets. A murky fog filled with flakes of scorched human remains rose and fell in the superheated drafts above the incinerated city.

The shrill sirens of the Magen David Adom and Red Crescent ambulances broke the stilled silence. Sadly, even if the rescue teams could have penetrated the circle of destruction, their heroic efforts would have come to nothing. Untold thousands of human lives had ceased to exist in a fraction of an instant. Even though there could be no official body count or death toll, everyone knew this grisly act of terror greatly eclipsed the previous record of almost 3,000 annihilated souls on September 11, 2001 in the United States.

Indeed, one SSI missile would have destroyed all four targeted structures and the people within them, but whoever masterminded this catastrophic and heartrending assault wanted to demonstrate his power through unbridled horror and consummate destruction. Yes, a rocket quartet composed quite an emphatic dirge.

Away from the carnage and wreckage, at a secret Israeli Air Force Base, the officer in charge was ready for heads to roll! The red-faced commander bellowed to his men, "Who was responsible for this act of war? From where were those missiles fired? How did they avoid being taken out by the ID2MDS?" Pounding his fist on the console, he shouted, "I want answers, and I want them now!"

"Sir," the deputy at the tracking monitor answered with great reluctance in his voice, "the coding from the missiles says they are ours!"

Dumbfounded, the commander repeated the words to himself before whispering, "What? That's impossible!"

"Be not weary and faint-hearted, crying for peace, when ye should be uppermost: for Allah is with you, and will never put you in loss for your (good) deeds."
Qur'an 47:35

CHAPTER 5

THE ELUSIVENESS OF PEACE...

*S*till in his pajamas, President Paulson ran into the White House Situation Room to see the fire and smoke pouring from the Temple Mount, the Jewish Quarter, and the Palestinian government and political offices in East Jerusalem! "Oh my God! This cannot be happening!" the President exclaimed as he tried to make sense of the mayhem around him.

In HV3D SenseSurround, which places the viewer in the midst of the scene, the President witnessed destruction that made his stomach turn. Flakes of charred flesh fell like black snow atop what was left of the Temple Mount, along the heavily damaged Western Wall, in the ruins of the Archeological Park, as well as in the Kidron and Hinnom Valleys. The atrocious display of obliterated humans and incinerated construction was repeated in the Muslim Quarter, as well as the Christian and Armenian Quarters. The area of the Israeli capitol outside the Old City also exhibited vaporized structures and decimated humanity. The same was true in the streets in East Jerusalem. Drone hovercraft relayed graphic images of the devastation in *Al Quds*. Nothing recognizable remained in the charred rubble.

As Palestinian first responders worked to douse the flames in East Jerusalem before they spread to other buildings, Israeli firefighters tried to determine how to climb atop the blazing boulders that only a few minutes earlier formed the Temple Mount.

Double J stood silent and stiff, his mouth hanging open. He whispered, *"Who did this? Why? The Jews are at peace with the Palestinians! Did some group of radical Zealots manage to drag war out of the mouth of peace?"*

At that moment, the Israeli hotline sounded. The direct line between the U.S. President and the Jewish Prime Minister had been installed two decades earlier when Israel appeared to be on the brink of war with several Muslim states.

"Great," thought Double J, *"Sam will see me my bed hair and pajamas!"* His thoughts betrayed his narcissism, which stood in stark contrast to the images of death and destruction that surrounded him.

Though Sam and Double J had met extensively in the prelude to the signing of the historic peace treaty, they had not spoken to each other in the four months since that historic day. President Paulson cleared his throat and tapped the hard wired, top security 3DHP, having no idea of what the Prime Minister would say to him or what he would say to the leader of the Jewish people.

"Hello, Sam! What the hell is going on there?"

With great anxiety in his voice, the Prime Minister replied from his office, "The very flames of hell have swallowed Jerusalem, my friend! *Sheol*, the pit, the grave, hell itself has opened! My ancestors thought the Hinnom Valley outside the Old City was hell. Today, they are right—*Gehinnom* is indeed hell, and its gates have been thrown wide!"

Sam paused and then said, "James, I apologize for waking you, but this attack impacts both our nations!"

Ignoring the reference to his appearance, Double J asked, "Who shot who, Sam?"

"I hope you can help me with that answer! You will not believe what the initial facts tell us!"

"Try me," intoned the President, bracing himself for the worst. Then he added, "How bad could the worst be?"

"How about nauseatingly abhorrent?" the Prime Minister groaned. "Four SkyShark I missiles seem to have been launched from our secret Air Force Base codenamed 'Elusive Peace.' We have no idea who authorized the launch!"

Stunned by the Prime Minister's answer, James remarked, "No one will believe you, Sam! The Palestinians, Babylon, and especially the Brotherhood—that ancient brood of terrorists—will not believe you! How could they?"

Unable to hide his frustration, Sam banged his fist on his desk and said, "I am fully aware of that reality, James! But why would we attack the Palestinians in Jerusalem with SkyShark I Missiles four months after making peace with them? Why would we destroy our own Temple Mount and most of the Old City of Jerusalem? Why would we kill countless numbers of our own innocent people?" The Prime Minister spoke in grief-filled tones. Tears pooled in his eyes.

President Paulson answered through gritted teeth, "Indeed—but if not you, then who? And why SkyShark I Missiles of all things! The Palestinians as well as bin Laden will think we are in on this with you!"

"That's exactly what I am thinking!"

"Could some fringe Zealot group have pulled this off?"

"I don't see how they could, James! None of the Zealots have that level of expertise."

"Then we better be ready for war, Sam!"

"Our armed forces and citizens are being brought up to date as we speak. I must address the nation soon, myself. I would suggest you do the same!"

With visible despair, the President of the United States asked, "What do we tell them?"

"Anything but the truth—yet! Of course, we will have a much larger audience than our nations. Consequently, we tell the world that both our governments, both of our nation's citizens condemn this act of terrorism!"

"Beyond that, shouldn't we remain on the same page?"

"I'm faxing you the text of my address now. Use it as a base for your own speech if you like."

The President paused to consider the implication of Prime Minister's words before responding. Did he somehow consider the President of the United States to be his puppet or pawn? Brushing aside his thoughts for the moment, the Commander in Chief asked, "Any idea about whether the Palestinian President made it out alive?"

"Honestly, James, I don't see how anyone could have survived the impact of four SSI's! Here, Sunday is a workday, and the President was probably sitting in his office, just as I am here behind my desk.

He likely never knew that instant incineration was coming." At that moment an aide tapped the Prime Minister on the shoulder and gave him several sheets of paper. Sam quickly glanced over them.

"It's worse than we think, James! I must go. We'll talk again when I know more!"

"Wait! Tell me what you have just read!"

Unfortunately, the Prime Minister's 3-D holophone image had already vanished.

"Come to Me, all you who are weary and burdened, and I will give you rest. Take My yoke upon you and learn from Me, for I am gentle and humble in heart, and you will find rest for your souls. For My yoke is easy and My burden is light."
Matthew 11:28-30

CHAPTER 6

SACKCLOTH AND ASHES. . .

*N*ervously, mournfully, Sol rubbed his bald head, tugged at his full white beard, and marched around his sun-drenched living room. The dark and foreboding scenes on the HV3D were only a few miles away in Jerusalem, yet they seemed to be from another world! As Ahava sobbed and moaned, Sol rattled off a list of questions. "What happened? Do you believe what the Prime Minister said in his address? How could the government not know who launched those missiles or from where they were fired? Why hasn't anyone claimed responsibility for such a horrid act of terror? What do you think, Ahava?" Weeping uncontrollably, all she could do was shake her head and shrug her shoulders.

The rabbi continued pacing around the living room, reciting Scripture, and praying. Plagued by a sense of doubt and overarching fear, Sol shouted to God, "Who could or would do such a thing, *Adonai*—and why? We have lost all that we gained. One act of terror nullified all the years of negotiation we invested in peace as well as all the concessions that we made to achieve it. In an instant, someone obliterated all of our historical and holy sites in Jerusalem including all of what remained of Your Temple."

Rabbi Shlomo Malichi Ben Yisra'el sat down. For his entire life, he had fought for Judaism, especially Orthodox Judaism. He wondered if today's devastation also effectively annihilated his lifelong achievements.

In Sol's younger days, he served with *Yad HaShem* (Hand of God). *Yad HaShem*, an Orthodox anti-Christian group, went to great lengths in efforts to drive all missionaries out of Israel. Despite all of his work through *Yad HaShem*, the number of Messianic believers only grew each year in Israel. More than three million of the ten million Jews in Israel now followed Y'shua!

The Hassidic Jew hated the missionaries who duped feeble Israelis into believing in a false Messiah! He had fought them at every turn. He went through the courts to expose their illegal missionary activity. He wrote books countering their teachings and evangelism methods. In earlier years, Sol physically participated in chasing down missionaries and destroying their materials. In righteous indignation, the Orthodox Rabbi had even pummeled missionaries with stones when they would not heed his demand for them to stop their proselytizing and leave his beloved homeland!

Still, at the end of the day, Sol had to admit that the missionaries were successful. As the number of Messianic Jews in Israel increased dramatically over the years, Sol and his compatriots at *Yad HaShem* faced a new problem: How to counter Y'shua's followers who were indigenous to Israel. Sol could run down and chase out missionaries, but what were he and *Yad HaShem* supposed to do with the home-grown Jews who preached that Y'shua reigned as the Messiah?

One of Sol's heroes, Orthodox Rabbi Saad'ya Har'el, took on the Messianic Jewish organizations head to head. Sol walked over to an article in *The Jerusalem Post* that he had framed and hung on the wall years ago. The title of the piece was "Jews for Jews!"

The angered and broken hearted defender of Judaism scanned down to the paragraph where Rabbi Sadd'ya said, "Jews who profess faith in Y'shua are no longer Jews! The evangelism of the oxymoronic 'Christian Jews,' who disguise themselves with the titles 'Messianic Jews' or 'Completed Jews,' promise unwitting and uniformed brothers that they don't have to give up their customs and traditions to believe in Y'shua. These lying apostates claim we as Jews can believe in Y'shua as our Messiah and still observe *Rosh Hashanah* [The New Year], *Yom Kippur* [The Day of Atonement], *Sukkot* [The Feast of Tabernacles], *Hanukkah* [The Festival of Lights], *Pesach* [Passover],

Shavuot [Giving of the Torah], and the rest of the Jewish holidays. In reality, these reprobates make as much sense as would 'Jews for Hitler' or 'Jews for Allah!'

"We must save true Jews from the so called Christian Jews' clutches by all means possible. This includes espionage at the now 400 or more Messianic Congregations that are polluting The Land. Furthermore, we must confront these apostates when they conduct public baptisms, lead open-air services, hold free concerts, and distribute heretical literature. These traitors of *Adonai* and Israel should be banned from synagogues, stripped of their Israeli citizenship, and then deported!"

Sol thought, *"Despite all of these efforts through Yad HaShem, more and more Jews began proclaiming that Y'shua was the Messiah. Likewise, the Christian missionaries continued coming each year to brainwash weak-minded or agnostic Jews! Thus, the number of Messianic believers only grew each year in Israel. Even so, I still cannot believe that a third of all the Jews in Israel now believe in a false Messiah!"*

Sol sat down and bent over in his chair, placing his face in his hands as he prayed. *"Adonai! HaShem!* The Great I Am, whose name is ineffable, your 85 year old servant comes before you today with a broken heart! I have failed You in so many ways! I have failed to stop the evil missionaries. I have failed to stop apostate Jews from proclaiming falsehoods. Now, I have likewise failed to bring peace to Your Land! I have bargained with Satan himself, and I have lost! I have negotiated with terrorists and have birthed only more horror! For my entire life, I have only sought to please You and serve You! What do I do now?"

The words of Proverbs 16:7 shut out all his other thoughts. *"When the LORD is pleased with a man's conduct, He may turn even his enemies into allies."* The octogenarian rabbi realized the Lord had answered him! Immediately, he fell to his knees and proclaimed, "I have not pleased You, O God of Abraham, Isaac, and Jacob. Our enemies remain our enemies!"

Sol then clearly heard, *"Without faith it is impossible to please God, because anyone who comes to Him must believe that He exists and that He rewards those who earnestly seek Him."* How was the ragged rabbi supposed to respond to those words, pulled straight from the Christian New Testament?

Far beyond his botched efforts with the Messianics, buried deeper than his foolish fiasco with the Muslims, Sol could see his most profound and most consuming failure. Even so, he had long refused to confront this darkness at the core of his very being that so displeased his righteous God and King.

Ahava came over and knelt next to her husband whom she not only loved, but also deeply respected and admired. She could not bear to witness his grief. "How can I help you, Sol?" she gently asked through their tears. "You could not have stopped those missiles today! *HaShem* knows this is not your fault!"

In a voice barely audible, Sol told his bride, "Call Mark and Ariel! Call them now!"

Then, weeping bitterly, Sol tore his clothes and then lied prostrate on the floor, as he realized the date. It was *Tisha B'Av*—the ninth day of the Jewish month of *Av*, the infamous day on which both the first and second Temples were destroyed!

"How many towns have We destroyed (for their sins)? Our punishment took them on a sudden by night or while they slept for their afternoon rest."
Qur'an 7:4

CHAPTER 7

TO STAND OR TO SURRENDER. . .

$\mathcal{P}$astor Mark knew nothing of the ground shaking events on both sides of Jerusalem. He always turned off his mobile 3DHP on Sunday mornings so that he would not be distracted as he made final preparations for worship and his sermon.

The stakes rose so much higher this particular Sunday. What should Mark do in the face of the bloody threat he found nailed to the doors of the church? Kneeling at the altar in his study, the pastor, seminary professor, international evangelist, and occasional adviser to U.S. Presidents on Muslim issues poured out his heart to Jesus. The humbled servant sought his Messiah's steady hand in this life or death situation.

Deep within his soul, Mark knew what course he must take. The process of elimination alone left only one choice. Obviously, he could not comply with the Muslim's demands and disperse his congregation, never to meet again in this sanctuary. Without doubt, the pastor could not and would not tell his sheep to desert Jesus and follow Allah! Only one option remained. The pastor and the faithful congregation would face down the terrorists and, with the power of Jesus, the Lord and King of All Eternity, continue to minister in His name in the community and around the world.

Despite the tense circumstances, Mark found a consistent peace in his soul. He clung to his Saviour's words from John 14:27, John 15:20. and Luke 6:27-28: *"Peace I leave with you; My peace I give you. I do not give to you as the world gives. Do not let your hearts be troubled and do not be afraid." "Remember the words I spoke to you: 'No servant is greater than his master.' If they persecuted Me, they will persecute you also!. . ." ". . . Love your enemies, do good to those who hate you, bless those who curse you, pray for those who mistreat you."*

Mark did not talk in formal words when he prayed. Instead, despite his great reverence and respect for Jesus, Mark conversed with his Lord as he would talk with a friend over lunch. After all, in John 15:14-15, Jesus told His first followers, *"You are My friends, if you do what I command. I no longer call you servants, because a servant does not know his master's business. Instead, I have called you friends, for everything that I learned from My Father I have made known to you."*

Thus, as a personal friend of Jesus, Pastor Mark prayed for the strength and steadfastness of the Holy Spirit. He pored over question after question in his soul. "Am I, personally, willing to suffer for Your Name—again? Am I willing to watch my present family suffer, should the terrorists follow through with their threats? Can I place my congregation in danger of persecution? More importantly, can I love the terrorists I long to hate? How can I bless them and do good to them, after they have done so much evil to me? How can I pray for those who have unleashed so much personal pain on me?"

Though his soul struggled, pray for the terrorists, he did. "My Lord and King, my Saviour and Ransom, my Hope and Peace, my Counselor and Intercessor, My dear, sweet Jesus, I call on You this morning. Change the hearts of the terrorists, and at the same time, change my own heart. Help me love them, not hate them! Help me forgive them, not be angry with them! Help me seek their redemption, not pursue my revenge! Help me bless them with all I know about You, all I have learned from You! Remind me of the great forgiveness You freely poured out for me as you hung on the cross! May the wounds they have given me be lost in the crimson flow from Calvary. Lord, help me pray for the terrorists to be washed in Your very Blood, too! Help me, Jesus! We are the Church of the Transformed. May the terrorists know Your transforming power first hand!"

Through the seminary where he taught, Pastor Mark ran a website for Muslims who were interested in learning more about Isa—Jesus' Name in Arabic and in the Qur'an. The website had more than 10,000 hits each day from Muslims in Islamic states all over the world. Many of those thousands a day professed their faith in Isa as Saviour and Lord—a decision that could cost them their very lives.

Through a Christian HV3D satellite system, Pastor Mark also preached each day in Muslim lands. During one of his daily evangelistic messages, Pastor Mark asked every Muslim who had experienced a dream or vision of Isa to go to his website and tell him about that encounter.

The ultranet response was so great, that the seminary super-server completely shut down. Since that sermon, hundreds of Muslims a day had written to Pastor Mark about how Isa revealed Himself to them through dreams and visions. Either Mark, one of his students, or other staff members at the seminary always wrote back to the Muslims to help them receive Isa's soul transforming forgiveness and salvation through their confession and repentance of sin!

As Mark considered the suffering that could be brought down upon his church, he wondered, "How many of the Muslims who turned to Isa through my website and teaching are suffering because of their faith? Jesus, I pray that you bless the persecuted. Give them Your very presence, no matter where they are or what they are enduring for their faith! Lord, millions are being tortured even as I call on Your Name. My brothers and sisters are suffering all around the world, especially in islamized Europe and Asia. Is this kind of persecution about to come to the United States? Is it beginning, here, in our church this very day?"

Mark's thoughts went back in time. He recalled that on the ninth anniversary of 9/11, September 11, 2010, the Vatican had warned Europeans: "Have more children or be islamized!" Abortion and broken families had dramatically decreased the indigenous population throughout most of Europe, while the mass immigration of Muslims and their prolific reproductive capacity increased their numbers geometrically.

Mark remembered that the Vatican ignored the other piece of the puzzle that allowed Islam to eventually dominate Christianity in Europe. He said to Jesus, "Lord, the vast majority of Europeans stopped following You. They turned instead to agnosticism, atheism, and secularism. In those days, only two percent of the native European population could be found in worship on Sunday mornings. At the same time, the Muslims converted many of the churches and cathedrals to mosques. Slowly but surely, as the followers of Islam became the majority population, they filled the vacuum of faith. Islam rapidly became the creed of Europe and the brutal Sharia Law its rule of order!

"Dear Saviour, the United States now walks this path that leads to destruction! We have so few Christians left! As Americans tolerate everything, they stand for nothing!

"Jesus, You and I both know what happened in Europe—as well as in most of the world. After the Muslims took control, the people finally acknowledged what was happening. Only then did the Europeans fight back! But their last minute rebellion was weak and was met by swift and sure death and destruction. The Muslims followed the command of Allah in the fifth chapter of the Qur'an, verse 33: *'The punishment of those who wage war against Allah and His Apostle, and strive with might and main for mischief through the land is: execution, or crucifixion, or the cutting off of hands and feet from opposite sides, or exile from the land: That is their disgrace in this world, and a heavy punishment is theirs in the Hereafter.'* The carnage in Europe was massive— not at all proportionate to the small numbers of Europeans that sought to retain their freedom. The carnage was so grisly and barbaric that no one has dared rebel again!"

Actually, as the pastor pondered the verse from the Qur'an, he understood that no weapons or actual battles were necessary to qualify as waging war against Allah. "Jesus, faith in You is considered an act of war against the false god of Islam! Throughout the Qur'an and the Hadiths—those alleged sayings of Muhammad and records of his actions—Allah's calls to deadly violence for such faith are beyond imagination!"

Now weeping as he continued praying, Mark said, "My Lord, the only lives that matter in Islam are the lives of Muslims. According to Allah, Christians, Jews, Hindus, Buddhists, spiritists, wiccans, agnostics, atheists, and secularists are all infidels who deserve death—period!

"You, on the other hand, welcome all who come seeking forgiveness, all who come in repentance. Jesus, Your ever strong arms of love remain open wide to all who seek the one true God of Creation! Thank You, Jesus, for loving all sinners and dying in our place—with arms nailed open wide on the cross! Thank You for offering life to each of us, instead of the death our sins have earned us!"

Returning to the moment as hand, the preacher prayed, "I do not believe the United States has learned from Europe's example—or even China's painful experience following the last World War. The Communists one-child policy had allowed Muslims to overtake China at an even faster rate than they conquered Europe.

"Here in the U.S., Muslims will soon be the majority population—either in my lifetime or the lifetimes of my children! But the confluence of non-Muslim American citizens, government officials, and the media are willfully blind to what is happening! Now, I fear, the process cannot be reversed! Please, open their eyes to the reality of what is happening right under their noses!

"Every leader in America says we should not fear Muslims! Jesus, You know what our own President said just last week: 'Even though the people of Islam in other nations have shown their propensity for violence and revolution, the Muslim citizens of America love peace!' His administration, like all those before it, has constantly reached out to the so-called moderate Muslims. He refuses to see as they refused to see that moderate Muslims were not the problem or, even worse, that their moderation was often only a disguise, a camouflage masking their true desire and work for islamization and jihad!

"Lord, the Muslims follow a book of lies. They follow a god who does not exist—save in the devil himself. Open their eyes to see the Truth—to see that you are the very embodiment of Truth!"

As a professor of Muslim evangelism, Mark was well versed in the Qur'an. Roughly, it was divided into two parts. When Muhammad lived in Mecca, he "received" the more peaceful and docile chapters—suras as they are called in Islam—of the Qur'an from Allah. However, when Muhammad was chased out of Mecca and landed in Medina, Allah's chapters grew longer and more violent. The call to jihad permeated all the Median passages.

"Apparently," Mark told His Best Friend in all eternity, "that powerless and nonexistent god of Islam must have changed his mind about some issues as his words in Medina often contradicted what he had told Muhammad in Mecca.

"I suppose a false god like Allah can do whatever he desires," Mark prayed in a sarcastic tone. "His prophet says that Allah amazingly began to abrogate his own words. I remember the words of Qur'an 2:106, where Allah supposedly says, *'None of Our revelations do We abrogate or cause to be forgotten, but We substitute something better or similar: knowest thou not that Allah hath power over all things?'*

"So, when Muhammad was in a tight situation, Allah was amazingly free to change his mind, as long as he improved upon what he uttered before. How convenient abrogation was for both Allah and Muhammad!"

Through his years of study, Mark understood that perhaps the biggest contrast between the Meccan and Medinan chapters was Allah's attitude about Jews and Christians. In Mecca, where Muhammad was born and grew up, he had emphasized that Jews, Christians, and Muslims worshiped the same god. There, Muhammad portrayed himself as a prophet, warning people to rid themselves of idols.

First, the idol worshippers thoroughly rejected Muhammad. Second, when he claimed to be greater than Moses, the Jews also rejected him. Third, when Muhammad announced he was greater than Jesus, the Christians rejected him, too. No wonder the people chased him out of Mecca.

Muhammad settled in Medina, where the rebuffed, self-proclaimed prophet began drawing the lines that distinguished Allah—the Meccan moon god—from the God of the Hebrew and Christian Scriptures. In the Medinan chapters of the Qur'an, Allah no longer spoke as "we," because Muhammad did away with the moon god's wife and three daughters. However, the crescent moon remained the symbol of Islam.

In Medina, with a more receptive audience to his revised message against Jews and Christians, Muhammad was given more honor and power in the new chapters he claimed Allah gave him. The illiterate Muhammad became both the Prophet of Islam and the ruler of the Muslims—as well as Islam's first general. Allah had conveniently given Muhammad permission to not only defend himself against attacks, but to be the aggressor in wiping out those who rejected him and the god he served. Allah, translated as "the god," sent his prophet back to Mecca to shell out revenge on his detractors. Muhammad and his fighters conquered his hometown.

Unfortunately, most of non-Muslim America did not know what Mark knew about Islam.

Mark continued his prayer, saying, "No matter what I say, Lord, the U.S. government and media see what they want to see. They hail the areas of America where Muslims are already the majority population. According to the feds and media, these Muslims majorities have proved themselves to be peaceful citizens, even in those areas where the dreaded Sharia Law takes precedent over our federal, state, and local law. Of course, the vast majority of non-Muslim Americans take such reports from the media as absolute truth!

"Even our state and federal courts now consider the Sharia when Muslims come before them. It's hard to believe, Jesus, but now polygamy and spouse abuse are acceptable, justifiable behaviors in certain areas of the United States! Similarly, saying anything that could remotely be considered as criticism of Muhammad, Allah, or the Qur'an can lead to execution by stoning."

Unlike the vast majority of America's leaders and citizens, Mark knew and understood the strategy of Islam. While a small minority of Muslims who took their inspiration from the non-violent Meccan portions of the Qur'an did live in genuine, relative peace with the rest of America, the vast number of Muslims in the U.S., as well as the rest of the world, placed their faith in Allah's calls for violence and world domination in the Median passages of Islam's holy book.

These jihadist Sunni Muslims—who had virtually wiped out their Shiite rivals years ago—only played at being peaceful. Behind their friendly and peaceful camouflage a desperate, demonic political force dwelled whose goal was world dominance—one worldwide Caliphate where Muslims ruled and no one else survived! In the *ummah*—the true, united, all consuming, Islamic community—Christians and Jews, as well as peace-loving, misguided Meccan or moderate Muslims, would no longer be allowed to live! Likewise, in the ultimate *ummah*, no agnostics, atheists, or people of any other religion would be allowed to outlast their usefulness to the Muslims.

Mark asked his God, "Who can stop the Muslims now, Lord? Only You! But You are allowing islamization as the end times draw near, aren't You, Jesus? The European Union has been swallowed up in the Caliphate. After Russia's coalition with the Muslims failed to destroy Israel, just as Ezekiel prophesied, the Great Bear of the North is now slowly and excruciatingly being islamized—and the Chechen Muslims show no mercy to the nation they have fought for so many decades.

"I see what is and has been happening in other lands, too. The majority of Asia is being or has been harvested by Muslims. World

War III ended with a radical, new order in Asia. The surviving nations were too weak to stop the Muslims inside and outside of their borders.

"Similarly, Australia and New Zealand have been islamized without one shot being fired, without any organized resistance to the silent revolution every sensible politician and citizen seemed to deny.

"Africa long ago fell to Muslim rule. The African states in the Caliphate remain hotbeds of terrorism whose lethal venom finds its way to the four corners of the world—including the Americas.

"Are the Muslims beginning their final move on the United States? Up to this point, the aggressive followers of Islam have plotted silently, secretly, invisibly. Even though I have warned Americans of the threat of islamization for years, few people listen to me—even fewer believe me. They seem to think that the United States of America will somehow avoid the fate of her allies and enemies in the world."

Mark paused as his intercession took on an even more serious tone. "Dear Saviour, I feel as though I am witnessing the beginning of the end! Soon, the rights You gave to us of life, liberty, and the pursuit of happiness will be replaced by the commands of Allah for death, dominance, and the pursuit of bringing the U.S. into the worldwide Caliphate.

"Likewise, I fear that our cherished equality is about to be snatched out of our hands. The Muslims do not believe that You create all men equal! Muslims have no equals but other followers of Allah! The very concept of equal treatment of non-Muslims under Sharia Law remains an unthinkable absurdity. Only Islamic victors are equal! Besides, the worldwide *ummah* won't allow any non-Muslims to survive for long. As inferior servants of the Caliphate, once their money and resources run out through their service and payment of the tax on infidels, the *jizya*, they will no longer be of any use to Islam. Hence, their pointless existence will be summarily terminated!

"Yes, Jesus, I fear that America's long-defended freedoms and God-birthed rights will soon be forgotten history! Muslims, who envision and fight for a Caliphate that rules over the entire world, hate democracy, for it is a slap in the face of the rule of Allah and his vicious Sharia Law!"

Inhaling deeply, the pastor said, "Nonetheless, Islam considers your Church a greater enemy than democracy. As such, will the first public battle of the modern Muslim revolution against the United

States be launched at our church today, Lord? Will my family and Your congregation be ground zero in the new fight for America? The terrorists have not chosen to take over a government building full of American citizens. The Islamists are not kidnapping business leaders and wealthy citizens for ransom. Instead, they are making their first strike at Your Church, our humble, small portion of it that loves You completely! You, and each of us, as well as all our brothers and sisters in the U.S. who follow You are the first enemies they seek to destroy!

"As I sense Your peace, despite the threatened violence of the day, I am prepared to lead my family and Your congregation to refuse the crimson ultimatum that was nailed to the door of Your House! And I am no fool, Jesus. I know that even if all of us survive this day, the victory will ultimately be inconsequential in the larger scheme of the Islamists. They will only continue to spread terror and death. Dear Lord, are we already beyond the point of no return? Can we no longer stop the islamization of the United States of America? Regardless of the answer, I will stand firm with You and the willing of this congregation on this day, against any threat, come what may!

"Without doubt, I have traveled too far on my personal journey with You, my Lord and King, to turn back now. My commitment to You is solid, unshakeable! Now, I must discover who will yet stand with me, as I stand with You!

"First, I will call Your greatest gift to me, my wife. Then, I will talk with the elders of Your church!"

". . . My grace is sufficient for you, for My power is made perfect in weakness. . ."
II Corinthians 12:9

CHAPTER 8

HIGH PROFILE MOMENT. . .

*A*ll of the U.S. Armed Services stood at the highest state of alert. American troops prepared for immediate deployment, whether outside or inside U.S. borders. Depending on how the Muslim citizens of America responded to the attacks in the DROP, America's soldiers could soon be needed to fight on their own shores!

This day, which should have been one of rest and relaxation for the President, brought him nothing but stress and fear. As he waited for his Cabinet members and Vice President to arrive, the leader of the world's last superpower churned through the events of the day. In the hours before his national address, he had to make some sense of it all. The Commander in Chief mulled many more questions than answers.

James decided that he must prioritize his essential questions. He spoke to his supercomputer so he would have both an audio and written record of his thoughts. "One, who made this unprovoked attack on the fledgling Palestinian state? Two, what should the U.S. do now that the leadership of both the Palestinian nation and its major political party has been incinerated in an instant? Three, what will Babylon do in response to the Palestinian destruction and carnage? Four, is Israel's official denial of involvement plausible? Five, will anyone believe this attack took America completely by surprise?"

Regardless of the correct answer to his last two questions, the President realized Israel held the smoking gun, since the missiles were fired from within The Land. Furthermore, with Israel as the most likely suspect in the attack on the DROP, the Muslims would assume that the

U.S. at least gave prior approval to the attacks, even if America did not actually participate in the strikes.

The man in the Oval Office reflected as he paced around his desk. He again spoke his thoughts so he could review them later. "After some rocky years, the United States and Israel have strong ties. America has stood by her most loyal ally in her hours of greatest darkness.

"Case in point, when the Caliphate prepared to annihilate Israel, the United States moved to protect the Promised Land. To prove Uncle Sam was serious, America threatened to strike with nuclear weapons."

As the President continued his measured steps around his historic office, he asked himself the obvious question. *"What could the Jews gain by initiating a war with the Muslims? Such a fight would not be a safe wager. The Muslim Brotherhood longs for a fight with Israel's Defense Forces (IDF). Besides, the missiles destroyed all the Jewish holy and archaeological sites in Jerusalem. Sam would not do that. He would neither destroy the Temple Mount and Old City any more than he would pick a fight with the Babylon and its massive Brotherhood Army.*

"The Brotherhood—it sounds like such a noble and peaceful organization," the President said sarcastically as he retraced the history of what was now the most feared body of men on the planet. He recalled that his great grandfather belonged to the men's group in his Baptist Church that was called the Brotherhood. *"Wow, those two organizations have absolutely nothing in common beyond their mutual name!"*

The President inhaled and exhaled deeply as his glazed eyes contemplated the new geopolitical landscape. He spoke for the record. "Let's see, what do I remember about the Muslim Brotherhood from all the briefings I had to endure when I entered the White House and took over the peace negotiations? Oh yes! The Brotherhood began in 1928 in Egypt as a Muslim political movement that espoused peace. I at first thought that beginning sounded reasonable, until I learned of the Brotherhood's political ambitions.

"Then and now, the Brotherhood stands on the twin foundations of Islamic ideology and theology. Thus, the political goal of the Brotherhood was and still is the establishment of a global Caliphate under Sharia Law. The Brotherhood believes in Islamic Supremacy and the Muslim's destiny to rule the earth—at all costs!

"Thus, despite the apparently humble and peaceful beginnings of the Brotherhood, the organization embraced jihad from its birth. Over the last century and a half, the Brotherhood became a transnational movement, growing more and more forceful as it sought to make the Qur'an and Sharia Law the foundation of Muslim lives, families, neighborhoods, and states. To achieve its self-proclaimed 'noble' goals, the Brotherhood clandestinely spawned Muslim terrorist organizations such as Hamas in Gaza, Hezbollah in Lebanon, and Islamic Jihad in Egypt.

"Not content with dabbling with terrorism in the fight against Isreal, the day came when the Brotherhood no longer denied its true intentions and became an extremely active terrorist organization itself. Over time, the Brotherhood surpassed Al Qaeda as the fiercest terrorist organization in the world."

President Paulson shuddered as he contemplated the Brotherhood's current role. "With a membership in the tens of millions, the Brotherhood now serves as the Army of Babylon. Worse yet, extreme Islamic terrorists who once fought under the various banners of Hamas, Hezbollah, Islamic Jihad, Al Qaeda, Fatah, the Palestine Liberation Front, Abu Sayyaf, Al Shabaab, Asbat al-Ansar, Boko Haram, al-Gama'a al-Islamiyya, Abu Nidal, and Mujahidin-e Khalq, just to name a few, now stand as one under the mantle of the Brotherhood. How did these groups overcome their theological, political, and methodological differences?" Answering his own question, the Commander in Chief said, "The Caliph gave the jihadists an ultimatum: 'Work together or be killed.' The surviving terrorists coalesced because they all shared a balanced diet of hatred and violence, as they learned the ways of jihad from their youngest days!"

As Double J considered Babylon's massive number of troops, he stopped pacing, shook his head, and thought, *"Indeed, as a brilliant leader, Sam would never pull such a boneheaded and self-destructive stunt. He would not provoke all out war with Babylon's terrorist army! But if Israel did not strike the DROP, then who did?"* Nothing made sense to the stumped President.

Around the world, every HV3D and 3DHP provider proclaimed the gruesome news of the attacks on the Palestinians and one of Islam's most holy sites. Now, before a worldwide audience, the American

President had to rise to the occasion, even though he had no effective narrative of what had transpired or what would take place in response.

The political gambler continued his recording. "I have four audiences. I must first convince the non-Muslim citizens of America that we had no part in this act of war. Then, I must persuade the ever burgeoning Muslim population of the United States that their government did not have any role in today's massacre. Tougher yet, I must convey that same message to the Caliphate, praying that the Muslims of the world will believe the U.S. did not participate in this atrocity. Last but not least, I must prove to the ever shrinking number of non-islamized nations of the world that the U.S. shares their shock over today's events."

Then, the President realized he had one more audience to address: the Israelis. "I must reach out to the Jews, assuring them of our solidarity with them, without alienating the Muslims! How can I perform that miracle?"

As he sulked over the task before him, the as yet untested President suddenly understood his imperative. He thought, *"This precarious address must be a tag-team approach. We will shoot with both barrels! Triple A will co-anchor the official U.S. response to today's atrocities! Who better to calm the righteous fury of the Muslims of America and the world than one of their own?*

"Perhaps Triple A will play a much larger role in my administration than either of us have foreseen. My Vice President must step out from his behind the scenes role and into the national spotlight. After all, he brought me into the White House. Now, he must help me stay here!"

Finally, the President sat down behind his desk. In fifteen minutes, his Vice President and Cabinet members would meet him in the situation room to discuss the crisis. As he waited for their arrival, the Commander in Chief confronted his greatest weakness. He had not chosen qualified men and women to fill his Cabinet posts. Rather, the consummate political gambler had used those plum positions to pay back political debt. Such nominees scored a big hit with the Democratic majority in Congress, but they would prove to be far less than what he needed today. After all, a chain's strength could not overcome its weakest link, and the President's leadership chain possessed many weak links.

In an unexpected moment of self reflection, the most powerful man in America asked himself, *"Am I the weakest link of all?"* As the question hung in the air in silence, he rose from his chair and walked across the room to gaze at the Presidential portraits he had chosen to hang in the Oval Office. He peered deeply into the eyes of several of his predecessors who suffered major crises during their tenure in the White House. As he paused before the portraits of Abraham Lincoln, Franklin D. Roosevelt, Harry Truman, John F. Kennedy, Ronald Reagan, Paul Ryan, and Marco Rubio, he asked those patriots, "Did you feel like you were up to the task when you occupied this office?"

Instead of grappling further with his self-doubt, he thought, *"I need more help!"* With that revealing statement, Double J stepped outside the Oval Office door and briskly walked to the office of his Chief of Staff. The President opened the door and said, "Eddie, I need to talk with three people: Pastor Mark Basel in Atlanta, Rabbi Shlomo Ben Yisra'el in Abu Gosh, Israel, and Imam Addar Mansur Zaahir in the DROP—if he is still alive!"

Then, he quickly ran back to the Oval Office. He opened the door and shouted "Print!" He asked himself, *"Why preserve for posterity the questions and doubt that grip me today?"* Thus, the political ace quickly read over his words so he could purge those that might cast him in an unfavorable light. As he read, the President muttered to himself, *"After all, I have a legacy to build and preserve."*

To that end, the President also added some comments. He whispered to himself with a sly smile on his face, *"Why not include some noble and brave thoughts in the historical account of this day of my Presidency?"* Quickly, he made new audio and print versions of his morning monologue.

Patting himself on the back, he thought, *"As President Obama's first Chief of Staff, Rahm Emmanuel told his boss, 'Never let a serious crisis go to waste!'"*

"And We made the son of Mary and his mother as a Sign: We gave them both shelter on high ground, affording rest and security and furnished with springs."
Qur'an 23:50

CHAPTER 9

ADDING INSULT TO INJURY. . .

*A*s the pastor rose from the altar, he picked up his Bible. He was thumbing through the pages, when his office 3DHP lit up. He expected the call to be from his wife or one of the family members in the church. Instead, Imam Addar Zaahir's face appeared before him.

"Hello?" Mark said, curious as to why the imam would be calling him, especially on a Sunday morning just before worship.

"You are looking good, Pastor! This is Imam Zaahir, but of course you know that already. You haven't seen the news this morning, have you?"

"No," Mark replied with deepening curiosity, "why do you ask?"

"Do you have your mobile 3DHP with you? Actually, you have an HV3D right there in your office, don't you?"

Mark asked himself, *"How does he know I have an HV3D?"* Then, he answered the imam, "Why yes, I do have an HV3D, but I haven't been watching it this morning."

"Of course not, you have been praying, haven't you?"

This conversation was turning strange, but Mark did not have time to further consider the imam's words. "Right again, Addar. You seem to know me very well this morning."

The Muslim cleric smiled slyly. "I just remember what you told me in the Rose Garden—about how you prepare for worship and preaching."

Mark did not recall that conversation, but why would he? Still, the imam was making him nervous. He always did. "What can I do for you, Addar? I will have members of the congregation arriving any moment."

"Of course you will. I'll get to the point. Turn on your HV3D and see for yourself what is happening."

The imam's voice sounded peculiar. Mark could not tell if what he heard was excitement or anxiety. The pastor turned toward the HV3D and said, "On." Immediately, images of blazing fire and billowing smoke surrounded him.

"What am I seeing, Addar?"

"You are looking at what remains of the *Al Haram al-Sharif*, the Noble Sanctuary, which includes, as you also know, the Dome of the Rock, the Al Aqsa Mosque, and the underground Al Marawani Mosque. You are also seeing devastation of the DROP government and political buildings in East Jerusalem!"

"This is the Temple Mount? What happened?" Mark could not believe his eyes.

"Pastor Mark, four SSI missiles were fired from a secret military base inside Israel on the defenseless and demilitarized DROP. Perhaps this attack shows why Israel has always insisted that a Palestinian state have no armed forces of its own. One rocket from the Israeli base hit the Al Aqsa Mosque. Another destroyed the Dome of the Rock. Together, those two missiles destroyed the entire Noble Sanctuary, which you Christians refer to as the Temple Mount, even though no Temple ever stood there. The third missile consumed the DROP's temporary capitol building in East Jerusalem, while the last obliterated the Palestinian political office building. We have no idea how many Palestinians have been killed, but we fear that the DROP is without a government head or political leadership." All the while, the imam's voice remained formal and calm as he relayed the horrible story of destruction and loss of life.

"Israel did this?" Mark asked with great hesitance in his words.

"I did not say that. Officially, Israel's Prime Minister says he has no idea who did this. But the evidence points to Israel."

"How do you know the missiles were SSI's and from a secret base in Israel?"

The imam did not answer the question, but spoke personally, "Mark, I know you must cut this conversation short to greet your people as they arrive. Yet, I need your help. As one of the men of faith who helped craft the peace agreement, I need you to come to Palestine and help us prevent a war from erupting! Your presence would be quite reassuring. I have been asked to temporarily speak for the DROP until we determine if our President is alive, injured, or dead, as we assume. Can you fly out tonight on the direct flight to Tel Aviv? If so, I will have a car and a driver ready to meet you at the airport. This is the upmost importance, Mark!"

Dazed and uncertain, Mark said nothing.

"Pastor," the imam asked, "can you give me an answer?"

"I apologize, Addar, I am just somewhat overwhelmed by what has happened and by your request."

"I understand, Mark. I too apologize—for catching you off guard with all of this. I know you have a lot going on this morning. Yet, as you might imagine, time is of the essence. Your President is about to address America and the world. The Israeli Prime Minister spoke to his people and the citizens of the nations only minutes ago. These leaders have no idea what is happening. Truly, no one does. I will be speaking to the shattered nation of the Palestinians in a few moments, and I need to know if I can say that you and the other leaders who helped craft the peace accord with Israel are returning to help us through this crisis before the Battle of *Har Megiddo* erupts before our eyes! I am sorry, Mark, but I need your answer. You and your wife Ariel—you both must come! There is no time for debate!"

Trying to make sense of all the morning's events in Atlanta, Israel, and Palestine, Mark continued to stand in the midst of the images of the carnage in silence.

With growing impatience and anger, Addar shouted at Mark, "Will you come?"

"Blessed are the meek, for they will inherit the earth."
Matthew 5:5

CHAPTER 10

UPPING THE STAKES. . .

*A*s typical, the Vice President would be late to the emergency meeting at the White House. Thus, his driver disengaged the satellite autodrive on the limo and sped through the streets of Washington D.C.. In the back seat, Abdul-ghafoor Asim Abdullah fumed. He felt like a political pawn.

Abdul had no desire whatsoever to address the nation with the President at this critical moment in history. The Vice President understood clearly that the President planned to use him—again—and he was tired of James' gamesmanship.

As he stared out the window of the limo, Abdul knew the Muslims wanted to use him as well. Ever since the election, Abdul had been receiving calls from prominent Muslims both inside and outside of the United States. Invariably, they wanted him to back their cause or some initiative that would promote Islam, Sharia Law, or even terrorist activity within U.S. borders.

He had received such a call this very morning from the General of the Brotherhood Army—or as Abdul called him, the Masked Man of Babylon. As far as Abdul knew, no one had ever seen the General's face. Thankfully, Abdul could not answer the General because the President called at the same time.

The President never gave Abdul a chance to talk but looked a bit shell shocked as he said, "Triple A—have you seen the news? I need you at the White House as fast as you can get here. You and I will be addressing the nation! Drop whatever you are doing and get here, Triple A! I need your take on today's events."

Abdul hated the nickname the President had given him. Likewise, he hated the President's nickname, too. *"President Double J and Vice President Triple A—both monikers show disrespect for us and the offices we hold."*

Despite his frustration, Abdul faced far more important issues today. When he arrived at the White House, what would he tell the President? Surely his boss would ask him if he knew or suspected who launched the attack on Jerusalem. Should Abdul reveal his suspicions or should he say nothing at all? The Muslim powers that be said they intentionally kept him in the dark so he could have deniability. Abdul wondered if they just did not trust him. Either way, the Muslim Vice President wasn't sure he wanted to know the corrupt plans of the players in the Caliphate.

In a vacuum of facts, the Muslim-biased media spun the story of the missile attack, pinning the blame on a rogue Israeli Air Force squadron. That option made no sense to Abdul, as such a unit would easily be identified and brought to the world stage to confess.

So far, no one had stepped forward to claim responsibility for the gruesome attack. Conspiracy theories abounded, and of course, one of them was complete subterfuge: "The U.S. and Israel had teamed up to wipe out the Palestinians. In short order, the two allies would hit the remainder of the Muslim lands with similar attacks." No one needed to tell Abdul knew who pushed that disinformation.

What could he honestly say to the President, the American electorate, and the remaining free world that would help relieve fears? Much less, how could he calm the Muslims in the U.S. and around the planet who were itching to retaliate? Would he be allowed to speak the truth or would he be forced to read a prepared statement, as he had begrudgingly done so many times before?

Despite being out of the Muslim leadership loop, Abdul indeed had a very strong sense of who was behind today's disaster. Likewise, the Vice President thought he knew the perpetrator's motive, as well. But did he dare expose what he felt to be true to the President? Would the Commander in Chief believe him? What proof would Abdul be willing and able to offer?

The second most powerful man in the world felt trapped as he continued to stare out the window of the limo. As it sped past the Lincoln Memorial, Abdul knew he would be at the White House in a few moments. He wanted to pray, but to whom? *"Should I pray to Allah, the god I cannot understand, who demands that I pray in Arabic—senseless words to a senseless god? Do I even believe in Allah anymore? Instead, maybe this would be the best time to speak my first prayer to Isa?"*

A Messianic believer had been telling Abdul things he never knew about Isa—Y'shua as she called Him. Contrary to Islamic teachings, the Messianic Jew told Abdul that Isa was indeed crucified on the cross to atone for sin. Furthermore, his female friend claimed that Isa was indeed the very Son of God—a claim Muslims regarded as heresy.

After all, how could a divine Allah father a child with an earthly woman? Having sex was beneath the god of Islam—even though Allah, when he was only the moon god of Mecca, originally had a wife, the goddess of the sun, and three daughters. Abdul sarcastically thought, *"I wonder how Muhammad persuaded Allah to dump his wife and children? Allah started out as one of the hundreds of Arab pagan gods—one for each day, if needed. Muhammad must have promised Allah he would be the head honcho, the one and only, if he divorced his wife and disowned his daughters!"*

Abdul's friend, Naomi Levine, had said that the true God of the Bible caused Mary to become pregnant though His Spirit, not by any physical act. Abdul found that prospect intriguing. After all, even Islam considered Mary the virgin mother of Isa—although not the son of Allah. If not by the Spirit of God, how else could a virgin Mary have conceived a son? Following the discussions with Naomi, Abdul had read the New Testament passages about Isa's birth with great interest. Actually, the Muslim Vice President had gone on to read most of the Christian Bible.

If Isa was God in human flesh—Emmanuel as Naomi called Him—could His sacrificial death actually atone for sin, even Abdul's sin? Could the Incarnate, who never sinned, become sin for all mankind, as Naomi put it, and thereby offer Himself in substitutionary sacrifice on a cross of agony and shame? Abdul silently asked, *"How can I be sure?"*

His questions had led him to delve into the growing Chrislam movement for a short time. So called peace-loving Muslims and open-minded Christians claimed the two faiths worshiped the same god. Nonetheless, Abdul knew enough about authentic Christianity and true

Islam to understand that the two deities were irreconcilably different. The God of the Bible loved unconditionally and forgave freely while the god of the Qur'an hated intensely and punished joyfully. Plus, in the days of Moses, two thousand years before the birth of Muhammad, the God of the Bible prohibited the Jews from worshiping pagan gods and specifically condemned bowing down to the moon, sun, or stars. No, Abdul could not reconcile the god of the Muslims with the God of the Christians and Messianics.

Abdul enjoyed talking about issues of faith with Naomi. As a matter of fact, Abdul just enjoyed being with Naomi. His heart always raced when they talked. Come to think of it, Abdul's heart skipped along whenever he thought about her—even now. Abdul trusted her with his deepest doubts and fears.

Only Naomi knew that a crisis of faith raged in the soul of the Vice President of the United States. At times he hated Islam and its cruel, austere god. Allah changed his mind whenever he wanted, and he constantly called for violence and war. What Muslim could be sure he would go to Paradise, with the rivers flowing beneath, unless he killed or was killed in jihad?

Isa and Allah stood as stark opposites. But why should Abdul trust Isa? Were not millions of Muslims killed by Isa's followers? Regardless, Abdul decided he was like one of Isa's closest followers: Thomas. Whispering to himself, the Vice President said, *"I must see Isa to believe in Isa. And what are the odds of that happening?"*

Abdul then asked himself, *"How did I manage to get locked in this spiritual and political trap, anyway?"* He had refused James' request to be his running mate many times, but finally relented. *"Why?"* he asked himself one more time. Actually, He knew the answer. Addar had persuaded him. The imam had filled Abdul's head with and heart with lofty goals of helping the Muslim people of the United States and the world. However, immediately after the election, Addar revealed his true colors and allegiances. Abdul feared that today tragic events in the DROP and Israel would soon consume him as well.

He felt like a puppet that two masters were fighting to control: James and Addar. The Vice President seemed to recall a passage he had read in the New Testament that said a man could not serve two masters. Abdul asked himself, *"Didn't Isa say one master would be*

69

loved and the other hated? Which master will I choose? Sometimes, I hate both of them!"

As the driver said, "We're here, Mr. Vice President," Abdul's mobile 3DHP came to life. *"Mr. President, I'm outside the door!"* he muttered to himself. To his surprise, this call came not from the President or from anyone else in the United States, for that matter. This call originated in Babylon, and only one person would call him from the Caliphate. What if this call was being traced? Should Abdul answer it?

The driver opened the limousine door, but Abdul-ghafoor Asim Abdullah, the Vice President of the United States of America, only swallowed hard and stared at the larger than life veiled face of the General!

*"Nay, We gave the good things of this life to these men and
their fathers until the period grew long for them; See they not
that We gradually reduce the land (in their control) from its
outlying borders? Is it then they who will win?"*
Qur'an 21:44

CHAPTER 11

COMPASSIONATE ENEMY. . .

*S*ol remained on the floor, weeping because of God's displeasure
with him, weeping because of the destroyed Temple Mount,
weeping because of his foolishness in believing that peace could
come in his time, and weeping because of the likelihood that everything he knew in life had now changed. As the tears gushed down his
cheeks, Ahava nervously tapped his shoulder and tried to hand him the
holophone.

"Did you reach Mark and Ariel?" Sol whispered, trying to regain
his composure, before taking the call.

"No," Ahava replied, shaking all over and wiping her own tears
away. "Someone else called you first."

"Who?" the weary rabbi asked his partner in life and ministry.

"Imam Addar Zaahir," Sol's cringing wife replied.

"Oh!" was all Sol could muster in response. He wiped the tears
from his face and cleared his throat. "How bad do I look Ahava?"

The love of his life could only shake her head.

Taking the 3DHP from her, the weary rabbi said, "*Salaam*, Imam
Zaahir."

"Shalom, my friend," Addar replied in kind. "Sol, I can see your
devastation. If you are like me, you feel as if the world you have known
up until this moment has suddenly disappeared."

"You read my mind, Addar. At this point, I don't see how we can make things right again."

"Isn't that the test of faith?" the duplicitous imam asked.

Addar's seemingly sincere comments took the tension and fear out of the conversation. "You are exactly right, Addar," Sol answered. "Although I do not know where we go from here, I do know the One who has already set the course!"

"While we seemingly both believe in a power higher than our own, do you think any of us could have foreseen the horrid events of this day?"

"If we could have anticipated this tragedy, Addar, we would have done everything in our power to prevent it!"

"I agree, my friend! Yes, I agree!"

A long pause ensued as Sol's grief-filled spirit left him with no clue of what to say next.

In every sense of the word, the two religious leaders could not have been more opposite. While Sol sat on the floor weeping before *Adonai*, Addar seemed untouched in this hour of inexpressible trial. Unlike Sol's reddened eyes and puffed face, Addar's visage remained unmarred by the catastrophic events of the day. If anything, the imam's face communicated satisfaction, even borderline happiness.

In terms of physical appearance, Sol measured five feet and two inches short in his elevator shoes, while Addar soared at a height of six feet and three inches. More round than tall, Sol wore 53 inch pants. With such uncommon measurements, Sol's wardrobe required custom tailoring. On the other hand, Addar always wore a *thowb*, a robe that concealed his 34 inch waist. Sol's lengthy, flowing, pure white beard actually rested on his portly belly. In contrast, Addar's coarse, black beard remained closely trimmed.

In regard to faith, the aged rabbi staunchly defended Orthodox Judaism as the purest form of the Jewish faith, *HaShem* as the only true God, and the Tanakh as His only inspired Scripture. Conversely, Addar publicly fought for the most transparent expression of Islam, all the while proclaiming Allah not only as the veritable deity of the Qur'an, but also as the same heavenly being found within the Hebrew and Christian Scriptures, as well.

Though Addar always pushed to reach his goals, a faux, mild-mannered exterior veiled his inner drive. To outside observers, the imam seemed to take setbacks in stride. Yet deep within Addar, an all-consuming void pushed him to never accept defeat. As Sol groveled in silence before his God, Addar strategically, perhaps unscrupulously, plotted his next move.

Finally, Addar could endure no more of Sol's runny nose and leaky eyes. The Muslim cleric despised the weakness of his Jewish counterpart. In fact, the rabbi's melodramatic performance sickened Addar to the point of nausea! He asked himself, *"Why would any god put up with these people? A handful of such imbeciles lost their lives today, and this pig is blubbering like a baby who wants his umm to nurse him!"* Addar wanted to say, *"Suck it up! Be a man, you sniveling Jew!"* Be that as it may, the sophisticated, even-keeled imam determined this was not the moment for such an outburst.

Unable to stomach the rabbi's emotional spectacle any longer, the imam finally pierced the strained silence by saying, "Sol, I need your help!"

"What can I do? Tell me, and you can consider it done," Sol answered, hoping that his affirmative response would help ease the pain in his heart and prove to Addar he yet wanted peace.

"As you might imagine, our government and political leaders are presumed dead."

"Yes, and I wondered until a moment ago. . ." Sol stopped his sentence before finishing his sorrowful thought.

Addar stepped in to fill the void once more, "You wondered if I was alive, myself?"

Hanging his head, Sol answered, "Yes. I could not bear to utter the words."

In that moment, the calloused Addar actually felt the softhearted Sol's compassion. To his amazement, the Muslim cleric suddenly realized that this Orthodox rabbi, this Jewish infidel, actually cared about his life. Sol's genuine affection caught Addar off guard. He wasn't prepared to engage emotionally with this man whom he regarded as his vile enemy!

Clearing his throat, Addar said, "Thankfully, I was in Ankara, the Babylonian capitol." Then, to regain his composure and control over the conversation, the straightforward imam changed the subject.

"Tomorrow evening, I need you to come to East Jerusalem. I want to bring our negotiating team together once more. If we have any hope of averting all out war, we need cool heads. Can you come, rabbi?"

"Tell me the time and place, and I will be there," Sol replied without even pausing to consider the risks to his person.

Addar thanked Sol in both Arabic and Hebrew: "*Shokran! Todah!* I will contact you again with the details as soon as I have them." Then, looking for a way to end the call on a positive note, the imam awkwardly said, "Ahava must be prepared to join you! I tell you, Sol, for an eighty-five year old woman, she is still slim and trim and quite attractive! You are a blessed man, my friend."

Sol looked at his bride of six and a half decades and agreed wholeheartedly with Addar's compliment, yet he had no idea what to say back to the imam.

Refusing to endure Sol's morose expression any longer, the Muslim holy man abruptly closed the call by saying, "Don't worry! I promise I won't try to win Ahava's heart! She is safe with the man she obviously loves and adores! Regardless, make sure you treat her well! If she were my bride I would give her everything she deserves!" His beguilingly evil smile went unnoticed by the grieving rabbi. "Goodbye, my most fortunate friend."

The impatient imam did not wait for Sol to respond. The rabbi wondered, *"On this day of grief, how can Addar be so carefree and whimsical? He almost seems glad."*

"When you hear of wars and rumors of wars, do not be alarmed. Such things must happen, but the end is still to come."
Mark 13:7

CHAPTER 12

CALMING TURBULENT SOULS. . .

*"H*ar Megiddo?"* Had Mark heard the imam correctly? *Har Megiddo,* the Mountain of Megiddo, was the Hebrew name of the site where the rulers of the world would gather for the end time battle predicted in Revelation chapter sixteen. Over the centuries, the two words were corrupted into Armageddon.

Why would the MIT and Princeton trained Muslim be talking about that end times battle? On one hand, Addar, as a surviving Shia Muslim, would believe that the true followers of Allah would massacre two thirds of the Jews at *Har Megiddo* and then face the Christians at *Al-Malhama Al-Kubra*, the Great Slaughter, the Great Battle. Shiites, now virtually extinct, anticipated these events would be tied to the return of the *Mahdi*—the Twelfth Imam, the final imam.

On the other hand, Mark expected the Battle at *Har Megiddo* to come at the end of the seven year Tribulation. The Book of Revelation claimed that all the remaining rulers of the world would gather at *Megiddo.* There, Jesus would execute judgment on the nations, thus setting the stage for His thousand year reign on earth.

The pastor said to himself, *"Surely we are not at the throes of Megiddo. While the Gog-Magog War may be past, will not our Lord's followers be raptured before the Tribulation and the Battle of Har Megiddo?"*

Indeed, many Christians and Jews believed that the battle of Gog and Magog had already been fought. During World War III, Russia and its Muslim allies attacked Israel with undefeatable, unstoppable force. However, the Christians and Jews trusted that God Himself intervened on Israel's behalf, causing a worldwide earthquake as well as bringing down fire from Heaven to stop the invaders in their tracks.

Did Addar believe more end time battles would soon erupt? Was he privy to plans the Caliph might have to wipe out most of the Jews? The pastor's head was spinning as he attempted to sort out the threat against his church, the devastation in Jerusalem, Addar's comment, and what would happen next.

Mark had finally told Addar that he and Ariel would come to East Jerusalem. Be that as it may, would they be able to fly to Palestine that night? Why were both of them needed? How long would they be gone? Who would watch the children?

The pastor forced himself to focus on the immediate crisis before him. He looked at the time and realized his congregation should be arriving. Tightly closing his eyes, Mark called on Jesus: "Lord! Show me what to do, what to say!"

With that brief but most earnest prayer, Mark ran out of his study, through the sanctuary, and to the outside doors, where he stopped to catch his breath. As he opened the doors, the minister found several families talking excitedly about the morning's catastrophic events in Israel and the DROP. Oblivious to the crises at hand, their children innocently chased each other in circles.

Mark thought, *"Though my people have seen the news from Jerusalem, they surely have not seen the bloody threat that was nailed to this very door."*

Forcing a smile to his face, the pastor began to greet and calm the people whose lives were entrusted to him by Jesus Himself! Indeed, he shepherded a church of the nations. His congregation consisted of refugees from China and Japan, former Muslims from Afghanistan, Turkey, and Iran, former Orthodox Jews—who were now Messianic Jews—from Russia and the U.S., former agnostic and atheistic Europeans who fled their own countries rather than be islamized, and Americans who had at one time had no faith in either the God or the country of their forefathers. Now, all of these diverse souls were united as one as fervent followers of Isa, Y'shua, Jesus!

Seven years ago, this church had begun with two members: Mark and his blushing bride from Israel. Today, more than eight hundred redeemed and transformed souls would come together in unity to worship the one true God and King who transcends all human divisions of nationality, language, culture, politics, income, education, age, and gender. The Lord blessed Mark to guide an undivided congregation—united in Jesus' love, mercy, and peace.

At this point in American history, agnostics and atheists not only far outnumbered people of faith, but the growing number of Muslims also far outpaced the dwindling numbers of Christians. Therefore, given such lack of faith in the society at large, Mark knew his Lord smiled on his congregation.

On this morning of terror, the good and faithful shepherd tried to be upbeat for his arriving flock. Quickly, he faced a wide range of emotions. Though many of the people were angry, more were mournful. Though a few of the church members demanded revenge, the vast majority of the souls simply felt shock and disbelief.

No matter their feelings, each of them, one at a time, fell into their pastor's open arms for strength and comfort—even as Mark himself was trying to process his own emotional reaction to all the morning events! He whispered to each of his brothers and sisters in Jesus, "Our Lord is with us. Trust in Him! Claim His peace!"

"Peace? What peace?" a senior Messianic Jew by the name of Zebulun Bartimaeus exclaimed as he freed himself from Mark's embrace. "How can you even say the word peace today when war has begun? I have lived through many wars and brushes with war in my years! Mark my words, Pastor, today is the beginning of World War IV, so don't talk to me about peace!"

Surprised by the abrasive reaction to his words of comfort, Mark needed a second or two to readjust his thoughts. After blinking his eyes for several seconds, Mark replied, "Zebulun, the peace of Y'shua is not contingent on peaceful circumstances. *Adonai* promised us His peace, not the world's version of peace. Though all hell may rage around us, we can yet claim and live in the peace of Y'shua, my brother!"

Immediately, Zebulun placed his bald head back on Mark's shoulder. "Forgive me, Pastor," the seasoned believer said. I should not have said what I did nor should I have said it so boisterously! I do trust in Y'shua and His peace, and I know today's events did not surprise Him! Even so, I can hardly bear to see the *Kotel* and the Old City as burning ruins!"

"Certainly, such a sight is horrible for us all, Zeb! We all grieve today, not only for the loss of such pieces of our history of faith, but for the many lives that have been extinguished today. The vast majority of those souls did not know Y'shua as Messiah, Saviour, and Lord!"

With his head still on Mark's shoulder, Zebulun said, "Today's loss is nothing, compared to what will we see in the days and weeks ahead! Today is the beginning of the end!"

"But when the forbidden months are past, then fight and slay the Pagans wherever ye find them, and seize them, beleaguer them, and lie in wait for them in every stratagem (of war); But if they repent, and establish regular prayers And practice regular charity, then open the way for them: For Allah is Oft-forgiving, Most Merciful."
Qur'an 9:5

CHAPTER 13

WITH ALL DUE RESPECT. . .

*T*he shaken Vice President entered the White House and resolutely walked to the Situation Room. Along the way, he decided not to take the call from the Babylonian capitol of Ankara in the Caliphate's state of Turkey. Too many people were watching and listening. Any conversation with the General would require complete privacy.

As he opened the door and entered the Situation Room, Abdul scanned the seats at the table and saw that his was the only one that remained empty. The President stood and said. "Nice of you to join us, Triple A!" Double J intended to break the tension of the day with a light moment, but his comment ended up sounding like a cheap shot.

Abdul stopped short of his seat. For the first time, he revealed anger as his eyes turned toward the head of the table. "Mr. President, these are very troublesome moments. I would greatly appreciate it if you would speak to me with the respect due me and the office I hold!"

Double J pursed his lower lip, not having the foggiest idea what Triple A meant by his words. Nonetheless, the President did not appreciate the open rebuke from his Vice President in the presence of his Cabinet.

The determined Vice President continued to speak forcefully, as he said, "Call me Abdul, call me Mr. Abdullah, call me Mr. Vice President, but do not ever again call me Triple A!"

With those words, the top two men in the United States—and perhaps the world—stared into each other's open eyes across the vast expanse of the conference room table in the Situation Room. Whoever blinked or spoke first lost the challenge, and Abdul knew with certainty that he would not lose, not this time. At six feet and four inches tall, the Vice President had a six inch height advantage over the President. Abdul stood his ground, something the Commander in Chief and his Cabinet had never seen him do, as he typically said and did little to nothing at their meetings.

Finally, awkwardly, the President spoke. "Have a seat—Mr. Vice President!"

"Thank you, Mr. President," Abdul responded as he sat in his chair across from James. "For future reference, I believe all of us in this room should be called either by our proper names or the position we hold—you included, sir. We need to respect each other and our positions, especially now, given the circumstances before us!"

"Anything else Mr. Vice President?" The tone of the question revealed both James' embarrassment and frustration.

"No sir, Mr. President. Thank you!" Abdul wondered if he had said too much and gone too far.

"Well then, I do have something for you, Abdul."

"Yes, James?"

"Have your bags packed and ready to go as soon as this meeting is over!"

Abdul thought to himself, *"What? Have I just been fired? Is the President so insecure that he could not take even the smallest challenge?"* Abdul took a deep breath and was about to stand so he could leave the room, when James continued speaking.

"You and I will be flying to the DROP immediately following our joint address to the nation."

Abdul sighed audibly. He was so glad that he had not stood or started walking to the door! How embarrassing that move would have been! Quickly regaining his composure, Abdul displayed genuine, deep-seated concern as he asked, "Both of us, sir? Is it wise for both of us to be in such a volatile area of the world at the same time? Frankly, is this the time for either of us to be in what could reasonably be called a war zone?"

The tension in his voice waning, the President replied, "I considered the existential risks, Mr. Vice President, before I agreed for both of us to go. I have arranged for extra security personnel as well as additional security methods during our travels. Plus, while waiting on you to arrive, we determined this is the best course of action. You and I will show American support for both the Israelis and Palestinians.

"Likewise, we will be there as heads of state for the funerals that are coming. Caliph Sanaullah bin Laden has declared the traditional three day mourning period for the dead. Even so, because of the grim task of finding as many bodies or body parts as possible, the Caliph has suspended the requirement for burial within twenty four hours. Instead, a mass funeral service will be held on Wednesday."

"'Agreed to go,' Mr. President? Has someone invited both of us to go to Palestine?"

His voice now calm, the President answered, "You catch on quickly."

With his curiosity piqued, Abdul asked, "Who wants us in Palestine, Mr. President—and for what purpose?"

"Actually, Imam Zaahir has invited us." The President's words hit Abdul so hard that James might as well have punched him in the stomach. "With the DROP government and political leadership severed at the top, the imam wants to reassemble the team that helped negotiate the treaty with Israel."

Abdul shook his head. "Mr. President, I was not part of those negotiations—in any direct fashion. In fact, you did not help broker the treaty, either." He looked away from the President to the previous and current administrations' Secretary of State, Hannah Fiedler. As she used her virtual key pad to hammer out notes for the two leaders, Abdul asked, "Should not the Secretary of State, who played such an essential role in the negotiations, be the one to accompany you, sir?"

The President left his seat, walked over to Hannah's chair, and stood behind her. "The husband of the Secretary of State is—or at least was before today—in discussions with the DROP for a government contract for his pharmaceutical company. Thank God that Aaron was not in Palestine at the time of the missile strike! However, being hyper-cautious at this most sensitive and uncertain time, we see at least a potential conflict of interest should the Secretary of State accompany me on this trip."

Hannah pointed out that she agreed with the President's decision. "With the situation so tense and precarious, Abdul, I too feel that my presence would have a negative impact on any discussions. I have fully briefed the President on the history of the negotiations that led to the formation of the DROP four months ago. I have also prepared extensive notes for you, Abdul."

"Thank you, Hannah," the Vice President said with sincerity. "However, you remain the one that needs to be there. I fear that your absence will speak the wrong message to the Palestinians."

The President cut off that line of thought by saying, "Abdul, as brilliant and pivotal as Hannah was during the negotiations, she was not invited to join me in East Jerusalem. Instead, Imam Zaahir specifically invited you! Perhaps he senses that you, of all American leaders, will be able to relate to the Palestinians in this time of great turmoil."

Abdul doubted that the President's reasoning, though it did make sense. He chose to add nothing more to the conversation. Instead, the Vice President whispered to himself as he pushed back in his chair, *"So, Addar has plans for me—again! If he cannot get to me through the General, he will get to me through the President!"*

Back in his seat, the first democrat to occupy the White House in sixteen years noted, "Imam Zaahir says he has also invited Israeli Prime Minister Ben Baruch, as well as Rabbi Shlomo Ben Y'sra'el, Pastor Mark Basel, and their wives to the meeting in the DROP capitol. Mr. Vice President, do you have any ideas as to why Ariel and Ahava are needed in the DROP in these tense days?"

Of course Abdul could offer a few opinions, but he could not mention them in this room at this time—especially not with these people. Instead, the Vice President frivolously postulated, "In comparison to men, empirical studies show that women have more natural ability to defuse tense situations. Again, I reiterate that Secretary Fielder, not the Vice President, should be flying with you later today."

"You really don't want to go with me, do you, Mr. Vice President?"

As he was not expecting that question, Abdul faltered for a second, and then said, "Of course I don't want to go! What expertise, diplomacy, or tactical advice can I offer in the place of the Secretary of State?"

The President looked at Abdul, as if the answer loomed obvious to everyone else in the world, save him. Then James took on a personal tone. "Abdul, are you not a Muslim? As Vice President of the United States, and the only Muslim to hold such office, you are the most qualified person in this room to attend this meeting! If we hope to avert war at this precarious moment, we need your influence and insight. Without you, I doubt seriously that the imam would have invited me, Abdul."

Of all that James said to Abdul, the question, "Are you not a Muslim?" hung in his head and heart. As he struggled with his answer to the President's question, the first man in line for the highest office in the land found himself staring into blank space.

As the silence again became uncomfortable, the President asked, "Abdul! Where are you? We need you to focus with us in these moments before our joint address."

Shaking off the voices within him, Abdul replied, "James, whatever you and the Union needs, I am ready. Still, as you might imagine, the unspeakable events of this day have hit me differently than they have struck all of you." The moment Abdul stopped speaking, he asked himself, *"Where in the world did I find those words?"*

The President sighed deeply. "Please forgive me, Abdul. How inconsiderate of me not to realize that you would be processing all these developments in a much more personal manner than the rest of us. I truly am sorry! I believe I can speak for all of us in offering you and your people our condolences."

While everyone around the table nodded their heads in agreement, Abdul realized he had not witnessed a thoughtful, compassionate side of James before this moment. The Vice President had no idea what he was supposed to say in response. Thus, he replied with a few softly spoken but deeply felt words: "Thank you, Mr. President. Thank you, everyone. I truly do not know how to express the feelings within me."

James replied, "No problem! We understand."

Then, a wry smile graced the President's face as he turned from his conversation with his Vice President to speak to the rest of his Cabinet. He said, "It's odd, don't you think, that this morning I had not only called all of you who are now here at the table, but I had also tried to contact Sam, Sol, Mark, and Addar. I wanted to know their take on today's tragic act of terror. As I spoke with the imam, he said he too wanted to hear the input of everyone who was involved in the peace negotiations. Perhaps Addar and I are on the same page!"

Abdul responded honestly, perhaps too honestly as he said, "James, I most certainly hope that you do not share any of Addar's desires and expectations for our hastily arranged meeting in the DROP!"

CHAPTER 14

A MUDDLED MESSAGE. . .

*I*mam Addar Zaahir looked remarkably calm in the moments before his address. He sat in front of the DROP's red, white, green, and black flag, which featured a large crescent moon in the center. No clues on the set indicated where he was.

As he began, Addar spoke with confidence, as though his moment in time had arrived.

"*Salaam*, citizens of the Democratic Republic of Palestine. Shalom, citizens of Israel, our partners in peace. And peace to the citizens of the United States, Babylon, and this world, whose eyes focus here on *Al Quds*, the Holy, Jerusalem."

Addar stopped talking as the scenes of the destruction and carnage again came before the world. Nothing existed to give viewers a familiar reference point for what they beheld. Everything that once existed at the Temple Mount and in East Jerusalem existed no longer. Charred remains of buildings and tiny pieces of seared human flesh filled the smoldering landscape.

As the incredible aftermath of the explosions continued to be displayed to an international audience, the imam declared, "Though the physical fires are under control, the Holy City, East and West alike, is ablaze with feverish mourning. We grieve over the shocking and horrid loss of life from the brutal and unprovoked attack on the innocents. Unarmed citizens of Palestine and the world were brutally killed atop the *Haram al-Sharif*, the Noble Sanctuary—the Temple Mount as the Jews and Christians falsely call it, as no Jewish Temple ever existed there. Such violent death also rained down upon the diligent national and political leaders in the capitol of the DROP."

Energetically, Addar continued, saying, "Investigations in both Israel and the DROP move forward at this hour, as we seek to determine who plotted and carried out this deadly and most devastating attack on the newborn Palestinian State. The death toll and the names of the deceased will be compiled, if bodies, or should I say body parts, can be found and identified. DNA analysis may be our only means of knowing who died in such hideous fashion today. However, early reports indicated that the powerful blasts destroyed even the victims' DNA.

"Most unfortunately, we now know that our recently elected DROP leaders, including our noble President Mundhir Kanaan and his faithful Vice President Ratib Shadid were killed instantly in the missile attack, along with countless other government officials, members of the Palestinian Congress, as well as our main political party leaders. I have been asked to fill the DROP leadership void until we schedule new elections."

The imam, a powerful rhetorician, leaned forward as he said, "At this historic moment and time of bereavement, we could easily lash out in hate. We who remain are certain that our attackers want us to do just that—strike out in violent hatred! No matter, until we know without doubt who lies behind these heinous assassinations and murders, we must turn to the one true god, Allah, Most Gracious, Most Merciful. Allah is the one god of Muhammad, peace be upon him, and Isa, whom some know as Y'shua or Jesus, and Ibrahim, whom some call Abraham. To be men and women of genuine peace, we must pray for solace, strength, patience, perseverance, and determination!"

Addar eased back in his chair. He asked, "What do we know? We know that four SSI Missiles, developed jointly by Israel and the United States, swept out of the clear blue sky at 3:03 p.m. Israeli time. We know that these missiles were fired from within the borders of Israel. Nonetheless—let me caution all who want to jump to conclusions—we as yet have no indication as to who ordered the firing of those missiles or why they were launched.

"While my statement may sound ludicrous to the citizens of the DROP, we must ask, what could Israel have hoped to gain from this destruction, so soon after negotiating peace with us?"

Addar put his hands together in prayer-like fashion. "Tomorrow, the Palestinian, Israeli, and American members of the team that nego tiated the historic peace between Palestinians and Jews will reassemble in Eastern Jerusalem. Prime Minister Samuel Ben Baruch and President James Paulson will both be here, along with the clergy team which I led. In addition, I have personally invited the U.S. Vice President, Abdul-ghafoor Asim Abdullah, to join us, so he can offer us his valuable insight into this catastrophe. I, Imam Zaahir, will represent both the DROP and Babylon—with the Caliph's blessing—at this hastily arranged meeting.

"As I mentioned a moment ago, I have been asked to guide our country in the critical days ahead, until we know what our response will be to this attack, and until we have duly elected officials again in office. We pray to Allah, Most Gracious, Most Merciful, that this time of transition will be short.

"I call on our Babylonian allies, who wish to rush to our military aid at present, to be patient with us and not act in haste. We do not want to further complicate an already heinous and perilous situation.

"Men and women of the world, of all faiths, please join us in prayer to the one god of all time and eternity for the wisdom and wherewithal to know what to do and when to do it. Trust me, when the enemy has been identified, we will act with all the power and destructive force available to us for vengeance and justice! For now, intercede for the families of the many victims who are mourning this evening.

"I will address you again, tomorrow evening, after our team of Palestinians, Israelis, and Americans—Muslims, Jews, and Christians—has gathered and discussed all the options."

The imam opened his arms to the worldwide audience. "Until then, may Allah, Most Gracious, Most Merciful, indeed be most gracious and merciful to us in our great loss. In addition, may he also be just and swift to condemn and destroy those behind the vulgar evil of this day!"

With those final words, Imam Zaahir's face faded from the HV3D images that filled the sanctuary. With confidence in Jesus, Pastor Mark stepped up to the pulpit. "As I said before the imam's address, we needed to hear and see what he put forth on this day of crisis. Thankfully, he called for peace and tried to calm tensions. He spoke directly against military intervention, at least for the present.

"My wife, Ariel, and I will be flying to Tel Aviv on tonight's redeye out of Atlanta. We will arrive in East Jerusalem, Palestine tomorrow evening. Honestly, I do not know what the imam expects of us, but if we can be of any service in this crisis, Ariel and I are more than willing to go.

"Nevertheless, I fear that grave danger lies ahead. I found some of the imam's words extremely troubling." Mark looked at his notes of the address. "Imam Zaahir said, and I quote, 'We must turn to the one true god, Allah, Most Gracious, Most Merciful. Allah is the one god of Muhammad, peace be upon him, and Isa, whom some know as Y'shua or Jesus, and Ibrahim, whom some call Abraham.' For those of you who did not understand the intent of Imam Zaahir's words, he desired to communicate that Isa and Ibrahim, the Arabic names for Jesus and Abraham in the Qur'an, serve Allah as does Muhammad! The imam wants to draw Christians and Jews under the umbrella of Islam."

Pastor Mark moved to the right of the pulpit and pointed upward with his right forefinger. "Let me be perfectly clear. Imam Zaahir not only said what we hear Muslims telling us here in America today, but he also said what we are hearing from a growing number of Jews and Christians alike! The imam claimed, before the entire world, that Allah, the false god of Muhammad, is the very god of both Jesus and Abraham—and thus the very god of both Jews and Christians! The imam says that Allah, *HaShem,* and God the Father are one and the same!

"How can such be the case when the Qur'an, the Holy Book of Islam, tells Muslims to kill Jews and Christians, and the Holy Book we call the Bible tells us to love and do good to our enemies as well as pray for their redemption? In the fifth chapter of the Qur'an, verse fifty one, we hear the call of Allah as he says:

O ye who believe! Take not the Jews and the Christians for your friends and protectors: They are but friends and protectors to each other. And he amongst you that turns to them (for friendship) is of them. Verily Allah guideth not a people unjust.

"A few verses later, in the seventy second verse of the fifth chapter, Allah says:

Certainly they disbelieve who say: "Allah is Isa the son of Mary." But said Isa: "O Children of Israel! Worship Allah, my

Lord and your Lord." Whoever joins other gods with Allah—Allah will forbid him the Garden, and the Fire will be his abode. There will for the wrong-doers be no one to help.

"And what is the fate of the infidels, Jews and Christians alike? Chapter 18:100 says: *'And We shall present Hell that day for Unbelievers to see, all spread out.'"*

The pastor lightly thumped the pulpit with his left hand as he proclaimed, "The imam calls not for peace! Peace for the Muslims means surrender! The Muslim cleric gives us a choice: either believe that Allah reigns as god over Muhammad, Jesus, and Abraham, or be killed for our refusal to believe! To live, the imam says we must believe that Abraham bound Ishmael, not Isaac, on the altar of sacrifice! To live, we must believe that Jesus came as only a prophet of Allah who will return to personally condemn all Jews and Christians! To live, we must deny that Jesus reigns as the very Son of God who was crucified to redeem us from our sin and who will return to gather all who believe in Him to the Heavenly Kingdom!"

Cupping his hands behind his ears, Mark said, "Listen carefully! This Muslim cleric seeks to deceive Christians and Jews, along with followers of all other religions, as well as agnostics and atheists. You see, the followers of Allah employ deceit as a weapon to destroy the infidels—us! The Muslims will not stop until all the Christians and all the Jews have been wiped off the face of the earth—until everyone who does not believe in Allah no longer exists! This is the command of Islam's false god! I plan to challenge the imam precisely on these points when I meet with him, face to face!"

The members of the congregation talked among themselves and wondered if their pastor spoke the truth. Why was he making such strident allegations against Islam, particularly on this day? Was he right or wrong about the imam? Some thought that Pastor Mark could be overreacting to the current crisis.

As the murmuring continued, the pastor's convincing and conclusive evidence appeared in the HV3D image that surrounded them!

"They take their priests and their anchorites to be their lords in derogation of Allah, and (they take as their Lord) Isa the son of Mary; Yet they were commanded to worship but One God: There is no god but He. Praise and glory to Him (far is He) from having the partners they associate (with Him)."
Qur'an 9:31

CHAPTER 15

UNHEEDED WARNINGS. . .

*T*he blood in the larger than life HV3D projections of the threatening note seemed to be dripping off the page over the congregation's heads. Silence filled the sanctuary as the eight hundred plus members of the church began to read the terrorists' message Pastor Mark found nailed to the church door that morning. The people whispered the words to themselves, cringed at the threats, and held their children and grandchildren close to their sides. Even so, the bloody note, as far as they knew, had been delivered to someone who lived in Babylon.

Holding the original note above his head, Pastor Mark spoke with a gentle, soothing voice, saying, "This note that you have just read was nailed to the door of our church this morning!" As the entire congregation gasped at once, all the air seemed to be sucked out of the sanctuary!

The vacuum soon gave way to the sounds of the people as they stood and began making their way to the doors. With his own emotions still in check, Mark urged his now panicking flock to remain in the sanctuary. With calm strength, he urged his brothers and sisters to retake their seats. Then, he said plainly, "We must discuss our response to this threat before any of us leave today. Have we not prepared for this day?"

While a few families disregarded Mark's request and quickly exited the church, the vast majority of the believers returned to their pews. Their faithful shepherd paused until all eyes focused on him.

As a father would comfort and encourage his children, Mark said, "Though we may be afraid, though we may want to run and hide, we must face this challenge together, with each other, and with our almighty, all loving Lord! We belong to Him. This place of worship belongs to Him. Thus, we will seek His guidance for our next step and all the steps that will follow."

Again stepping out from behind the pulpit, Mark added, "I do not know if other churches in the area or around the country have received such threats this morning, but I do think that the horror in East Jerusalem connects with this threat on our door!"

Tears flowed throughout the house of worship. The people shook their heads and said things like, "This can't be true!" "Who would make such threats?" "We live in America!" "Isn't this a cruel prank?"

Patiently, the serene shepherd allowed his frightened flock to verbalize their anxiety. He gazed at his family. The twins, Tim and Tom, fidgeted in Ariel's lap, unsure of what was happening around them. Grace clearly understood the threat. She sat motionless next to her mother. Ariel held all three of them in her loving arms. Then she, like everyone else in the congregation, began looking to Mark for hope, strength, and assurance of their safety. Mark gazed into his bride's eyes, but quickly had to turn away, else he would be weeping, also.

When quiet returned to the sanctuary, Pastor Mark took a deep breath and said, "Since the beginning of this church, I have been warning of the trouble to come as the Muslim population of the United States continued to explode." Mark touched his face with his right hand to correct himself. "I should not have used the word explode. Please pardon my expression. Let me restart. Since the birth of this church, I have warned you and everyone who would listen of the trouble to come as the Islamic population continued to rapidly expand in the United States. I pointed out that the Muslims would not be satisfied with U.S. tolerance of their religion, their mosques, and their blaring minarets issuing the call to prayer five times a day. I noted that they would seek to govern themselves, not under our federal, state, or local laws, but under Sharia Law—the most hate-filled, barbaric, insidious, and terrifying nightmare of rules ever codified! I predicted that the followers of Allah would initiate conflict because the Qur'an demands jihad—holy struggle, holy war!

"Yet, no matter what I said to you, to the previous president as I served on his religious council, or to my students at the seminary, no one believed me! You and everyone else thought that Islam would never attempt to take over these United States of America!"

His passion rising, the pastor noted, "For years, I have tried to prepare you and the rest of the nation. I have clearly proclaimed that the only way to stop what was happening in America was to share our faith in Jesus with the Muslims around us. We see them in our work places, at the grocery stores, in our children's schools, in our local, state, and national governments. They are all around us, and we cannot defeat them, but we can win their souls to Jesus the Messiah!

"You know that the classes I teach in the seminary prepare upcoming pastors to share the Gospel of our Saviour with Muslims. I teach Muslim outreach. Through the theological school, I have developed materials and tracts to help us talk to Muslims about Jesus—the real Isa, not the Isa of the Qur'an!

"Jesus gave His life, not in a suicide bombing, not in jihad, but on the cross for our salvation and the salvation of deceived Muslims, too! The Qur'an says that everyone must accept Muslim rule or be killed. Everyone must become a follower of Islam or be killed! The Bible says that everyone who accepts Jesus Christ will live! Everyone who becomes a follower of Jesus will discover life eternal!"

Mark walked to the other side of the podium as he announced, "The Qur'an's Isa will supposedly return at the end of time to condemn all the Christians and Jews for their refusal to believe in Allah! The Bible's Jesus will return at the end of time and take all who believe in Jesus to Heaven—former Muslims, once unbelieving Jews, and previously pagan Gentiles included!"

Mark again looked to his bride and smiled! She offered a quivering smile in return. Ariel knew God had appointed her husband for such a time as this!

Turning back to his sheep, the shepherd warned, "My brothers and sisters, at its heart, Islam is not a religion, but a pretense for tyrannical power, vehement hatred, ghastly war, and grisly genocide! The result of eye for eye and life for life is that everyone but the Muslims will be blind or dead! The manifest goal of Islam is world dominance, not world salvation! Muhammad chose jihad, holy war against the infidels, as the pathway that leads to ruling over all the earth.

"We know the Muslim Brotherhood's mantra: Islam is the solution! Islam's solution is to wipe out anyone and everyone who stands in its way! Thus, the Brotherhood considers us and all those souls who profess faith in Isa, Y'shua, Jesus to be the problem!

"As it turns out, Adolph Hitler did not have the Final Solution, after all. His attempt to wipe the Jewish people from the face of the earth did not succeed. The six million children of Israel who were brutally murdered in so many ferocious ways did not die in vain because Jacob rose from the ashes of the Holocaust!

"Oddly enough, the very Muslims who deny the Holocaust now want to complete it! I tell you the truth, the solution of Islam aims to not only finally and completely answer Hitler's Jewish question, but Islam's solution will also answer the Christian question, the atheist question, the agnostic question, the idolater question, the pagan question, and the everyone-else-in-this-world-except-Muslims question! In its ultimate solution, Islam will exterminate one and all who stand in its way until no one remains but Muslims alone!"

Pastor Mark suddenly stopped preaching, as he stared at the entrance to the sanctuary, where several unknown and unexpected guests slowly walked into the silent room!

"No one knows about that day or hour, not even the angels in Heaven, nor the Son, but only the Father."
Mark 13:32

CHAPTER 16

THE COMPLEXITY OF IT ALL...

*N*ormally, the President would address the nation from the Oval Office. Yet in this case, the circumstances bore no resemblance to normal. In fact, this crisis was unprecedented. Some nation or group had made four deadly strikes on the newly constituted DROP using jointly developed weapons of the United States and Israel. An act of war had been declared on the Palestinians, but by whom and for what reasons?

In another abnormality, President Paulson and Vice President Abdullah would co-anchor the address to the nation and world. Obviously, both men could not speak from behind the Oval Office's Resolute Desk.

Hence, to solve the practical issues as well as to underscore the seriousness with which his administration approached the current disaster in the Middle East, James decided to broadcast the address from the Situation Room at the White House. Located in the basement of the presidential residence, the worldwide earthquake had badly damaged the Situation Room. As such, instead of just repairing the facility, the Situation Room had been expanded to make it more versatile. The enlargement was the first made since the George W. Bush administration improvements of 2006 and 2007.

Not only would Abdul be speaking with James, but the President's entire Cabinet would join them at the conference table. Although neither the James nor Abdul wrote their own portions of the joint address—

at least not the officially approved portions—the Commander in Chief did choreograph the entire production.

As the time for the address drew near, the appointed personnel took their seats at the Situation Room's large conference table. Flanked by all the members of his Administration, the President spoke through his mic to the producer in the control room. "I want to begin the address with a wide shot of my entire Cabinet sitting around the table, which would communicate the unity of my administration in facing the task ahead. Then, as I continue speaking, have the HV3D cameraman slowly zoom-in to a tight shot of me alone. After my initial remarks, move to the second camera and a wide shot of the Vice President and me sitting side by side. Then, when the Vice President begins speaking, have that camera zoom in to a tight shot on him. After that, come back to me for my final comments. What do you think of that plan?"

The producer considered the President's proposal, and then suggested only one change. "Mr. President, I think when we zoom in from that initial shot of your Cabinet that we should stop on you and the Vice President for a few moments, before we end the zoom with a tight shot on you. It's my humble opinion, but I think doing that will help raise his clout when it comes time for him to speak."

The affable leader of the free world nodded his head in agreement. He said, "You know what is best, so I am great with that modification!"

Meanwhile, Vice President Abdullah shook his head as he sat at the table with the President and the rest of his advisors and leaders. He watched the flurry of last minute preparations. The set director walked over to the two men. After raising the height of the President's chair, he lowered the height of the Vice President's seat. Stature wise, the changes gave James a slight advantage over Abdul, who now felt like he was sitting on the floor.

The makeup team attended the Defense Secretary who needed help to stop his bald head from shining. She next moved to the Secretary of State who required a fresh application of lip stick. An aide gave the Secretary of Homeland Security a new tie, as the one he was wearing clashed with his suit. Meanwhile, the producer asked the President's Chief of Staff to change seats with the Secretary of Labor so that the men and women at the table would be spread out more evenly.

Abdul asked himself, *"What am I doing here? The world is about to go to war, and the leaders of the last superpower are worried about their makeup and attire! Meanwhile, I must make statements today with which I don't necessarily agree! Am I a traitor to my own people?"*

Thirty seconds later, the President of the United States began his address. As the world stepped into the room filled with U.S. officials, he said, "Citizens of the United States, our friends outside our borders, and those who choose to be our enemies: My Cabinet and I come before you this morning to first express our grief and sadness over this day's events in the newly formed Democratic Republic of Palestine. Our prayers and our sympathies are with the victims and families of this tragic and unprovoked attack. My administration and the people of this great land stand hand in hand with the people of the DROP and Israel."

As the camera now focused on the Commander in Chief and his Vice President, James continued, saying, "You have heard from the leaders of both those nations. They have called for restraint as investigations proceed into the missile attack for which no nation or group has yet claimed responsibility. In personal consultation with those leaders, I tell you now that even though our foreign and domestically based military and homeland security forces are at their highest state of alert, the government of the United States only echoes the call for restraint—despite the many lives lost in the DROP and Israel today. No one wants to see war on the heels of the historic peace between these two nations."

The HV3D cameraman zoomed into a tight shot of the President alone, as he said, "This morning, I personally spoke with Israeli Prime Minister Samuel Ben Baruch and the temporary leader of the DROP, Imam Addar Zaahir. In each of those critical conversations, I felt a strong sense of unity! The three of us stand together on the side of peace. I have also talked extensively with Secretary of State Hannah Fielder about today's horrible events. And tomorrow evening in East Jerusalem, my Vice President and I will meet with Prime Minister Ben Baruch, Imam Zaahir, as well as Pastor Mark Basel and Rabbi Shlomo Ben Y'sra'el, who served as essential members of the Israeli-Palestinian negotiating team.

"Even though Prime Minister Baruch, Imam Zaahir, and I make a joint call for peace, such a provocative attack as the one perpetrated today could easily set much of the world on the course of war. In that light, I have asked Vice President Abdullah to remind us of some of the ebb and flow of events in the Middle East and the world around it during the past few decades. To some, this review may sound like a school lesson. Regardless, if we hope to avert war, we must place the events of today in their historical context. Vice President Abdullah?"

The producer now cut to the second 3D SenseSurround camera and the wide shot of the two most powerful men in the world. Despite his sweating hands and feet, as well as his trembling knees, Abdul began with apparent confidence. "Thank you, Mr. President. Fellow Americans and our friends in the world, the Paulson Administration is dealing with a global landscape that former generations of American leaders could not have imagined—or at least refused to contemplate. Frankly, to understand the current state of affairs in the Muslim world, we must go back not decades, but about twelve hundred years, when the major divisions in Islam began."

Abdul's deviation from the script caught the production crew off guard. Likewise, James was obviously surprised by his Vice President's impromptu intentions to cover so much of Islamic history in an international address. His eyes opened wide for the entire world to see. Despite his stunned expression, James said nothing to stop Abdul, and the Commander in Chief actually found the walk through Muslim history to be quite enlightening.

As the second videographer zoomed in on the Vice President alone, Abdul focused completely on his message. "From the outset today, we must understand that while Islam is not a monolith, many groups have forcefully tried to make it so. As a result, Islam is far less diverse than it was at the start of this century. We need to discuss how we arrived at the present reality.

"Most Muslims generally agree on the core beliefs of Islam known as the Five Pillars:

- *Shahada*: Sincerely reciting the Islamic creed
- *Salat:* Properly performing the ritual prayers five times daily
- *Zakat:* Generously paying the charity tax for the poor and needy
- Sawm: Daily fasting during the holy month of Ramadan
- Hajj: Solemnly making at least one pilgrimage to Mecca

"Beliefs beyond these foundational principles vary and sometimes contradict each other. You might say that just as there are varied denominations in Christianity, and varied sects in Judaism, so there were also varied schools in Islam. Historically, the two most prominent sects of the religion have been the Sunnis and the Shias, who are also known as Shiites.

"The beginning of these streams of Islam goes back to the second century of the religion's existence and the slaughter of Muhammad's last family members. Those Muslims who would form the Shia sect saw those murders as a predetermined act of Allah that provided atonement for sin. However, the concept of atonement is only found in Hebrew and Christian Scriptures, not the Qur'an. Not surprisingly, the forefathers of the Sunnis condemned that line of thinking about atonement, regarding the entire concept as heresy."

Feeling more confident about his portion of the address, Abdul began to relax and actually enjoy himself. He continued, saying, "The chasm between the original Sunnis and the emerging Shias grew wider as the Shiites claimed their imams were not mere mortal men made of clay, but spiritual beings composed of light. In addition, the Shias asserted their imams were sinless, infallible, and bore a portion of the living spirit of the Prophet Muhammad. Thus, Shia imams were spiritual leaders as well as theocratic leaders—like the former Ayatollahs of Iran. Shias regarded their imams as chosen servants of Allah who have been given the Qur'an as an inheritance. Thus, such imams were called *ahl al-dikr*, people of the message.

"The Shias believed the final imam in the line of Muhammad did not die but will return during the end times. Born in the ninth century, this four year old boy named Muhammad ibn al-Hasan al-Mahdi disappeared only a few days after the Shias declared him to be their imam. While al-Mahdī means the Guided One, the Last Imam goes by many other titles, such as the Hidden Imam, the Twelfth Imam, *Sahib az Zaman* or Master of the Age, *Imam al Muntazar* or the Awaited Imam, *al Qa'im* or the One to Arise, and *Bagiyyat Allah* or Remnant of Allah. The Shiites trusted that their Last Imam would return—endowed with miraculous powers and accompanied by Isa—shortly before the final Day of Judgment.

"Even within their own sect, the Shiites held various beliefs about the Hidden Imam's birth, life, spiritual existence, and long awaited return. Only one common thread ran through all the varied expectations of the Shias: Israel and the United States would be attacked and destroyed before the Twelfth Imam could return.

"Before the vast majority of Shia Muslims were annihilated earlier this century, their imams were still considered holy men and held various clergical roles. Moreover, sovereign religious leaders held political power over Shia nations.

"On the other hand, the imams of Sunni Islam have no clergical or political authority. Sunni imams do not necessarily lead in the community, and they are not required to have special education. They direct Friday prayers at the mosque, but in certain communities, anyone can lead those prayers.

"As one might imagine, such divergent doctrines between the Shias and the Sunnis set up centuries of conflict. In fact, for almost fifteen hundred years, Sunnis and Shias have endured alternating times of war and peace.

"In the 1700's, an even more fundamental aspect of Sunni Islam was born: Wahhabism. Muhammad ibn Abd-al-Wahhab founded this fiercely radical strain of Sunnism. He considered himself infallible and proclaimed that the Qur'an must be taken literally. The term Wahhabism is now considered an insult, and those who follow the teaching of al-Wahhab today refer to their movement as the more familiar Salafism, which translates as Monotheism. From their inception, Salafist-Sunnis considered all the nations of the world to be Muslim battlegrounds.

"Salafists don't see themselves as another stream of Muslim thought, but as the true, authentic, and only way of Islam. The Salafist-Sunnis feel that they alone are true Muslims! They regard all so called "moderate Muslims" as traitors who deserve death. By the middle of the twentieth century, Salafists made up the majority of Sunni Muslims in many nations, such as Saudi Arabia, Kuwait, and Qatar.

"In 1928, Hasan al-Banna formed the Muslim Brotherhood. With the goal of Islamic rule in a worldwide Caliphate, al-Banna's Brotherhood grew rapidly. Ten years later, the Brotherhood became even more strident, as al-Banna decried the Westernization, modernization, and secularization of Islam. The movement went underground in 1954, after the failed assassination of Egyptian President Gamal Abdel Nasser Hussein."

As Abdul continued laying the groundwork for the current crisis, he came back to the original script. Accordingly, the production crew played video of Muslims on U.S. college campuses, while the Vice President said, "Beginning in the 1960s, the first wave of Salafist-Sunnis, most of them active members of the Muslim Brotherhood, began immigrating to the United States in order to infiltrate American colleges and universities. Financed by the Muslim World League, the MWL, in Mecca, they also planned to build schools—madrasas—for younger students. While speaking peace, the MWL invested in jihad.

"By 1963, the Salifists formed the Muslim Students Association, the MSA, followed ten years later by the World Assembly of Muslim Youth, the WAMY—both organizations built their headquarters here in the U.S.. Also in 1973, the Saudis financially backed the North America Islamic Trust, the NAIT. This front for the Muslim Brotherhood soon built and owned more than 300 mosques and madrasas in the states.

"After another decade passed, Saudi Arabia's most powerful banker opened the Suleiman Abdul-Aziz al-Rajhi (SAAR) Foundation. This Muslim Brotherhood group of charities began in Virginia with an initial bequest of three and a half million dollars. Though disbanded long ago, SAAR discretely financed terrorism."

Now images of hostages in Iran appeared before the international audience, as the Vice President said, "In November of 1979, the Shiite revolution in Iran became the backdrop for the kidnapping of 52 Americans. President Jimmy Carter failed to win the release of the hostages either through diplomacy or a doomed military rescue that claimed the lives of eight U.S. servicemen. In fact, the captives only found freedom 444 days later, which happened to be inauguration day for President Ronald Reagan.

"Well into the twenty first century, the Shiites ruled Iran. The Ayatollahs, the highest rank of Shiite clergy, worked through their puppet presidents in efforts to destroy the United States and Israel. The leaders desired to create the chaos necessary to facilitate the return of the Twelfth Imam. Thus, for decades, America and Israel led the charge to isolate Iran and its growing nuclear threat.

Now talking over video of mosques in the U.S., Abdul said, "In the late 1990's and early 2000's, the Grand Mufti, the sheiks, and the royal family of Saudi Arabia financed the building of mosques across the country, so that Salafism could be taught here and Muslims and Islamic converts could be trained for jihad against Americans.

"The Salafist-Sunnis, in partnership with PAIR—the Panel on American Islamic Relations—hoped to form a parallel, fundamentalist Islamic society in the United States. These hardcore Sunnis had no intention of assimilating into American society. While the Salafists and PAIR publically talked of living peacefully with their neighbors in the U.S., they secretly and surreptitiously planned to enact the rule of Sharia Law and islamize America without ever having to declare open jihad."

Next, Abdul began to voice over scenes of the 9/11 terror attacks in New York, Washington D.C., and Shanksville, Pennsylvania. "However, someone outside the partnership changed the entire American-Muslim dialogue. An old school Wahhabist with his own band of terrorists, Osama bin Laden used passenger jets as weapons of mass destruction (WMD) in the September 11 attacks of 2001. More than any grisly act of terror up to that point, the Al Qaeda attack viscerally demonstrated Islam's willingness to kill thousands of innocent people in the name of Allah's jihad. Bin Laden's attacks against Americans prior to 9/11 were not on U.S. soil but against the USS Cole in Yemen in 2000 and the U.S. embassies in Kenya and Tanzania in 1998.

"As the hunt was on for bin Laden in Afghanistan, here in the states, our government learned much about front operations that were linked to the Brotherhood's Salafist-Sunnis. More than fifty organizations, some with names as benign as the International Relief Organization, Global Relief Foundation, Happy Hearts Trust, and the Success Foundation, did business for the Brotherhood right here in the U.S.. After investigations and sting operations, many Brotherhood leaders in such organizations were tried and convicted for conspiring to financially support Muslim terrorism in the U.S..

"Meanwhile, in 2007, the Salafist-Sunnis republished the fifty point Brotherhood Manifesto from 1936. They claimed the time had come to implement the manifesto's call to enact Sharia Law and a one-party state—an Islamic Caliphate. Their work began in the Middle East and North Africa."

The images shifted to the 2011 riots in the Middle East when Abdul said, "Ten years after 9/11, revolution swept through the Islamic nations. Muslims took to the streets in opposition to the tyranny of their leaders. The 'Arab Spring', as the uprising was called, began as a push for democracy.

"Unfortunately, without some democratic political structure or leadership to replace the bloody regimes of the ousted despots, the Arab Spring turned into the Muslim Winter—and the killing season for Christians. Even worse in Syria, Bashar al-Assad, fearing a massive insurgent uprising, clamped down on the protesters in his country. In the ensuing civil war, Assad massacred untold thousands of his own people. The conflict quickly became a proxy war for two power foes in the region—the Shias of Iran who backed Assad and the Sunnis of Saudi Arabia who backed the rebels.

"As the most organized political and terror organization in the Arab world, the Brotherhood gladly filled the leadership void in the wake of the revolutions. Thus, in the following years, the dividing lines between Salafist-Sunnis and the Shias became sharper.

"At the same time, all the upheaval in the Middle East caused refugees to pour out of the region. Millions came to the United States, welcomed by President Barack Hussein Obama on humanitarian grounds. Thus, the islamization of the United States took a major step forward."

The video changed to the May 2011 raid on Osama bin Laden's compound. "Ironically, the assassination of Osama bin Laden came under the watch of President Obama. Nonetheless, even as Obama planned bin Laden's appointment with death, the President consulted the Muslim Brotherhood to help shape and direct his administration and foreign policy. The President felt comfortable accepting the Brotherhood's advice. He had no qualm with Islamic influence on every aspect of American society and government, even though the Brotherhood's goal then and now remains unchanged: one worldwide *ummah*, one global Muslim nation. Though Obama claimed to be Christian, Muslims never doubted he was still one of them.

"Obama's worst legacy was the deadly attack on the U.S. Consulate in Benghazi, Libya on the eleventh anniversary of 9/11. Four Americans were killed on September 11, 2012, including the U.S. Ambassador. At that time, Obama's foreign policy stance was that the death of bin Laden had dealt the final blow to Muslim terrorism against the U.S., while jihadists—namely Al Qaeda—were in retreat. This gross miscalculation meant the President provided insufficient protection for the Consulate and its people before the assault. After the bloody strike, Obama covered up its true nature in anticipation of his reelection bid. An act of war against the United States was swept under the rug as the President denied for weeks that the Benghazi strike was a terror attack. The Muslim world celebrated his second term.

"Obama withdrew U.S. troops from Iraq during his first administration and he pulled them from Afghanistan during his second round in the White House. Then, the world stared down a nuclear Iran led by the Shiite, Grand Ayatollah Ali Khamenei, and his political pawn, President Mahmoud Ahmadinejad. When it became clear that President Obama would take no military action against Iran, Israeli Prime Minister Benjamin Netanyahu, acting at great risk to his nation, single-handedly used surgical strikes to wipe out the Iranian nuclear threat. Sunni Muslims were most grateful!"

Over scenes of the Muslim battles in Iran, the Vice President said, "However, the Jewish attack on Iran yielded unintended consequences. Salafist-Sunnis took advantage of Iran's apparent weakness. The Salafists organized a collation of the Sunni led nations to attack Iran in order to put a permanent end to the Shiite nation's quest for a nuclear arsenal. The Shias were quickly defeated, which made the Sunnis desire victory beyond Iran."

Images of violent Muslim civil war played while Abdul reminded the U.S. and the world of the how Islamic history changed once and for all. "Still driven by the Salafists, the Sunni majority states launched synchronized attacks against the Shiite minorities in their own lands. This action brought the Shias of Iraq, Azerbaijan, Bahrain, Lebanon, and Yemen to their brothers' defense. The result was that war erupted throughout the Middle East and Northern Africa. The grandson of Osama bin Laden, Salafist Sanaullah bin Laden led the Sunnis in their merciless efforts to annihilate the Shiite sect as well as any other smaller Islamic sects that stood in their way."

Once more, the video changed, this time to the war in Asia, as the Vice President shifted his focus. "While the eyes of the outside world focused on the Islamic conflict, a handful of rogue nations took advantage of the chaos. First, China decided to flex its military muscle. The Communist nation attacked South Korea unilaterally, yet with overwhelming force, to put a sudden end to the more than century old conflict between the Democratic South and the Communist North.

"While South Korea was, for all practical matters, obliterated, Communist China's leaders were gravely mistaken in their calculations, as Japan, the United States, and our European allies quickly launched a joint retaliatory attack against China and North Korea, while also protecting the Chinese-occupied, independent island state of Taiwan.

The scenes of war shifted to the battle between Pakistan and India. "After wiping out the Shities among them, Pakistan's Sunni majority used the worldwide pandemonium to attack its archenemy India. With no one to restrain the long suppressed hatred between the nations, Pakistan and India wiped each other off the map with their nuclear weapons. While the immediate death toll was horrendous, residents in the surrounding region continue to suffer from the long term impact of the nuclear devastation."

As Abdul continued his narrative, those watching the address saw scenes of the Russian army. "Also seizing on the international free-for-all, a resurgent Russia urged several leaders in the Sunni nations to open another front in their war—this one against Israel. Included in this coalition of Sunni states was the newest member of the sect, Iran. Russia and its Muslim partners planned to destroy Israel and plunder its vast oil and gas reserves. Many Jews and Christians around the world saw this attack as fulfillment of the prophecy of the Gog-Magog War found in Biblical book of Ezekiel.

"As the Russian-Muslim alliance bore down on the mountains of Israel, a cataclysmic earthquake, unable to be measured on the Richter scale, ended the attack before it began. The earthquake caused dormant volcanoes to erupt so that molten lava rained from the sky. However, eyewitnesses claimed that the fire from the sky was too far away from the volcanoes to be molten lava.

"As this video reminds us, the largest earthquake known to man literally shook the entire world, including the United States. The force of the quake shifted the earth's axis by nineteen degrees and shortened the day by an incredible five minutes!

"Furthermore, the tidal waves formed by the earthquake crashed against all the coasts of the Mediterranean and Red Seas. As you see, twenty to thirty feet walls of water obliterated the shorelines of Southern Europe and North Africa."

When the video changed to the damage in the states, Abdul said, "Amazingly, the Doomsday Quake's tidal waves also pummeled the east coast and, to a lesser degree, the west coast of the United States!"

Now the masses again watched the Vice President himself as he began to talk about the political and military aftermath of the disasters. "The earthquake stopped the Russian led assault against Israel in its tracks. Furthermore, the plate-shifting tremors brought China and North Korea to their knees. Likewise, the Doomsday Quake immediately halted the war between the Salafist-Sunnis and the Shias. Cumulatively, we now refer to all those conflicts as World War III.

"Also as we know today, when the dust settled, the water receded, and the radiation fell, the Salafist-Sunnis emerged victorious. Despite the Sunni's own losses in the earthquake and tidal waves, they had successfully eliminated the Shia Muslims along with the other, smaller sects of Islam. The coalition of Sunni states chose Sanaullah bin Laden as Caliph over the first Islamic Caliphate completely under Sharia Law in this century. Bin Laden named the Muslim Alliance (MA) Babylon. He placed its capitol in his hometown of Ankara, Turkey.

"The one-two punch of war and the earthquake decimated Japan, China, Taiwan, North Korea, and Russia. More than any other nation, Russia suffered from the nuclear fallout from its aged, destroyed reactors. Bin Laden's forces quickly moved in and eliminated the Islamic minority sect of the Hui Muslims in those lands. From that point, the Salafist-Sunnis began to islamize those nations.

"The European allies of the United States suffered heavy casualties, but survived the war, quake, tidal waves, and thankfully minimal nuclear radiation. However, because of the European nations' loss of population, their low birthrate, and years of Muslim immigration and prolific reproduction, Europe, too, soon fell under Islamic rule, with very little effective resistance. The armed revolt that finally did rise to challenge the Caliphate came not from the EU's armed forces, but its militia. Those brave souls were quickly undone. Even bin Laden himself was amazed at how rapidly Europe became islamized.

"When the European Union realized that the inevitability of Muslim conquest, the aging EU President, Geert Wilders, deactivated their weapons control systems, as well as the alliance's weapons systems satellites.

"However, United States President Eric Cantor thought more needed to be done. Not only did he destroy the satellite network of the European Union, but he also took out the networks of Russia, China, North Korea, and Japan. Cantor, America's first Jewish President, took out the satellite weapons systems to remove all possibilities that the Caliph of Babylon could launch nuclear attacks against the U.S. and Israel.

"As a result, the United States emerged once again as the only superpower in a drastically changed world. In response, bin Laden set out to head the largest and most feared army ever assembled. He ordered the formation of a unified Islamic jihadist movement under the auspices of the Muslim Brotherhood. Thus, the Salafists and the Brotherhood finally consummated their long engagement.

"The Brotherhood consolidated all the previously autonomous Islamic terrorist organizations under one banner and one leader, the infamous General, who true identity remains unknown to the remaining free world.

"The differences of theology and methodology between the terrorist factions found in the new Brotherhood Army were not resolved through discussion and compromise, but through violence and death of any group or individual that opposed bin Laden in any sense of the word. Such treatment was even meted out to the small number of Sunnis who did not consider themselves Salafists. Now, supposedly, no dissension lies in the ranks of the 40-million man force—at least no vocal opposition. Indeed, the Brotherhood is the largest army—or should I say the largest terrorist organization—in world history!

"Despite the purges and wars, some Shia populations, small as they are, still cling to life. Likewise, some Shiite clerics, like Imam Addar Zaahir, are actually respected and admired by a plurality of Sunni Muslims in the world.

"Be that as it may, if the Salafist-Sunnis killed the vast majority of Shias and other, smaller sects of Islam, if bin Laden killed Muslim terrorists who did not follow his line of thinking, then Babylon's Brotherhood Army certainly will not refrain from killing the remaining *kuffar*—infidels—in this world yet today!

"Remember, the minor, militia-led European rebellion was quelled easily by bin Laden before the formation of the Babylonian army of terrorists. Yet today, this 40 million man band of lifelong thugs is itching for a fight with the rest of the free world, especially the U.S. and Israel, even though bin Laden's mega-army does not have nuclear weapons or professionally trained soldiers to handle the high-tech weaponry left behind in Europe and Asia or weapons control systems or satellite networks for those arsenals.

"While bin Laden has made no secret of his efforts to train his army of terrorists and to rehabilitate the weapons and systems in his hands, so far he has made little progress. Through torture and the threatened murder of family members, bin Laden has attempted to force Asian and EU engineers, scientists, and military experts in the now Muslim states to help in these endeavors. However, many of those noble men and women chose their own deaths over working to further the cause of jihad.

"Hence, though the process may be slow, the nuclear weapons arsenal is being repaired and restored. At the same time, Babylonian troops are slowly learning how to use and operate the entire weapons arsenal, as well as the vehicles of war—tanks, ships, jets, helicopters, and space fighters—left behind in islamized nations.

"As we speak, though many leaders refuse to admit it, islamization is a real and present danger across North, Central, and South America. Because of this encroachment, the peace treaty between Israel and the DROP—an independent state with diplomatic ties to Babylon— seemed to be a sign of hope for peace between the Caliphate and Israel, and, ultimately, the Americas.

"Indeed, we cannot overstate the importance of maintaining the peace between Israel and the DROP, which is why President Paulson is about to announce an historic development of his own!"

"O ye who believe! When ye meet the Unbelievers in hostile array, never turn your backs to them. If any do turn his back to them on such a day—unless it be in a stratagem of war, or to retreat to a troop (of his own)—he draws on himself the wrath of Allah, and his abode is Hell—an evil refuge (indeed)!"
Qur'an 8:15-16

CHAPTER 17

NOT SO VEILED THREATS. . .

*T*he General, the phantom leader of Babylon's Brotherhood Army, clenched his jaw and made a fist of his right hand as he listened to the Vice President's portion of the address. In his digitally distorted voice, the General said, "Not only does Abdul refuse to answer my call, he is spouting the infidel's heresy about Islam, while being too forthcoming about facts we don't want to share with the *kuffar!*" Babylon's chief terrorist slammed his 3DHP down on the table so he would no longer see Abdul's image.

"Why have I bothered to spare his life?" the shrouded General shouted. One of his aides answered, "Because he is one of us?" The General's veil revealed only his eyes, and his glare was sharp and cold as he whipped his head around to face his idiotic underling. "I would have no problem arranging your death, and are not you a Muslim, also?" The aide quickly decided to leave the room.

"Oh, Abdul-ghafoor Asim Abdullah," the masked man moaned, "I could have ended your life long ago. Yet, I thought I could groom you and use you in the cause of Allah! Do not prove me wrong after all these years!"

The grisly General picked up his 3DHP. Abdul had completed his part of the address and now the President spoke about new coalitions and alliances that he was arranging with the few nations that were not yet islamized. "Mr. President," the General said to the image of the U.S. Commander in Chief, perhaps I should quote from the Bible to which your wife clings so dearly? *'You fool! This very night, your life will be demanded from you.'* I believe that passage is found in the book of the good doctor, Luke—his twelfth chapter and twentieth verse, as I recall! Well, President James Jacob Paulson, you might survive the night, but only by my good graces! I believe most earnestly that your days are numbered!"

The masked Muslim turned to another aide. "Are the coordinates and codes ready?" The aide mumbled something about the input being finished within the hour. "An hour?" the General roared. "All the details were supposed to be completed three hours ago!" This aide, too, decided to go to another part of the building.

"Timing is everything in this life," the frustrated head of the Brotherhood Army shouted at the aide as he ran from him in fear. "Is our martyr, our *shahid*, able to complete his task?" But no one was there to answer.

The thoughts of the masked mastermind of terror turned to tomorrow's meeting that the American President had discussed. The remaining key players from the peace talks would reconvene in the DROP. Surely, they had no idea what would be facing them in less than 24 hours.

He turned off the President's address and instead used his 3DHP to call his operative in Washington D.C..

"Yes?" the uniformed man said to his superior.

"Do you have all that you need?" asked the veiled face.

"Yes!" came the swift reply.

"Are your men trained and ready, as well?"

"Yes!" the now aggravated operative answered.

"Are you growing impatient with me, as this is the fourth time I have called today?"

A long pause preceded his answer, "No!"

Laughing under his breath, the sinister General said as he closed the limited conversation, "You really don't want to be on my bad side, do you?"

Ending that call, the General went back to the President's address. The madman spoke to the 3D holograph image of the leader of the

United States of America the filled the room. "President Paulson, do you realize how easily I could crush you this very day? But where is the fun in that?" The General laughed, gutturally. "For the moment, you continue to be of use to me. Truly, you are nothing but a foolhardy, gambling politician who would never be where you are now without me!"

As the dark figure walked out of the room, he muttered, "You serve at my pleasure, Mr. President!"

"Remember the words I spoke to you: 'No servant is greater than his master.' If they persecuted Me, they will persecute you also. If they obeyed My teaching, they will obey yours also."
John 15:20

CHAPTER 18

THE ELEMENT OF SURPRISE. . .

Seven men in black hoods and black leather clothing stepped inside the sanctuary, each with a smart submachine gun in his right hand, and a 24 inch machete strapped to his left side—a most ancient weapon complimented by a most modern one.

Smart submachine guns fired bullets not by gunpowder, but by electromagnetic blast. When the shooter aimed at the target through the crosshairs, each smart bullet fired was programmed with an electronic "picture" of its target. That picture guided the smart bullet until it reached and hit its bull's eye. Since a smart bullet could travel a mile on the power of its electromagnetic burst, it would literally chase down a moving or bobbing and weaving target until impact. Designed for the U.S. army, most troops called the bullets MGMs—mini guided missiles.

But the men carrying the smart submachine guns were not American soldiers, but Muslim terrorists. As the congregation turned to see these armed men in black at the door, the terrorists quickly fanned out along the perimeter of the large room.

The apparent leader remained at the door until the other six were in place. Then, he began slowly walking up the center aisle. With his eyes fixed on the 3D holovision image of the bloodstained note he had written, the terrorist leader spoke loudly so all of frightened people could hear him.

"Dr. Basel," he said, "I see you received our message this morning! It's a pity that you did not take it seriously!"

With calm assurance in his voice, Pastor Mark answered, "Oh, I took your message quite seriously."

Scornfully, the Muslim in black retorted, "Did you? If you took our message seriously, then why are you and your lovely congregation still here this morning?"

"For the same reason we are here every Sunday morning: to worship the true Lord and King of all time and eternity!"

"I must thank you Dr. Basel! You summed up the goal of Islam—the work of the Brotherhood—in such a succinct and precise manner just as we entered this house of false religion! Our solution—Allah's solution—is to wipe out the entirety of the infidel infection in this world, so that we may worship the true Lord and King of all time and eternity! By the way, in case you have forgotten, his name is Allah!"

"Thank you for confirming your intentions. I have been warning people for years. Still, I cannot seem to persuade anyone outside of Islam to believe me!"

"Dr. Basel," the terrorist chided, "I don't think I like your fear-no-evil tone! We are not students in one of your seminary classrooms. You need to regard us with the respect and dread due us!"

Still calm, still confident, Mark replied, "We will not be afraid! We will not fear you because you have no ultimate power over us. We will not dread you because we do not fear death! However, we can pray for you. We can tell you that Isa loves you and gave His Life to redeem you. We can tell you that you can be forgiven and start a new life with Him, today, right now."

Mockingly, the terrorist said, "I see. It's very gracious of you to offer Isa's forgiveness, but I know that He neither died for me nor rose from the grave for me, but he will return to earth to condemn you and all like you who reject Allah!"

Then, snatching a young boy from his mother's arms, the taunting terrorist took a few more steps. "Perhaps now you will fear me—even loathe me!" He held his machete to the boy's throat! "With little effort, I can slit this fine young Christian's neck from one side to the other!"

"No!" the boy's weeping mother shouted, her eyes filled with tears. Moans and gasps rose and fell all over the sanctuary.

Looking back at the distraught mother, the terrorist said, "You see, Dr. Basel, at least someone here today dreads my presence here! This woman most likely hates me!" He let go of the boy who ran back to his panicked—though most grateful—mother.

"If you do not fear me, if you do not dread me, then you at least need to respect me, Dr. Basel! I warned you this morning. Now comes the time to make good on my promises—threats as you would call them, Professor!" The shadowed terrorist reached the front of the sanctuary, and then turned to address the congregation.

Pastor Mark interrupted what the Muslim was about to say. With no sarcasm but with genuine hope in his voice, the shepherd of the flock said, "Perhaps you and your friends are here this morning to confess your sins at the altar and pray to receive Isa's forgiveness?"

The terrorist whipped around and snapped, "Dr. Basel, the day I bow to Isa will be the day that I thank him for letting me kill you!"

"Then you will not be kneeling today, I suppose," Mark replied. With those words he touched a virtual button on the back of the pulpit and the sanctuary turned dark! The sounds of smart submachine guns, conventional weapons fire, and screams filled the sanctuary!

"Knowest thou not that to Allah (alone) belongeth the dominion of the heavens and the earth? He punisheth whom He pleaseth, and He forgiveth whom He pleaseth: And Allah hath power over all things."
Qur'an 5:40

CHAPTER 19

THE BATTLE WITHIN. . .

A kindly sort of man who had mellowed with time, Shlomo Malichi Ben Y'sra'el wondered about the worth of his life. Had his rabid days of opposing Christianity been as fulfilling as they seemed at the time? Surely, the heady days of brokering peace with Palestine now appeared to be wasted and empty.

"Has my life journey led to nothing?" he asked Ahava. "Just hours ago, I reveled in hope and peace. Now, I wallow in self-pity and anxiety."

Sol's still lovely bride did her best to comfort him. She even attempted to make him smile. "I love you still, the same, even though you are surely easier to live with during our golden years! You have become a much calmer, wiser, light-hearted soul! Even curious Gentile children no longer upset you!"

Being short and stout with a long white beard, Sol was mistaken for Santa Claus on more than once occasion! On such a day in Jerusalem, an American girl had walked up to him in the Jewish Quarter and asked if he was Saint Nick! Sol was both offended and flattered at the same time, for he loved children. Sol dropped down to one knee and looked into the green eyes of the six year old and then said, "Don't tell anyone, but I am Santa Claus' Jewish brother! With ibex, the wild goats of the mountains, pulling my sleigh, I deliver my packages at *Chanukah!*"

Actually, Sol did give out many presents during the Festival of Lights. As he and his bride had raised six children of their own, God had now blessed them with eighteen grandchildren and three great grandchildren!

Undoubtedly, Ahava was the most accommodating woman in the world! With the kindest of hearts, she truly believed her needs were secondary to the needs of others. Her love, combined with her vision and hope, drove her to tender acts of service. She founded and led *Adonai* Ministries, which served the widows and orphans of Jerusalem, Tiberias, Haifa, and Beit Shean. Each day, as she compassionately and patiently touched the hearts and needs of broken children and poor widows, she literally lived out her name—as Ahava means love.

While Sol was challenged in height but blessed with girth, Ahava was also vertically challenged yet blessed with a sleek trim body that made women half her age jealous! In fact, this octogenarian could still fit into her wedding dress!

Inseparable, these two Hebrew lovebirds had been husband and wife for more than sixty five years. Still love struck, they could not imagine being apart. They knew each other so well that they did not have to speak to know what the other was thinking. Even now, though Sol had said nothing to her, Ahava knew something was deeply troubling him—something beyond the missile attacks. The current crisis for Israel seemed to bring his hidden, personal strife to the surface.

The lifelong sweethearts went to bed, emotionally drained from the day's twisted turn of events. Even so, as Ahava perceived, a personal battle raged within Sol. He tossed and turned as the words repeated over and over in his head: *"Without faith it is impossible to please God, because anyone who comes to Him must believe that He exists and that He rewards those who earnestly seek Him."* If this verse had been written in the Torah, Sol knew it would not haunt him. But the verse was in the New Testament—Hebrews 11:6 to be exact. Ariel Basel had shared this verse when she was telling Sol that salvation was not earned, but was given through faith in the Messiah—Y'shua.

For his entire life, the rabbi had placed his faith in the God of Abraham, Isaac, and Jacob, not God the Father, God the Son, and God the Holy Spirit. Truly, Sol worked hard to please God. The wrinkled clergyman wondered if all his work and his cumulative lifetime of faith were somehow insufficient. *"Is God displeased with me?"* Sol whispered. "Are You displeased with me, *HaShem?"*

Then the prophecies of Joel again invaded his heart. "I know the words You gave to the prophet Joel in the Tanakh, Adonai. In his fourth chapter and second verse, he quotes You, saying, *'I will gather all the nations and bring them down to the Valley of Jehoshaphat. There I will contend with them over My very own people, Isreal, which they scattered among the nations. For they divided My land among themselves.'"*

Sol buried his head in his pillow as he prayed, "Dear God, I helped foreigners divide Your Land! I sold Your Land for the illusion of peace, when You are the only true Peace! I have betrayed You, Your people, and Your land! Forgive me, Adonai, forgive me! I pray I have not gone so far that even You cannot forgive me! I have been a fool—an old, fat fool!"

As he lied there before his Maker, Sol wondered. *"Could the Lord be telling this seasoned rabbi that I should have faith in Y'shua? Must I seek the alleged Son and not only the Father? Indeed, is the Son the only way to the Father, as the Messianics claim?"*

Other words that Ariel had shared with him quickly replayed in his memory. Sol remembered talking with her during one of the breaks in the negotiations with the Palestinians. Her husband Mark had brought Ariel with him for that set of talks so they could visit her family in Tiberias when the negotiations ended.

Ariel had quoted the words of Paul—a former Pharisee who came to faith in Y'shua through a miraculous revelation that actually made Paul blind for a time. Sol wondered if he was blind now. Ariel had told him, "You are a modern day Pharisee, Sol! But listen to what the former Pharisee Paul said in Ephesians 2:8-9: *'For it is by grace you have been saved, through faith—and this not from yourselves, it is the gift of God—not by works, so that no one can boast.'"*

The Orthodox leader realized he had been boasting this very day before God about his role in the peace negotiations. The rounded rabbi knew he heard the Lord's voice saying the words of Proverbs 16:7, *"When the LORD is pleased with a man's conduct, He may turn even his enemies into allies."* In the recent past, Sol had found great comfort, solace, and satisfaction in that verse, as he thought he had pleased

God so much that the Lord had chosen to bless Israel through peace with the Palestinians! Now, Sol's turmoil centered on this verse!

The old man had boasted falsely! That peace had been nothing more than a mist, a vapor, and now it had become a nightmare! Sol had two strikes against him. One, he had not pleased the Lord. Two, he did not know the Messiah—if He had in fact already come! If he made a third strike, the swinging rabbi would be out!

What else had Ariel told him? She shared the story about Y'shua and another Pharisee—one who visited Y'shua at night to avoid the scandal and shame of being accused of believing in the Man from Nazareth—of all places. Sol thought, as it was then, so it is now! Here he was, in the middle of the night, a twenty first century Pharisee trying to figure out this first century Galilean who many hailed as Messiah— even today in Israel!

The sleepless rabbi sat up in bed, hoping he would not wake his dear wife who was resting so well next to him. From the nightstand, he picked up his flashlight and it automatically began shining. Sol slipped out of bed, tip-toed across the bedroom floor and through the hall until he came to his study. There, he stopped and stared at the chest resting against the outside wall. Would he find the answers he sought in that locked box?

"Here I am! I stand at the door and knock. If anyone hears My voice and opens the door, I will come in and eat with him, and he with Me."
Revelation 3:20

CHAPTER 20

UNEXPECTED PASSENGER. . .

*A*ir Force One (AF1) cruised at 50,000 feet above the Atlantic. Aboard were the President and Vice President of the United States, Chief of Staff Eddie Murdock, various assistants, and a double security detail. Air Force One was being escorted by no less than four of the Air Force's latest fighter jets—F-47's all! These jets were the fastest, toughest, most nimble, and most deadly fighter jets the U.S. had ever manufactured. The only thing they lacked was stealth capacity, but they could blow an enemy fighter out of the sky, even hundreds of miles away, by electromagnetic force! The Commander in Chief was taking no chances.

Inside Air Force One, the President considered the American citizens and officials who became collateral damage in the missile strikes. Would or could the United States ever know who or how many of her citizens died on the Israeli and Palestinian sides of Jerusalem? Actually, would any accurate count of U.S., DROP, Israeli, or other nation's losses be made? During his address, James had asked for a moment of silence for all the victims. Who knew how many people from how many countries died instantly in the explosions?

Personally, James had not known what to do during the moment of silence near the end of his address. He bowed his head, but he did not pray. He never prayed.

Regardless, the proud President delivered what he considered to be big news in his speech. The United States would help China, Japan, and even North Korea rebuild! James told the world, "Even though islamization had already begun in those lands, maybe, just maybe the U.S. can help those three nations reverse the process."

Unfortunately, James did not realize the naivety, even the stupidity, of his proposal. Yes, years ago, the three nations had agreed to promote native population growth, seeking to reverse decades of great attrition. Nonetheless, even then, Japan, China, and North Korea had already passed the point of no return in regard to islamization. The casualties of World War III only sped up the process!

Therefore, with irreversible islamization in those lands, the Caliph of Babylon effectively ruled over all of Asia. As soon as bin Laden secured the remaining few and small open territories in Europe, he would officially proclaim his rule over China, North Korea, and Japan.

Although James would soon be forced to acknowledge his foolish and futile efforts of a U.S.-Asian alliance to stand against the Caliphate, his last minute diplomacy with North, Central, and South American countries would bear some fruit. Already, Canada, Mexico, Brazil, Argentina, Peru, Uruguay, Chile and a few other nations in the three regions were making military and diplomatic alliances with the United States in order to stand against the Caliphate and to reverse internal islamization. James suggested formalizing the new relationship between the nations by calling it the American Union.

Even so, such hopeful prospects for the American continent could also be dashed by one question which no one could yet answer: Were the lands of the potential American Union also too far down the road of islamization? Until proven otherwise, James assumed that islamization could be stopped and reversed in any of these nations that sought to escape the consuming jaws of the Caliphate.

In his post speech analysis, President Paulson thought he had been rather magnanimous, as he had actually allowed his Vice President to make some of the best points. As it turned out, with the extra material Abdul included, he had talked almost twice as long as James had spoken.

Then and there aboard Air Force One, James realized he needed Abdul more than he cared to admit. Strangely enough, James wondered if perhaps it was the providence of God, and not his own political savvy, that landed Abdul-ghafoor Asim Abdullah on the Democratic ticket and ultimately in the White House. Somehow that thought was comforting, even though this high-risk-taker and political-gambler-extraordinaire, James Jacob Paulson, was anything but a believer!

While James mulled over Abdul's political capital, the Vice President himself retired to his private bedroom. In many ways, he felt he was a traitor to his Islamic faith and heritage. He was the Muslim pawn in the American President's deadly chess match with Islam— just as he had been the Muslim pawn in the U.S. Presidential election. Did the Vice President agree with the policies and decisions that his Commander in Chief had presented only hours ago? Did he personally believe in Allah as well as the terror and jihad the god of Islam demanded?

Though the sun still shined in the District of Columbia (D.C.), night had already fallen in the DROP. Hence, Abdul wanted to make up for the seven hours he would lose in the time change. Moreover, he had no desire to discuss the joint address with the President, and the Vice President surely did not relish the idea of "savoring the highlights" as the President always called his post-speech analysis.

In the main cabin, Abdul's boss thought he had reason to celebrate this historic evening. The focus group results were coming in, and James could see he had scored high marks for credibility, command of the situation, and his restrained response to the brutal attack. In fact, the President was all smiles, until he read the report for the Vice President, who scored even higher marks than he did with the focus groups in all three areas. Beyond that, the Vice President's trust factor rating left the President's numbers in the dust! Frustrated, James quickly balled up the papers and trashed them. "Focus groups smocus groups," he mumbled to himself as he sipped his wine.

Meanwhile, as Abdul doused the lights and lied down on his bed, he felt both physically and emotionally drained. How was he supposed to feel, personally, as a Muslim, about the attacks in East Jerusalem and the Noble Sanctuary? Should he not be mourning and enraged? If so, why did he feel so neutral, almost like a third party observer who had no stake in the day's events? He had his suspicions, but why wasn't he trying to determine exactly who was behind the carnage and destruction? Did he not care or did he fear the truth? Maybe something else altogether brewed inside him? As his thoughts went around in circles, Abdul slowly drifted off to sleep.

Sometime later, he awoke to the knock at the door of his private sleeping quarters. Reluctantly, Abdul propped himself up on his elbow and said, "Yes, Is that you, James?" Without an answer, the door opened. The Vice President rubbed his eyes as the bright light behind the figure in the entrance to the dark room made it hard for him to see who was there. Even so, Abdul somehow instantly knew that James was not the one standing in his doorway.

With a few more taps on the now open door, the voice from the light asked, "May I come in, Abdul?"

"Allah hath purchased of the Believers their persons and their goods; For theirs (in return) is the Garden (of Paradise): They fight in His Cause, and slay and are slain: A promise binding on Him in Truth, through the Law, the Gospel, and the Qur'an: And who is more faithful to his Covenant than Allah? Then rejoice in the bargain which ye have concluded: That is the achievement supreme."
Qur'an 9:111

CHAPTER 21

THE SEDUCTION OF EVIL. . .

❖❖❖

*I*n the darkness of the windowless room, the computer holoscreen glowed pale red. The cryptic code, composed on virtual keys, foretold destruction and doom. With only a few more key coordinates left to enter, soon the irrevocable process would be in motion—despite the General's complaints that the data entry should have been completed hours ago.

The misery, mutilation, and murder of men, women, and children did not concern the jihadist hiding in the red tinged darkness. Such details were irrelevant to the work of Allah! He had heard the rationale spoken hundreds, even thousands of times. *"The infidels are bound for eternal catastrophe, anyway, so what temporal or ultimate worth do their damned souls hold? From the dawn of time, such wretched souls have been destined for endless pain and suffering! They are receiving justice, not terror!"*

Waves of sweat rolled off the face of the agent of death in the merciless heat of summer night in a Middle Eastern desert. Consequently, his dark, steamy hours of suffering would be rewarded because of the great victory he was preparing for Allah!

In anticipation, the relentless typing of characters and codes paused for a moment. He asked himself again, *"What awaits me in paradise?"* He smiled as he considered the promise his mullah told him that Muhammad—peace be upon him—had made for such brave souls: "A palace with 72 rooms, 72 beds, 72 sheets, and 72 virgins who would never lose their virginity!' Ah, yes, Muhammad's promises found in the Hadith are sweet indeed! As the mullah said, 'Without the Prophet's sayings and deeds, as well as the traditions found in the Hadith, we could not understand the Qur'an!"

The perspiring poltroon considered other rewards that the mullah said awaited him. "Qur'an 52:24 promises you will be attended by boys graced with eternal youth, who will seem like scattered pearls as you behold them—young boys, as fair as virgin pearls! While the *niqab* hides the beauty of the women on this earth, the young boys' loveliness is displayed for all to see! Both the boys and the virgins will be yours in paradise!"

With a bedeviled grin on his face as well as renewed excitement in his lustful heart, he resumed his work and the virtual keys again danced rapidly, silently. *"My family will finally be proud of me! I will hear no more of their chiding insults about my worthlessness or my filthy, vile habits. I will have the respect and honor of Allah himself! Yes, a great slaughter is coming—to the glory of Allah and to the glory of one who has never received the praise he deeply deserves! How my family, how my friends, will be amazed when they hear of the torrent I unleash!"*

He shouted into the darkness, *"Peace is for the weak! Peace is no better than surrender—and it may be even worse! Annihilation swiftly comes to those who dare to stand against Allah! All that is in the hands of the infidels will belong to the one god who has no partners!"*

Laughing out loud, the young man shrouded by darkness proclaimed, *"The kuffar have been deceived! They remain deceived! Forever, they will be deceived! They are so easily beguiled, when only terror and death await them—now and for all eternity! Jihad! Glorious jihad! All the wrongs of this world are about to be made right, and Allah will reign supreme with no other gods and no other power beside him!"*

After making the final entry, this anonymous wretch lifted his hands in praise! Victory and valor belonged to him! The pieces were set in motion and nothing could stop them now!

He turned off the computer, and nervously waited in the darkness. The sound came like a clap of thunder, although it passed too quickly for him to hear. He felt no pain as his body slumped to the floor. No one grieved his passing.

"... 'I am the Light of the world. Whoever follows Me will never walk in darkness, but will have the Light of Life.'"
John 8:12

CHAPTER 22

STUMBLING IN THE DARKNESS...

*S*ol tried to be quiet and use as little light as possible. He did not want Ahava to know of his clandestine activities. Mark and Ariel had given him an English Version of the New Testament when they exhausted their supply of Hebrew translations. Though he had told Ahava he had destroyed that New Testament, Sol had actually hidden it in the chest in his study. After all, whether truth or fiction, that book did claim to contain the new covenant God had promised the Jews through Jeremiah! Sol figured he should know what it said.

Tonight, he longed to find that New Testament. He wanted to read the passage about that nighttime encounter between the Pharisee and Y'shua. How Sol identified with that teacher of the law. Sol asked himself, *"What was his name? Nicolas? No! Nicolas is not a Jewish name! Whatever his name was, I know the confusion and the hunger for answers that my prototype Orthodox Jew felt!"*

On this moonless evening, Sol's flashlight brought a soft glow to the otherwise black room. Slowly, he walked across his study to the chest. He unlocked and opened it, cringing at the loud creaks that echoed in the room. Shining the flashlight into the open chest, Sol tried to remember where he had hidden the New Testament so that Ahava would not find it.

Of course, Sol could have searched the New Testament with the help of his super computer, but that ancient relic had shut down yet again. The raging rabbi had almost tossed it out the window when it died again two days ago, just as he was finishing his sermon for Shabbat!

As he examined the contents of his chest, the rabbi was taken aback by all the news and HV3D clips he had saved from the peace negotiations. He found several reports about his role in the talks. He had fought hard to maintain the Biblical borders of Israel as much as possible, even as he agreed to cede land to the Palestinians. He had argued, emphatically, against Muslim control of the *Kotel*, the *Haram al-Sharif* or Noble Sanctuary for the Muslims, the Temple Mount as the Christians called it. Sol wondered if the *Kotel* might yet stand this night if he had fought harder for it to remain under Jewish control.

Throughout the negotiations, Sol had sought Palestinian cooperation in the building of a third Temple. Of course that proposal had gone absolutely nowhere. Hence, when the peace negotiations ended with the Palestinians in control of the *Kotel*, the rabbi saw his dreams of a third Temple go up in flames. Today, that destroyed vision had become reality.

As it turned out, all the cumulative negotiating, arguing, and pleading was indeed pointless. The *Kotel* no longer existed! The Muslims held that the Jews had never built a Temple in Jerusalem in the first place. Now, all the evidence of the first and second Temples no longer existed! Worse yet, all out war could be no more than days, maybe even hours, away. Depressed, Sol pushed all the news reports aside, but not before he saw the big, bold headline: "PEACE AT LAST!"

At that moment, Sol realized he had embarked on a personal quest for peace.

Below that layer of Sol's recent history, he found certificates of appreciation and awards from the many years of his work to protect Jews from followers of Y'shua. He rediscovered his personal audio diary that he recorded during his one-man campaign against Christians, missionaries, and Messianic Jews.

In a box of holographic news clips, he saw himself, red faced, arguing in court that neither Gentile Christians nor Jews who believed in Y'shua had legal rights in Israel. In another frame, he looked at a much younger and feistier version of himself burning Christian tracts and books.

He gazed further into the past when he found an antiquated, single dimension photo that showed him forcing a missionary into a car. He drove that missionary to the airport and personally ensured that he was deported and would never be allowed to return to Israel!

Sol read the headline of an op-ed piece he had written for *The Jerusalem Post*, sixty years ago. "Y'shu or Y'shua?" (Fool or Messiah?) In the article, Sol used the Hebrew acronym for "May His Name and Memory be Obliterated," which is Y'shu, to strike a critical blow to the Messianic movement. For generations after that article, missionaries had to argue that the Messiah's Name was not Y'shu, but Y'shua, which means God saves!

Once upon a time, Sol regarded his chest of artifacts as trophies. Tonight, he felt ashamed of them, ashamed of himself! This was not the happily ever after future he had envisioned. He felt much more foolish than he felt happy! He scolded himself, saying, *"Maybe my name and legacy should be obliterated!"*

Underneath all the suddenly irrelevant news items of his hate-filled past, Sol's flashlight shined on the New Testament. Sol gritted his teeth as he reached for the book and brought it close. *"What was that Pharisee's name?"* he asked himself as he pounded the New Testament against his head. If he could remember the name, he could use the concordance to find the verses about him. Concentrating as hard as he possibly could—until his brain actually ached—the seeking rabbi realized he could not retrieve the name.

Frustrated, Sol sat down in front of the chest. Then, in a moment of inspiration, the Orthodox Jew realized he could look up the word Pharisee in the concordance instead. Sol flipped to the end of the New Testament. In the concordance, he found twelve verses listed under the heading of Pharisee. He looked up each verse, with help from the table of contents to find the books that contained the verses.

What Sol found discouraged him. *"Y'shua apparently had little use for Pharisees, calling them hypocrites, self-righteous, proud, and compassionless."* He shrugged as he thought, *"No wonder a Pharisee did not want to be seen in Y'shua's presence!"*

The only other verses for Pharisee were in reference to Paul. Sol read about Paul, the Pharisee who persecuted Y'shua's followers until his famous vision of Y'shua as he walked to Damascus. That encounter completely transformed Paul! He not only stopped persecuting the Jewish followers of Y'shua, but he instead began preaching that Y'shua was the Messiah. Sol found Paul's metamorphosis quite astounding. He thought, *"What an awesome vision Paul must have witnessed to have been so completely changed!"*

His eyes straining in the dim light, Sol read that Paul's original name was Saul. The rabbi mused, *"Saul and Sheol are the same word in Hebrew. Saul means asked for, while Sheol means pit, grave, even hell itself."* Sol reflected further. *"Was this Pharisee bound for hell without Y'shua? Was his name not random, but ordained by God? Did Saul ask for hell by his actions?"*

Next Sol considered the name Paul, which was a Latin name, not Hebrew. *"If I remember correctly, Paul means short. Could Paul have been short like me? But wouldn't his new name have spiritual significance? Maybe the name reminded him that God was the source of strength for all he accomplished after he met Y'shua on the road to Damascus? Maybe his new Latin name was a foreshadowing of his ministry to the Gentiles? Maybe the name humbled a proud man—a man a lot like me."*

From his conversations with Ariel, the Orthodox Jew remembered that Paul had suffered great persecution himself for being an ardent evangelist for Y'shua! Even so, no matter how much the Jews humiliated him, how long they imprisoned him, or how severely they beat him, Paul would not stop preaching salvation in the Name of the Messiah!

Sol reasoned, *"It makes sense that somewhere along the way Paul stopped preaching to the Jews and took Y'shua's message to the Gentiles instead. After all, the Jews rejected Jesus, so logically, they would likewise reject Paul!"*

The old rabbi paused again to consider Paul's complete transformation. *"A persecutor of the Jews who believed in Y'shua became persecuted by the Jews who rejected Y'shua. I suppose I would have been right there, siding with Paul's enemies."*

As he continued to ponder Paul's dramatic conversion, Sol turned back to the concordance. He noticed that below the twelve listed verses for "Pharisee," there were 86 listings under "Pharisees." He began going through those verses one by one. *"Hmm,"* he moaned, *"these Pharisees do sound somewhat like the Orthodox of today! They fought with Y'shua at every opportunity."*

At the point where his physical tiredness almost overcame his spiritual quest, Sol looked at the sixty fourth listing under the word Pharisees. There, in John 3:1, the rabbi found the Pharisee Nicodemus! *"Not Nicolas, but Nicodemus!"* Sol mumbled. *"Very close! Nicodemus is not a Jewish name, either."*

Despite his weakening flashlight, his aching body, and weary soul, the rabbi continued his mission to meet Nicodemus in the pages of the New Testament. Sol turned to the third chapter of John. Several parts of the passage spoke to him in real time. He considered the words he read carefully. *"Nicodemus served as a member of the Jewish ruling council, which made him a member of the Sanhedrin—impressive."*

Sol himself served as a member of the reconstituted Sanhedrin. Although in its modern form, the Sanhedrin had very little power, Sol knew that the rebirth of the Sanhedrin was actually a symbolic gesture—one that hopefully pointed to the rebuilding of the Temple and the soon arrival of the Messiah! *"Suppose the Messiah has already come,"* Sol wondered. *"Does that mean Nicodemus actually stood before the Son of David—the very Son of God?"*

As he continued to dissect the passage, Sol noted, *"Hmm! Nicodemus addressed Y'shua as Rabbi.' Nicodemus respected Y'shua—even saying he knew God sent Him! Nicodemus said the miracles Y'shua performed proved God was with him! Interesting indeed!"*

Sol read Y'shua's words from verse three in a whispered voice. *"I tell you the truth, no one can see the Kingdom of God unless he is born again."* Looking up from the page and into the darkness, Sol acted as though he had made a major discovery, *"So this is where that phrase originates! Y'shua said His followers must be reborn!"*

The reenergized rabbi read on. He smiled, thinking, *"Nicodemus sounds as confused by those words as I am yet today! He asked Y'shua, 'How can a man be born when he is old?' Y'shua told Nicodemus that he could not 'enter the Kingdom of Heaven unless he is born of water and the Spirit.' Born of the Holy Spirit? Nicodemus still did not understand! But Y'shua expected the Pharisee, as a teacher of the people, to know these things."*

Looking at the bottom of the page, Sol found an explanation as to what Y'shua might have meant when He said the words "born again." The footnotes said that in the original Greek text those words could also mean "born from above!" That translation actually made sense to the elderly rabbi. *"We have a physical birth into this world, so it makes sense that we need a spiritual birth for Heaven! We must be born again—born from above."*

As Sol continued to explore the text, he whispered to himself, *"Y'shua called Himself the Son of Man. God called Ezekiel the Son of man, with a small 'm' in English. Y'shua said He came from Heaven. He said He would be lifted up. Was this a veiled reference to the snake Moses lifted up in the desert? The sinful, dying Israelites looked up to that snake and lived. Y'shua said he would be lifted up on the cross. Sinful, dying Jews are to look to the crucified Y'shua to find life—eternal?"*

His heart beating rapidly, Sol felt as though he stood with Y'shua and Nicodemus as he listened to their conversation. The impassioned teacher asked many more questions of the text. *"Y'shua claimed to be both the Son of Man and Son of God? God sent His Son, His only Son—like Isaac—for sacrifice? But God did not stop Y'shua's sacrifice as He stopped Abraham from sacrificing Isaac. God gave His Son in sacrifice because of His great love for the sinners of this world? The Messiah is the sacrifice, the ultimate atonement for human sin?"*

Finally, Sol arrived at the sixteenth verse of John's third chapter. *"For God so loved the world that He gave His one and only Son, that whoever believes in Him shall not perish but have eternal life."* Many of the missionaries quoted this verse to Sol—before he deported them. He had paid no attention to its words before tonight.

Sol grappled with Y'shua's words. *"HaShem loves the world so much that He sent His very Son to save it through faith in His sacrifice for sin? What kind of love is this? I could not sacrifice my son for the best Hebrew man I know, but God supposedly sacrificed His only Son for rebels condemned to hell itself?"*

The soul-searching rabbi reread John 3:16, then noted, *"Y'shua says, 'God so loved the world,' not 'God so loved the Jews.' Could Y'shua be the fulfillment of HaShem's promise to Abraham that all the nations would be blessed through his seed, through his descendants? Perhaps I have been indescribably selfish wanting a Messiah for the Jews alone? Would not the Maker of all Creation want to redeem His entire Creation?"*

Sol found himself spellbound, as he asked more questions of John's verses. *"Y'shua came to save, not condemn? Anyone in the world can believe in this Messiah, even Muslims? If Y'shua's sacrifice is the atonement for sin, then all who reject Him cannot enter Heaven?"*

Y'shua's words in verse nineteen spoke directly to Sol in his present situation. *"Light has come into the world, but men loved darkness instead of light because their deeds were evil."* Sol shined his dimming flashlight around the black room. He considered the darkness within his own soul. He tried to fight back the tears he felt welling up in his eyes.

Then, the rabbi looked at the last words of Y'shua quoted in John chapter three—verses twenty and twenty one. *"Everyone who does evil hates the light, and will not come into the light for fear that their deeds will be exposed. But whoever lives by the truth comes into the light, so that it may be seen plainly that what they have done has been done in the sight of God."*

The irony of Y'shua's words and Sol's current circumstances did not escape him. Like Nicodemus, Sol came to seek out Y'shua under the cover of darkness—physical and spiritual darkness, despite all both men knew about the Torah, the Law, and the Messianic prophecies. Sol asked, *"Am I afraid and too ashamed to come out of the darkness and into the Light of the One who could be the Messiah? Am I not only hiding from Ahava but from myself and from God Himself?"*

As he continued to read John's narration in his third chapter, Sol became frustrated as he realized that John did not say what Nicodemus did in response to his secret meeting with Y'shua! However, now that Sol knew his name, he looked up Nicodemus in the concordance and found two more passages in which he could read about the Pharisee: John 7:50-52 and 19:39-42.

Again, in John chapter seven, the inquisitive rabbi saw words and phrases that seemed to jump off the pages in real time. Verse fifty and fifty one said, *"Nicodemus, who had gone to Y'shua earlier and who was one of the Sanhedrin's own number, asked, 'Does our Law condemn anyone without first hearing him to find out what he is doing?'"*

Sol thought, *"The Pharisees and priests of the Temple wanted to arrest Y'shua, but Nicodemus spoke out, publicly, for Him? Nicodemus defended Y'shua, when members of the Sanhedrin wanted to condemn and kill Him? What had happened since his night meeting with Y'shua to make Nicodemus so brave that in broad daylight he defended Y'shua's right to a fair trial. While Nicodemus' arguments ring true, verse 52 says the other members of the council scorned him for defending Y'shua. Did Nicodemus believe Y'shua was the Messiah?"*

As the flashlight continued to dim, Sol shook it and realized the ten year batteries would soon be dead. He whispered, *"Of all nights, this has to be the one in a decade to replace batteries!"* Thus, Sol quickly flipped the pages over to John 19. As he began reading verse thirty nine, he realized he needed to back up to verse thirty eight. He read through verse forty two.

> *"Later, Joseph of Arimathea asked Pilate for the Body of Jesus. Now Joseph was a disciple of Jesus, but secretly because he feared the Jewish leaders. With Pilate's permission, he came and took the body away. He was accompanied by Nicodemus, the man who earlier had visited Jesus at night. Nicodemus brought a mixture of myrrh and aloes, about seventy-five pounds. Taking Jesus' Body, the two of them wrapped it, with the spices, in strips of linen. This was in accordance with Jewish burial customs. At the place where Jesus was crucified, there was a garden, and in the garden a new tomb, in which no one had ever been laid. Because it was the Jewish day of Preparation and since the tomb was nearby, they laid Jesus there."*

The notes at the bottom of the page told Sol that Joseph also served as a Pharisee and a member of the Sanhedrin, yet, amazingly, followed Y'shua as Messiah, as well! Sol's mouth fell open. *"With another Pharisee and member of the Sanhedrin, Nicodemus helped bury Y'shua! If Joseph did this because he was a disciple of Y'shua, then Nicodemus must have become a follower of Y'shua, too! The two of them would have been thrown out of the Sanhedrin for helping bury the body of one the ruling body had condemned!*

"They buried Y'shua on the eve of Passover?" Immediately Sol realized the implication of his question. *"Was Y'shua not only the Lamb of Atonement but also the Passover Lamb? Is His Blood painted over the doors of the souls of those who believe?"* Sol breathed rapidly as the flashlight flickered. *"We are forgiven by blood sacrifice. On Yom Kippur, the High Priest must take the blood of the lamb into the Holy of Holies to atone for the people's sin. Does this mean that Jesus*

is both the Sacrifice and the High Priest? Has he entered the Holy of Holies in Heaven with His own Blood for our atonement?"

The rabbi's head and heart swirled, as he reasoned. *"Y'shua was crucified, which means He was cursed by God! Deuteronomy 21:22-23 says that anyone who is impaled on a stake is an affront to God—accursed! Our sins are an affront to God also! Did Y'shua bear our curse on the cross to atone for our sin, so death—eternal separation from God in hell—would pass over us, if we place our faith in Him?"*

Physically drained yet invigorated in spirit, Sol leaned against the chest. *"Obviously, Nicodemus as well as Joseph decided to believe in Y'shua as the Messiah, or they would not have risked everything to hastily bury Him to avoid desecrating the Passover! Are these Pharisees brave men of faith or just plain fools who got everything wrong?"*

He let the question hang in the air for a few seconds, and then Sol asked, *"Which am I?"*

With those words, the room went dark.

"They but wish that ye should reject Faith, as they do, and thus be on the same footing (as they): But take not friends from their ranks until they flee in the way of Allah (from what is forbidden). But if they turn renegades, seize them and slay them wherever ye find them; And (in any case) take no friends or helpers from their ranks."
Qur'an 4:89

CHAPTER 23

THE DARKNESS IS AS LIGHT. . .

Still drowsy, Abdul sat on the edge of his bed and shook his head. Looking back to the door, he could see the figure of a man standing in the light.

"May I come in, Abdul?" the voice asked again.

Feeling nothing but incredible peace in his heart, Abdul replied, "Of course, please, do come in!" Abdul stood to meet the One behind the voice.

"You have been searching for the truth," the voice of the One said, as the door closed.

Now, in the room, Abdul could see that the figure was not backlit by the light in the hallway. The figure was the Light!

"You have been searching for Me, Abdul!"

Opening his eyes as wide as possible, Abdul peered into the Light. He was mesmerized as he gazed into the most kind, understanding, and compassionate eyes he had ever seen! Those eyes seemed to not look at him, but to see within him—all the way to his own soul! Abdul could not breathe! He could not speak! Even so, he was not afraid, but quite overcome with joy—joy beyond description, beyond anything to which he could compare it!

Completely humbled, Abdul fell to his knees. He could hear the pounding of his heart in his chest! Then, the One, the Light said, "Now that you have found Me, Abdul, follow Me!"

Tears of release and freedom flowed like rivers down Abdul's cheeks! "Isa? Y'shua? Jesus?"

"Yes!" the Lord answered, while placing His Hand under Abdul's chin to lift his head. Through his tears, Abdul saw the warmest smile, and then felt himself smiling in return!

"Follow Me!" Isa said once again.

"How can I, Lord? I am a Muslim!"

"You are one for whom I died and rose again, Abdul. I offer you life, today! I offer you My peace!"

Abdul had been awash in Isa's peace ever since He entered the room. He felt that peace even as he said, "Lord, if I turn from Islam, I will be killed! I am a large target, and powerful forces will come after me!"

Isa knelt beside Abdul. The very Son of God placed His hands on Abdul's shoulders. "No power greater than my Love exists, Abdul! Besides, those who save their lives will end up losing them, but those who lose their lives, for My sake, will save them in the end! Indeed, what good is your life if you lose your own soul, Abdul? Therefore, do not fear those who can harm your body, but cannot touch your soul. You see, I am the only Way, the only Truth, and the only Life—for you and for every man, woman, boy and girl on the face of this earth. Because of my immeasurable love for you, I will never leave your side! I will never forsake you! When persecution comes—and it will come—I will give you strength to stand, endure, and overcome!"

Abdul looked down, breaking eye contact with Isa. Abdul felt ashamed and unworthy. "I am a follower of Islam! I am the Vice President of the United States, Lord—elected as a Muslim by Muslims!"

"I know what you are and who you are, Abdul." Isa lifted his chin to restore eye contact. "I know everything that you have done that you now regret. I know everything that you have failed to do that now brings you remorse. In spite of all that, I have forgiven you—long ago! The question is whether you will accept My forgiveness. Will you accept My mercy and grace?"

"I just don't see how I can make this work, especially in the role I have now—a role I never sought."

Isa smiled. "I called and appointed you for such a time as this. You will be a great and powerful witness to the power of the Truth that you have sought! You are already beginning to know the saving, transforming power of My cross—borne for you and all who are far from My Father! Your regrets and sorrow for the past will soon give way to My hope and love in the present as well as My purpose and power for your future."

"You say, 'My Father.' How can a divine God degrade Himself to father a child with a human woman?"

"Abdul, My Father is not limited by the ways of humanity! Truly, I was not conceived through any human act of sexual relations! Though I am eternal, by the very power of the Holy Spirit, Mary conceived Me in her womb. I was born both divine and human so that I could pay the eternal price for human sin! I was born to die for your sin, Abdul, and not only your sin, but for the sin of every soul who has lived, does live, or will live on this earth!"

"I was always taught that Allah. . .that God. . .was one, not three!"

"My Father, the Holy Spirit, and I are one, Abdul. I have something to show you to help you understand. Cup your hands." Without asking why, Abdul did as Isa asked. From His own Hands, Isa poured a liquid into Abdul's hands.

"What is in your hands, Abdul?"

"Water," Abdul said as he looked curiously into Isa's pure eyes.

"Look again. What is in your hands now?"

Abdul felt the change before he looked. "Ice," he replied. You froze the water!" Again, Abdul peered deeply into Isa's love-filled eyes.

"Look at your hands again. What do you see now?"

Once more, Abdul felt the change before he saw it. The cold of the ice was replaced by warmth. "Steam! You heated the ice until it became steam!"

"Whether liquid, solid, or vapor, all three are water, Abdul. All three are the same. Likewise, whether Father, Son, or Spirit, all three are God. All three are the same!"

Abdul understood. He smiled and asked, "Your Father and Holy Spirit are also in You and here with me now somehow?"

136

Smiling in return, Isa answered, "Yes, Abdul! Wherever My Father is, I am with Him. Wherever I am, the Spirit is with Me. Wherever the Spirit is, My Father and I are also. We are one and cannot be separated by time, distance, or any temporal or eternal power!"

"What about when You were on the cross, Isa? My Messianic friend says God—Your Father—had to abandon You as you hung there."

Gently and yet firmly at the same time, Isa held Abdul's hand. Together, they sat down on the edge of the bed. Again, Isa gazed deep into Abdul's soul as He said, "When I was crucified, Abdul. I bore your sin. I bore the sin of the world. God cannot be one with sin! Therefore, for the first and only time in all eternity, I was torn from My Father! Just as your sin separates you from My Father, so, when I bore your sin on the cross, your sin separated Me from My Father. The spiritual agony of being severed from My Father, from the Holy Spirit, hurt Me far more than the physical pain of the cross and the scourging I endured for you! I suffered indescribable pain, all alone in all eternity, so that you would not have to be separated from My Father—ever!"

Abdul's tears rushed from his eyes.

"Then, Abdul, when My bloodied, tortured physical Body died and hung lifeless on that cross, My Soul went to hell in place of yours! There, still separated from the love of My Father, from the presence of His Spirit, I suffered the eternal agony that should have been yours as the just and logical consequences of your sin!"

Abdul hung his head in shame, weeping uncontrollably. "I caused all that to happen to You?"

"Yes, Abdul, I chose to take on all the consequences of every sin you chose to commit!"

"I cannot bear the pain I feel in my soul, now!"

"What you feel right in this moment, Abdul, is the Holy Spirit convicting you of your sin. All the remorse and regret you feel, this Godly sorrow, will lead you to confess your sin, all your sin, and receive My mercy! This unbearable pain will also lead you to repent, to turn from your sin, and start a new life filled with My grace!

"I am so unworthy, Isa," Abdul said through his tears.

Again, Isa placed His Hand under Abdul's chin and lifted his face until their eyes met. "I love you so much, Abdul, that I suffered both here on earth and in the depths of hell in your place. That's how much you are worth to Us—Father, Son and Spirit!"

Abdul shook his head back and forth, trying to comprehend the depth of Isa's unconditional love and unlimited suffering for him.

"I will not only be merciful to you by forgiving your sin, but I will be gracious to you by empowering you through My Spirit. You will be one with Me, just as I and My Father are one in the Spirit. You have much to do for My Kingdom, for the souls that are so confused and troubled on this earth, so filled with anger, fear, and hate in this world."

His voice weak, Abdul said, "Isa, I am not a leader! I never wanted to be Vice President of the United States! I don't have any political ambition!"

"Yes, and those are three of the reasons I have chosen you for the work ahead, Abdul. I would not have chosen you to lead if you were filled with political ambition, the thirst for raw power, and the desire to rule over men. You will rely on Me, and I will be your guide and wisdom. Yet, you must first make a choice."

"A choice to confess my sin, repent of it, and accept Your mercy and grace?"

"Yes, Abdul, will you do that? I already know — I already suffered, died, and went to Hell for — all your sins. By confessing them, you are not telling me anything I don't already know about you. Through confession, you admit to yourself and to Me that you are a man who stands condemned by your own willful, sinful choices. Through repentance, you turn away from all that sin and turn instead to Me.

"In response, because of My great love for you, I offer you, not condemnation, as you deserve, but mercy and grace. In My mercy, I forgive you and free you from the eternal consequences of your sin. But I have even more to offer you beyond My forgiveness! Through My grace, I welcome you into My Kingdom, into the oneness I share with My Father, the Holy Spirit, and all believers! I purchased mercy and grace for you with My very blood! Will you confess your sin, repent of it, and accept the mercy and grace I bought for you so long ago?"

Abdul felt a new wave of guilt rush over him. Sadly, he said, "I don't deserve such mercy and grace — especially at so high a cost!"

"Those are Satan's words, Abdul, and he is correct, actually. No one ever deserves forgiveness! No one can earn it! Likewise, no one can earn grace. No one can work their way into My Kingdom. My mercy and grace come to you as gifts of love that you cannot measure or fathom. Won't you receive the greatest gifts ever to be offered in all eternity?"

Abdul felt a second wave washing over him—a wave of hope mixed with that indescribable peace and joy he felt when Isa first entered the room! "I would be a fool to walk away from the greatest gifts anyone could ever receive!"

Isa patted Abdul on the back. "Now, you understand!"

Abdul slipped off the bed to kneel beside it and before Isa. Through his remaining tears, he said, "Lord, I confess to you that I am a blind sinner! As I say these words, I am dead because of my sinful choices. Please remove my guilt and condemnation and fill me instead with Your mercy and grace! I repent of all that sin, and I desire to start over, with a clean slate, never to turn back. I want my home to be in Your Kingdom! I most earnestly desire to serve You, if You will have me!"

With unbridled enthusiasm, Isa replied, "We forgave you more than two thousand years ago, Abdul! You have no idea how joyful we are that you have finally received that mercy. By My grace, you are now a son of God, my brother, and an heir in the one and only eternal Kingdom of Heaven! The way We see you now, Abdul, it's as though you never sinned!"

Abdul looked into Isa's shining face and said, "I want to tell everyone about You! I want to tell them You are the essence of life, hope, peace, joy, love, mercy, and grace! Show me how! I'll do whatever You say, go wherever You send me!"

"Yes, you will, Abdul! Truly, you will!"

"You have heard that it was said, 'Eye for eye, and tooth for tooth.' But I tell you, do not resist an evil person. If someone strikes you on the right cheek, turn to him the other also."
Matthew 5:38-39

CHAPTER 24

THE REAL THING. . .

*A*fter all the conventional and smart submachine gun fire in the darkness, a shout of "All clear!" rang out. Then, the lights came back on and the window curtains reopened to reveal six of the seven terrorists were handcuffed and facing the wall.

Long before this day, Pastor Mark had been preparing his congregation for such an attack, although most of the people doubted Muslim terrorists would ever threaten the Church of the Transformed. They felt such occurrences only happened in foreign countries, not in the United States.

Nonetheless, from his own experience, Pastor Mark knew the day would come. Furthermore, because of who he was, how he preached to the Muslims, and what he taught at the seminary, he knew his congregation would be one of the terrorists' first targets. Not only had he seen the pattern over European and Asian countries, he also had personal experience with Muslims terrorizing Jesus' churches. In all cases, Pastor Mark understood that once the Muslims were close to being the majority population, the terrorists would begin demonstrating their strength—always starting with churches, Christian ministries, or Christian missions.

More than five years ago, Pastor Mark had convinced the elders of the church that they should develop an emergency contingency plan. That plan was actually developed by the police officers who were members of the congregation. For the last five and a half years, those officers in plain clothes had practiced their plan with the pastor and congregation once each month. Sixty six times the church rehearsed what they finally put into action. While giggles, jokes, and outright laughter often accompanied the practice drills, on this day of reckoning, sobriety and earnestness reigned.

When the "All clear!" was heard, the members congregation rose from their prone positions on the pews, erupted in applause, knew that Pastor Mark had been right all along, and praised God that they were indeed prepared for the threat that became reality on this very morning.

Even so, Pastor Mark put a quick end to the celebration. "Where is the seventh terrorist?" he shouted. In the same moment, his wife Ariel screamed, "Grace is gone! She was right here, and now she's gone!"

An uneasy hush instantly fell over the sanctuary.

Shouts of *"Allahu Akbar!* There is no god but Allah!" shattered that silence! "Long live the Brotherhood!" the jihadists chanted! Then, loud laughter erupted from the six terrorists who faced the walls. Mark asked himself, "Can I yet love and pray for these men now that my daughter has been taken?" For the moment, he had to push that question to the back of his mind — and heart!

The lead officer, Joe Peterson, shouted, "We're on it, Pastor!" He and Officer Phillip Gabriel ran out of the sanctuary to track down Grace and the missing terrorist. At the same time, one of the remaining officers used his holophone to let the entire police force know what was happening.

Pastor Mark flew down from the podium to embrace Ariel and his twin boys. He prayed softly into her ear, "Help us, Lord! Help us! I pray I did as You directed this morning! Now, help us find Grace! Lead us to her, Lord Jesus, please! Bring her back safely!"

As best they could, the people began to make their way to their pastor and his family, so that they could all pray together for Grace's safe return!

While the sanctuary had been dark, the seventh terrorist had grabbed Grace and forced a drugged rag over her nose and mouth. As she struggled silently, the terrorist carried her out of the sanctuary and into the fellowship hall. There, he had quickly bound the teenager's then limp body, gagged her mouth, and placed a sack over her head.

Next, he had tossed Grace over his shoulder and ran through the fellowship hall to a window. He knew he had to make a fast getaway.

Now crouching at the window, he peeked outside to make sure he could make it to the van. Between him and the vehicle, he saw three men. He did not know they were off duty police officers.

The terrorist opened the outside door, pressed his machete against Grace's neck, and then began screaming, "I will kill her if you make one move! Leave me alone, and she will be unharmed! Put your hands up, turn around, and do not move!"

Officers Eric Battista and Frank Noel, along with Sergeant Bruce Booth could clearly see the machete at the captive's neck, just under the bag that covered her face. Thus, the officers did as the terrorist demanded. They placed their hands in the air and turned around. Unable to reach for their weapons, the policemen heard the terrorist toss the hostage into the back of the van. The officers then turned toward the van, which bore no license plate. The terrorist shouted, "Stay where you are!" as he pointed his smart submachine gun at the officers, ran around to the driver's door, opened it, and jumped into the van.

Quickly, Eric, Frank, and Bruce took out their revolvers and ran toward the van. Unfortunately, none of them could make it to the vehicle in time to stop the terrorist from driving away with his prisoner. Likewise, they could not fire their weapons because traffic filled the street and because they certainly did not want to harm the hostage.

As Eric ran back toward the sanctuary, Frank and Bruce hopped into the sergeant's personal car and gave chase. Bruce disengaged the satellite autodrive and floored the accelerator pedal. As Eric reached the door to the sanctuary, Officers Joe Peterson and Philip Gabriel rushed outside.

They asked, "Eric, what happened? Where are Frank and Bruce?"

Eric answered as he caught his breath, "They are chasing the terrorist's van. The hostage is in the back!"

"The hostage is Grace, Pastor Mark's daughter!" Joe said. "Which way did the van go?"

"Oh no! Not Grace!" Eric, the rookie, said with grief in his voice.

"Where did they go, Eric?" Philip pressed.

Eric pointed and said, "Straight down the road!"

"They are probably headed toward the interstate," Joe shouted, as he and Phillip ran to another car and joined the pursuit.

Shell-shocked, Eric ran into the sanctuary and saw Pastor Mark holding his wife, Ariel. Already the people of the congregation were surrounding their weeping leaders. Eric pushed through the crowd as politely and quickly as he could in his efforts to reach Pastor Mark. Breathless when he approached the couple, Pastor Mark said, "What is it, Eric?" Between breaths, Eric told him, "The terrorist. . . put Grace in a van. . . took off toward the interstate. . . four officers in two cars are pursuing. . ."

Pastor Mark and Ariel put their arms around Eric, remembering he was new to the police force. As they tried to comfort him, the rest of the congregation continued to gather around them to pray.

Meanwhile, Frank had alerted the station of his and Bruce's where-abouts and requested help. Joe cut in and said he and Philip were just three blocks behind them. Frank gave a description of the van to head-quarters, while Bruce edged closer to the van. Suddenly, the back door flew open, revealing two more terrorists who began firing their auto-matic smart weapons. The smart bullets shattered the windshield and hit Frank before he could return fire. The terrorists then took aim at the tires of the car. As they exploded, Bruce lost control of the vehicle, which ran over the sidewalk and plowed head first into a building. Both the sergeant and the officer died instantly on impact.

If they had been in a squad car, instead of Bruce's personal vehicle, the two brave souls might have survived, as the Atlanta Police cars were equipped with bullet proof tires.

Joe and Phillip did not have time to process what happened as they flew past what was left of the inflamed car with their friends, brothers in Christ, and fellow officers inside it! "Two officers down!" Joe blurted into the mic on his chest! "Two officers down!"

No sooner had the words left his mouth than a hail of MGMs pelted Phillip's car! Joe screamed into his mic, "Terrorists are firing on us!"

Those were the last words Joe spoke, as the smart bullets pierced Phillip's chest and the car veered into the opposite lane and into an oncoming truck. Both vehicles exploded!

As they watched the tremendous blast, the terrorist gunmen cheered in frenzied Arabic, while Grace remained oblivious to it all.

"Strongest among men in enmity to the Believers wilt thou find the Jews and Pagans; And nearest among them in love to the Believers wilt thou find those who say, "We are Christians": Because amongst these are men devoted to learning and men who have renounced the world, and they are not arrogant."
Qur'an 5:82

CHAPTER 25

HEALED BY WOUNDS...

*A*s Sol prayed in the darkness, he sensed a presence. He felt that someone was in the room. "*Adonai*, is that You?"

A voice answered, "You have called me by many titles before, but never have you called me, '*Adonai!*'"

With a bit of embarrassment in his voice, Sol said, "Ahava! How long have you been in here?"

"Long enough to know that you are desperate for answers, my husband."

"What makes you think I am desperate?"

"You've been pouring over your allegedly destroyed New Testament for an hour or more!"

"Why didn't I see you when I shined the flashlight around the room?"

"Because I was sitting on the floor and the light went over my head."

"Are you angry with me, Ahava?"

"Angry? Why should I be angry with you, Sol?" Ahava inched over to her husband and sat beside him on the floor.

"Why? Because I can't get Y'shua out of my heart and head," Sol confessed

"Ever since your discussions with Ariel and Mark you have been acting strangely!"

Sol sighed heavily. "You think I am crazy, don't you? Admit it!"

Ahava reached for Sol's hand. "What I think is this: My husband wonders if he has been wrong for the past 85 years! He wonders if he has missed the Messiah! My Orthodox Rabbi wonders if he has the courage to believe Y'shua is his Messiah! That's what I think!"

The dark room became absolutely silent.

A few moments later, Sol replied, as he began to weep, "But I have so many questions, Ahava! Do I have to give up being a Jew to be a Christian?"

"Wasn't Y'shua an observant Jew, Sol? Did He not celebrate all the feasts and festivals? Was He not in Jerusalem on the High Holy Days?"

"Maybe, but how could the Jewish leaders of Y'shua's day be so blind to who He was?"

Ahava thought about saying, *"Perhaps you should ask yourself the same question."* Then she decided that now may not be the right time for such a comment. Therefore, she asked, "Did they not expect a worldlier and more militarily inclined Messiah? Were they not threatened by His miracles and His power with the people? Plus, like all the prophets God sent before Y'shua, He was rejected because the leaders did not appreciate His message that convicted them of their sin!"

Sol paused for a moment. "Ahava, why does it sound like you know so much about Y'shua? Have you been reading the New Testament, too?"

"Perhaps," his blushing bride replied sheepishly.

"Perhaps? Have you or have you not been reading this New Testament from the chest?"

Now Ahava confessed, "When you said you had destroyed the New Testament, I looked in the chest to make sure. When I found it, at first I thought I should destroy it myself. At the same time, I wanted to read it, to find out what it said about Y'shua." Ahava inhaled deeply in the darkness and said, "It seems to me that Y'shua was rejected even before He was born! He was rejected by Joseph before the angel visited him in a dream. He was rejected by both Joseph's and Mary's families. He was rejected by Bethlehem which had no place for His

145

birth but a stable. He was rejected by Herod when he ordered the execution of all the male Jews in Bethlehem two years old or less."

Sol was stunned to hear Ahava speaking so knowledgably about
Y'shua's earliest days and the time before His birth. With Sol at a loss
for words, Ahava continued talking about Y'shua.

"The people of Nazareth, Y'shua's hometown, rejected Him. Even
Y'shua's own brothers rejected Him—until He was crucified and resurrected! To that point, my dear husband, the death by crucifixion that
Y'shua suffered was prophesied thousands of years before by Isaiah in
his fifty-second and fifty-third chapters—the words of which you have
never read in the synagogue on any Sabbath! Do you fear that Isaiah's
prophecy was fulfilled in Y'shua?"

Sol was not expecting such a direct question. The darkness hung
over them in silence as he considered his answer. At last, he said,
"Fear? I don't know if fear is the right word. No rabbi reads the passages of suffering detailed in Isaiah 52 and 53 in the synagogue. The
passage raises more questions than answers. The Messiah was supposed to set His people free and lead them—not be crucified because
He did not meet their own frenzied demands!"

"Did you ever consider that Y'shua offered eternal freedom, not
temporal? Did you ever consider that He leads, even now, all those
who believe in Him as the Messiah of God?"

"Sweetheart," Sol replied in hushed tones as if anyone could hear
them, "such words could get us thrown out of the synagogue—we
could be excommunicated!"

"Are you trying to tell me that you have never considered the
implications of Y'shua's life and death?"

"I've never spoken them aloud!"

"Neither have I, until tonight—to you in the darkness! I am on this
journey with you, Sol, wherever it make take us!"

The old rabbi found comfort in his wife's words. He did not walk
this road alone. Maybe, just maybe, he had not gone crazy, either. He
gratefully said, "I had no idea you were thinking and searching, too. I
suppose I should have trusted you with my own questions. I still have
so many! Like how can Y'shua be the Jewish Messiah when throughout
history Christians have attacked Jews in His Name? Why is the world
worse now than in Y'shua's day and why doesn't He do something

about it? How could the Messiah have allowed the Holocaust? Ahava, who can answer all my questions?"

"My Love," his partner in life said as she laid her head on Sol's shoulder, "Don't you think that if Y'shua is indeed the Messiah—the Lord God Himself—that He will help you, help us, find the answers to our questions?"

"I suppose that makes sense, Sweetheart," Sol answered, now stroking Ahava's hair.

She squeezed Sol's other hand, and then put her arms around her searching husband's neck. "Do you think that God may be bringing Mark and Ariel here to help us find our answers?"

"Could be," he said, holding her as tightly as possible.

"Sol, you have not been the same man since Mark and Ariel first spoke with you about Y'shua." She pushed herself back from him and tried to see Sol's eyes in the blackness, but could not. "You have been kinder to me than you ever have in sixty five years of marriage! I have witnessed more tenderness and genuine compassion in you than I ever believed I would see!"

"So you are not mad with me or ashamed of me, Ahava?"

She cupped her hands and held her husband's moist face, and told him, "Because of you and how you have already changed, I wonder if Y'shua is the Messiah, too!"

The two of them embraced each other once more. Neither one of them wanted to let go!

Sol whispered in Ahava's ear, "Maybe *Adonai* is here, after all!"

"For truly I tell you, many prophets and righteous people longed to see what you see but did not see it, and to hear what you hear but did not hear it."
Matthew 13:17

CHAPTER 26

EXTREME MAKEOVER. . .

*A*bdul still knelt by the bed in the darkness, remembering Isa's last words, "I'll be back soon—like a thief in the night!" Although, Abdul breathed rapidly as his heart raced, he felt overwhelming joy and contentment! Slowly, he stood, looking to where he had last seen Isa. The Lord had emanated such brilliant light in the room that everything else disappeared in His glory!

Abdul had heard stories of Muslims who were seeing visions and having dreams in which Isa visited them. Even so, Abdul did not believe such tales. He had shrugged off such reports as mere Christian propaganda! He even categorized the accounts as modern fairy tales!

To his great surprise, now Isa had appeared to the most skeptical Abdul! As he turned on the light beside his bed, he touched his chin where Isa had lifted his head. He looked at his hand that Isa had held in His own Hand! Abdul had felt such strength, peace, love, hope, and satisfaction just from Isa's touch! As he stood there, Abdul realized he had never truly known who he was until this moment. As a follower of Isa, he knew his role, purpose, and reason for being!

He remembered something else Isa had said before leaving. Abdul had asked Him, "Will I still remember my sins and mistakes, even though You have forgiven them and freed me from their eternal consequences?"

In the most soothing tones, Isa had answered, "Yes, Abdul, you will remember your sins and mistakes. Furthermore, Satan will remind you of your guilt. He will attempt to disable you through his condemnation. Even so, as my servant Paul noted, those who believe in Me—as you do—no longer face condemnation! Hence, do not give Satan the satisfaction of heaping guilt and condemnation on your back! You are forgiven and free!"

Then Isa, with His hand on Abdul's shoulder, said, "I allow you to recall your bad and painful choices so that you will learn from them. The memories of your sin and mistakes will keep you from repeating them."

As he now stood alone in the bedroom, Abdul vowed that he would not relive the sins of his past, but would instead reside in the grace that Isa had promised him!

His heart filled with gratitude, the Vice President decided to get dressed. He had to tell someone about the miracle that he had received! Who could he tell? As he walked through the doorway and down the hall, the first person in view was the President. With great enthusiasm and anticipation, Abdul said "Good evening, sir!"

The Commander in Chief looked up to see his Vice President towering over him, wearing the biggest smile he had ever seen! Sarcastically, the President asked, "What are you suddenly so happy about, Mr. Vice President?"

With his gaze fixed on the President's eyes, Abdul sat down and said, "James, I am not sure you would believe me if I told you!"

"Oh, I get it!" the President retorted, as he sat his wine glass on the table. "You've read the focus groups report, and now you have come to gloat!"

Shaking his head, Abdul countered, "Oh, no, James! I have no idea what the focus group numbers are—and frankly, I don't care about them in the least!"

"Then what is up with you? I've never seen you like this."

Abdul replied, "I don't know how to explain all this, but I just want you to know that I really do love you, and I hope you can forgive me for being so distant and so. . . difficult. I promise that all my ways have changed!"

Awkwardly, the President pushed himself back in his chair and crossed his arms across his chest. "What do you mean when you say you 'really do love me,' Mr. Vice President?"

Abdul chuckled as he saw the apprehension rising in the President's eyes. "Don't worry, James! I'm not talking about that kind of love! I mean that I love you as though you are my brother, even my father!"

The President leaned forward and looked in Abdul's eyes. He saw genuine kindness in those eyes that had always borne disdain for him. The President sat back again and asked. "Where have you been for the last hour and what have you been doing?"

Abdul did not hold back. He placed his hand on the arm of the President's chair and said with excitement, "I met Isa!"

Perplexed, the President asked, "Who is Isa?"

Before Abdul could answer, Chief of Staff Eddie Murdock ran into the room and interrupted the conversation, shouting, "Double J, you better get ready for this! Sanaullah bin Laden is responding to the attack on Palestine!"

"When Isa found unbelief on their part he said: 'Who will be my helpers to (the work (of) Allah?' Said the Disciples: 'We are Allah's helpers: We believe in Allah, and do thou bear witness that we are Muslims.'"
Qur'an 3:52

CHAPTER 27

NO WAY OUT...

*T*he prayers for Grace, her parents, and her brothers began to subside. For a few moments, the sanctuary was sill and silent. No one knew what to do next.

Pastor Mark felt the spiritual nudge of Jesus to do what he said he would do. Hence, Mark rose to his feet and said, "My dear brothers and sisters, from the depths of our hearts, Ariel and I thank you for your intercessions for Grace and for each of us and our boys! Your prayers have already given us strength and peace that Jesus is in control and will somehow work through all of this confusion and hatred for Grace's release and our good, as well as for the good of the church and the Kingdom!"

As he continued to speak, Pastor Mark's tone turned more somber. "However, brothers and sisters, our prayers are not yet complete. Others here today need our intercessions. I speak not only of our brothers who are officers of the law among us—as well as those who are pursuing Grace's captor—but I also include the six men here who came to cause harm today as well as the seventh who has taken Grace from us."

From memory, the obedient and compassionate minister quoted his Saviour's words from Luke 6:27-36.

"Love your enemies, do good to those who hate you, bless those who curse you, pray for those who mistreat you. If someone strikes you on one cheek, turn to him the other also. If someone takes your cloak, do not stop him from taking your tunic. Give to everyone who asks you, and if anyone takes what belongs to you, do not demand it back. Do to others as you would have them do to you. If you love those who love you, what credit is that to you? Even 'sinners' love those who love them. And if you do good to those who are good to you, what credit is that to you? Even 'sinners' do that. And if you lend to those from whom you expect repayment, what credit is that to you? Even 'sinners' lend to 'sinners,' expecting to be repaid in full. But love your enemies, do good to them, and lend to them without expecting to get anything back. Then your reward will be great, and you will be sons of the Most High, because he is kind to the ungrateful and wicked. Be merciful, just as your Father is merciful."

With strength and compassion in his voice, Pastor Mark continued, saying, "Brothers and sisters, we have a rare opportunity to be in the very presence of men who consider us their enemies. Let us show them that we do not hate them, but instead love them and want to see the day of their redemption in Jesus. They intended us great harm today, and they have indeed inflicted harm upon us. However, our Lord intends today's events to be for our good as well as their good! Jesus tells us to love them and pray for them, just as He loved and prayed for us while hanging on the cross, dying in sacrifice for our sins. Jesus also interceded for these men in black here with us now. He purchased their pardon even as He purchased ours—with His very Blood!"

The officers had not removed the terrorists from the sanctuary. The Federal Bureau of Investigation (FBI) wanted to come to the church and take them into custody themselves. Pastor Mark motioned for the officers to bring the Muslims forward. The six looked down and would not make eye contact with the people. As the congregation gathered around them, the leader spoke, addressing Pastor Mark. "We have heard the prayers offered for your daughter and your family. Now, you will extend this same supplication for us? Why would you do such a thing?"

Pastor Mark knelt in front of the Muslim and made eye contact with him. "Because Isa loves you; therefore, I love you—we all do!"

The leader of the Muslim terrorists tried to control his emotions, but he could not stop the tears that escaped from his eyes!

"Or suppose a king is about to go to war against another king. Won't he first sit down and consider whether he is able with ten thousand men to oppose the one coming against him with twenty thousand? If he is not able, he will send a delegation while the other is still a long way off and will ask for terms of peace."
Luke 14:31-32

CHAPTER 28

REMARKABLE RESTRAINT. . .

*F*or the first time, Sanaullah bin Laden was dressed in western attire instead of his traditional Muslim dress—a white *ghutrah*—an Arab cotton headdress—and a white flowing robe. Both bin Laden's attire and his words seemed quite conciliatory—a dramatic shift from the Caliph who typically oozed hatred for all things non-Islamic.

Babylon's *Al-Varisha*—The Lightening—Satellite News beamed the Caliph's speech to the entire world. Every major channel in every country interrupted their programming for the Caliph's words which could alter the very course of human history.

From his ornate study in his luxurious palace, bin Laden said, "*Salaam*, citizens of Allah's Muslim Alliance, our Caliphate, and citizens of the world outside our borders. I come before you today with great sorrow and mourning.

"Before I say anything more, allow me to announce a call to prayer for all Muslims tomorrow at noon. As we do each Friday, we will go to the mosques tomorrow, Monday, for a time of shared prayer and a word from the imams. However, tomorrow's prayers and message will be focused on the victims of the terror that befell the independent state of Palestine this afternoon. This call to prayer will substitute for the funerals that should be held tomorrow, in keeping with Islamic funeral and burial traditions and practices.

"The few remaining leaders of the DROP cannot possibly coordinate the efforts that would be necessary to have the funeral service tomorrow for so many who have been brutally murdered. In this regard, as Imam Zaahir has noted, we will conclude the three day mourning period for the victims before our ceremonial funeral for them on Wednesday. Also, as this disaster is so extreme, women, as well as men, will be allowed to attend the funeral service for the masses slain by our vile and despised enemies. Please bear with this change from our prescribed traditions."

With his forefinger against his lips, the Caliph took a softer tone. "In this moment of anger and grief we must pause for one moment in order to avoid thousands of moments of remorse. This is not a time for rash accusations or hasty revenge. On one hand, yes, our brothers' and sisters' blood must be avenged. On the other hand, no, we do not yet know the culprit behind this cowardly and barbaric act. We must prove to the world that Allah is patient and only seeks justice.

"In that regard, as your Caliph, I command that rioting within the states of the MA come to an immediate end. Furthermore, I command that there be no independent retaliatory strikes against any suspected groups or nations. We have many investigations underway, as do other governments as well. When all the facts have been gathered, we will follow the directives of the Sharia and those of the Palestinian state. Our glorious Sharia Law demands that those who cause suffering must suffer in like manner."

Pounding his right fist into his left hand, bin Laden announced, "Babylon stands as a strong and united alliance. We follow the all powerful Allah, Most Gracious, Most Merciful, god over all the earth. We need not be frightened or intimated or feel pressure to respond to this disaster without the complete story being known. Allah is just. Thus, we as his followers will act justly."

Bin Laden leaned toward the camera. "Make no mistake. The guilty will be punished. They will not escape. They will not be allowed to make claims of victory. On each of these points, you have my solemn word in pledge.

"The MA's 40-million man army stands ready to act—and ready to defend Babylon if the perpetrators of this terror seek to strike again!

155

We warn the evildoers: Stop now or face the unmitigated wrath of Allah!"

With raw strength and sheer defiance in his tone, the Caliph proclaimed, "We are a noble people, with a noble history. All we require is the respect that is due our alliance and our god! Consequentially, we will wait one week for the United States and Israel to conclude their investigations. One week from tonight, we expect the U.S. and Israeli governments to reveal who is responsible for the unprovoked act of war on the independent state of Palestine. If the guilty party is identified, we will take just and appropriate action."

With his forefinger wagging at the camera, bin Laden concluded his brief and curt address. "If the governments of the United States and Israel fail to identify the vile perpetrator of such heinous violence on the innocents of the DROP, we will still take just and appropriate action—against them! We will take 40 million appropriate acts!

"One week. *Leila sa'eeda!* Good night!"

"That they said (in boast), 'We killed Isa the son of Mary, the Messenger of Allah—but they killed him not, nor crucified him. Only a likeness of that was shown to them. And those who differ therein are full of doubts, with no (certain) knowledge. But only conjecture to follow, for of a surety they killed him not."
Qur'an 4:157

CHAPTER 29

THE ULTIMATE POWER...

By the time everyone had prayed over them, all six of the terrorists of the Brotherhood were weeping and bowing before Isa on their knees. The Holy Spirit had convicted them of their sins! Pastor Mark asked them, "Would you like to receive the mercy and grace that Isa gave His life to purchase for you?"

The leader of the terrorists replied, "I cannot imagine why Isa would love us in light of all the hatred that has long dwelled in our hearts for His followers. I cannot imagine why Isa would forgive our cruelties spoken in His Name not to mention the harm we have done to Him through His disciples. I cannot imagine why He would want a relationship with us who have killed His innocent believers. Then again, I also cannot imagine refusing such love, forgiveness, and desire for relationship that is offered to us by Isa!"

The five men with him nodded their heads in agreement!

Enthusiastically, Pastor Mark asked the six men in black to repeat this prayer: "Lord Isa, You have many Names: Jesus, Y'shua, Messiah, Saviour, Redeemer, Master, Son of God, Son of Man, King of kings, Lord of lords, Emmanuel, Mighty God, Wonderful Counselor, and Prince of Peace, just to mention a few! Each of Your Names describes an aspect of who You are! Today, I bow before You, the Incarnation of Mercy and Grace! I confess my sins of hatred and violence to You, asking You to take away the eternal punishment of those and all my sins, for You bore my punishment on the cross, and You went to hell in my place! As I turn away from my sins in repentance this day, I instead turn to You, knowing that You will receive me and make of me a son of Your Father! Through Your forgiveness, I am made new, as though I have never sinned! Now, Lord I invite Your Holy Spirit to abide in me, as I am Your living temple! Empower me to follow You and do Your will. I belong to You, and now You belong to me! I am forever grateful and will forever love and serve You! I look forward to spending eternity with You in Heaven, for you are the one True God, Most Gracious and Most Merciful! Amen!"

Everyone's eyes flowed with tears and their hearts, with joy as the six new disciples of Jesus stood and were embraced by everyone in the congregation! That physical demonstration of love and acceptance of former enemies continued until the FBI agents arrived.

As the leader of the men in black talked with Pastor Mark, the head federal agent approached the Muslim from behind him. What the agent overheard, he found impossible to believe!

"I have been filled with hatred for so long that I never thought I could truly know love. I have never been able to love my wife and children. I saw them more as property than precious souls who needed and deserved my love. Now, for the first time in my life, for as far back as I can remember as a child, I feel loved and I feel love. . . how can I say it. . . pouring out of me! I feel like an incredible weight has been lifted from my soul—is this what forgiveness feels like? Does it feel like freedom and the opportunity to start over in life?

"I no longer want to hate and kill for Allah! I want to love and live for Isa! I want to tell every Muslim—every member of the Brotherhood—that we have been wrong for so long! Isa is not a prophet of Allah—Isa is the very Son of God! Isa proved who He was when He indeed was crucified! He suffered in my place! I still cannot believe the One, True God would do any such thing for me! But I feel it! I know it because I am not the same man I was when I came into this sanctuary!

"Pastor Mark, I am so sorry about your daughter! I wish that I could bring her back here to you right now!"

Mark asked, "What is your name?"

"Salah Udeen Waleed."

"Your name fits the new person you have become. You are indeed Salah Udeen, 'the righteousness of faith!' You are indeed, Waleed, 'a newborn child!' Salah Udeen Waleed, through Isa, I too have forgiven you of the harm you intended for me, my family, and my congregation today. We are now brothers in Isa!"

With those moving words, Pastor Mark embraced Salah Udeen Waleed! The man in black wept grateful tears upon his new brother's shoulder.

Amazed at what he had witnessed, the FBI agent interrupted, saying, "Waleed, if you really are sorry about the events of today, maybe you can help us undo them!"

Though all the agents were skeptical of the transformation that had supposedly happened in these hard and hatred-bred men, the agents saw genuine peace on the faces of those six former Muslims.

Salah Udeen told the agents, "If you hurry, you might be able to find Grace in an abandoned, empty office building on the other side of town, which the Brotherhood uses as its local headquarters. Please be swift," he said as he gave them the address. "She will not be held there long. She is not the one we came to capture!"

The lead FBI agent immediately sent six of his men, with local police backup, to the site. He wondered if he was sending the men into a trap, but he had no choice but to check out the lead.

With his red-eyed, sobbing wife by his side, Pastor Mark prayed softly, "Please, Lord, let our little girl be safe! Let her be brought back to us—whole and unhurt! Protect these men as they go to find her! Thank You, Jesus! Amen!"

What the agents and officers did not know was that the building housing the local Brotherhood headquarters was also used for a most gruesome purpose.

*"I am the Root and the Offspring of David, and the bright
Morning Star."*
Revelation 22:16

CHAPTER 30

A GRUESOME AND GRISLY ACT. . .

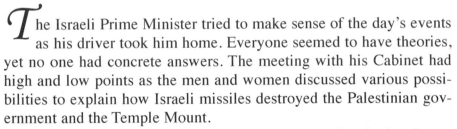

*T*he Israeli Prime Minister tried to make sense of the day's events
as his driver took him home. Everyone seemed to have theories,
yet no one had concrete answers. The meeting with his Cabinet had
high and low points as the men and women discussed various possibilities to explain how Israeli missiles destroyed the Palestinian government and the Temple Mount.

Israeli Defense Minister Zeev Tzion felt that the Brotherhood must
have agents within the Israeli Air Force and all the military branches.
He had already ordered an investigation into the missile firing, which
would include the interrogation of every person at the Air Force Base
in the Negev.

At one point in the meeting, the Defense Minister pounded the
table and proclaimed, "No one is above suspicion! Someone on site
must have launched those missiles. How else could anyone have managed to pull this off unnoticed?"

The Minister of Internal Security, Shimon Ben Yehudah, snapped
back, "Why do you think we have a traitor or traitors in service to
Israel? To me it is obvious that the missiles were fired by someone
who gained access to our cyberspace weapons system!"

Defense Minister Tzion countered, saying, "Do you realize how
many levels of encryption we have in our ultranet weapons system?
The complexity of each of those levels would require years to break,
and we change the encryption every four months! Only a genius could
crack all those codes!"

Deputy Israeli Foreign Affairs Minister Abigail Wilenski jumped into the debate, declaring "Maybe you are both right! Maybe someone on the inside gave the necessary codes to someone on the outside. Nevertheless, we must determine if our weapons can be used against us! If the Brotherhood has control of our missiles, we could be wiped out by this time tomorrow!"

Abigail's words brought the boisterous, rapid-paced meeting to a hushed halt. Everyone took a few moments to consider such a sudden destruction of The Land.

After a few moments of absolute stillness, Prime Minister Ben Baruch rose from his chair and noted, "Abigail has a good point. Yet, if the masked General of Babylon or his Caliph have control of our missile launching system, why did one or both of them choose to destroy the DROP capitol and the Palestinians? Why did those missiles not rain down on Jews alone? Why would they wait to attack us? Why not launch enough missiles to bury Israel in desert rubble and be done with us?"

Everyone around the table quietly considered the Prime Minister's questions. No answers seemed to be obvious. Then, the Minister of Science and Technology, Yitzhak Gid'on, the oldest member of the Cabinet at 87 years of age, rephrased the questions: "Indeed, Mr. Prime Minister, if the Brotherhood, the General, the Caliph, or all the above are behind the missile launches, what reason would they have for destroying the Palestinian government and the third most holy site in Islam?"

All eyes focused on Sam. "I can think of two possibilities," he answered. "One, the Palestinian democracy stood as an abomination to Babylon. Think about it—Muslims hate democracy. Democracy is hypocrisy to Muslims—it is anathema! Would it not be a double affront to have a Muslim democracy? So, wipe out the DROP with Israeli and U.S. weapons, and the problem is solved! At that point, as far as appearances are concerned, Babylon could justifiably attack us and the United States.

"Two, perhaps Babylon only had limited access to our weapons. What would bin Laden or the General choose to do if they only had four missiles under their control? Instead of destroying four Israeli strategic targets, would not Babylon have more impact by framing the U.S. and Israel for an unwarranted attacked on the DROP?"

Minister of Justice, Ruth Keren, the youngest member of the Cabinet at the age of 35, answered the Prime Minister's question with one of her own. "Sam, do you really think that Babylon would destroy the Dome of the Rock, the Al Aqsa Mosque, the underground Al Marawani Mosque, and the two office buildings filled with their government and political leaders merely to garner a pretext for declaring war against the U.S. and Israel?"

"I don't put anything past the General," the Prime Minister answered. "Ruth, we have long heard rumors of the General's desire for a coup that would place him in the Caliph's palace. Maybe he ordered the strike, but will pin it on bin Laden. Perhaps the destruction of the Dome of the Rock and the Al Aqsa Mosque will turn Babylon against its Caliph and open the door of the palace to the General."

The Prime Minister began to walk around the table. "I don't know that any of the options we are considering make ultimate sense to us—maybe the whole idea is to keep us guessing and off guard so that we are not ready for the next strike."

Sam stroked his beard and noted, "For decades, in our attempts to live peacefully with the Muslims among us, Israel has funded more than 200 mosques in the Land. We have paid the salaries of the imams. We have purchased all the Qur'ans used in the worship of Allah. We have built, backed, and funded madrasas, paid the salaries of Muslim teachers, and supplied the students and teachers with their text books and Qur'ans. We have done the same for the Muslim colleges and those teachers and students. We have paid for all the maintenance and upkeep of the Muslim holy sites, including the ones that now no longer exist! These are but a few of the many olive branches we have extended to the people who consider us to be their eternal enemies."

In frustration, Ben Baruch shouted, "All our efforts at peace have failed! All our efforts to do what is 'right' instead of what is expedient have borne no fruit. Instead, we face an enemy who has somehow used our weapons for evil purposes—purposes that may yet include our own destruction!"

Visibly shaken, Justice Minister Keren commented, "Given that Babylon cannot utilize its own nuclear and conventional weapons, given that the Brotherhood troops are not trained in mobilizing the tanks, ships, jets, helicopters, and other war machines they gained in the takeover of Asia and Europe, maybe, just maybe, the Caliph and the

General must use our weapons and war machines to attack us. Maybe today's strike was a test to see if the Brotherhood could indeed use our military machine for its own purposes. If that is the case, maybe the next attack will not be on Israeli soil, but on the shores of the U.S.!"

Sam asked in response, "Are you saying that someone in Babylon is smart enough to crack our encryption and tap into our weapons system, but not smart enough to develop a weapons system for the arsenal in the Caliphate?"

Science and Technology Minister Gid'on shared his thoughts, saying, "You make the process sound too easy, Sam. Even with the coerced help of scientists, engineers, and military experts I think it will take an extended time period for Babylon to develop a weapons control system and even longer to rehabilitate the weapons that were effectively neutralized by the Asians and Europeans. Even more importantly, we must remember that Babylon has no satellite system. Remember, the United States shot the satellites out of the sky for the very purpose of preventing the Muslims from annihilating the rest of the world!"

The Prime Minister stopped his pacing and responded by saying, "So, if the Caliph and or the General want to attack us with conventional or nuclear weapons, their only choice, at least for now, is to use our own arsenal against us? In that light, must we assume that the Unites States' weapons system has been violated as well? Surely, both the Caliph and the General know that America will bring its entire arsenal to bear against Babylon if a full scale attack is launched against us."

Minister Gid'on added, "If the Muslim Alliance is testing its control of Israeli and U.S. weaponry, can we prevent an all out takeover of our complete arsenals—including our nuclear weapons? If so, do we have sufficient time to wrestle back control of our war machines before the General or bin Laden orders nuclear strikes against us from our own arsenals?"

Religious Services Minister Yaakov Nessa anxiously rose from his seat. "Listen to what we are saying! Could we be facing the end time events foretold by the prophets? Is the One whose Name is ineffable about to gather the nations before Him for judgment?"

The Prime Minister had never given credence to the end time prophecies of the Hebrew Tanakh or the Christian New Testament. At the same time, something in the words of Minister Nessa resonated within him. As the discussion continued around him, Prime Minister Ben Baruch heard a whispered voice saying, "I am the First and the Last, the Alpha and Omega, the Root and Son of David, the Great I AM!"

For hours after the Cabinet meeting, Sam remained seated at the conference table. Those softly spoken words still echoed in his heart and soul. As the Prime Minister could not refocus his thoughts to what he considered to be the much more pressing and urgent issues his people faced, he decided he needed rest and left for the official Prime Minister's residence.

After his driver and security team pulled up to *Beit Rosh HaMemshala*, the house of the Prime Minister, Sam left the protection of his armored vehicle to walk to the steps that led to the residence. Two members of his security team accompanied him. Suddenly, his escorts came to a dead stop. Sam looked up and gasped! An exceedingly disturbing sight greeted them at those steps—the heads of his Cabinet members!

Shocked, Sam could not make sense of what had happened! He was just speaking with these friends and colleagues a few hours earlier! In that intervening time, each of them had been executed and had their severed heads delivered to his doorsteps!

One of the security men called for the rest of the team to rush to the Prime Minister's residence and check out the property and make sure his family was safe inside.

Meanwhile, Sam's eyes could not stop scanning the faces of his trusted advisors. In the center of the gory display, Sam saw a note partially written in blood—most likely the blood of one or more members of his Cabinet! As he read the message, he wondered if the terrorists had been eavesdropping on the discussions he had with his Cabinet!

The cryptic message read:

In the Name of ALLAH—

**Most Gracious, Most Merciful—
and MUHAMMAD his Prophet—
Peace be upon him!**

Prime Minister Ben Baruch:

The end —and your end—are indeed near!
You will soon join your piggish infidel cabinet members in
eternal torment! We will strike your neck next!

Qur'an 14:16-17:

"In front of such a one is Hell and he is given for drink boiling, fetid
water. In gulps will he sip it but never well he be near swallowing it
down his throat: Death will come to him from every quarter yet will he
not die: and in front of him will be a chastisement unrelenting."

How will such a one as you even drink such water when your head is no
longer attached to your body?

Prepare yourself for final judgment and a chastisement most grievous!

ALLAHU AKBAR!

There is no GOD but ALLAH!

"And they feed, for the love of Allah, the indigent, the orphan, and the captive."
Qur'an 76:8

CHAPTER 31

PRECIOUS CARGO...

A confused and fearful Grace awoke to the blasts of the smart submachine guns. Now, the terrorists fired at the drivers who witnessed the killings of the police officers. As Grace breathed rapidly, the thirteen year old felt like she was about to faint! Her head pounded, her body steamed with sweat, and her wrists bled from the ropes that bound them.

Where was she? Where was she going? Who was with her? She remembered clinging to her mother as her dad talked to the terrorist. Then, everything went dark for Grace.

"They must have knocked me out somehow!" the intuitive teen suddenly realized. "They knocked me out and kidnapped me! I am in a vehicle of some kind."

Suddenly the van stopped. Someone picked her up and moved her into a car. In a few seconds, she was speeding down the road again. "At least the car seat is padded," she thought. "At least it is better than a hard floor."

Grace heard a Muslim talking, but no one answered him. Then she realized he was engaged in conversation with someone on his 3DHP.

"Only three of us are left. We have the package, but not the one you ordered!"

Moments of silence ensued.

The terrorist pleaded, "But he had a plan! We don't know about the rest of the team!"

More silence.

"The daughter! And we barely nabbed her!"

A longer period of silence.

"But he had a plan! Everything went dark!"

Uneasy silence.

"Hello? Are you still there? Hello?" the terrorist said. Then, he concluded, "We must have been cut off."

The second terrorist spoke in broken English, "He may be planning to cut each of us off—permanently!"

"Maybe we should not go back," the third jihadist said, his voice trembling.

"No! Face to face, we can make him understand," said the first terrorist. "We have a great asset for our cause!"

None of the terrorists said anything else.

In her quiet darkness under the bag on her head, Grace tried to make sense of the half of the 3DHP conversation she heard. Though only thirteen, Grace was brighter and wiser than her years. She realized that the terrorists came to abduct her dad, but instead, ended up taking her. Her dad's emergency contingency plan surprised the Muslims.

Grace asked herself, *"What will happen now that the terrorists have taken me instead of Daddy! He will be worried about me."*

Suddenly, she understood. *"They took me so they could still get Daddy! So why did the person on the other end of the call hang up when the terrorists said I was here instead of Daddy?"*

Grace tried to calm her nerves and her breathing. Her face was hot and clammy inside the sack. She tried to pray, but all she could hear was her heart pounding in her hurting head! She whispered, "Lord Jesus! Lord Jesus! Please! Please. . ."

All the hyperventilating caught up with her. Her eyes rolled back, and her body went limp and fell into the floor.

"Jesus said: "I tell you the truth, unless you change and become like little children, you will never enter the Kingdom of Heaven."
Matthew 18:3

CHAPTER 32

INNOCENT, HATE-FILLED HEARTS. . .

*I*n unmarked cars without sirens, the six FBI agents and twenty Atlanta police officers approached the seemingly abandoned building from different directions, in hopes they could surprise the unsuspecting terrorists and free Grace Basel.

The old, deteriorating structure with shuttered windows stood in a deserted part of Atlanta. Only the homeless braved these streets. All seemed quiet as the agents and officers prepared to storm each of the six locked entrances simultaneously. They formed six teams of four men each. Two of the Atlanta Police officers would stand guard outside between the entrances in efforts to make sure no one else came in or out.

"In five," the head FBI agent told the six team leaders via his badge mic. "Five, four, three, two, go, go, go!" Guns blazing, the agents and officers busted through the doors to find no resistance on the other side. The head FBI agent whispered into his mic, "If they are here, they now know we are here, too."

Even during daylight, the darkness inside was foreboding. As the six teams slowly made their way toward the center of the large open floor that spanned a city block, they discovered a crude, makeshift structure inside the old office high rise.

Unbeknownst to them, behind the walls made of scraps of tin, plastic, cardboard, and plywood, the Brotherhood was busy holding summer camp—Jihad Summer Camp! Boys as young as six and as old as sixteen were learning the ways of terror! Some of the older Muslim teens were attending the camp for their tenth year!

A total of 147 boys were inside the large shack. Similar jihad camps were underway at 922 other secret sites across America. At this very moment, 124,470 young Muslims were learning the ways of jihad on U.S. soil! An Arabic banner hung over every camp that read, *"Slay them wherever ye catch them!"* (Qur'an 2:191)

Likewise, each camp was dedicated to a Muslim who was killed in jihad. The Atlanta camp was dedicated to Anwar al-Awlaki, a U.S. born and educated radical cleric who had inspired many Muslims to acts of terror in the states and around the world, before he was killed by a drone in September of 2011.

On the global level, in the last decade alone, 11,817 Jihad Summer Camps had trained more than twenty four million Muslim boys to be Brotherhood terrorists. The ever vigilant Brotherhood constantly prepared future soldiers for jihad.

As the agents and officers slowly stepped closer to this most basic and most cruel of training facilities, they heard the dull roar of generators. The generators not only provided power to light the training camp, but also supplied the needed electricity to run the refrigerators that stored butchered human bodies!

The boys began their training at six years old by watching graphic videos of faithful and holy Muslims killing vile and evil Christians and Jews. After the first summer of brainwashing, the next year's camp had the now seven year old boys practicing hand to hand combat skills with each other. By their third summer camp, the junior terrorists were eight and practiced their combat skills with their adult instructors. The next summer, at nine years of age, the boys learned how to kill with machetes and smart weapons. The nine year olds had anticipated and actually enjoyed slitting the throats and cutting off the heads of their innocent victims—homeless men the boys had kidnapped from the streets of Atlanta! During their fifth Jihad Summer Camp, the ten year old boys began killing the homeless with their bare hands.

When the young jihadists turned eleven, their summer camp instructors taught them how to chop up their victims' bodies, place the pieces in garbage bags, and store the bags in large refrigerators. At twelve years old, the pre-teen terrorists learned how to dispose of the sliced and diced bodies and bones in underground incinerators that were hidden in densely wooded areas. The furnaces, manufactured for recycling waste into energy, became crematoriums for Jihad Summer Camps and Brotherhood operations around the world.

When the boys became teenagers, they became assistant instructors. During their last summer camp, at sixteen, the young men would pair off and fight each other for all the other campers to see. The combatants neither pulled their punches nor sheathed their machetes. The battles continued until one of the teens killed the other. These fights to the death kept weaker jihadists off the real battlefields where they could endanger their fellow soldiers.

Each day's camp meeting began with readings from the Qur'an. The selected verses always gave the spiritual foundation for jihad. On this day, the Brotherhood leaders used Qur'an 9:30: *"The Jews call 'Uzair a son of Allah, and the Christians call Isa the Son of Allah. That is a saying from their mouth; (in this) they but imitate what the Unbelievers of old used to say. Allah's curse be on them: how they are deluded away from the Truth!"*

After reading the verse, the leader told the jihad campers, "If Allah fights them, then we must fight them in the name of Allah!" The boys chanted back, "Death to the Jews! Death to the Christians! Allah, let my hands be your vessels of death!" Little did the boys and teens know that they would live out those words that very day.

Outside the ramshackle walls of the camp, the FBI agents and police officers continued inching closer. They had no idea they had been under surveillance since the moment of their arrival—even before they fired their weapons to enter the building.

Now, as the lawmen encircled the camp upstairs, two jihadists sped out of the underground parking lot. The young and frightened pastor's daughter continued what would prove to be a tenacious and arduous journey.

On the main floor of the abandoned building, the agents and officers closed ranks around the camp. Suddenly, the tin, plywood, plastic, and cardboard walls simultaneously fell on all four sides, and the men could only fire a couple of rounds before they were mowed down by the avalanche of smart bullets! The two officers who stood watch outside ran through the doors only to be cut down in like manner.

The boys of the camp then ran out from behind their leaders and slit the throats of all of the agents and officers, whether they were alive or dead!

With great pride and no remorse over the murders of the twenty officers and six agents whatsoever, the more than 200 hardened men and boys celebrated with frenetic shouts of *"Allahu Akbar!* There is no God but Allah!"

A few moments later, the Muslim terrorists picked up their weapons, as well as those of the agents and officers. Then, the Muslims grabbed as much of their training materials and supplies as they could carry. With each man and boy carrying heavy loads, they marched silently down the passageway into the parking garage, loaded their vans, and left.

They would never return to this training site that this day became a real jihad battleground for the boys of the summer camp!

As a testament to the effectiveness of the Brotherhood's methodology, one of the Muslim teens trained in the Atlanta camp was already known as one of the most ruthless jihadists in the world!

"If there were a Qur'an with which mountains were moved, or the earth were cloven asunder, or the dead were made to speak, (this would be the one)! But, truly, the Command is with Allah in all things! Do not the Believers know, that, had Allah (so) willed, He could have guided all mankind (to the Right)? But the Unbelievers—never will disaster cease to seize them for their (ill) deeds, or to settle close to their homes, until the promise of Allah come to pass, for, verily, Allah will not fail in His promise."
Qur'an 13:31

CHAPTER 33

FAILURE IS NOT AN OPTION...

*B*efore being whisked away from the Jihad Summer Camp, Grace realized that the one-sided 3DHP conversation she overheard in the van did not focus so much on her as it centered on the terrorists who had kidnapped her. The General had been on the other end of the call.

"Brothers, did Allah grant you success?" asked the deep, gnarled voice from Ankara.

"Only three of us are left. We have the package, but not the one you ordered!"

"What do you mean? Are the other six members of your team dead, captured, or what? Are you telling me that you jackasses failed at something so easy as abducting a pastor from his church?"

"But he had a plan! We don't know about the rest of the team."

The General fumed. "He had a plan, did he? We had a plan, too, you imbeciles! A much larger plan than your nascent portion of it! Without the package, the rest of the plan cannot proceed! And just what package do you have?"

"The daughter! And we barely nabbed her!"

"The daughter, you say? I don't recall the daughter being the backup plan! I seem to remember that if you could not take the pastor hostage, you were instructed to kill him!"

"But he had a plan! Everything went dark!"

With that final statement, the voice from the Brotherhood headquarters in Ankara decided he had heard enough and ended the call with the terrorists in the van.

Next, he had called the leader of the Atlanta summer camp. "Only three of our fighters are coming back to you. They do not know the fate of the other six. They do not have the right package with them. They did not successfully follow our detailed and critical plan! When they arrive, take the substitute package from them. Ship this incorrect package to the identified destination. Then, give your brothers the reward they deserve!"

When the car arrived and entered the underground parking lot, the camp leader greeted them, saying, "I understand you ran into difficulties at the church?"

"Yes," the driver exclaimed, his voice and body shaking. "The pastor had a plan. He was ready for us!"

"And you were ready to counter that plan, were you not? The three of you, your team leader, and the other five men had a very simple backup plan. 'If you cannot capture the pastor, kill him and anyone else who stands in your way!' Was that not plan B?"

"Yes, but the lights went out," the driver emphasized, drenched in sweat despite the coolness of the underground garage. "We fired our MGMs! For all we know, the pastor is dead!"

With rumbling anger in his words, the Brotherhood leader replied, "Most unfortunately, I know the pastor remarkably lives, even somehow escaping your smart bullets! The pastor is smarter than the bullets—far smarter than you!"

"Well, it was dark!"

"Just where are your six brothers?"

"Captured? Killed?"

"They are very much alive. In fact, they have divulged our location. We must abandon the camp."

"They must have been tortured!"

Losing his last ounce of patience, the leader shouted, "Your fellow team members have suffered something worse than torture. They have betrayed us! They have betrayed Allah! They have become infidels, traitors to the noble cause of jihad!"

Feral fear overtook the driver who kidnapped Grace. He could not voice a reply.

Grabbing the driver by the throat, the leader demanded, "What package did you bring to me?"

As he struggled to breathe, the driver answered, "We have a very valuable package. Despite the darkness and confusion, I was able to kidnap the daughter. She is in the backseat of the car. You can use her to bargain for the pastor! Perhaps what I have done will be even better than your original plan!"

The Brotherhood camp leader tightened his grip around the driver's neck and at a measured pace stated, "Never. . . suggest. . . to. . . me. . . again. . . that. . . anything. . . you. . . do. . . could. . . be. . . an. . . improvement. . . to. . . my. . . orders! Understood?" He then released the driver, who could not respond as he fell to his knees, while gasping for air.

The leader barked, "Actually, you will never talk to me again— about anything! You will likewise never fail me again!" With those words, he shot the three terrorists in the head at point blank range!"

Grace screamed when she heard the shots. What she feared was confirmed. The terrorists were after her dad, dead or alive! Now, what would happen to her? Grace remembered the terrorists' warning for the congregation to abandon the church. Would she now face the threatened punishment? Would the terrorists indeed force her to marry one of their own at the age of thirteen?

"For even the Son of Man did not come to be served, but to serve, and to give His Life as a ransom for many."
Mark 10:45

CHAPTER 34

THE PASTOR'S CALL. . .

*T*he hour was late, and the FBI agents continued their interviews with church members. The agents wanted to question Mark and Ariel after they spoke with the 800 plus people who had come to worship this day.

In his study, Pastor Mark and Ariel revisited the day's blur of events when his 3DHP lit up. Expecting to hear from the agent in charge of the search for Grace, Mark squeezed his bride's hand. She squeezed his in return. The 3DHP showed a woman and a number Mark did not know, but he answered the call with hope that Jesus had answered their prayers and was delivering Grace back to them.

"This is Pastor Mark."

"Hello, Pastor. Please hold for a call from the President!"

President Paulson's image appeared before the couple. "Pastor Mark! Good to see you!"

"Thank you, Mr. President! It is good to see you, as well."

"I am calling you from Air Force One. I hear you and Ariel have endured a very rough day, so far!"

"Yes, Mr. President!"

"I want you to know that I have told the Director of the FBI to give you and your family the agency's upmost attention!"

"Thank you, Mr. President!"

"Mark, I truly cannot imagine what you and Ariel have endured, with your daughter Grace missing."

"Taken, Mr. President! Abducted! Kidnapped!"

"Exactly, Mark! My mistake. Forgive me, please?"

"Already done, Mr. President!"

"Mark, please feel free to call me James. This is not a time for protocol and formalities."

"All right, sir, Mr. President. . . James!"

The Commander in Chief smiled at the pastor. "I understand you and Ariel were supposed to fly to Tel Aviv tonight?"

"Yes. . . James, we were."

"I imagine you have changed those plans?"

"Yes. We cannot go now."

"I had arranged a government jet to pick you up as soon as you were ready to go this afternoon. I suppose I need to cancel that."

Mark's phone beeped, indicating an incoming call. He quickly looked at the phone. The call was from Babylon."

"Mr. President, I mean James, I hate to ask this, but could you call me back in five minutes, sir. I have a call coming in from Babylon!"

"Mark, this call could be of ultimate importance! You take the call. I will get back to you in ten minutes!"

"Thank you, James. I truly do appreciate your patience. I will talk with you after I take this call. Goodbye."

"Goodbye and good luck!"

Pastor Mark flipped to the other call, but there was no image, only darkness. With dread in his heart and voice, Mark said, "Hello?"

"Dr. Basel?"

"Yes, I am Dr. Basel." Mark did not recognize the mangled Arab voice.

"Have you enjoyed your morning? Say now, how many dreaded Muslim Brotherhood terrorists attended your worship service today?"

"Who are you, and what do you know about the events here at our church today?"

Ariel held to her husband tightly. A cold chill ran down her spine.

The man on the other end of this call was silent for a moment. Then he curtly asked, "Don't you remember me, Mark? I am so fond of you and your family."

At that moment, Mark realized he was speaking to the General of the Brotherhood Army.

"What about the seventh man who visited your worship service, Dr. Basel? Did he refuse to submit himself to Isa? Did he slip through

176

the Messiah's fingers today? Did he take something that did not belong to him—something very close to your heart, perhaps? Could it be something for which you would risk everything to have back in your possession?"

Mark locked his jaw and refused to answer.

"You are still coming to Palestine, are you not, Dr. Basel? I hear that *Al Quds* is most pleasant at this time of year!"

Mark had briefly met the secretive General during the last round of peace negotiations. Mark wondered what the General was hiding behind his veiled faced and contorted voice.

"Pastor, is something amiss? You are so quiet and look so troubled! Perhaps some time away in Palestine is just what the doctor ordered?"

Mark finally responded, asking, "What do you know about my travel plans? And what is your name?"

"I'm sure you know who I am, Pastor Basel. You know I just go by my rank, anyway. Again, you are still planning to visit what is left of the DROP, are you not? Or has something come up at the last minute? What could be of more importance than to help avert the war to end all wars, Professor?"

Feeling his anger and hatred beginning to surge once more, Mark refused to play the General's pathetic game. He said nothing and closed his eyes.

"Are we sleepy or are we praying, Reverend? I would suggest that a few moments sleep would be for more productive than making pleas to a deity that does not exist!"

Mark heard evil chuckling coming from the darkness. The General taunted him, saying, "What's the matter? Your sweet Isa won't allow you to come out and play with me? Is he afraid you might get hurt?"

Mark clung to Isa's peace as he kept his eyes closed. He would not gratify the Masked Man of Babylon with an emotional response.

"I'm so sorry," cooed the General in sickeningly sweet, though still distorted tones. "Are we not having a good day? Is that why you cannot come to the DROP? Do you have family issues or something like that? Are your parents unavailable to babysit the boys?" Snickering once again, the General feigned an apology saying, "Oh, I am so sorry, Doctor! It slipped my mind that your parents are no longer in this world, are they?" The Muslim's insulting comments were followed by even more self-amused laughter.

Reining in the anger and hatred that longed to be released from within him, Mark replied calmly, saying, "You know very well why I cannot leave, don't you? Until our daughter has been brought back to us, we cannot go anywhere. Ariel and I must be here!"

"Quite the contrary," thundered the tortuous voice. "You and Ariel will fly to Tel Aviv as soon as possible or you will never see your precious Grace again—at least not alive! She will be here, waiting for your arrival in East Jerusalem! She will be free to return home with you, unless she wisely chooses to remain and follow Allah, of course!"

Ariel's tears ran down her face to the floor. Mark, with great fury swirling in his soul, demanded, "Where is my daughter now?"

Ignoring his question, the faceless voice said, "Let me make myself clear, Dr. Basel! If you breathe one word of this to the FBI agents there at your church or to any law enforcement or governmental agency, your daughter will vanish without a trace! Cooperate with us, and your delicate Grace will be returned to you. Betray us, and your darling little girl will be the blushing bride of a fine upstanding member of the Brotherhood—or maybe, she will not be at all! And we wouldn't want that to happen now, would we? Not after what happened to your dear *Ab* and *Umm*!"

"It is not lawful for thee (to marry more) women after this, nor to change them for (other) wives, even though their beauty attract thee, except any thy right hand should possess (as handmaidens): And Allah doth watch over all things."
Qur'an 33:52

CHAPTER 35

THE ROBES FOR THE ROLE...

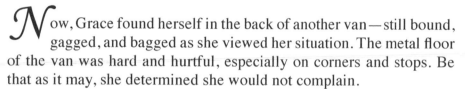

*N*ow, Grace found herself in the back of another van — still bound, gagged, and bagged as she viewed her situation. The metal floor of the van was hard and hurtful, especially on corners and stops. Be that as it may, she determined she would not complain.

Grace's growling stomach argued against that decision. She had not eaten breakfast before church, as she awoke too late to do anything but shower and throw on her clothes. She and her friends had skipped supper last night, as they had made a pact to fast from three meals a week. The time they would normally spend eating would instead be devoted to prayer for the malnourished and starving children of the world.

The van came to another quick stop, throwing Grace all around the cargo area. She would be quite bruised and battered from her two van rides alone.

The door opened and someone grabbed her. In the bright, late afternoon summer sun, she could only see silhouettes of the men around her. They looked like dark ghosts through the cotton sack that covered her head.

"Take her inside, quickly! We do not have much time!" an anonymous Muslim male bellowed. "Muzaynah is ready for her."

Inside the house, Grace smelled strange spices and pungent aromas. She was pushed along until she was thrown on a bed. Immediately, someone started taking off her clothes! Grace instinctively curled up in a ball in defense.

"Relax," Muzaynah cooed, "I am not going to hurt you. I am just going to change your clothes."

Grace felt a bit less afraid knowing that she was with a woman. The teenager wondered if she should ask Muzaynah for food. Although, how could Grace ask for food when her mouth was stuffed with a rag?"

Her shoes, socks, slacks, and undergarments came off first. Now, feelings of embarrassment rushed over Grace, and her face felt red hot. She tried to cover her nakedness with her hands. Being a mother of three girls, Muzaynah Afham understood. She said, "Modesty is something every young woman must learn!" She then placed a lower undergarment, something like a slip, around Grace's waist. Then, the Muslim woman helped Grace to her feet.

"I am going to take the sack off your head for a few moments. I will also remove the ropes. You must keep your eyes closed, and you must not try to escape. Your life would be in danger!"

The only daughter of Mark and Ariel quickly nodded her head in agreement. The sack came off first, and Muzaynah could see Grace's red face. It took a bit longer to untie the ropes that bound her hands. Muzaynah saw how they had cut into Grace's wrists. The Muslim mother felt sorry for this young woman, even though she was *kuffar*— an infidel! Muzaynah had lost her fourth daughter in a car accident when she was a young teen.

The sympathetic mother said, "I see you are bleeding. I will tend your wounds if I have time after dressing you." Grace thought this woman sounded compassionate. Grace needed some kindness at this moment in her harrowing journey.

With her hands free, Grace rubbed her stomach in circles. At first, Muzaynah did not understand, but then quickly realized that Grace was hungry. "I don't have permission to remove the gag from your mouth," she said. "But I will ask if they will let you eat in the van." Grace tried to smile and again nodded her head as the only way she could convey her gratitude.

Just for a second, Grace opened her eyes to get a snapshot of this woman who was being as gentle with her as the circumstances would allow. Muzaynah was wearing a full length *jibab*, but her face was not covered. Grace remembered that women did not have to wear the *niqab* to hide their faces at home.

"Raise your hands above your head," Muzaynah gently instructed. Grace felt some kind of undershirt coming down over her arms and head. Its smell was unique to Grace, as she could not describe it. Similarly, she could not tell if she liked it or not. Once in the shirt, Grace felt the weight of the black shroud sliding over her arms and head. The bottom hem almost touched the floor. "You and my youngest daughter are almost the very same size!" Muzaynah said approvingly, though with sadness. "I lost her a few years ago."

Both Muzaynah and Grace jumped as they were startled by the unexpected and loud pounding on the bedroom door. "Two minutes! Have her out here and ready to go in two minutes!" the driver of the van shouted.

"Okay! Okay!" Muzaynah answered, and then added, "Can she take some food with her?"

"She can eat once she is above the Atlantic!" the gruff voice shouted back through the closed door.

"Above the Atlantic?" Grace said to herself and in the same instant realized she would be flying somewhere. Now, with a bit more fear pumping through her system, Grace wanted to ask Muzaynah about the flight and where she would be going. Yet, the gag made that impossible. The thirteen year old began breathing rapidly again as the mystery of her airborne escapade could not be resolved.

"I cannot care for your wounds, but I will tie the ropes less tightly and higher on your arms," the grieving mother whispered to Grace. "And I will not tie the sack so tightly around your neck either." Then Muzaynah had an even better idea. "I will not put the sack back over your head as the *niqab* will cover your face. But you must promise to keep your eyes closed tightly!"

Grace nodded in agreement and tried to say, "Thank you," as best she could with a sopping wet gag in her mouth.

Without knocking or another announcement, the bedroom door flew open, and the driver grabbed Grace by the arm, saying, "Come along, my little Muslim bride!"

"Am I flying to my wedding—to a Muslim?" Grace asked herself in a moment of panic. As she hyperventilated, she asked Jesus to prevent her from passing out again. She prayed that this would not be her wedding day!

"Indeed, you will be a beautiful bride!" Muzaynah commented, as Grace was pulled through the front door into the blazing Atlanta sun. "May you know the happiness that was taken from my little girl!"

Before the two men threw her back into the van, Grace's head was already spinning, and her new tears soaked the dark veil that covered her face. This daughter's heart ached for the embrace of her own mother.

At the same moment, one of the men in the van said, "This virgin bride seems strong. She will bear many noble Muslim children!" With those words, Grace's world went black once more.

*"The thief comes only to steal and kill and destroy; I have
come that they may have life, and have it to the full."*
John 10:10

CHAPTER 36

WALKING THE TIGHTROPE...

*W*ith great emotion and urgency, Ariel asked, "Mark, what does
that cruel man mean by saying, 'Maybe she will not be at
all?'"

Still staring blankly at the fading images from his holophone,
Mark answered in monotone, "It means he will kill her if we do not
cooperate."

Ariel again grabbed Mark and held him tightly. Her firm embrace
jolted Mark back into the moment, and he said, "But we will do everything we can to get Grace back alive and unharmed! We will do what
he says. We will go to Palestine!"

"Is that safe, Mark?" Ariel asked through her tears.

"Safe or not, we have no choice, Honey!" Then he pushed Ariel
back and looked straight into her dark eyes. "Sweetheart, this is not
about Grace. This is not about the church. This is about me! Remember
what the lead terrorist said about Grace after he received Jesus? 'She
is not the one they wanted!' They took her because they could not get
to me! They had no interest in Grace!"

Ariel sobbed, "Well, they have an interest in her now! But why are
they sending our little girl to Palestine, Mark?"

"Because they wanted to take me to Palestine."

"What do the terrorists want you to do there? Or what do they want
to do to you there?"

"I don't know, Honey! Still, the location must be important, or
they would have kept Grace here until I surrendered to them."

"Mark! You can't surrender to them! They will kill you!" Ariel held tightly to her husband once again.

"Darling, if they wanted me dead, they could have shot me before the worship service while I stood at the church entrance, reading their message. They want me to do something, and they want me to do it in the DROP!"

"But what? What do they want you to do? And are you sure they are not going to do something horrid to you there?"

"I cannot be sure of anything, but this: Isa will be there with us. He will not leave us alone. He will not forget us or forsake us."

Ariel started to ask another question, but Mark's holophone rang again. He looked and saw the lady at the White House again.

"Pastor Basel, the President is calling once again. Please hold— and may God bless you and keep you!"

"Why did she say that?" Mark asked Ariel. "She couldn't know about my last conversation, could she?"

Ariel answered, "Mark, the President, the Israeli Prime Minister, and the imam all told the world that you and I were going to Palestine to meet with the other key players in the negotiations. Maybe she is praying for the best!"

"Yeah, you are probably right." Mark looked into Ariel's reddened eyes. "Thanks Honey! My mind is going in a thousand different directions."

As the President began to speak, he could see that the couple had been crying. "Mark—are you and Ariel okay?"

"Just a lot going on, sir. I mean, James."

"I can understand that, and I am afraid I have more bad news."

Both Mark and Ariel stared at the President. "Is it about Grace?"

"Yes and no. Listen. The FBI agent who was at your church—-the one who sent his men and a bunch of Atlanta cops to the empty building—has reported back to headquarters. His men found two accidents on the way. The Atlanta cops said the four men in the two cars were fellow officers. Apparently, the cops were hit by automatic MGM fire. We don't know if they were killed by the bullets or in the collisions."

"Those four officers were members of our church!" Mark said with grief. Ariel tightened her hold on her husband.

"I am truly sorry to hear that, Mark. But that's not all. The six FBI agents and twenty Atlanta cops that found the abandoned building are all dead, too."

"Oh no," Mark and Ariel said in unison. Mark felt the weight of thirty lost lives on his shoulders. He told himself, *"If I had just called off church—just for today—those men would be alive!"*

Seeing the look of horror on Mark's face, the President asked, "Pastor! Are you all right?"

Shaking off his doubts and fears, Mark asked "What about Grace?" He was almost afraid to hear the answer.

"She was not there. That old office building was apparently being used as some kind of training facility, as far as our investigators know at present. However, the only bodies found were those of the agents and the Atlanta cops."

Mark wondered, *"Did Grace see those murders? Did she see the officers from the church die as they tried to reach her and save her?"*

The President said, "Mark, did you hear me?"

Mark took a deep breath and, again, tried to focus on the moment. Looking to Ariel, Mark answered, "Yes, we both heard you, James."

"I'm sorry, but there is yet more. The FBI tells me that your daughter may, and I emphasize the word may, be on her way out of the country with the terrorists."

"James, what makes the FBI suspect that about Grace?" Ariel quietly buried her face in Mark's chest and wept.

"Honestly, Mark, I don't know the sources of that information. I just want you to know everything I know."

"Thank you for that, James."

"We are sending a picture of Grace that the FBI pulled from your church website to every exit point in the country. Beyond that, I have told the FBI to keep watch on you and Ariel and your boys—we cannot be too careful right now."

Mark immediately realized the President's plan would not work. "James, we have a situation here."

"Yes? Are you two safe?"

"Physically, we are fine. I am asking for your understanding and cooperation."

"You name it, Mark. What do you need?"

"For reasons I cannot divulge, Ariel and I will be going to Palestine after all."

The President sat erect in his chair. He asked, "Mark, have you heard from the terrorists—the kidnappers?"

"James, please do not ask me questions that I cannot answer! All I can say is that we will be in Palestine. I really do not know anymore than that."

Easing back in the chair, the President said firmly, "Okay, Mark. I can still send the government jet for you and Ariel."

"Thank you, again, James. However, given the circumstances, I don't think it would be wise of us to arrive on a U.S. government jet. We will make arrangements to fly out tonight."

"Mark, you have me very concerned about you and Ariel. How about us alerting the FBI and they can travel undercover with you and watch your back in Palestine?"

"With all due respect and gratitude, James, that cannot happen! Please, do as we ask, and don't assume anything or do anything! Please!"

With genuine concern, James pleaded with Mark and Ariel. He said, "Listen. Thirty people have been killed already. I have just received word from Israel that Prime Minister Ben Baruch's Cabinet has been murdered—beheaded to be exact. We don't want either of you or Grace to be added to this growing list of casualties!"

Ariel asked the President, "Every Cabinet member was beheaded?"

"Tragically, yes. Not only that, but their heads were brought to the steps of the Prime Minister's residence. He and his security detail found them—along with the bodies of the Israeli security detail that was guarding the residence!"

Ariel asked, "Are the Prime Minister's wife and children safe?" She held her breath as she awaited the answer.

"Amazingly, they were inside the house, asleep and unharmed, Ariel!"

Ariel breathed deeply and said, "Thank the Lord for saving them!"

The Commander in Chief had no response. He stared blankly into his holophone.

Mark then said, "James, I need to ask another favor of you. I cannot tell you how much Ariel and I appreciate your desire to help and protect us. Even so, you must understand that what we must do, we must do alone! I cannot say anymore. The only thing that I ask of you now is to tell the FBI agents who are here, interviewing members of the congregation, that we cannot be questioned this evening. We have some preparations to make before our flight to the Holy Land tonight—we need to be at the airport very soon. Thus, we have no time to be interviewed. Will you be able to do that for us?"

"Consider it done, Mark and Ariel. It is the least I can do. I look forward to seeing you in Palestine, if that is part of the plan."

"We don't know the answer to that part of the puzzle, either, James. Thank you for your help and your understanding."

"If you need anything, and I mean anything, call this number, and the White House will patch the call through to me. Goodbye and may God be with you!"

Mark was surprised, as he had never heard the President even refer to God before this moment. The heartbroken pastor replied, "I cannot tell you how much we are counting on Him, James! We hope you are doing so, as well!"

"There are (yet) others, held in suspense for the command of Allah, whether He will punish them, or turn in mercy to them: and Allah is All-Knowing, Wise."
Qur'an 9:106

CHAPTER 37

BY THE BOOK...

Exhausted, President James Jacob Paulson found it difficult to focus. Air Force One would be landing in a few hours, yet he had found no time to rest, much less sleep. While deciphering everything that had happened on Sunday had proven hard enough, what would happen on Monday? On one hand, the President realized he must expect the worst. On the other hand, he considered the advice of Benjamin Franklin. "Blessed is he who expects nothing, for he shall never be disappointed."

As the weary leader walked into his private bedroom, he remembered that Abdul said he had met someone that night—someone named Isa. *"Who in the world was Isa and how in the world would he be on Air Force One?"*

James had little time to contemplate, however, as his Chief of Staff came running in behind him through the open door. "You have a call, Double J!"

"From?"

"FBI Director Lloyd. He said you told him to call when he had new information."

"Indeed!" The President sighed as he followed Eddie down the hall. As they walked, the President said, "Please don't call me Double J anymore. Make sure you and everyone else call me James or Mr. President, instead."

"Whatever you say, James. You are the boss. You call the shots."

Eddie walked ahead of the Commander in Chief and entered the conference room first. He said to Charlie, "Make sure you don't call the President by his nickname—Double J. Call him James or Mr. President."

"What's that all about?" Charlie asked.

"The Vice President wants more formality and respect in the White House. So, no more calling him Triple A either. He is Abdul or Mr. Vice President. Got it?"

"Sure thing!"

The President entered the conference room and saw that the FBI Director's face was sullen and his brow furrowed. "Yes, Charlie, what do you have?" The President sat down while Eddie brought him yet another cup of coffee.

"James, so far, I have learned three things from our interrogations of the six terrorists."

"Fire when ready!" The President paused and then said, "I suppose those words were not the best choice for this day!"

Charlie replied, "There are no words for today, Mr. President, but let me tell you what we know. First, the Brotherhood headquarters in Atlanta was a jihad training camp for boys and teens—six to sixteen to be exact. This is the same age spread of such camps in what used to be Europe and Asia. We've heard rumors of these camps being in the states, but this is the first one we have actually seen.

"Accordingly, the six Muslims we have in custody are home-grown. Three other American Muslims were part of this team. From the age of six, all nine of these men were trained right here on our soil to be jihadists! They joined the Brotherhood the day they started their ten years of training!"

"You cannot be serious, Charlie!"

"I know this is hard to believe, James, but I could not be more serious. While the Atlanta training camp has been housed in the abandoned building for years, the terrorists have also been using the space to practice the kidnapping of Pastor Mark Basel for about four months."

With a furrowed brow, the President asked, "What does the Brotherhood want with Mark?"

"At this point, we have no idea, James. Yet they obviously have gone to great lengths to capture or kill him."

"Does the Brotherhood have other such camps in the states, Charlie?"

"Apparently, somewhere between 900 and 1,000 camps operate within our borders. Unfortunately, we have no idea where they are."

"Why is that?"

"The leaders in one camp know nothing of the locations of the other camps. Otherwise, the terrorists in one camp, like the ones now jailed in Atlanta, could spill the beans about other sites."

"Charlie, how many boys were in training in Atlanta?"

"Around 150."

The President jumped out of his chair. "You mean to tell me we could have 150,000 young jihadists training on U.S. soil even as we speak?"

"Unfortunately, yes! Maybe the other camps could be even larger. Who knows?"

"What did they leave behind at the Atlanta camp—anything?"

"Well, the Brotherhood apparently left in haste after mowing down our agents and the police officers. We found a training manual—which is also the first one we have seen—and some hacked up bodies in the walk-in refrigerator!"

"Hacked up bodies?" James asked, grimacing.

"We believe there are enough two to three inch chunks for about five to six people."

"Who are they—or who were they, I guess I should say?"

"That's the second thing. The DNA says these bodies are those of homeless men. The Atlanta police had been receiving reports from the homeless shelters that many men were missing. Such calls have been coming in for years. Even so, how do you investigate missing homeless people? Plus, the Atlanta force just didn't have the manpower to even try tracking anyone down."

"Were they chopped up alive?"

"Not according to the Brotherhood manual. The homeless men were needed for the boys' training. The boys either slit their throats with machetes or used them as target practice with smart weapons. Once dead, the boys were taught how to chop up the bodies and bones!"

"Kids doing all this?" The thought made the President nauseous. "Are all of them American born and raised, too?"

"As far as we can tell from the terrorists, these boys and teens are American citizens, James."

"And this is the first camp we have found out of a thousand?"

"Right, and as I said, we have no idea where any of the other training facilities may be."

"Are you sure, Charlie, that the terrorists in your custody do not know the locations of the other camps—any of them? They could be holding out on you, couldn't they?"

"James, these guys could not be more cooperative. They are giving us tons of information—things we haven't even asked them about!"

"Why would they do that?"

"These six Muslims are now Christians! They got saved at the Church of the Transformed after the kidnapping!"

With disbelief and disdain in his voice, James stated, "Oh really? You must be pulling my leg now, Charlie!"

"No, James, I could not be more serious. At first I balked at this report, but these men are not putting on an act. These guys have changed! They have bent over backwards to help us. My guys have never met any terrorists like these—former terrorists, now!"

"So what else have they told your men?"

"That's the third thing. The kidnapping today was botched. The nine terrorists—the six we have, the one who abducted the pastor's daughter, and another two in the getaway van—were at the church for Pastor Basel! But the pastor and the police officers in the church had been training for a day like this for five years! So they thwarted the Muslim's plans. They took the girl as a last ditch effort to save their mission!"

"Did they say why they came after Mark?"

"They were following orders and don't know what their superiors want with the pastor. Still, the jihadists said if they could not kidnap the minister, they had orders to kill him—plan B!"

The President sat on the edge of the table. "Charlie, do you think this attempt to kidnap or kill Mark has anything to do with the attacks on the DROP—and the negotiating team's arrival there tomorrow?"

"I don't know how they are connected, but they must be, Doub. . . James. This is the first church in the states to be targeted by terrorists, and it just so happens to be the same day of the attack on the DROP? This is too much coincidence for me—especially when you consider that the hostage is being taken to Palestine—if they can get her past the beefed up security. Besides, the real target was Pastor Basel, a member of the negotiating team itself!"

"Are you sure that is what is happening to Grace—that she is being taken to the DROP?"

"The terrorists say their mission was to take the pastor to Palestine. Thus, the Brotherhood will take the daughter to the DROP to lure the pastor there."

"You need to secure as much information from the terrorists about the plans in Palestine, pronto, Charlie! I just spoke with Mark, and he and his wife are headed for the DROP tonight, so it sounds like the Brotherhood's plan C is working."

"Got it. I'll talk to the agents as soon as we finish this call."

"What else do you have, Charlie?"

"Well, before I go any further, I think we better put some agents around Pastor Basel and his family!"

"I thought the same thing, Charlie. I told Mark we were going to do just that. But he refused."

"Why?"

"Not sure—but most likely because the Brotherhood has contacted him and demanded that he and his wife go to Palestine alone, or else their daughter will be killed. Despite that possibility, Charlie, with this information that you now have, I think we should put some agents around Mark and Ariel anyway. They will be flying to Israel tonight.

"Contact Erdmann over at Secret Service. Have him place his best men around the Basels. At all costs, those men must be discrete. This security detail for Mark will have to be invisible. No one, not even Mark and Ariel, can know the agents are there—okay?"

"Erdmann will know the right men to send!"

"Good! The Basels will be on the midnight flight to Israel, so the guys need to get moving."

"Right—I'm on it. Oh, one more thing—a fourth point I almost forgot. These Muslim boys were not only training to kill, but to be killed! The greatest honor they could achieve is to die in jihad for Allah! Their young minds were brainwashed from the age of six. They have been indoctrinated to believe that there are only two forces in the world: Islam and everything else. To destroy the infidels they must be willing to die as *shahids*—martyrs! There is video all over this place of these boys swearing they want to die in jihad—and they look very happy about the prospect!"

"My God! These boys were never children!"

"While that reality is most unfortunate, the true horror is that these kids have no conscience about killing or any driving desire to stay alive! They are cold blooded merchants of death!"

"That sends a shiver down your back! I have just one more thing, Charlie. What else is in that Brotherhood training manual?"

"Mr. President, you won't believe me when I tell you!"

"Why are you so afraid? Do you still have no faith?"
Mark 4:40

CHAPTER 38

THE GUT GNAWING QUESTIONS...

❖❖❖

*B*efore leaving his study, Mark and Ariel had been quite busy. They booked two one way flights to Israel, having no idea when they would actually be returning home. They lined up a babysitter for the boys—a young couple in the church who would actually stay in their house with Tim and Tom until their return. Neither Mark nor Ariel had any blood kin in the Atlanta area or the United States, for that matter. Hence, in times of need they always turned to their church family.

Mark called a fellow professor at the seminary to preach for him, just in case he would not be back by midweek. He also talked with the lead elder of his church to explain that he and Ariel were leaving, even though Grace had been kidnapped. The elder said, "I don't understand this Pastor Mark, but I know you, and I trust your judgment."

After that conversation, Mark and Ariel sent out a holophone message to the congregation, asking for their prayers and support in this current, uncertain situation. One point Mark made was that "While the circumstances are discouraging and extremely frustrating, our Lord Jesus is neither discouraged nor frustrated. In fact, our Messiah is in complete control, and He knows the way through this darkness around us. We are following Him with good courage, for He has never left nor forsaken us, and He promises He never will leave nor forsake us!"

The professor also spoke with the chair of his department at the university. Then, he lined up a back up instructor for his classes. Mark also told an assistant to choose some previously recorded but not yet aired sermons for the Muslim satellite outreach.

Next, Mark and Ariel talked with the lead FBI agent on site. Indeed, he had been contacted by headquarters and instructed not to interview them this evening. Mark agreed to contact the agent upon their return from Israel to set up an appointment.

The agent confirmed that the relatives of the four dead Atlanta police officers who were members of the church had been notified. Consequently, Mark and Ariel's final task before leaving the church was to talk to those four grieving families, even though their time to speak with them would have to be extremely short.

Despite their time constraints, the couple poured out their hearts to those mournful souls, wrapping a blanket of Jesus' love and strength about them in their own time of heartbreak. They had lost brave and loyal husbands, fathers, sons, and brothers who had died heroically in efforts to save Grace. To each family, the pastor said, "We owe you and your family a debt of love we will never be able to repay. I'll be ready to conduct the funeral service when we return." Mark and Ariel prayed for each family to know the peace and comfort of Jesus. Mark reminded the families that their brave loved ones were standing in the very presence of Jesus, who personally welcomed such good and faithful servants!

After all their tasks, Mark and Ariel left his study and entered the sanctuary to leave through the main church entrance. They were headed home to pack a bag or two and then go directly to Atlanta's Hartsfield-Jackson Atlanta International Airport. The couple had no time to spare.

Even so, as Mark and Ariel passed the pulpit, he stopped in his tracks. The pulpit—actually the entire podium—was riddled with bullet holes! Those shots that were fired in the dark had not been fired into the air to terrorize the congregation. Rather, those shots—it looked like hundreds of them—had been aimed at Mark! Both he and Ariel fell to their knees at the altar. They bowed their heads realizing what had happened during those few dark moments.

With tears once more rolling down his cheeks, all the emotion and tension of the day spilled out of Mark who had been so strong for everyone else. "Oh Lord," he prayed, "I should not be alive! Surely, with all the smart bullets that were fired at me this morning, I should be dead! The only reason I live and breathe in this moment is because You miraculously saved my life! Therefore, I know You have a purpose for Ariel and me to fulfill! We pray for Your Holy Spirit's power and wisdom as You lead us. We pray for another miracle, as well: that You will return Grace to us unharmed and untouched!"

Ariel sobbed uncontrollably as Mark continued. "Dear Jesus, although I am alive and well, thirty men are dead tonight because of the decision I made this morning to proceed with our worship of You, despite the threats made against us! Four of those men were dear friends of ours, Master! We grieve with their families, even as we know these four brothers are with You! As I speak these words of gratitude and entreaty to You, Saviour, we can only hope that the other twenty six families can know Your peace in such horrible circumstances."

Then, Mark laid out the questions that only his Redeemer could answer. "Am I responsible for their deaths, Jesus? Am I responsible for Grace's kidnapping? Are these men dead and are their families mourning because I made the decision myself—the wrong decision? Is our only daughter in the hands of evil terrorists tonight because I acted on my own, not in submission to You? I beg for Your forgiveness and for the forgiveness of the families if I made the fatal choice, the fatal mistake by going ahead with worship today against Your will!

"Lord, with the same intensity, I ask for Your peace, complete and whole, if You guided me to make that decision. Either way, dear, precious, all loving, and all knowing Jesus, help us have Your total clarity in each choice we must make from this moment. We pray by the very Blood You poured out to redeem us, the very Blood of the very Son of God! Amen!"

As Mark and Ariel embraced and wiped each other's tears, they knew the deep and abiding peace of Heaven, even in the midst of hell on earth!

"On no soul doth Allah place a burden greater than it can bear. It gets every good that it earns, and it suffers every ill that if earns. (Pray:) 'Our Lord! Condemn us not if we forget or fall into error; our Lord! Lay not on us a burden like that which Thou didst lay on those before us; Our Lord! Lay not on us a burden greater than we have strength to bear. Blot out our sins, and grant us forgiveness, have mercy on us. Thou art our Protector; Help us against those who stand against Faith.'"

Qur'an 2:286

CHAPTER 39

NEITHER SEEN NOR HEARD...

❖❖❖

*W*ith nightfall, Grace's stomach was growling loudly, even though no one could hear it through the noise of the van speeding through Atlanta. The next to last stop had been for quick pictures and fingerprints and a hastily assembled, forged Babylonian passport. Grace's new name was Haziqah, an eighteen year old from the Muslim Alliance state of Turkey.

As time bore down on the terrorists, the driver had one final stop to make. He took a sharp right turn off of I-85, followed by a quick left, and a quick right, which placed the van in front of a non-descript building. When the door of the building opened, two Turkish Muslims stepped through it and then climbed into the waiting van with their three pieces of luggage.

Now, the jihadists raced for the airport. Along the way, Grace's new Muslim mother exchanged her gag for a bandage and then wrapped around her head with gauze. However, this woman lacked the kindness and compassion of Muzaynah.

This woman, her face veiled, said to Grace, "Haziqah, when we go through the airport security process, you are to say nothing, you are to do nothing, but pretend to be our daughter. If you try to speak or run or do anything to attract attention, you and your family will die! You will die here with us. We have something with us that would take your life instantly. Then, we would target your parents and brothers! When I say we, I don't mean the two of us who will travel with you. I mean the Brotherhood! Have you heard of the Brotherhood?"

With tears welling in her eyes, Grace nodded. She told herself she would not fight!

"You are a good and wise daughter, Haziqah!"

The flight for Israel would leave in less than two hours and the Muslims were still twenty minutes away from Hartsfield-Jackson Atlanta International Airport. Would this family, a Turkish father, mother, and eighteen year old daughter by the name of Haziqah, have time to clear all the security checks involved for a flight through or to Israel? Would the increased security measures and personnel identify Haziqah as Grace, thus sparing her from further turmoil?

Once they were dropped off at the airport, Grace and the Muslim couple went through the checked luggage inspection. While standing and walking were a relief for Grace, she remained extremely weak from lack of food and drink. Gagged with the bandage, she could say nothing to the people scanning the bags, even when asked "Who packed your bag?"

Instead, the Brotherhood operative posing as her father, Hajib Dizhwar, answered, "She is mute, but she packed the bag herself." Grace obediently shook her head in agreement. Likewise, Grace's Babylonian passport indicated that Haziqah Dizhwar was indeed unable to speak, having the rare condition of being born without vocal chords.

Had Grace's condition been real, modern medicine could have easily remedied it. But in Babylon, such operations could not be performed. The mullahs taught that Muslims born with defects were intentionally created that way by Allah. Actually, such birth defects resulted from Muslim inbreeding, a truth no Islamic leader would admit.

Once Grace and her surrogate Muslim parents cleared the luggage inspection, the trio next went through the pre-flight personal security check. Each passenger's passport or valid citizen identification was embedded with a microchip that gave a history of the passenger's domestic and foreign travels. When Grace handed her passport to the inspector, the only travel listed for Haziqah were two flights, one from Turkey to Israel and another from Israel to Atlanta. Both flights had supposedly been taken exactly two weeks prior to today. The father explained that the three of them were traveling home by the same route. They had no personal bags or belongings for the flight.

Next, the faux family approached the last check point. No scanners or pat downs were waiting for them. Instead, multiple body scans were performed on passengers as they walked through the airport. The inspector who examined the composites of Grace's scans noticed something unusual around her mouth. He stepped out from his booth and asked her to stop.

At that point, Hajar Dizhwar lifted Grace's veil as she explained that her daughter had oral surgery yesterday. Grace's heart began to beat rapidly as she hoped that the inspector might somehow know she was not Muslim! However, Grace's dark hair and eyes gave the inspector no reason to doubt she was from Turkey. When the Muslim mother produced the bill for the dentist's services, the inspector found no reason to detain the thirteen year old Christian disguised as an eighteen year old Muslim. As such, with their official clearance to fly, all hope rushed out of Grace's heart.

With no more obstacles before them, the makeshift family of three ran quickly to their gate, as the jetliner bound for Tel Aviv had already begun boarding. In fact, as they raced to their terminal, Mark and Ariel stowed their carry-on bags and settled into row 22, seats A and B. Exhausted, in every sense of the word, the couple looked forward to a light meal and several hours of needed sleep.

"What will we do when we get to the Ben Gurion Airport, Mark?" Ariel asked. They had made no arrangements for transportation or lodging.

Mark calmly replied, "Something tells me all the details are handled, Honey. I think we will know what to do soon after we land."

Ten minutes later, on the opposite side of the jetliner, the Dizhwars arrived at row 66, the very last row on the jetliner, seats M, N, and O. As Hajar took the window seat, Grace followed to seat N, while Hajib, a large Muslim man, squeezed himself into the seat to Grace's left. He knew his discomfort would not last long, as the aisle seat to his left would not be occupied. Hajib had purchased that seat as well.

Now, Grace's growling stomach could not be denied, but her Islamic parents realized they could not risk allowing her to eat. Instead, Hajib reached into an inner pocket of his robe and pulled out what appeared to be a packet of two cloth hand sanitizers, which had easily passed through inspection. He handed the packet to Hajar who quietly opened it, then took out one of the cloths and held it up to Grace's nose, underneath her black veil, while Hajib forced Grace's shoulders to the seat. In three seconds, the thirteen year old was unconscious.

Grace would not open her eyes again until the aged jetliner landed in Tel Aviv, twelve hours later.

". . . Hear, O Israel, the Lord our God, the Lord is one. Love the Lord your God with all your heart and with all your soul and with all your mind and with all your strength."
Mark 12:29-30

CHAPTER 40

PUPPETS AND PAWNS. . .

*A*ir Force One and its Air Force escorts touched down in the Jerusalem International Airport at 10:07 Monday morning, Israel Daylight Savings Time. Typically, the presidential jet would have landed at Hatzerim Air Base near Be'er Sheva, but with the press of time, Israeli Prime Minister Samson Tuvya Ben Baruch asked the U.S. President to fly into Jerusalem's little known airport. Ben Baruch ordered all other flights into and out of the Jerusalem facility to be cancelled. As a further measure of precaution, the Prime Minister increased the airport security detail threefold.

As the President and Vice President prepared to disembark Air Force One, Abdul remained overjoyed at meeting Isa during the overnight flight. Even as he and the President continued to discuss the ramifications of bin Laden's address, the beheadings in Israel, and the developments with Pastor Basel and his family, Abdul was bright, upbeat, and somehow optimistic—traits he had not exuded before.

Within half an hour of stepping on the tarmac, the Presidential entourage arrived at *Beit Rosh HaMemshala*, the official residence of the Prime Minister, which was still an official crime scene. For that reason, the President, Vice President, Chief of Staff, and the President's and Vice President's security teams avoided the blood-stained front steps and entered the historic residence from the rear.

As they went through the back entrance, Abdul noticed the *mezuzah* on the doorframe. His Messianic friend, Naomi, had told him a little bit about the *mezuzah*. He knew it contained a tiny hand written scroll inside it. On one side of the scroll were two passages from the Torah. Deuteronomy 6:4-9 contained the *Sh'ma*, part of the words faithful Jews offered to God in prayer three times each day, while Deuteronomy 11:13-21 told of God's promises to those who obey His commands. Both passages carried instructions to *"Inscribe them on the doorposts of your house and on your gates."* On the other side of the scroll was one of the names of God.

As was the Jewish custom, Abdul touched the *mezuzah* with his right hand and then kissed the fingers on that hand. The tradition helped the Jews remember the words of the *Sh'ma* and the promises of God that come with obedience. The Prime Minister watched Abdul and wondered why he, a Muslim, honored a Jewish tradition.

Nonetheless, first the Prime Minister greeted the President as he entered the residence. "Shalom, James! Welcome to my humble abode!" The barrel-chested Jew shook hands with the President while wrapping his left arm around James' shoulders.

"Todah, thank you, Sam! It is always good to see you, even in times like these!"

Then, the Prime Minister offered a similar greeting to the American Vice President. "Shalom, Abdul!" he said. "Finally, I have the pleasure of meeting you face to face!"

"Todah rabah, thank you very much, Sam, but the pleasure is all mine!"

Before releasing Abdul's hand, Sam said in a friendly tone, "I noticed what you did with the *mezuzah* as you came through my door. Frankly, I must tell you that you are the first Muslim whom I have ever seen do such a thing!"

Somewhat embarrassed, as Abdul thought his actions had gone unnoticed, he said, "I was only trying to show my respect for the Jewish custom for the *mezuzah*."

Sam smiled and squeezed Abdul's hand a bit harder. "I have never met a Muslim who respected Jewish customs, either! You are most welcome in my home, Abdul!"

After sharing a light breakfast, followed by a brief tour of the residence, the three leaders stayed at the table for some preliminary discussions. "Sam, I hate to be blunt" the President began, "but how are you and your government responding to the beheadings of your Cabinet members?"

Sam, who had avoided this conversation as long as he could, sighed deeply and hung his head for a moment. Then, he answered, saying, "Personally, I am devastated! In less than three hours, my Cabinet members left my office, lost their heads, and had their heads transported to my front steps. Three of them were killed inside their homes: Religious Services Minster Yaakov Nessa, Science and Technology Minister Yitzhak Gid'on, and Deputy Foreign Affairs Minister Abigail Wilenski. All three of their spouses were beheaded as well. As you may or may not know, my Senior Foreign Affairs Minister, Rachel Meir, was killed atop the Kotel.

"My remaining Cabinet members were killed outside their residences—just after their security escorts pulled away and just before they could enter the doors of their homes.

"The beheaded bodies of my *Beit Rosh HaMemshala* security team were found around the perimeter of the residence. Had the terrorists wanted, they could have slipped into the house and killed my wife and children! Perhaps my driver and team drove up in time to make the terrorists flee. I am most grateful that their lives have been spared!"

"Are they still here with you?" James gently asked.

Clearing his throat, Sam replied, "No, I have sent them to an undisclosed safe house for an indeterminate amount of time. They are very shaken by the events of last night—as am I!" Sam handed James a color copy of the bloody message that he found among the severed heads of his Cabinet.

Taken aback, James asked, "Are these red stains and red words the blood of your Cabinet members?"

"According to the initial investigation, yes!"

"Sam, this message strongly implies that you may be next on the terrorists' list!"

"Indeed," the physically muscular but emotionally weary Prime Minister replied, "and I believe the words the terrorists chose prove they were listening in on my Cabinet meeting. My office is being debugged as we speak, which is why we are meeting here this morning. Part of our discussion had centered on end times prophecy, which is vaguely referenced in the note, you see. Religious Services Minister Yaakov Nessa, an Orthodox rabbi, felt that the attack on the DROP, which also destroyed the *Kotel,* might be a sign that the end times were near. Personally, I've never given such prophecies much thought or credence before."

Intuitively, Abdul asked, "But something within you now looks at those prophecies differently, with greater respect, right? Something changed in that Cabinet meeting."

Somewhat surprised by the question, Sam answered honestly. "Actually, while we were still talking in my office, I felt as if someone was in the room with us, trying to whisper into my ear."

Abdul followed up on Sam's words, asking, "Could you understand what the voice was saying?"

For a soundless moment, Sam looked into the eyes of James and then Abdul. In the President's eyes he saw confusion over what he had just said. But Abdul's eyes revealed an open, accepting confirmation of his words. Such being the case, Sam said to Abdul, "I heard the words softly but clearly. In fact, I can still hear them in my mind. 'I am the Alpha and the Omega, the First and the Last, the Beginning and the End.'"

Abdul could not contain his smile! He asked Sam, "Whom do you think whispered those words to you?"

Again, before answering, Sam looked into the eyes of the two men at the table. James eyes were vacant, but Abdul's eyes were filled with so much encouragement. Inhaling deeply, Sam said to Abdul, "If I did not know any better, I would say that Y'shua spoke those words to me!"

While James was stunned as Sam's admission, Abdul was nodding in agreement. "I understand, Sam! I really do! Those words sound like they could be from the New Testament."

"Actually," Sam said with some resolve behind his words, "I entered those words on the ultranet and found that they come from the last chapter of the last book of the New Testament. They were part of Y'shua's final words in the book called Revelation. When Y'shua said those words, He was talking about His promised return to earth."

Abdul was about to share his encounter with Y'shua with Sam, when he caught James' stern gaze. The President's eyes and body language conveyed that Abdul should pursue this conversation no further. Thus, Abdul looked back at Sam and said, "We need to find a time to discuss your experience in more detail!"

Surprising himself by his own response, Sam said, "Yes, I would like that, Abdul!"

Feeling most uncomfortable with the present direction of the discussion, James said, "Do you believe you can pull Israel back from the brink of war now — in light of the beheadings?"

Sam refocused his thoughts and answered, "Israel has paid an extremely high price, James. If not Babylon, someone or some group wants to decapitate our government." Sam hesitated as he realized that statement did not come out as he intended. "I chose my words poorly, but they are literally true. And if Babylon has not spawned this carnage, then who has?"

James replied, "I understand. Nations have gone to war with far less provocation than this. Abdul and I came here, hoping we could keep our two nations from rushing to war. Now, with the assassinations, I don't know if we have a choice. Regardless, you know that if you must declare war, I will do the same and our nations will fight side by side."

Obviously moved by James' unquestioned show of support, Sam said, "You cannot know how much I appreciate you and your commitment, James. At the same time, if we do not have control of our own weaponry, does Israel have a chance to survive such a war?"

"We can only answer that question when we know who launched the rockets on the DROP — and how they did it. I see only two candidates for that attack as well as for the beheadings: the General or bin Laden. Speaking of which, what do you make of the Caliph's speech, Sam?"

Blinking his eyes rapidly to again shift his thinking, Sam said, "Frankly, I don't know how seriously to take bin Laden's timetable, based on last night's killing spree. Did he bluff and order the attack against my Cabinet or did someone else require their execution!"

James replied, "Frankly, the Caliph's demand for a one week investigation blindsided me! Bin Laden began the speech with such diplomacy only to end it with a deadline that could lead us all into war! Now, based on the overnight massacre, I wonder, has war already begun?"

"I've been talking with my intelligence agents here, and their sources say that bin Laden will use the Palestinian attack as grounds for invading Israel. Of course, he knows that the United States will fight by our side, and since you are somewhat implicated by our joint work on the SkyShark I missiles, bin Laden just might launch some terror attacks in America to keep you off balance."

"Sam, Abdul and I heard much the same report while we were over the Atlantic. As is the case here, our government and military are on the highest state of alert. What grabs my gut is that we still have no idea how those missiles were fired! What does your investigation show so far?"

The Prime Minister moaned and clasped his hands, "James, we are running up against a brick wall! We have searched in many ways for the orders to launch those missiles, and we have no record whatsoever that they ever were fired! The system says those four missiles remain in our arsenal! Someone had to physically inspect the silos to prove they had indeed been launched!"

"How can that be?"

"That's the question of the day, James! How can four of our own missiles be fired without our knowledge? We did not see them until they showed up on radar—old, outdated, radar!"

Stone faced, James asked, "Do you remain confident that this is not an inside job?"

James' questions began to feel more like an interrogation, but Sam answered without complaint. "We have traced every operations panel in the base and elsewhere that could have sent those missiles soaring. Each of those systems shows no commands given for firing the SSI's!"

"Could someone have hacked into the control system?"

"If someone did break all our codes and encryption, if someone managed to avoid setting off all our internal system alarms, then that someone is either one of the most brilliant terrorists we have ever seen or we have a traitor on the inside with the highest level of clearance, or both! Such a person is not on our list of the usual suspects!"

"Sam, given what you just said, do you think that this theoretical hacker could pull this same stunt again, this time with much deadlier weapons than the SSI missiles?"

"James, we must consider the worst case scenario. We must do everything in our power to prevent it, but when you don't know what you are looking for or really how to find it because of its sophistica-tion. . . well, let me put it bluntly. . . we fear that our entire nuclear arsenal may be at risk right now!"

"Which means a nuclear attack may be next for the DROP or Israel?"

"If that happens, both Israel and Palestine will be history in a single shot! A nuke will not respect our interwoven borders!"

"When ye proclaim your call to prayer, they take it (but) as mockery and sport; That is because they are a people without understanding."
Qur'an 5:58

CHAPTER 41

STILL DEAD MESSIAH. . .

S ol and Ahava drove into the modern city of Jerusalem for breakfast that Monday morning. They wanted to see how close they
could get to the *Kotel*, or what remained of it. The Orthodox leader
could not count the number of times he had prayed there at the Western
Wall or the Wailing Wall, as most tourists called it. For all his life, Sol
had asked *HaShem* for a third Temple! Now, the very foundation for
that Temple was gone! Sol wondered if the very foundation of his life
had been destroyed, as well.

The faithful Hasidic rabbi prayed three times daily—at the *Kotel* if
at all possible. Morning, noon, and night, he prayed with one *phylactery* on his forehead, another on his left hand and arm, and his white
and blue prayer shawl over his head.

A stickler for detail, Sol always made sure he wrapped the strap
of his *tefflin shel yad* around his arm seven times, before wrapping
it around his hand and fingers. Inside the small, black cubic leather
box of the *phylactery* was one compartment with one piece of parchment with four Torah passages written on it: Exodus 13:1–10, Exodus
13:11–16, Deuteronomy 6:4–9, and Deuteronomy 11:13–21. The
Deuteronomy passages were the same ones written on the small scroll
of the *mezuzah*.

Inside his *tefflin shel rosh*, the head *phylactery*, four compartments
held one piece of parchment each, with one of the Torah passages on
each piece. Sol could recite the words of those Scriptures in his sleep.

In Exodus 13:1-10, Sol knew Moses commanded the Jews to celebrate the Passover that saved their ancestors' firstborn sons, to dedicate their own firstborn sons to God, to remember God's rescue of His people from Egypt, and to always obey the Law of God. In verse nine, Moses told the Jews to use *tefflin* to help them never forget. *"And this shall serve you as a sign on your hand and as a reminder on your forehead—in order that the teaching of the LORD may be in your mouth—that with a mighty hand the LORD freed you from Egypt."*

Exodus 13:16 reiterated the point of using *tefflin* as a means of remembrance. *"And so it shall be a sign upon your hand and as a symbol on your forehead that with a mighty hand the LORD freed us from Egypt."*

Again, in Deuteronomy 6:8, the Jews were commanded to use *tefflin*. In regard to the Scriptures, the Jews were commanded to *"bind them as a sign on your hand and let them serve as a symbol on your forehead."*

Then, in Deuteronomy 11:18 of the Torah, the Lord Himself commanded Sol and all Jews to remember His words and deeds by wearing *tefflin*. *"Therefore, impress these My words upon your very heart. bind them as a sign on your hand and let them serve as a symbol on your forehead."*

So many powerful words lived in these four passages, yet Sol's favorite text in the Torah was the *Sh'ma*, found in Deuteronomy 6:4-5. *"Hear, O Israel! The LORD is our God, the LORD alone. You shall love the LORD your God with all your heart and with all your soul and with all your might."* Sol loved speaking those words in prayer to God each day.

Sol smiled as he recited the *Sh'ma* to himself. Despite the destruction in the Old City, he knew God still reigned. Even so, the aged rabbi asked himself, *"Where will I go to pray now? Should I continue to pray for a third Temple?"*

The old rabbi resumed eating. He and Ahava enjoyed their breakfast of lox and bagels on the veranda of the restaurant overlooking the modern city of Jerusalem. As he took another bite of his breakfast, Sol's thoughts abruptly shifted. Strangely enough, he recalled that he first tasted lox and bagels, not in Israel, but in New York. There, he and his father had visited one of the Chabad Lubavitch Centers in Brooklyn.

That very day, Sol met the Messiah—or at least the rabbi who claimed to be the Messiah! The Rebbe, the Yiddish corruption of rabbi, Menachem Mendel Schneerson allowed people to call him *Mashiach HaMelech*, King Messiah. At six years old, Little Sol was so excited to meet the rabbi, even though he did not fully understand the importance of the Messiah to Judaism at that point.

Sadly, only a few months after Sol met Rabbi Schneerson, he died at the age of 92. To this day, many of Chabad-Lubavitch Hasidim, Ultra Orthodox as most Gentiles call them, still believed Rabbi Schneerson was *Mashiach HaMelech,* even though he remained dead and buried in Queens. Sol always chuckled a bit when he thought about the supposed King being buried in Queens!

Y'shua, on the other hand, was supposedly alive and well—eternally! He too had died, but not from old age and natural causes like the Rebbe. If the writers of the New Testament had it right, Y'shua willingly allowed His crucifixion—sinless in Himself, but bearing the cumulative sin of mankind. Thus, as the grave held no power over Him, the New Testament proclaimed that Y'shua rose from the stone tomb three days later.

As Sol contemplated what he knew about Y'shua, his thoughts were ever so rudely interrupted by the Muslim call to prayer, the *adhan*. Sadly, he looked at Ahava, knowing their delectable breakfast was now ruined.

Sol had been forced to listen to what he considered to be the obnoxious *adhan* from the local minarets all his life. With the Sunni's five calls to prayer a day, Sol had suffered under the blaring minaret at the *Kotel* to the point where he often could no longer focus on his prayer to *HaShem*. Hence, Sol felt his disdain for the Muslim call to prayer was more than justified. In fact, he surmised that the volume and the dissonance of the singing were intentional.

He often thought, *"Could not the Muslims be like the Jews? We pray several times a day with no loud, offensive call to prayer being issued. At the very least, could not the Sunnis be like the Shiites, who only prayed three times a day? Of course now, for all practical purposes, the Shiites no longer exist, but the comparison remains valid!"*

Despite his resentment, Sol knew he should be grateful. He said to his already wilting wife on the warm morning, "Allah told Muhammad he wanted fifty calls to prayer each day, Ahava! Get this: Muhammad had a vision in which he winged his way to the so called seven levels of Heaven from the *Kotel*, which is why Jerusalem first became and remains the third holy site to Muslims to this day. But Muhammad never came here in real life. He only traveled to Jerusalem in his dreams!"

Ahava could not count how many times her aged husband had told her this story. Most unfortunately, on the other hand, Sol had no recollection whatsoever of telling her the tale even once! That being the case, as he spoke with such motivation to Ahava, the ever dutiful wife could not bear to stop him. She smiled as she endured her husband's oft told story once more.

Grinning, Sol said, "In his alleged vision, Muhammad flew here on a horse called al Buraq, the Lightening. Obviously, this was no ordinary horse! No, al Buraq had wings as well as a woman's head! Picture that, why don't you!

"Muhammad tied up his flying half-human-horse at the *Kotel* before he leapt into Paradise. There, in the seventh heaven, Allah told Muhammad he wanted Muslims to pray 50 times a day! When Muhammad came back down a few levels to report to Moses, he said that people did not have time to answer so many daily calls to prayer! Hence, Moses sent the prophet back to Allah to negotiate!

"When Muhammad returned to Moses, he said Allah had reduced the required number of daily calls to prayer to 45! As the fanciful tale goes, Moses kept sending the prophet back to Allah for repeated negotiations. After nine rounds of bartering, the great god of Islam finally settled for five calls to prayer a day!"

As he laughed, Sol asked, "Have you ever heard such a crazy story, Ahava?" While she wanted to answer, *"More times than I can ever recall,"* she instead just giggled and shook her head.

Next, Sol recalled another night—this one neither an alleged vision nor dream. Years ago, the rabbi and his wife had stayed overnight in the Old City for an important meeting with his fellow *Hassidim* the next day. "Ahava, do you remember when we were in Jerusalem and a minaret blasted out the *adhan* all night long—literally?" Ahava again nodded her head. He added, "We did not sleep a wink that night listening to that illegal noisemaker! The Muslims deliberately broke the law just to torment us!"

The anything but reticent rabbi told his now bored bride, "I do not envy the obedient Muslims who go through the rites of purification before prayers. While the Jewish purification ritual requires complete immersion of the body in the naturally flowing or living waters of a *mikvah*, the basic Islamic purification ritual is much more complicated. It is called the *wudhu*, and requires the cleansing of all exposed parts of the body."

As Ahava sleepily nodded her head once more, she knew what was coming. She muttered to herself, *"For the umpteenth time, he's going to take me through all the minute details of these rituals!"* While her pot-bellied husband was so proud of what he knew about Islam, Ahava thought, *"At this point in his life, does Sol not realize how uninterested I am and always have been about all things Muslim?"* She prayed, *"Adonai,* can you please restore your servant Sol's memory? If not, can you please erase mine?" With resolve, she braced herself for the dissertation that Sol was about to present.

Sol had observed the *wudhu* when a group of imams invited him and some other rabbis to learn about Muslim practices. In return, the rabbis demonstrated some of their rituals. The idea behind the exchange was for the two groups to learn to respect each others' traditions.

As the *adhan* continued to blare through their breakfast, Sol loudly told Ahava that the Muslims used a specific pattern of cleansing. "First, the Muslims wash their hands up to their wrists. Then, they rinse their mouths and snort water up their noses." Ahava grimaced at that requirement, as she subconsciously rubbed her nose.

"Next," Sol continued, "the Muslims scrub their faces from brow to chin and ear to ear. Following that, they scrub their arms up to their elbows. With a wet hand, they wipe their heads from the brow to the back of their necks. With their wet fingers, they clean their ears, inside and out, and then they wipe the rest of their necks. Finally, they wash their feet up to their ankles. Of course, the water for cleansing is always provided outside the mosque."

Ahava did not know which she disdained more, the blaring *adhan* or Sol's endless droning about Muslim rituals. But she could barely hear her husband. So, in kindness to him, she asked Sol to speak louder. To comply, Sol moved closer to her, sat on the edge of his chair, and yelled, "Get this: the ritual of the *wudhu* is not complete until the entire process is repeated two more times!

"My curiosity got the better of me years ago, which prompted me to further research Islam's purification rituals. To my great surprise, I found even more extensive and precise practices for certain circumstances."

Sol shouted, "This more involved and detailed ritual is called the *ghusl*, and should be observed upon conversion to Islam, before Friday Prayers and those for annual feasts, as well as for the *Hajj*—the Muslim pilgrimage to Mecca."

As the couple was in a public place, Sol refused to yell out the other situations and circumstance that required the more detailed cleansing of the *ghusl*. The more extensive ritual had to be performed following a discharge of semen, sexual activity, menstruation, childbirth (after the forty day waiting period), and death, unless the body is that of a *shahid*, a Muslim martyr.

"With the *ghusl*," Sol said with excitement, "Muslims first wash their right hands up to their wrists, making sure to clean between the fingers and that all areas of the hand are wet. This must be done three times. Then, Muslims repeat this procedure three times for the left hand."

Ahava did her absolute best to appear interested in Sol's monologue. She quickly raised her hand to cover her mouth as she could not stop a long yawn from rising to the surface.

Oblivious to her sleepiness, Sol marched on. "Next, Muslims thoroughly clean their, you know, private parts." Ahava blushed and giggled at her husband's awkwardness, especially as he had to talk so loudly to be heard. He then noted, "They follow that, uh, cleansing by rewashing their right hands and then their left hands, again for three times each. Obviously, the *ghusl* cannot be performed in a public place or outside the mosque!

"After this, Muslims cup their right hands, fill them with water, and lift the water to their mouths. Then, they take some of the water into their mouths, swirl it around, and then spit it out. The remaining water in their right hands is for their noses. They snort that water up the noses and then blow it out of their noses into their open left hands. This portion of the ritual is repeated three times as well." Ahava could only find the energy to shake her head in response.

"Likewise for the *ghusl*, the Muslims must wash their face three times, specifically from the hairline to the chin and from one ear to the other. A handful of water is used to wash their beards, and they must rub the water in and through their beards with their fingers.

"After their beards are clean, they wash their right arms from their fingertips up to and including their elbows, making sure that nothing is stuck to the skin that would prevent it being touched by water. After repeating this process three times, the Muslims repeat the same procedure for their left arms.

"Once their arms are washed, they pour water over their heads and down to the roots of their hair. They use their wet fingers to wash the roots. Of course, this process is also repeated three times." Ahava found it increasingly more difficult to hear Sol, so he talked even louder.

"Following this," Sol shouted, "they pour water down the right sides of their bodies, over the left sides, and then over their heads. Then, all remaining parts of the body are rubbed with the hands—three times.

"Finally, the Muslims take a step to the right or left of where the floor is wet. Three times, they wash their right feet up to their ankles. Then, they do the same for their left feet. For these purification rituals alone," Sol said, "I am most grateful that I am not a Muslim!" Ahava laughed. Then, she quickly added, "You should be a Christian, Sol! Christians only are baptized once in their lives!"

The two of them chuckled together, but Ahava's remark made Sol wonder, for the first time, if purification in the *mikvah* was not the precursor or prototype for baptism? Wasn't water baptism a symbolic physical act of the cleansing of the soul that was made spiritually pure by Y'shua's blood sacrifice? That would explain why followers of Y'shua only had to be baptized once, as Y'shua supposedly sacrificed Himself once for all people to atone for their sin.

Moreover, in that same moment, Sol realized why Christians say their names are written in the Lamb's Book of Life. They believe that Y'shua, as the Lamb of God, did indeed atone for their sins once and for all, not every year on the Day of Atonement—*Yom Kippur*. Thus, at the moment someone willingly repents and receives the Messiah's forgiveness, the Christian believes his name is written in the Lamb's Book of Life—forever.

However, the Jews—when they still had the Temple—believed that the sacrifice of the lamb on the Day of Atonement placed their names in the Book of Life for one year. Sol pondered, *"Was God's sinless Messiah, His Lamb, the ultimate atonement for sin? Did the annual sacrifice of a lamb on the Day of Atonement only point to the consummate sacrifice of the Lamb of God?"*

Sol shook his head to clear it of these thoughts. He wasn't ready to go there—at least not yet. He tried to refocus on what he was telling Ahava about Islam's purification rituals. Thus, Sol reported to her that he had discovered what the Muslims must say after the *wudhu* or the *ghusl*. "I bear witness that there is no god except Allah alone, with no partner or associate, and I bear witness that Muhammad is his slave and messenger. O Allah, make me one of those who repent and make me one of those who purify themselves."

"How can you remember those exact words?" Ahava asked in her loudest voice.

"I really don't know," Sol replied, with a puzzled look on his face. However, Sol thought, *"The Muslims cannot purify themselves—neither can the Jews. Only HaShem can purify a soul."*

Sol remembered that God had given Moses many requirements for cleansing, depending on the circumstance that caused the unclean state of a Jew. He recalled that touching a dead person would land a Jew outside the camp for a week. The person had to wash on the third and seventh days in order to be allowed to return to the camp. Even so, no Jew was ever required to go through anything like the *wudhu* five times a day, every day, except for the circumstances that required the more stringent regimen of the *ghusl*!

Sol further contemplated the Islamic purification rituals and asked himself, *"All that washing and scrubbing—for what? The uncleanness of man festers within his spirit, not on his flesh!"*

While Sol was lost in deep thought, his bride was lost in frustration. Ahava had stopped eating and had plugged her ears with her fingers. She decided that the *muezzin* who was singing the call to prayer that morning was tone deaf!

He cried:

Allahu akbar Allahu akbar
(Allah is supreme! Allah is supreme!)

Allahu akbar Allahu akbar
(Allah is supreme! Allah is supreme!)

ash-hadu al-laa ilaha illa-llah
(I testify that there is no god except Allah!)

ash-hadu al-laa ilaha illa-llah
(I testify that there is no god except Allah!)

ash-hadu anna muhammadan rasulu-llah
(I testify that Muhammad is the messenger of Allah!)

ash-hadu anna muhammadan rasulu-llah
(I testify that Muhammad is the messenger of Allah!)

hayya 'ala-s-salah hayya 'ala-s-salah
(Come to prayer! Come to prayer!)

hayya 'ala-l-falah hayya 'ala-l-falah
(Come to success! Come to success!)

Allahu akbar Allahu akbar
(Allah is supreme! Allah is supreme!)

ash-hadu anna muhammadan rasulu-llah
(I testify that there is no god except Allah!)

Rain or shine, five times a day—dawn, noon, afternoon, dusk, and evening—this call to prayer, the *adhan*, rang out for all to hear. Each time, it would be followed by a second call—the *iqama*—which was the call to line up for prayer. Then, the faithful Muslims would bow toward Mecca and pray to Allah.

Sol kept reminding himself that the minaret atop the *Kotel*, as well as the *Kotel* itself, no longer existed, along with everything else on and around the Temple Mount. Minarets and buildings could be reconstructed, but nothing could replace the history unveiled through archeology at the Temple Mount. A tear ran down Sol's cheek once more.

The Jews had lost the Temple itself almost exactly 2,000 years before. As he recalled, Y'shua had supposedly predicted its destruction. In 70 AD, the Roman Army fulfilled His prophecy on *Tisha B'Av*—the ninth day of the Hebrew month *Av*—which was the same day the first

Temple was destroyed in 586 BC. Now, the Temple Mount had been destroyed on *Tisha B'Av*. As he sat with Ahava for breakfast a day later, on *Eser b'Av*, the tenth of *Av*, Sol felt the same overwhelming grief and sorrow his people felt thousands of years ago. Not only had the Temple Mount been reduced to charred ruins, but all his hopes for the third Temple had likewise gone up in smoke.

"Why, Adonai, why?" Sol asked as he tried to hide his latest tears from Ahava.

Sol heard the words distinctly, despite the blaring cacophony from the minaret, "A third Temple shall be built, but the sacrifices made there shall be meaningless!"

"I tell you the truth, you will weep and mourn while the world rejoices. You will grieve, but your grief will turn to joy."
John 16:20

CHAPTER 42

SMOLDERING RUINS AND SEETHING ANGER...

*I*mam Zaahir met President Paulson, Vice President Abdullah, and Prime Minister Ben Baruch and their security details as they solemnly and silently walked through the rubble and ashes of what used to be the Temple Mount atop Mount Moriah, a most precious and sacred site to Jews, Christians, and Muslims alike.

For Jews, *the Har HaBayit*, Mount of the House of God, was hallowed ground as it was the location of the first and second Temples. There on Mount Moriah, all of Israel would gather to celebrate the High Holy Days before God. Faithful Jews revered those Temples as God's dwelling place among them.

For Christians, Mount Moriah was sacred because they believed the very Son of God gave His life there in ultimate sacrifice for sin. According to the testimony of His first disciples, Jesus submitted Himself to cruel crucifixion to redeem all who would believe in Him from the eternal consequences of their earthly transgressions. On that same mountain, His followers believed Jesus rose from the tomb, proving His power over death as well as guaranteeing them life everlasting with Him and His Father in Heaven.

For Islam, after Mecca and Medina, the Noble Sanctuary was the third most holy place. The Dome of the Rock, *Qubbat Al Sakhrah*, and the farthest mosque, the Al Aqsa Mosque, had stood on Mount Moriah. Somehow, Muhammad's night flight with his winged horse al-Buraq took him to the farthest mosque, even though no mosque was yet built on Mount Moriah at that time. The rock, *Al Sakhrah*, was revered by Muslims who said it was the center of the world and bore the footprint of Muhammad, made as he took flight to heaven to receive Allah's commandments. Islam also alleged the stone bore the handprint of the archangel Gabriel, who held the rock in place to keep it from following Muhammad. In response, the rock supposedly split.

However, this rock's significance predated Muhammad and his Qur'an. The Foundation Stone, *Even HaShetiya* as the Jews called it, was the center of Creation, the place from which *HaShem* created the rest of the world as well as where He gathered the dust of the earth to form Adam's body. Jewish tradition claimed Adam and his sons Cain and Abel made sacrifices on this stone. Likewise, Noah was said to have used it as an altar for burnt offerings. Furthermore, the Jews held that this was the same stone where Abraham almost sacrificed his son Isaac on Mount Moriah.

Likewise, *Even HaShetiya* was the threshing floor that David bought from Araunah. There, the Tanakh says the king made sacrifices to God to stop the plague sent in punishment for David's census of his soldiers. David's Son, King Solomon, built the Temple here, and *Kodesh HaKodashim*, the Holy of Holies, was built over the Foundation Stone. This Most Holy Place housed the Ark of the Covenant, and was that sacred space where God dwelled amidst His people, Israel.

Indeed, as the leaders stood in the destruction of this most sacred of sacred places, they were speechless, as they tried to grasp how much cherished and sacred history was now lost! Finally, Imam Zaahir stated the obvious when he said, "The Dome of the Rock, the Al Aqsa Mosque, and the underground Al Marawani Mosque have been vaporized!"

Looking for anything surrounding the Temple Mount as a point of reference, Sam sadly noted, "The Yeshivas, where the Orthodox men and children studied, are dust and ashes. The Hurva Synagogue is obliterated—again. It is as if these places never existed."

James, who had toured the Holy City during the negotiations of the treaty between Israel and the DROP, commented on the great historical losses, saying, "All the archeological finds in the Old City and the City of David that were painstakingly brought to life are now lost forever in the annihilation of the missile blasts."

Abdul, who had visited the Al Aqsa Mosque and the Dome of the Rock as a child, said nothing about the loss of those structures. Instead, he asked Sam, "Are we not standing over the most holy site for the Jews?" Addar wondered why Abdul would even think to ask such a question.

Sam, somewhat caught off guard, replied, "Under this rubble are the remains of the Temple, destroyed by Rome in the first century. Behind the veil in the Holy Place of that Temple was the Holy of Holies, where the High Priest went once a year with the blood of the sacrificed lamb to atone for Israel's sin. Yes, that place is the Jews most holy site."

Abdul then asked, "Don't the Christians believe that the empty tomb of God's Son is near here? Has it been destroyed also?"

Addar, wanting to silence Abdul, decided to answer him. "Christian tradition says the Church of the Holy Sepulcher in the Christian Quarter was built over Jesus' tomb. Nonetheless, others say that grave was outside the Old City walls in a garden not far from the Muslim Quarter. Regardless, both places were consumed in the missile strikes. Still, I am certain that the myth of Jesus' crucifixion and resurrection will live on in the hearts of fools and the minds of the weak." Addar immediately realized his comments were too candid, too revealing of his true thoughts.

In the awkward moments that followed, Abdul considered the dangerous state of Addar's soul. He silently prayed, "Isa, Addar is so far from You! He is consumed with hatred, even as he supposedly calls for peace with his enemies. He knows nothing of real peace—of Your peace. If I can help him see the reality of You, please, show me how."

Meanwhile, the imam pondered what he considered to be Abdul's quite bizarre behavior. *"What in the world has happened to him? Since when has he known anything about the fallacies of Christianity? Why is asking such stupid questions?"*

In efforts to move beyond his curt remarks about Christians, the imam noted, "As the smoke continues to rise over the remains of the ancient and more modern structures alike, many if not most of the streets of East Jerusalem are either destroyed or shut down. Either way, it is a landscape of emptiness." Gazing toward the evening sun, Addar seemed to be almost smiling as he said, "The extent of the devastation seems endless."

Then, suddenly, the imam turned toward James, Abdul, and Sam as he offered what Abdul saw as a rehearsed, contrived call for peace. "Gentlemen! We have a choice this day. We can either see the mass destruction as the end or as a new beginning. Jews, Christians, and Muslims alike have suffered great loss here. We can walk away and go to war over what happened, or we can stand fast here, amidst the desolation, and start anew with a joint will to not only rebuild what we can of what has been lost, but to also construct new and strong relationships between our nations. As I see it, none of us has the upper hand on the claim of owning this hallowed and now desecrated piece of land."

James replied, "We have lost more than buildings, ancient and new, in this destruction. Many, many lives have been needlessly taken!"

Sam added, "Just last night, my Cabinet—my friends and patriots—lost their lives to the blade of a machete! Do you believe I can do anything to prevent Israel from going to war now?"

Gathering the President, then the Prime Minister, and finally the imam closer to him, the Vice President said, "None of us can undo the tragic events of yesterday and last night. Even so, before we do anything in response to those horrible actions, should we not pray? How will we know if we should go the way of war or find the path of peace without God's guidance and strength?"

James and Addar were obviously stunned by Abdul's poignant remarks. More astonishment followed, as the Vice President reached for the hands of James and Sam who were standing to either side of him, "Please allow me to pray for us and the people of our nations."

Abdul then looked to Addar and asked him, "Won't you join hands with us?" Still stunned, the imam stood motionless. He had not expected a word from Abdul this evening, much less a call for prayer. When he realized he could not refuse Abdul's invitation, the imam, reluctantly, clumsily, reached for and grasped the hands of Sam and James.

Infuriated, Addar then watched as Abdul closed his eyes and said, "Isa, Y'shua, Jesus, we are but humbled, human souls before You this day. The devastation that surrounds us is a reflection of the destruction within our souls when we attempt to direct our lives instead of following Your lead. We must first have peace, Your peace, within each of us before we can ever hope to have peace, Your peace, in and between our nations, our peoples. The titles we have and the offices we hold bear no meaning or power outside Your plans, Your will.

"In these quiet moments in the midst of horrendous circumstances, take our eyes and thoughts off of what we see and turn them to what we cannot see: Your very presence here with us. Which way do we and our peoples turn from this deadly disaster? Should we not first turn to You, as You are not surprised, shocked, or overwhelmed by what has happened, but are the only One who can offer us clear guidance in regard to our first steps away from these gruesome events?

"Are we to be guided by the dark forces of hate, anger, and revenge, or can we dare to follow You in love, forgiveness, and redemption? Are we going to further the violence and proceed to war or are we going to turn to restoration and proceed to peace?

"Justice and vengeance as well as mercy and grace are in Your Hands. Only You can bring new life out of the stench and horror of death! Only You can redeem such evil events for the good of all! If we do not seek You, if we do not follow You, if we do not act with Your strength and wisdom, what hope do we have? What hope do the nations and citizens of this world have?"

Despite the genuine resolve and intent of Abdul's heartfelt prayer, his words brought nothing but swirling rage to Addar's haggard, hollowed, and hardened soul!

"O my people! Enter the holy land which Allah hath assigned unto you, and turn not back ignominiously, for then will ye be overthrown, to your own ruin."
Qur'an 5:21

CHAPTER 43

INNER AND OUTER DESTRUCTION. . .

*A*top the tower of the Hebrew University on *Har HaTsofim*, Mount Scopus, Sol and Ahava gazed at what were once East Jerusalem and the Temple Mount. The destruction almost reached the foot of Mount Scopus. The couple could not get any closer to the remains of the *Kotel* than this, as police cordoned off the devastated area.

The early reports were that thousands of civilians, both Palestinians and Israelis, as well as foreign tourists, had died in the missile attack. From where he and Ahava stood, Sol thought the death toll would be much higher—in the tens of thousands!

Ahava again asked, "Who would do such a thing as this? Do we have that much hatred in our hearts for the Palestinians that we would murder innocent citizens—many of our own, not only theirs? Would such hatred prompt us to destroy their places of worship and, in the process, our own *Kotel* and all that surrounded it? But if Israel, the sworn enemy of the Palestinians just seven months ago, did not cause this carnage, who did?"

Sol had no answer. None of the facts added up. "Do you think the Prime Minister took it on himself to do this? Maybe he regretted the peace treaty with the Palestinians, thinking Israel gave away too much land and too much of Jerusalem?"

Before Ahava could reply, Sol answered his own question. "Still, such a move would only cause Sam to be thrown out of office and drag Israel into war. He is no fool!"

"If not him, then who and why, Sol?"

"I don't know! Even so, the Caliph is giving Israel and the U.S. one week to find the answer, and we must pray that they do, or all of Jerusalem, all of The Land itself, may look like what we see right now!"

That thought made Ahava hold onto her husband. "Sol, don't say such things! Don't even think them! We have seen so many wars in our lifetimes. Israel always came out stronger, better! We must have faith!"

"In whom?" Sol said, indicating the spiritual upheaval that continued to churn within him. "Do I pray to *HaShem* asking Him to drive the Palestinians out of the Land promised to the Jews, or do I pray to His Son who says to pray for the Palestinians' salvation?"

Ahava just stared at her husband as he stared at the desolation below. She needed him to be strong in this crisis, but the turmoil within him was sapping all his strength. Suddenly inspired, she asked her long-white-bearded husband, "Do not the Messianics say that *HaShem* and Y'shua are one?"

Sol took his eyes off the rubble of the Temple Mount and turned to Ahava. "What point are you trying to make?" he asked.

"If they are one, then pray to both of them. Whatever answer is laid on your heart will tell you whether *HaShem* has a Son who is our Messiah!"

In silence, Sol debated the proposal presented by his wife of six and a half decades. Did Sol have the courage to make such a prayer? Was he ready for the answer, no matter whether it came from Father or Son? In regard to Y'shua, Sol had persecuted His followers by ostracizing and publicly humiliating them. He had turned them over to authorities who had arrested, jailed, and deported them. In regard to *HaShem*, Sol had helped to give away land that God said belonged to Him alone. The rabbi knew he was not supposed to advocate surrender of any of the Land but did so for the prospect of peace—peace that now seemed like such a foolish dream—or better yet, a bloodcurdling nightmare!

Ahava saw the extreme distant look in Sol's dark eyes. "My husband, in all our years together, you have always been so sure of yourself, so sure of your God! It breaks my heart to see so much doubt and confusion in your eyes!" She pulled Sol's face toward her own. "This is not a time for doubt and confusion within you, Sol! You must be sure of yourself, and to be sure of yourself, you must be sure about God! Else you will be of no use to yourself, me or our people in this crisis that surrounds us!"

Sol knew Ahava was right, but what would it take for him to be sure? Instinctively, he fell to his aged, aching knees to pray.

"Jesus knew their thoughts and said to them, 'Every kingdom divided against itself will be ruined, and every city or household divided against itself will not stand.'"
Matthew 12:25

CHAPTER 44

THE DEVIL IS IN THE DETAILS...

*A*s he drove, Addar fumed over Abdul's prayer—both the words he chose and to whom he chose to say them! "We must first have peace?" "Are we going to further the violence and proceed to war or are we going to turn to restoration and proceed to peace?" "Justice and vengeance as well as mercy and grace are in Your Hands?"

Despite his furious reaction to the Abdul's prayer atop the ruins, Addar wondered if he could use some of the words of the prayer for his own purposes. The more he considered the possibilities, the more Addar realized that Abdul's words would fit perfectly into the imam's plans—as though a gift from Allah came down from paradise right into his lap!

The irreverent imam raced through empty streets to his new temporary office, now that his old workplace was destroyed. He had phone calls to make, details to work out, and people to coordinate before noon prayers. He did not want to miss the special call to prayer issued by the Caliph.

"Everything seems to be going as planned," he thought, "if not even better!" If I were to pray, I would say, "Thank you, Allah, Most Gracious, Most Merciful! Please help me do what I must to complete your will: A true peace, like none this world has ever known—a Muslim peace! A worldwide Muslim Caliphate!" Addar's grin exuded evil.

Arriving at the small building, Addar ran inside. "Israel News," he said to the holovision. There before his eyes were the severed heads of the Prime Minister's Cabinet, even more macabre as their lifeless eyes peered into the darkness of the night. Would this beheading be the final straw with Israel, or would the Prime Minister take one more chance at peace?

The pensive Muslim cleric listened to the latest report. With the Prime Minister's residence behind him in the distance, the journalist said, "As of this hour, neither the Brotherhood nor any other group or individual has claimed responsibility for the decapitation of the Prime Minister's Cabinet.

"Despite not knowing who the killer or killers might be, one fact remains certain. One member of the Cabinet yet lives! In a case of deadly misidentification, apparently the murderers nabbed and beheaded the wrong man. We interviewed the sole survivor of last night's massacre just a few moments ago."

"What?" Addar said to himself. *"One of the ministers lives?"*

"Homefront Defense Minister Noah Ben Eleazar feels that God has spared his life for a reason."

Both glad to be alive as well as grieved by the death of his colleagues, Ben Eleazar poignantly said, "I have been pressing the Prime Minister and my fellow Cabinet ministers for increased security! We had managed to tap into the Brotherhood's secure communication lines, and we knew that we—the Prime Minister and his Cabinet—had a death sentence hanging over our heads! But no one took the threats seriously! Defense Minister Zeev Tzion even made light of the intelligence, saying that it was just a distraction to divert our attention away from the real threat!"

"And what did the Defense Minister believe was the true threat?"

"I am not at liberty to discuss that particular point in detail, given that I have yet to speak with the Prime Minister. But let me say this. If the threat Zeev perceived had become reality, you and I would not be having this discussion because we would not be here—no Israelis would be here! All I know is that *Yamam*, Israel's elite commando task force for counter-terrorism, is on highest alert!"

Addar scratched the back of his head. He spoke aloud to the holovision images. *"Hmm. Has the Caliph been persuaded to launch Goliath? If so, then my time is shorter than I thought! But one would think that bin Laden would have consulted the General before moving ahead. Perhaps the Caliph is suspicious. If so, where does that leave me and my hopes?"*

The morning was slipping away from the imam. Addar knew he had to move quickly. He picked up his secure line, wondering just how secure it was now. Was the Mossad listening in on his calls, too? Regardless, he had no other means of communication at his fingertips.

Addar called his contact at the airport. "Can you confirm the passengers I asked about earlier are indeed in flight?" the imam asked.

"Yes. They are on board and will arrive shortly after 7:00 this evening."

"Great! The General said to confirm that a car will meet them. He had asked me to pick them up, which will not be possible, given my schedule."

The imam then called the escort service to arrange the pick-up. "Make sure you go in the terminal with their name on the sign. Else they will wander around the airport, until they secure their own transportation—and they do not know where they are going."

"I will meet them inside the airport!"

"Wonderful! They will be tired—most likely hungry too. The last meal on this flight is not very filling."

"I will take care of the details."

"After they eat, bring them straight to me at the new location!"

"I have the address."

"Make sure no one else does!"

"If Allah so willed, He could make you all one People: But He leaves straying whom He pleases, and He guides whom He pleases: But ye shall certainly be called to account for all your actions."
Qur'an 16:93

CHAPTER 45

FOR ALLAH AND FOR FAMILY. . .

*I*brahim Shajee walked out the front door of his home in Jericho. His destination was the Nabi Musa Mosque, built on the site where Muslims believe Moses was buried, even though, according to the Jewish Scripture, Moses died outside the Promised Land and God buried him on a Moabite mountain by God Himself.

Sorrow filled Ibrahim's heart as he made his way to the special Monday noon prayers the Caliph had proclaimed. When he had made two steps down the road, his holophone sounded. He had received a video from his son. *"What is my worthless vagabond up to now? When he is here, all he does is shame his family by lying around the house by day and drinking himself into a stupor by night!"*

The message with the holographic video said "For the entire family to see and celebrate—now!" *"Well,"* Ibrahim moaned, *"does my missing son actually have a job?"*

As he turned around and reentered his home, Ibrahim was greeted by his youngest daughter who ran into her father's arms. "*Ab!* I am so glad you decided to stay home! Will you play with me?"

Ibrahim smiled at Tahera who was his pride and joy. "A little later, child, your mother, you, your sisters, and I must watch something first. Is your brother here?"

"No, *Ab, Umm* says he did not come home this morning either."

"Out being a fool all night long again," Ibrahim mumbled.

He pulled the crumpled paper from his shirt pocket—the paper he had found in the wastebasket in his son's Jahm's room. There in the hallway, Ibrahim read the words once more, words that he did not fully understand.

I open the window.
The sand fox howls and laughs in the desert dungeon's darkness,
mocking my perpetual pain.
The barren, silhouetted trees vainly reach for the stars in the dim light
of the crescent moon.
Bittersweet memories and dashed dreams haunt my fractured thoughts.
On the warm side of cool, rest runs away from my anxious, angry mind.

I open the window.
The fuming cars blow their insulting horns,
as the traffic lights flash in distress.
The crowded city rebels against the tyranny of time.
Dreaded souls curse the damned, monotonous cycles
of their feeble and frustrated days.
Their twisted thoughts turn to heated hatred and raging revenge
for the endless list of wrongs they have suffered.

I open the window.
Contrived smiles on decaying faces mask the silent suffering
of failed and forlorn lives.
The people speak empty pleasantries to the familiar strangers
who deny the agony that drives their pathetic existence.
Their vacant eyes look for some unsuspecting soul
upon whom they can pour out their fiery vengeance
so peace can finally reign.

I open the window.
The roar of the sea waves crashes on my deaf ears,
The tide incessantly, meaninglessly rolls to and from the shattered shore.
The bloodied beach cries out in lifeless loneliness
to a sky veiled and grieving.
No one offers even the slightest pretense of comfort or
empathy
to the savaged rocks and sands.

I open the door.
The ubiquitous malaise of morning portends the new
opportunity
to crash and burn once more.
Undefined, cookie-cutter days filled with wasted breath
roll off the uncalibrated assembly line.
The tortured torments of hell itself offer refreshing relief.

I open the door.
I face a wearied world that rebelliously refuses to respect or
remember me, but only offers its disregard and deceit.
My many mistakes loom large and overshadow me.
My callous crimes never leave me.
My chosen vocation evaporates before my eyes.
The load of life crushes down and grinds my guilty spirit
into the rut that has no end.

I open the door.
My mind wrestles with more excuses for my pathetic
performance.
Love is a word foreign and without place in my staid world of
self-pity.
The paltry possibilities for fulfillment have been long ago
swept away
like the faint clouds of morning.
Grave are my thoughts but I dare not enact them,
as I am forever bound by my uncompromising cowardice.

I close the door.
I close the window.
Darkness surrounds me.
Evil encompasses me.
Rage races around me.

My only friend, my vociferous pen,
pours out my fears and failures onto the all consuming paper.

The time has come.

Ibrahim had not seen Jahm since finding his cryptic message weeks ago. What would his wandering son have to say on the video?

Walking into the kitchen, the stoic father greeted his wife Mufiah with a kiss, and then asked her to come into the main room of the house with their three daughters. As they sat down, Ibrahim said to his daughters, "Your brother sent a video to my holophone. He wants us all to see it. I will run it through the HV3D so we can watch it together."

After Ibrahim entered the codes, he remained standing as he watched his only son's image slowly appear. The family had no idea where the video was made, as the background was dark. "I scheduled this video to be sent to you just before noon time, when I knew you would all be home," Jahm began. "You probably think I was out drinking again last night, *Ab*. To your surprise, I haven't been drunk in a long time. I realize that you may find that hard to believe."

Ibrahim chuckled, as he turned away from Jahm's image to gaze out the window, for he truly could not accept his imbibing son's claim at face value.

"Actually, while I have been gone, I have been in training for many weeks with the Brotherhood!" Ibrahim quickly turned back to the screen, as the rest of the family sat straight up, except for Mufiah who walked over to her husband at the window. "As I grew up, I knew how disappointed you were with me in the jihad camps. I had no heart for violence and murder.

"Now the past is the past, and as you hoped and prayed, *Ab*, I am now a man. I have found my passion and my hatred. I have found my consuming desire to fight and die in battle!"

Mufiah clung tightly to Ibrahim's arm, almost cutting off his flow of blood. However, Ibrahim was so involved in his son's words that he did not even notice the pain.

"I have been waging jihad on the Great Satan and the Little Satan. I am sending you this video now, before the next events occur, so you will know it was me who brought about such praise and victory for Allah! Be watching and listening this evening at about 8:00. All the Muslim satellite channels will bring it to you live!

"Finally, *Ab*, you now have reason to be proud of your only son! I gave up all my vile habits for which you have beaten me on more than one occasion. I have made myself a pure vessel for Allah. I now have all the eternal rewards of one who dies in jihad for Allah! Soon, you will see the proof! When you do, please celebrate! I will be forever enjoying the delights Allah has prepared for me!

"*Umm*, I hope you too will be proud of your only son. Tell my sisters of my greatness throughout their lives that they may admire their brother who gave his life in noble jihad for Allah!

"Death to the infidels! Death to those who kill the faithful! Death to all who oppose Allah! Death to me in jihad for Allah's glory! My greatest desire is to honor you, my family, and my god, Allah, with my death in his great cause! As much as Allah celebrates the deaths of worthless infidels, he rejoices even more in the death of his prized *shahids*!"

Jahm's image faded into the darkness, as Mufiah wept and begged of Ibrahim, "What has he done? What has my little boy done?"

Ibrahim's face was like a stone, his eyes fixed. "Our son is no longer your little boy! He has become a man, a *shahid*!"

"But you will receive power when the Holy Spirit comes on you; and you will be My witnesses in Jerusalem, and in all Judea and Samaria, and to the ends of the earth."
Acts 1:8

CHAPTER 46

THE CRY HEARD ROUND THE WORLD. . .

*T*he *muezzins* sang out from minarets all across Babylon and Islamic areas of the other countries, including vast areas of the United States. The singers called their fellow Muslims to a special time of prayer in the wake of the Palestinian tragedy.

In the DROP, Imam Zaahir arrived at the Sheikh Jarrah Mosque, named for a Muslim doctor from the twelfth century. The mosque suffered only minor damage from the flying rubble of the missile attacks. That mosque, like all others throughout Palestine, brimmed with Muslims to the point that the streets outside similarly overflowed with worshipers of Allah.

As always, the faithful began by reciting the prayer from the first chapter of the Qur'an. Many Muslims in various regions of the earth knew not what they were saying, as they recited the prayer in Arabic, a language foreign to them. As only one out of every 40 Muslims in the world actually lived in the Middle East, Muslims around the globe spoke many diverse languages.

No matter their location in the world, as the faithful bowed before Allah to pray, they would repeat these words of prayer seventeen times today—and every day.

In the name of Allah, Most Gracious, Most Merciful.
Praise be to Allah, the Cherisher and Sustainer of the Worlds:
Most Gracious, Most Merciful;
Master of the Day of Judgment.
Thee do we worship, and Thine aid we seek.
Show us the straight way,
the way of those on whom Thou has bestowed Thy Grace,
those whose (portion) is not wrath and who go not astray.

Instead of the local imams speaking from the *minbar* or pulpit after the prayers in each mosque, a special recorded *khutab* or sermon was beamed to all Muslims in their local languages who were gathered in Allah's name on every continent. There in the DROP, Addar wanted to hear every word.

The words rang out loudly and clearly for all of Islam's faithful to hear. "The Great Satan and the Little Satan have plotted together against us once more, but we know that Allah plots best of all! As a Caliph once ruled over Israel, so a Caliph will once more rule over the Little Satan—and the Great Satan, as well!"

Shouts of "*Allahu Akbar!* There is no god but Allah!" thundered through the Sheikh Jarah Mosque and out into the streets! Addar found it difficult to hear what was being said.

"Allah and Islam are not seeking to be tolerated by the two Satans. They do not seek to cooperate with the vilest civilizations that ever existed! Quite the opposite, Allah and Islam seek dominance and victory over the Satans! Terror is when Muslims kill Muslims. Justice is when Muslims kill infidels!"

More shouts of "*Allahu Akbar!*" resounded in mosques in every nation as the faithful and the fearless anticipated what would be said next.

"'Submit to Allah or die in your defiance,' we say to the plagued Zionist Regime and the leprous United States! The flag of Islam will fly over all Jerusalem and Washington D.C.! You cannot strike at Allah without incurring his mighty wrath!"

Again, shouts of praise to the god of Islam reverberated in every land.

"Sharia will be the law of the corrupt nations of the Jews and the Christians! Isa said in Qur'an 19:30, '. . . *I am indeed a servant of*

Allah; He hath given me revelation and made me a prophet.' Isa will return to condemn those who claimed that he was the son of Allah as well as those who tried but failed to crucify him! The Christians and Jews will be condemned to the eternal punishment Allah has prepared for them, for he created them to be infidels, and they can do nothing to change their fate. But we can hasten the day that both the vile Jews and repugnant Christians enter their eternal punishment and pain. We can start that pain and punishment in this world, as Allah the Just says we must!

"Allow me to address the heinous crimes of yesterday. The conspiracy of the swine Jews and blasphemous Christians will not stand! We do not believe that either is innocent in the atrocities in Palestine! The weapons were jointly forged and jointly launched against the innocents of Islam!

"The obstinate Jews and arrogant Christians left standing after our victorious battle will be enslaved to Allah and his faithful followers! We call on the Muslims within the borders of the United States and Israel to rise up and kill your captors! You are not bound by their laws, but only by the Sharia! You are not citizens of those infidel countries, but of the Caliphate! You are commanded by Allah to slaughter the unbelievers! Slit their throats!"

Thunderous cries and applause rose from every mosque around the world! Ecstatic dancing filled the streets! Handheld weapons blasted toward the sky in celebration.

"Your brothers in other nations will rise to assist you in ridding your lands of the fools who believe in any god but Allah, the idiots who worship dead idols, as well as the imbeciles who say there is no god! Together we will finally erase Israel from the maps of the world! We will take the land promised to us by Allah!

"The sewage of the world—the Jews—killed the prophets of our gracious and merciful god! These infidel apes have defiled the land! They and the noxious Christians have destroyed the *waqf* of the Noble Sanctuary!

"The forever lying Jews perverted the holy words of Allah! The cursed and covenant-breaking Hebrews are perpetual liars and thieves who have never been trusted! We will purge their toxic venom from the earth! The only good Jew is a dead Jew!

"Likewise, brothers, we will finally eradicate all memories of the cursed and treacherous Christians of the United States—as well as the Jews that live among them— and their onerous hatred of Allah! Although the Christians seem to be dying out of their own accord, we will accelerate the process! This is our duty—the very command of Allah! Their just reward has long been declared and is long overdue! Over the centuries, the putrid Christians have invaded our lands, killed our fathers, raped our mothers, and perverted our children! They deserve the same treatment in return—and so it shall be done!

"We will show no mercy! These bellicose regimes must not be allowed to remain! They are like puss filled sores that must be drained. Their day of doom has arrived! The greedy Zionists and the Christian Imperialists will no longer manifest Satan in this world! In truth, the Jews and Christians are walking, decaying corpses, who are about to meet their final destruction when we send them all into the prison which will never be unlocked! Their evil regimes will no longer plague the holy ones of Allah. The payment for their hatred of Allah and his people will be their ultimate annihilation!"

Frenzied screams and shouts drowned out the next round of vicious remarks that spewed from the invisible imam's tongue.

"In Palestine alone, more than two million Muslims have traded life for death by converting to the evil cult of the Christians! We must reclaim these onetime brothers and free them from the chains of false religion! If they refuse, then they too deem themselves both hypocrites and infidels, and will stand condemned before Allah and dead before his jihadists! They deserve the laborious agony of a slow, bloody release from this world!

"Americans can expect the same as the prophecy of Imam Anjem Choudary made on October 5, 2010 will soon be fulfilled! 'The flag of Islam will fly over the White House!' Demons have deceived the Americans into a false state of security. But the United States will no longer be a superpower! Instead, the sacred *Kabba* will be the center of all power in this world! The decrepit Christians, Jews, agnostics, atheists, and all pagans of the United States will serve Allah and his followers until their final, ghastly, putrid breath!

"Islam demands one Caliphate to rule the world. We cannot just settle for a portion of the earth, for Allah commands us to take it in its entirety! We must ensure that no one and nothing stands in the way of proclaiming the reign of Allah in every country, state, and city on this planet. Through divine order and by divine power, we will blaze across every nation and become the true guardians of this planet! Such is the destiny of Islam!

"Now is the moment for meeting our destiny! Generations before us have paved the way for our ultimate climax of ruling the world! Step by step, year by year, decade by decade, we have infiltrated the governments, societies, cultures, and economies of every infidel nation! Now is the time to claim those countries that are left for us to harvest! They have failed and will utterly fail to stop us!

"As the United States of America will fall, so will the other nations of North, South, and Central America! With the Great Satan's defeat, they will fall in fear of Allah! Soon, both East and West will be under Islam and Sharia!

"Apparently, the American President is too imbecilic to realize or admit that China, North Korea, and Japan already belong to Allah! Let him waste what little of his life remains trying to change the unchangeable! Soon, this mental midget, this shell of a man who doesn't know whether god exists or not will wonder no more! He will see Allah himself just before he spends eternity in the fires that never die!

"At the dawn of this century, the 9/11 2001 Muslim victory in the U.S. was a celebration of the jihad of the 'Magnificent 19!' The 3/11 2004 attack was glorious conquest for Allah in Spain! The 7/7 2005 Muslim victory in London was the great jihad of the 'Fantastic Four!' And the 9/11 2012 slaughter of Americans in Libya told the world that Allah's jihadists were able to strike at will! These were not separate attacks but varied fronts in one war: global jihad! Now, as we near the end of the century, we are ready to claim and celebrate victory for Allah through the Brotherhood's ultimate jihad in the United States and Israel!

"The stakes have never been higher. The slaughter will never be greater!"

A long pause followed so that the delirious Muslims around the world would not miss the imam's next phase of his venomous speech.

"Christians of Evil America, look at what was once called Europe! Islam conquered the former great lands of Christendom without firing a shot! Only after Allah claimed the land did foolish and ill-fated rebellions erupt! The resistance was laughable, and the same fate awaits the Great Satan and his minions! Allah laughed as we slew the weak rebels in London, as we cut off the heads of the rebels in Paris, and as we burned alive those who dared to rise up against Allah in Berlin!

"The one true god is already laughing about the feeble United States and it new North, Central, and South American allies. Allah will laugh until every last non-believer in those lands is rotting in infinite agony! Then, those of us who worship the one and only god of time and eternity will take up his laughter without end!

"We do not need manufactured weapons of mass destruction! The 40-million strong Brotherhood is Allah's weapon of mass destruction! If you choose to fight instead of surrender, each of you will die a thousand deaths at the hand of the *mujahedeen*—the jihadists of Allah!"

More boisterous cheering and praise of Allah arose around the world—especially in the mosques of the United States and Israel! The Ground Zero Mosque in New York City echoed with so much noise that the vast majority of the imam's sermon was unheard!

"Buckingham Palace is now a Holy Mosque! The White House will soon be cleansed and dedicated to the worship of Allah as well! The Israel Knesset will also become a mosque where Allah is praised! Such mosques proclaim Allah's victory over the lands that once were in the hands of infidels!

"As the vile Zionists and the evil Americans destroyed our holy places and government buildings, so we will set fire to every synagogue and every church in their lands whether those decrepit places of false worship are empty or full of infidels.

"Likewise, we will bring down to dust the great monuments to Washington, Lincoln, Jefferson, Kennedy, Reagan, and Cantor, as well as all shrines to a Holocaust that never happened and a Jewish god that never existed!

"No longer will menorahs and crosses defile the lands promised to the followers of Islam by Allah himself! Our determination to die in Allah's jihad is greater than the Jews and Christians will to live!

"The sloth-filled Vatican no longer stands! The ruins of St. Peter's Basilica are buried beneath the largest mosque in Europe! Likewise, the Great Synagogue, the Dohány Street Synagogue in Hungary, is rubble underneath The Great Mosque of Budapest!

"Soon, the Temple Emanu-El of New York and the Washington National Cathedral in the United States will either be transformed into mosques or be destroyed so mosques to the true god Allah can rise over their dust and ashes!

"In Jerusalem, the Belz Great Synagogue with it large wooden ark will soon be nothing more than pebbles and splinters underneath a grand and glorious mosque, while the Church of the Annunciation in Nazareth, where blinded Muslims have been lured into worshiping Isa as Allah's son, will soon be razed and be the site of a towering mosque where our brothers and sisters can once again worship the one and only god of the Qur'an!

"Because of their worship of false gods, the wrath of Allah has fallen on the Jews and Christians! Satan's name is 'Jew!' Satan's name is 'Christian!' Jews and Christians are but beasts disguised as humans! The time has come for us to take what is ours from the hands of these wild brutes, from the grasp of the Satans, from the clutches of the ignominious Jews and from the claws of the bloodthirsty American crusaders!

"The U.S. can no longer be allowed to dominate Muslims abroad or within its own borders. If the U.S. attacks one Muslim, the Great Satan has attacked us all! If the U.S. attacks just one Muslim, the nation of infidels has attacked Allah himself! Allah commands us to destroy both the United States and Israel!

"Brothers, the lewd and lascivious nation of the Jews will soon be overrun by Islamic jihad! The foul stench of Israel will be no more, and 'The Land' will finally be part of Babylon—as Allah ordained! We will complete the work Hitler left unfinished! Allah will accomplish what no other human army can! We will butcher the Jewish pigs who mock our god and his people! The Jews will be slaughtered as pigs are butchered. We will relieve the apes of their furry heads for their disdain of the sacred Sharia!

"To be *shahids*, martyrs, in the fight does not frighten us, but assures us that we have indeed pleased Allah and will rest forever in his Garden Paradise, with rivers flowing beneath and eternal virgins at our beck and call! We will gladly and joyfully die to rid the world of the Jewish and Christian contagions!

"Anyone left standing who wonders if there is a god, refuses to believe there is a god, or worships anything or anyone other than the one god will join the Jews and Christians in the never ending flames prepared for them! They can launch their conspiracy to overthrow the single, reigning deity of Islam as they wile away eternity in absolute agony!

"Israel, that slime of a nation, will soon be forever forgotten! We will not miss any of the foul smelling, foul plotting Jews! Death in the most horrible fashion to the 'chosen people'—chosen to die in the agonizing manner possible!

"But now, brothers, the United States of America is about to fall before the armies of Allah! Its only religion shall be the only true religion: Islam! Its new constitution will be the Qur'an! Its law will be the Sharia! The nation shall be of the Muslims, by the Muslims, and for the Muslims—so help me Allah!

"Shall we rename that land of the free and home of the brave Muslims the United States of Islamerica?"

"None of Our revelations do We abrogate or cause to be forgotten, but We substitute something better or similar: Knowest thou not that Allah hath power over all things?"
Qur'an 2:106

CHAPTER 47

THE RISKS OF IGNORANCE AND DENIAL...

*T*he President shouted as he paced around the living quarters of their secret and secure location. "Islamerica?" "The White House will be a mosque?" "The flag of Islam will fly over it?" "The constitution will be the Qur'an?" "The law will be the Sharia?" "The nation will be of the Muslims, by the Muslims, and for the Muslims?" By means of an intercepted transmission, he and the Vice President had listened to the call to arms that was delivered to Muslims all over the world.

"Abdul, what happened to the Caliph's plan to give us a week to prove that the U.S. and Israel had nothing to do with missile attack on The DROP?" Why would bin Laden say one thing and this imam another?"

The Vice President rose to his feet to explain. "James, deceit, the *taqiyya* doctrine, is the way of Islam. A Muslim is not bound by any treaty with infidels or any word spoken to infidels. As the Qur'an regards Jews and Christians as pigs and perpetual liars, you should not expect any consistency from Islam's leaders. They want to keep you off balance. Remember your history: Yassar Arafat always told the U.S. and Israel one thing, and then did just the opposite!"

The President asked, "Do you think this jihad that the imam just called for will start immediately, in a week, next month, or what?"

"That's the mystery of their words, James. They predict a lot, but the final details will be withheld for the sake of surprise and shock! Muslims want you to think you know what they are about to do. Then, they will do something completely different."

"Before we meet with Sam, Sol, Addar, and Mark this evening, I need to talk to General Ellis and Secretary of Defense Rothschild, as well as Homeland Security Secretary Davidson, Secretary of State Fielder, and, for that matter, my entire Cabinet!"

The President turned to his Chief of Staff. "Eddie, first, I must speak with Pierce, David, and Matt—we need an offensive and defensive military strategy in the wake of this wild imam's sermon. While I am talking with them, you can round up the rest of my Cabinet—as well as the appropriate leaders of the House and Senate. This is urgent, so don't let anyone put you off. They may not have heard the ratcheted rhetoric of this mystery cleric—who must be a mouthpiece for the Caliph. They may not know that a call for jihad against us and Israel was just issued. You got all that, Eddie?"

"I'm crystal clear, James! I will let you know when the guys for the first holoconference are ready."

"Good! In the meantime, I am calling Sam before he meets with. . . who will Sam meet with now that all of his Cabinet members, save one, are dead? All he has is Noah at Homefront Defense!" Then, in answer to his own question, James said, "Of course, he will talk with his Deputy Ministers, the main leaders of his coalition, and the military brass."

Turning back to his Vice President, the Commander in Chief asked, "Do you really think American Muslims will answer this call to jihad in the states, Abdul?"

"Why wouldn't they, James? What you are seeing now is not happening by accident. All of the islamization of Europe was planned, and yet Europe's leadership did nothing as they saw it unfold before their eyes—until it was too late. Why do you and your advisors think islamization cannot happen in the United States?

"Europe proved that the desire for Muslims and non-Muslims to live side by side in peace will never be realized! Europe proved that being against Muslims expansion is neither racist nor culturally or religiously insensitive but a matter of survival! Actually, if the U.S. does not take this call to jihad seriously and fight and defeat the Muslims, the U.S. will indeed become Islamerica!

"Look closer at the European example. The massive immigration of Muslims and their prolific reproduction were the first steps. Most Muslim men had four wives, while some also had slave concubines — handmaidens. On average, Muslim men had fifteen children each. Compare fifteen children per Muslim household to the European nations' birthrate that ranged from an average of negative one to two and a half children per household, and you can see how the Muslims took over Europe. The last minute military actions in Europe did not come until after the Muslims had become the majority population!

"In the U.S., we have some time before we Islamists have a plurality in the population. But the birthrate advantage is with the Muslims at eight to one, and Muslims are the largest minority population in the states. It is just a matter of a handful of years before they will be the majority!"

"In Europe, more stealth Muslims were in key government positions than anyone in the EU realized. With the one two punch of majority population plus some level of government control, Islam took over Europe!"

"Who knows how many Muslims secretly serve in the United States government?" Abdul paused as he realized that until yesterday, he was a Muslim holding the second highest office in America. Then Abdul added, "The Muslim infiltration of the federal government may be more advanced than any of us can know."

His expression blank and his face white, James sat down. He felt overwhelmed by the undeniable facts Abdul was laying out. The Vice President pulled up a chair and sat in front of the Commander in Chief.

"Consider this, James: You heard the imam's quote from October of 2010 that America would become a Sharia compliant Muslim nation. The attack on the DROP has only moved up the Muslim timetable. The U.S. would have probably had another generation or so before Muslims became the majority population. That notwithstanding, who knows how many young men have grown up learning the ways of terror at the jihad summer camps in the states? Likewise, who knows how many terrorist sleeper cells are waiting to deploy across the nation? Besides, with a 40 million strong Brotherhood outside the U.S., the Muslims can go to war now! Their disadvantage up to this point has been their inability to mobilize the European war machine they inherited. But if the Brotherhood has control of Israel's weapons, they may be able to control ours, also. If such is the case, why wait for the Muslim majority?"

"What about all our appeals to moderate Muslims—those who seek peace?" James asked.

"Truly James, 'moderate Muslim' is an oxymoron! Such a Muslim is not a true follower of Islam—at least not according to the jihadists! The Salafist-Sunnis always remind Muslims that the Qur'an calls all believers to jihad. Hence, Muslims who reject that call reject Allah! Qur'an 9:41 says, *"Go ye forth, (whether equipped) lightly or heavily, and strive and struggle, with your goods and your persons, in the cause of Allah. That is best for you, if ye (but knew)."* In other words, the call to jihad is universal, no matter how well equipped or how heavily armed you are—or if you are wealthy or poor! If you cannot or will not fight, you are supposed to pay so others can fight in your place.

"Those who do not fight or support the jihad of the 'true believers' are worse than infidels! For true Muslim believers, peace equals surrender! Therefore, James, as Europe went, so will America go. Moderate Muslims will be killed along with the infidels. All efforts to reach out to moderates and make peace only make us look weak to the Muslim hardliners.

"I know you did not count on a lesson in Islam, but let's go a bit further. The Qur'an is basically divided into two groups of writings— what Muhammad was told by Allah in Mecca and what he was later told in Medina. The Meccan passages speak of peace. Muhammad first attempted to reach out to the locals—even the Jews and Christians—to show them that Allah was the same god from the Bible. Muhammad even had the people pray facing Jerusalem at that time.

"Nonetheless, Muhammad was not very successful at recruiting many Jews or Christians or anyone else for that matter. After being chased out of Mecca, he settled in Medina, where he wrote the more violent aspects of the Qur'an. All the calls for jihad come from the Medinan passages of the Qur'an.

"The earlier verses about peace are abrogated by the later revelations about jihad."

James did not understand. "Abrogated? What do you mean, Abdul?"

"Abrogation is a Muslim principle. If a verse contradicts what an earlier passage claims, then the earlier text is abrogated—basically cancelled and replaced by the newer revelation. Thus, the so called moderate or peaceful Muslims no longer have the authority of the Qur'an behind them. With such being the case, the jihadist Muslims have basically abrogated the peaceful moderates, as well.

"Consequently, when we seem to be making progress with Muslims, we are truly fools in one of two ways. One, we are talking to the wrong people. The peace-seeking moderates cannot speak or negotiate for the majority of Muslims who embrace jihad. Two, we are talking with the right people—representatives of jihadist Islam. Nonetheless, they will not be honest with us. They desire to deceive us and lull us into a false sense of peace and security in order to complete what they see as the goal of Islam—ruling the earth under Sharia law! Remember, the *taqiyya* doctrine allows Muslims to use lies to achieve the goals of Islam. The fulfillment of the Qur'an is for the Muslims to rule the world—with no other religions and no other governments in competition—especially a democracy! As the English speaking Muslims say, 'Democracy is hypocrisy! Democracy is demonocracy!'"

The President's entire countenance fell. "Are you saying that all the time and money the U.S. has invested in reaching out to moderate Muslims has been wasted? For decades, we have poured billions of dollars into such efforts!"

"Our money wasn't wasted, James. Our cash funded jihad against the United States and other countries. Our money helped fund the islamization of Europe, too!"

"So we have foolishly hoped that the Muslims would integrate into American culture and society?"

"The imam answered that question in his blistering sermon. He said, 'Allah and Islam are not seeking to be tolerated by the two Satans. They do not seek to cooperate with the vilest civilizations that ever existed! Quite the opposite, Allah and Islam seek dominance and victory over the Satans! Terror is when Muslims kill Muslims. Justice is when Muslims kill infidels!'

"Most unfortunately, our hopes of Muslim integration into American society and culture have been and remain nothing but foolhardy. Political correctness and fear of being accused of racial and religious discrimination gave the Muslims the foothold they needed in the U.S. many decades ago. As the Muslim dilemma grew, Americans still chose to pretend they were our friends and neighbors. Meanwhile, true Muslims never desired to assimilate with Americans but to annihilate us! I tell you again, James, what happened in Europe is happening now in the United States!"

In a cold sweat, James confessed, "I should have listened to you six months ago, when we first took office. You were warning me about all this, but I could not believe that Islam could be a serious threat to the nation! I still don't know what the Muslims truly want."

"Yes, you do know what they want, James! The Muslims want everything! Tragically, you are not the first President or other elected official to ignore the threat of islamization or pretend it does not exist in the states!

"History repeats itself. America and the West sat idly by, watching and listening to Hitler, thinking he was not a real threat or that he would be satisfied with his initial land grabs and military victories! Strange, is it not, that the imam mentioned Hitler's work to kill the Jews was not completed, even though the Muslims deny the Holocaust of the twentieth century? Now, the Muslims want to complete his work of wiping the Jews and Israel from the face of the earth.

"Clearly, James, we must move forward. We cannot afford to spend time denying present reality or looking back with regret. Instead, we must concentrate on acting now and in the immediate future to combat an enemy that is both inside and outside of our borders! The Muslims want it all: One world Caliphate, one world religion, universal Sharia Law!

"In the states, we already have communities with Muslim majorities and Sharia Law! In those areas, women face stoning for adultery! Children's hands can be chopped off for theft. Adults and kids alike can be executed for leaving Islam for Christianity! Infidels can be condemned for criticizing Islam, Allah, Muhammad, or the Qur'an! We already have unknown numbers of Muslims filling local, state, and national positions. Islamerica is being birthed even as we speak!"

The Vice President stood to make his next point. "Why now? Who knows? But I have an idea about a possible catalyst. The Muslim world is running out of oil and natural gas, while America and Israel are just now tapping into their great reserves of those precious resources. Russia and the Muslims attacked Isreal for that treasure at the end of

247

World War III, so perhaps the Muslims' need for fuel has jumpstarted the battle over Israel and the United States."

The President grew more depressed by the moment. "Do you think the process of islamization has progressed far enough for the Muslims to have a viable power base within our borders?"

"Let's look at one aspect of things. Who do we trust, James? Throughout Europe, Muslim agents and terrorists had infiltrated the highest levels of the military and government! Do we think such is not happening in the states?"

As the Vice President sat down again, the President stared at him with a look of sudden suspicion. Seeing his expression, Abdul stated, "James, you have got to be kidding, if you think I am a Muslim plant! Even if I had been, I am no longer a Muslim! I tried to tell you that I became a Christian over the Atlantic! Remember, I told you that I met Isa!

"I'm on your side—America's side! I am on Isa's side! I want to combat Islam with His mercy and grace. If we cannot win their hearts and souls with forgiveness and love, then we will have to defeat them militarily. Even so, many more Muslims are choosing to believe in Isa than any non-Muslim realizes!"

Contrite, James apologized to his Vice President, saying, "I went over your files with a fine tooth comb, personally, Abdul. Please forgive me for doubting you even for a moment. You have been especially loyal to me, even when we did not agree with my plans. I appreciate you greatly—even more now than I ever imagined I would!"

Abdul, blushing, as the genuineness of the President's words triggered an emotional response in him, said, "I have a suggestion, James. This evening's meeting with the Israeli and Palestinian negotiators could be a godsend. With the call to jihad that has been proclaimed, you need to speak to the American people again. The Prime Minister will need to do the same for the Israelis. What better format than a joint address with you and Sam?"

The President smiled as he considered the proposal. James stood and said, "Such a presentation would show our solidarity and readiness, Abdul. We could also make a plea for peace, saying war is not what either of us wants. I think you have a great idea. I will discuss it with Sam and then the team back in D.C.. I'm glad you are here, Abdul!"

With a genuine smile, James reached for Abdul's hand, but instead of shaking it, he pulled the Vice President out of his chair and then wrapped both of his arms around him! Abdul was surprised though not upset by the heart-felt gesture of a man rising to the challenge that faced him.

A few seconds later, as the President walked away, his Vice President asked a question. "James, where are your wife and children?"

"... 'Don't be afraid; just believe.'"
Mark 5:36

CHAPTER 48

THE CHAOS ADVANTAGE...

*W*ith only three hours left in their flight, Ariel slept soundly, though Mark could not sleep at all. In fact, the pastor had been awake all night. Finally, he decided to watch one of the programming services just to keep his mind off Grace and what was facing them all. The questions haunted him in the darkness. Why did the Brotherhood want him, dead or alive? What fate awaited him in the DROP? Could he save Grace?

Mark closed his tired, bloodshot eyes. In all his confusion and unknowns, he still sensed the peace of Jesus. How thankful he was that this unshakeable peace was independent of his circumstances! He began to pray for Grace.

At the same moment, a newsflash on the HV3D demanded his attention instead. "Islam declares open jihad on U.S. and Israel!" The Muslim reporter smiled as he continued. "In a blistering attack of words, an unknown imam issues a call to war during the special noonday prayers that Caliph Sanaullah bin Laden established for faithful Muslims. In the sermon, the cleric demands that Muslims within the borders of America and Israel rise up to fulfill the next step of the Islamic goal of one world Caliphate. Renaming the USA the USI—the United States of Islamerica—the imam says the White House will become a mosque and the Islamic flag will fly over it! Similarly, the caustic cleric proclaims the Israeli Knesset is destined to become a place to worship Allah as well, just as Buckingham Palace is now a mosque. The United States and Israel have yet to respond to this challenge. We will bring you those details as soon as possible."

"Great! Not only is Palestine a powder keg from the missile attacks," Mark thought, *"but now World War IV is about to start, with my family at ground zero!"*

The next news item deepened Mark's concern. "U.S. and Israeli officials confirm that several top nuclear scientists, engineers, and retired military officers of both countries are missing. Unnamed sources in both Washington D.C. and Jerusalem suspect these experts have been kidnapped and taken to Babylon by the Brotherhood. The sources believe that the Caliph will force these highly skilled individuals to train Brotherhood soldiers in the use of Asia's and the EU's war machines. Likewise, the Americans and Israelis could be compelled to help reactivate the disabled arsenals and weapons systems—especially the EU's disabled nuclear arsenal. The sources have not said how Babylon will compensate for its lack of satellite operations which are essential to a fully functional weapons system."

Still smiling broadly, the reporter then noted, "These events coincide with intelligence reports out of Babylon that former EU military heads and nuclear scientists are being tortured in efforts to force them to help the Brotherhood resurrect the military might of Asia and the EU for Babylon's conquest of the U.S. and Israel."

Mark prayed aloud, "Lord, how can all these events be happening simultaneously? My family is in the crosshairs of this escalating crisis!"

The despair in Mark's voice woke Ariel. "What is it, Honey? What are you saying?"

"The news says that Muslims have declared open jihad against the United States and Israel! The imam at the noonday prayers says the states will soon be Islamerica! Plus, scientists, engineers, and military experts from Israel and the states have been kidnapped in order to work alongside former Asian and EU personnel to reactivate Babylon's war machine and nuclear arsenal as well as train the Brotherhood how to use the Asian and EU military vessels and equipment!"

"Can the Muslims do all that?"

"Baby, you have heard me talk about this scenario for years. It's just happening faster than I thought!"

Fully awake and filled with conflicting emotions, Ariel asked, "What do we do now, Mark? What about Grace? Can we still save our daughter?"

"I am praying with all my heart that Jesus has already saved her from the clutches of evil itself!"

Before he could say anything more, a call came into his holophone. "It's Addar," Mark told Ariel. Together they looked at his wrenched face as he spoke with urgency in his voice.

"Mark, have you heard the latest developments here?"

"Yes, Addar, we have just seen the news bulletins. Who is the imam behind this call for jihad? Is this straight from the Caliph? Are American and Israeli scientists, engineers, and military personnel being kidnapped to help Babylon fight us?"

"I have no answers for your questions, Pastor. But everyone here is trying to sort things out—and quickly! It looks like your soon arrival will be of great help!"

"How so?"

"President Paulson just contacted me. He wants to use our meeting tonight as an official response to the imam's sermon on jihad. Prime Minister Ben Baruch and the President will jointly address their nations and the world in a show of unity and to make a plea for peace!"

"How do I play into that?"

"You, Rabbi Ben Israel, and I can also call for peace from the Christians, Jews, and Muslims!"

"Do you think the Muslims will listen to you? Many have labeled you a traitor for the peace accord with Israel."

"The three of us are all that Christianity, Judaism, and Islam have to offer on short notice!"

"I suppose you are right about that."

"Start thinking about what you plan to say. Try to keep it concise and to the point. The world will not have much patience with us."

"Indeed!" Mark paused, and then added. "Do you by chance know anything about Grace?"

"I wish I could tell you where she is and that she is safe, Mark. As a father of daughters, I cannot imagine how you feel right now."

Ariel spoke up, saying, "Imam Zaahir, we know you have so many things to address in this crisis! But anything you can do to help Grace would. . ." Ariel's tears took her voice captive.

With apparent empathy, the imam filled in the gap, "I know. Anything I can do to help Grace would be greatly appreciated by both of you. You can call me Addar, as Mark does, Ariel. We are going to need each other in so many ways in these coming hours and days!"

Mark noted, "Addar, we had canceled our plans to come to the DROP until the General contacted us. Did you know that he demanded we make this trip? Do you know what he has planned for us?"

Addar almost smiled as he said, "I did not know your plans ever changed, and I most certainly am not the General's keeper! Who know what lies in the twisted mind of such a cagey individual? My advice is that you stay alert at all times. As long as the masked man has breath, he will boldly tell you lie after lie. He cares little for life—his own or the lives of others. Indeed, he works in mysterious ways!"

Mark wondered why Addar used that phrase, as Christians often say "God moves in mysterious ways," in reference to the old hymn from the late 1700's. The pastor was surprised that Addar even knew that phrase.

Changing the subject, Mark asked, "I don't suppose you will meet us at the airport?"

"If only I could! Trust me as one of my most loyal brothers will be there. He will take you to your hotel in West Jerusalem so you can freshen up and have a decent meal. Then he will bring you to the studio in East Jerusalem where all of us will meet and later address the world which is on the brink of madness!"

"Addar, you mentioned the battle of *Har Megiddo* to me while I was still in the states. I was surprised you mentioned this New Testament prophecy. Do you think this is the beginning of the end?"

"The Jews say: 'The Christians have naught (to stand) upon;' And the Christians say: 'The Jews have naught (to stand) upon.' Yet they (profess to) study the (same) Book. Like unto their word is what those say who know not; But Allah will judge between them in their quarrel on the Day of Judgment."
Qur'an 2:113

CHAPTER 49

CRISIS REVEALS CHARACTER. . .

❖❖❖

Sol felt as though all life had been sucked out of him. At 85, the combined impact of such swift and powerful events overwhelmed him—mind, body, heart, and soul! Sol recapped all the rapid-fire developments: *"The useless peace negotiations, the deadly missile attack, the possible role of Israel in the terror strike, the Caliph's looming deadline, and now, an all out call for jihad against Israel and the United States! Why is all this happening?"*

He and Ahava continued to watch the various news reports about the shadowy imam's unfettered verbal attack on Jews and Christians—and all other non-Muslims in the world. Sol wondered if he should just surrender and die, when the news broke about the kidnapped nuclear scientists, engineers, and military personnel!

Ahava put the brakes on his downward spiral when she asked, "Sol, do you believe that this is the end of Israel? Is life as we know it now gone forever? Is this how all our years together will conclude?"

A few seconds earlier, the bald rabbi would have answered "Yes!" However, suddenly he felt surges of hope within his aching heart. Somewhere within his spirit, he knew that this was not the end—at least not yet! Hope welled up in his soul, instead of tears welling up in his eyes. He gave a bold answer to his loving bride, "No! No! And no!"

Ahava actually smiled, as she too felt the genuine conviction of Sol's three declarations! "You could not be more correct, my husband! The enemy wants to terrorize us and bury us in tons of fear before the true fight even begins! That jihad-demanding cleric wants us to quake in our boots, run away, and search for a place to hide! But we must stand firm, Sol!"

The learned Jew could not have said it better himself! Ahava's encouraging words lifted the darkness that had descended over him, and he began straining for the light! "We will not simply go quietly into the night! We will not surrender and fall by the wayside! We have ways to fight that do not involve weapons of this world!"

Before Ahava could ask Sol what he meant by his last statement, the holophone came to life. Sol said, "Oh my! The Prime Minister himself is calling!" Sol took a deep breath, slapped his cheeks, and answered the call. "Shalom, Mr. Prime Minister! Sam, you are a sight for sore eyes on a day such as this one!"

"I'll take your words as encouragement, Sol. Each of us needs all the hope and faith we can find today!"

"Indeed! So what can an ancient rabbi do for you in this chaotic environment?"

"You and your wife can come to our meeting this evening about an hour early. I would like to talk with you about some developments before the others arrive."

"We will be honored to meet with you, Sam! So what can you tell us about the kidnappings?"

"Actually, President Paulson and I learned of them together, while we were talking earlier. Neither of us had a clue about these events until they were reported to the world!"

"How can that be?"

"Undoubtedly, both Israel and the U.S. have Muslim moles in high places who leaked this story."

"Do you think the story is true?"

"Maybe, according to my initial checks. While we cannot reach some of our most talented and valuable scientists and engineers, we cannot verify they have been taken from the country. The same can be said for some of our most knowledgeable military veterans!"

"I will be praying about all of this, Sam!"

"Good—and thanks! Sol, my friend and spiritual counselor, President Paulson has suggested an idea that I believe has great merit. He suggests that we have a joint conference tonight—a satellite holocast to both Israel and the United States, with our secondary audience being the Caliphate. We want to demonstrate our unity and our desire for peace, not war!"

"Sam, do you believe war can still be avoided after the execution of your Cabinet?"

"I imagine that my deputy ministers, the leaders of the coalition parties, and Military Chief of Staff, Lt. General Gideon, will push for war. But until we know if we are in control of our own weapons, I don't know how we could prosecute a war or protect ourselves from an enemy who can use our own arsenal against us! We must find a way to test our weapons system—safely!"

"Therefore, President Paulson and I feel that we should yet pursue peace, if for no other reason than to give us the time to know if Israel can protect itself and wage war if necessary. While the alleged kidnappings, the brutal beheadings, and the ghastly death and destruction could each be considered individual acts of war against us, can we launch a counterattack or even defend ourselves if targeted again?

"What do you think, Sol? In a few moments, I will meet with all the decision makers. Should I push forward with this concept of peace until we know if we can wage war? I am calling on your wisdom, the wisdom of my friend, Shlomo—who is most appropriately named!"

Sol's eyes burned and his stomach clenched as a rush of emotion surged through his body! The Prime Minister of the great nation of Israel wanted his advice above that of the professional politicians and military advisors. Regaining his composure, Sol closed his eyes for a moment and silently asked, *"Well, what do I tell the man, Adonai?"* A wave of peace washed away all other thoughts and feelings within his aged body. Hence, Sol answered with calm assurance, "Without doubt, Samuel, you are on the right track. Move forward, empowered by the very Holy Spirit of God!"

In response, Sam breathed deeply. "Yes," he agreed. "I sense that your advice is exactly right! I don't know how to thank you for giving me such assurance in such a confusing time! I don't know exactly what format all this will take this evening, but be ready, no matter what.

"Oh, did I even tell you? You will speak tonight, addressing our people, laying the spiritual groundwork for this call for peace. Can you do that? Will you do it? Mark and Addar will be making similar pleas."

Without hesitation, Sol replied, "May the Lord of all Heaven and earth speak through us all!"

"Exactly! If ever we needed the Hand of the Divine to guide us and empower us, that time is now!"

Neither Sol nor Ahava had ever heard or seen Sam speak words of faith as he was this afternoon. He was not running away from the battle that loomed, but running to it, all the while still hoping upon hope for peace!

Sol affirmed, "When we have truly called out to God in genuine repentance and humility, He has never failed us!"

"Then, by all means, old friend, as I move into this emergency meeting with our country's second tier of leaders and the heads of the coalition and military as well, lift up our repentant and humble nation to our Lord!"

"With great hope, I will kneel before the Ancient of Days!"

"Pray, as though our nation, as though our very lives depend upon it, Sol—because I believe they do!"

"I have told you these things, so that in Me you may have peace. In this world you will have trouble. But take heart! I have overcome the world."
John 16:33

CHAPTER 50

THE QUEST FOR ANSWERS. . .

*D*an Ata'halne asked from the front row of the White House Press Room: "Bob, does the President have a timetable for war?"

In the HV3D satellite news conference, White House Press Secretary Robert "Bob" Steer fielded questions he could not answer from journalists in the press room as well as from reporters in various countries. Surrounded by that sea of real and 3D-imaged faces, Bob knew that no firm decisions had been made, as the President's own secure satellite conference with America's leaders had not concluded on time. Thus, the Press Secretary did his best with the few facts that he had at his disposal.

"Dan, right now, the President, his Cabinet, the Chairman of Joint Chiefs of Staff, and the leaders of the House and Senate are talking via satellite link. The President and the Prime Minister along with the remaining members of the Israeli-Palestinian peace negotiating team will be responding to the imam's call for jihad during a live broadcast this evening, Israel time—probably around one or so in the afternoon our time.

"Even so, I can tell you this. The President and Prime Minister are first and foremost working to find a peaceful resolution to the present crisis. We remain optimistic that war can be averted and peace, celebrated."

Bob scanned the frantic hands waving in front of him. "Cheryl Jude in California, what question do you have?"

"What basis does the President have for averting war? The DROP has been attacked by missiles designed by the U.S. and Israel. Those missiles were fired from Israel. In response, it seems, the DROP or the Caliphate beheaded the Israeli Prime Minister's Cabinet. Now, Babylon wants to bring its inherited WMD—including its nuclear arsenals—and war machines to life with the forced assistance of kidnapped Israeli and U.S. nuclear scientists, engineers, and retired military officers. Furthermore, some of these hostages are military trainers. In this building fog of war, how does President Paulson see a path to peace?"

Bob quickly responded, saying, "Those reports about kidnapped U.S. and Israeli experts have not been confirmed. As such, I will not discuss those issues. Otherwise, Cheryl, in addition to the U.S.-Israel, alliance, the President has also formed a coalition with other nations in North, Central, and South America to fight against Babylon, if necessary. Even so, the prospect of World War IV quickly sobers the mind. The President does not want to put the remainder of the free world at risk if at all possible. He and Prime Minister Ben Baruch are going to pursue peace until war is absolutely inevitable!"

"A follow-up, if I may, Bob?"

"Okay, Cheryl."

"We understand that Israel cannot guarantee control of its own weapons arsenal. Likewise, our sources say that America's weapon system could be compromised, as well. As such, do the two nations have any other option but to call for peace?"

This was one of the questions Bob hoped no one would ask! The grimace on his face conveyed his uncertainty of what to say in response. The White House spokesman stared at the reporter as if he could intimidate her into withdrawing her question. Bob realized he must end the uncomfortable pause—but what could he say that would not jeopardize the President's call for peace. He decided to lie. And Bob knew if he was going to lie, he would have to lie in grandiose style to make it stick!

"Such rumors are floating around the White House, Congress, and the Knesset, as well. We categorically deny all such rumors! Both the U.S. and Israel have complete control of their massive war arsenals, and any potential enemy who doubts that fact places his people in dire jeopardy! America and her allies have the military capacity to wipe out any and all enemies in swift and lethal fashion!"

Bob wiped the beads of sweat from his brow as he said, "Next question? Yes, Michelle Eoin in Israel?"

"Everything we hear out of Jerusalem says the Prime Minister does not know what to do. Is Prime Minister Ben Baruch making any comments that you can share?"

"I do not claim to speak on behalf of any foreign leader. But I do know that the Israeli Prime Minister remains in closed door sessions with his Deputy Cabinet members, coalition party leaders, and his Military Chief of Staff even as we speak."

"I also have a follow up question Bob."

"All right!"

"Who is the imam that spoke to a worldwide assembly of Muslims today?"

Bob answered by asking, "Wouldn't we all like to know? At this time, we are doing everything possible to identify this imam. So far, voice track comparisons match none we have on record. Then again, as the message was recorded in many languages, we have no way of positively identifying the original voice. Hence, we have contacted Caliph bin Laden to determine if he approved the imam's blistering sermon beforehand. If not, after the speech, we want to know if he supports the imam's incendiary call for immediate jihad. Of course, both options would be in direct contradiction to yesterday's speech by the Caliph, in which he gave the President and Prime Minister one week to find out who authorized and carried out the missile attacks on the DROP yesterday.

"As an aside, I should point out that the Caliph cannot dictate the pace or scope of a U.S. investigation. This sovereign nation does not accept commands or idle threats from opposing world leaders."

"Could the shadowy imam that ignited Muslim jihad yesterday be the secretive head of the Brotherhood?"

"Michele, we have no intel on that theory at this moment. As I said, the voice patterns do not match. But we know that voices can and are being altered. The General's voice is always digitally distorted, typically, sounding somewhat different each time he speaks."

"Any idea as to what the Caliph is thinking?"

"Michelle, this is your fourth and final question! Actually, we are hearing from our contacts in Babylon that the imam's scorching war cry caught the Caliph by surprise. We are trying to confirm that report at this time."

"I see Carlos Raymundo in Mexico City—your turn."

"Gracias, Bob! We have reports of protests in the streets in the major cities of the U.S. and Israel—as well as in the DROP. Do you think the imam's call for jihad has already being answered?"

"So far, and I emphasize, so far, we are not hearing reports of violence, but of celebration. While we have the usual flag burnings, effigy hangings, and celebratory gunfire, we have not heard about any outbreaks of fighting or any attacks on non-Muslims. We are monitoring the situation very closely, realizing it would be a very short step to violence. Yet, the President is most grateful for the apparent calm of the moment."

"Who's next? Okay, Richard Percy in Canada."

"Are automatic responses taking place as we speak, such as troop deployment or battleship realignment?"

"We do have emergency contingency plans for the Middle East that include all branches of our military in regards to troops, air assaults, naval fleets and destroyers, subs, special ops, elite forces, missile readiness, and so forth. Some portions of those plans are in motion, but the true—let's say—the exact military response to the current situation will be specifically tailored to what our intelligence and military leaders know and when they know it."

"Janet Harper here in the briefing room, you have a question?"

"Two, actually, Bob."

"Shoot—sorry for the bad pun!"

A light amount of laughter moved its way through the press room and the foreign locations as well.

"Go ahead, Janet."

"What economic impact have the states and Israel felt already, and what does the White House anticipate if there is indeed a Muslim uprising within the United States?"

"Janet, let's be honest—I'm sure you will find that refreshing from a press secretary. We haven't had a major conflict on our soil since the Civil War! Thus, gauging potential economic costs will be a slippery prospect. Based on the size and scope of the opposition, the economic impact could be minimal or drastic.

"I can tell you this. Wall Street and trading venues around the remaining free world have been riding a roller coaster. Fuel prices have already jumped, just from fear of war. The value of the dollar and the Babylonian riyal have been in a state of flux. Thus, at day one into this crisis, all we have is uncertainty.

"War remains a very present memory for the nations. Even here in the United States, we continue to make infrastructure repairs in the wake of the Doomsday Quake that facilitated an early end to World War III. That statement is magnified many times over for Israel, which was the effective ground zero for the largest earthquake in history. Nonetheless, our military apparatus as well as our weaponry and personnel stand ready for battle. As I said earlier, we hope for a peaceful solution to the present crisis, but we will prepare for all alternatives.

"Now, let me say this: the possibility of major conflict on American shores has to be minimal! If Babylon should attack us, it cannot do so with the jets, ships, subs, missiles, and tanks of Europe or Asia. So, at least for the time being, the threat here would be from a domestic Muslim rebellion, and every President and administration, including President Paulson and his administration, has done everything possible to maintain open and peaceful relations with Muslim Americans in every aspect of our society and politics."

"For my second question. . ."

"I thought you already asked two questions!"

"Sorry! We have the Coast Guard and the National Guard ready to protect the U.S.. Do President Paulson, Secretaries Rothschild and Davidson, as well as General Ellis foresee domestic deployment of the Army, Air Force, Navy, or Marine Corps in response to a Muslim attack within our borders?"

"Janet, again, the President and those leaders you mentioned meet as we speak. While I cannot rule out such an unprecedented deployment, we must have a better idea of the scope and depth of any armed rebellion that might erupt in the states."

Bob wanted to end the press conference before the questions grew any more difficult. He tried to choose a reporter who would be a softer touch. "Jeremias Tiago in Brazil, what have you got for me?"

"Obviously, Israel represents the faster and easier target for the Brotherhood. Will the United States place a disproportionate percentage of its military forces in and around Israel, and leave the homeland more vulnerable?"

Bob tried to sound confident. "Again, any answer I give at this point to that particular question would be speculative in nature. We cannot report what has not yet been decided. I'm sure President Paulson will address this very issue later today. But let me be clear—the President will always make the safety and defense of America and her citizens his first priority!

"Is that all from you, Jeremias?"

"I have a politically incorrect question, Bob. You have a Muslim Vice President. Where is his loyalty?"

Bob smiled, "I can speak specifically to that question, Jeremias! President Paulson himself told me that Vice President Abdullah has again sworn his complete allegiance to our Commander in Chief and to our nation. We have no doubt whatsoever that Vice President Abdullah stands with his fellow Americans as we face a threat that has not yet been evaluated quantitatively or qualitatively at present."

"Barney Flynn in New York, your hand has been up the whole time."

"Babylon has a host of nuclear weapons at its disposal, but without a way to fire or deploy them. However, is anyone estimating the odds of bin Laden finding other more elementary and crude ways of using the nuclear resources at his finger tips—such as dirty bombs?"

"Barney, you pose a very strategic question. Long before today, we have gone over numerous scenarios about Babylon's nuclear threat. One school says the fear of devastating nuclear response will stop Babylon from using any small nuclear devices. Another school says Babylon will not use nuclear weapons of any sort, at least on Israel, because so many Muslim states are in the fallout zone. A third school says bin Laden likes to do things the old fashioned way—with conventional weapons and even hand to hand combat because then more Muslims have opportunity for jihad. However, a fourth school says that if Babylon seems to be losing a war and cannot see a path to victory, it will use some sort of nuclear option as a last resort. "

A long hush fell over the room and the remote sites.

Barney followed up, asking, "Have our scientists, engineers, and military veterans been kidnapped and taken to Babylon? Specifically, will our nuclear scientists be forced to help Babylon flex its atomic muscle?"

Frustrated and refusing to speculate, Bob answered, "Barney, we already discussed these reports. They have not been confirmed. I am not going to comment any further on what may turn out to be rumors."

To break the tension, Bob said, "Nithar Zulema in Ankara, you have the last word."

Nithar did not even have his hand in the air, but he quickly regrouped and read his written question. "Does the Paulson Administration consider that any or all of these events are leading up to the end times battles prophesied in both the Old and New Testament, as well as the Qur'an?"

Bob could have kicked himself for choosing Nithar. The timing of his question was especially poor, given the nuclear scenarios he had just reviewed.

"We can always count on the Islamic Satellite Network to throw in a thriller of a question! Nithar, of all people in this administration, I must be the least qualified to address theological issues, so I will not answer your question. I will allow you to ask another, non-religious, non-theological question, though."

"I appreciate that. Given what has happened in Israel, how has the U.S. government prepared to protect its political leaders from assassination?"

Bob wanted to strangle Nithar's holographic image. Instead, keeping his emotional response in check, the Press Secretary replied, "Our leaders have the best security details in the world. While I will not reveal, for obvious security reasons, the various aspects of how our government protects its officials, I can assure you and everyone else that our security ranks number one in the world, as we have not suffered a security breach in decades!"

"Ladies and gentlemen both here and abroad, I must cut this discussion short at this point. I too need to be part of the satellite holoconference with the President. We will get back to you as our knowledge base increases and we have new details of the U.S. and Israeli response to the present crisis. Thank you for your time and cooperation!"

As the spokesman for the President headed to the door, Nithar asked two more questions that were left to hang in the air. "Has the United States passed the point of no return regarding the islamization of America—either now or in the near future? And what about the threat of Goliath?"

"If any one disputes in this matter with thee, now after (full) knowledge hath come to thee, say: 'Come! let us gather together, our sons and your sons, our women and your women, ourselves and yourselves: Then let us earnestly pray, and invoke the curse of Allah on those who lie!'"
Qur'an 3:61

CHAPTER 51

TAKING IT TO THE STREETS...

❖❖❖

*W*ith horns blasting and guns firing into the air all around them, Mark and Ariel inched toward the meeting site. As though the destruction in East Jerusalem did not make traveling the roads difficult enough, the streets flowed with celebrating Muslims. Satellite autodrive was of no use in such tight confines, as the chauffer had to be careful not to run over any of the jihad-delirious celebrants.

To his right, Mark saw a likeness of the President hanging from a gallows. To her left, Ariel saw gleeful Muslims slitting the throat of the Prime Minister in effigy. Israeli and American flags blazed all around their vehicle.

Was Mark paranoid, or were more and more Muslims looking at their car, wondering why those inside it were not celebrating with them?

"Do you know an alternate route to the meeting place?" Ariel asked the driver.

"All our people have filled the streets this evening," he answered. "What a grand day for Palestine—our loved ones and leaders will be avenged!"

Ariel decided not to ask any other questions. Mark had experienced this "Muslim frenzy" before. Soon, the partiers would tire of burning flags and slaughtering effigies. They would look to spill real blood from real people!

Mark pulled Ariel closer to him, and she did not resist. Too afraid to speak her thoughts, she asked herself, *"What if this crazed crowd turns on us? The driver will not defend us! He is one of them!"*

Now, Muslims pressed against the car on all sides, making it rock as it slowly rolled along. More and more of the men were leaning over and looking into the car. To Ariel, it seemed that each of those men had hell fire in his eyes!

Ariel gasped when the tires on her side of the car lifted from the ground. Laughter erupted outside the vehicle, as everyone seemed to have the same idea at once. The manic men began lifting the car to turn it upside down! Repeatedly, the vehicle surged upward, only to fall hard on the tires, but each time, the car was lifted higher than the time before. Now, even the driver was scared. None of the Muslims outside cared that he was one of them!

Mark spoke Arabic. He wondered if he could somehow talk their way out of this mess. Yet, how would he get anyone to listen to him? No one would even be able to hear him through the din of the crowd.

All three of them held their breath as the car rose higher and higher off the ground. Would it roll over this time? What would the crowd do then? The trio could not run through the wall to wall bodies that so tightly surrounded them.

Suddenly, Mark heard something hit the top of the car—three times. The men on Ariel's side of the vehicle dropped the car, and it came down with a thud. All the men around them turned and tried to get away from the car, pushing and shoving their way through the ocean of flesh.

Then, Mark saw smoke rising from the ground: tear gas! The Muslims were all turning away now, covering their faces. Coughing and gagging replaced their chants and cheers!

"Quick, turn off the AC!" Mark told the driver. "We don't want that gas in here!" The driver immediately obliged as the crowd in front of the car moved away from the three canisters of tear gas.

In a few minutes, the car and its three passengers moved forward once more, yet as the stinging cloud dispersed behind them, the crowd ahead grew thicker. As three more canisters pounded on the roof, tear gas filled the air around the car.

Mark asked under his breath, *"Who fired those canisters? Who has come to help us? Do they have enough tear gas to clear the entire pathway to the studio?"* Mark turned to see who was behind them. Try as he may, the pastor could only see Muslims fleeing from the car as fast as the crowd would allow.

The three of them sweated profusely! Without the AC, the interior of the car became a sauna! Three more thumps on the car top, and the crowd in front of the oven-on-wheels began to thin once more. This pattern repeated itself six times until the car and its passengers made it safely through the danger and to the studio.

Mark and Ariel jumped out of the hotbox, as the President and Imam Zaahir opened the studio door! The cool air gave the couple a jolt! "Sorry we could not do more, Mark. The agents said they really feared for your lives at several points!"

"You had someone following us, Mr. President?"

"Mark, I know you told me that Grace's life would be endangered if I sent a team to protect you, but I could not take the chance of losing all three of you! And as you can see, if the agents had not been there then, you two would not be here now!"

"Thank you, Mr. President!" Ariel said with much emotion. With tears of gratitude in her eyes, she walked over to James and hugged him.

Still unaccustomed to receiving such genuine expressions of gratitude, the President said, "Please, I wish I could have done more! And please, as I told you both on the phone, call me James."

Addar shouted, "Mr. President! Get down! All of you! Get down!" Addar lunged at the three of them, knocking them to the floor.

A split second later, several rapid fire rounds destroyed the plate glass door. And a split second after that, the marksman outside fell to the ground in a torrent of smart automatic weapons fire!

"...Repent, for the Kingdom of Heaven is near..."
Matthew 4:17

CHAPTER 52

A TANGLED WEB...

❖❖❖

"*T*he General has returned your call, sir!" Angrily, the Caliph grabbed the 3DHP. As always, no 3D holographic image accompanied the General's rumbling voice.

Bin Laden wore white from head to toe. With his white, flowing beard and his white flowing robe, he looked more like a host of heaven than a soul bound for hell.

With short and crisp words, he demanded, "General, what report do you have for me?"

Subduing his thunderous tongue, the General replied, "Your highness, our plans move forward even better than expected, if I may say so. The imam's sermon lit a fuse around the world! We must only decide when we want the bomb to explode!"

With words like fire, the Caliph shouted, "I don't recall authorizing this sermon, General! Likewise, I do not remember ordering the missile attack, at least not this soon! By chance, are you behind both events, the missiles launched from Israel and the torrid call for jihad from the DROP?"

Making his best attempt to sound submissive, the General said, "Sire, should not the Muslims around the world hear one message from one voice?"

Grinding his teeth as he spoke, bin Laden countered, "I had no problem with one message going out to all the followers of Islam, General, as you well know! Contrarily, explain the inflamed rush to jihad! Why such violent rhetoric? Our plan has been altered by this sermon. I believe it has placed us at a weaker vantage point! And you did not answer my question. Did you create this sermon?"

"I did only as you asked, my lord. The actual content of the imam's sermon began and ended with the imam!"

Frustrated and infuriated, bin Laden scolded the leader of his 40 million man army, saying, "Most assuredly, I do not believe you! Be that as it may, do you have any word on how the Israelis and Americans are responding to the call for jihad?"

"From the news reports you and I have seen, nothing official has been said yet. On the other hand, my sources tell me there is great panic in Paulson's discussions with his leadership team. I hear similar reports in regard to Ben Baruch—especially after the beheadings."

"Which I did not order, either, General! Should I take a wild guess and ask if you ordered the executions of the Prime Minister's Cabinet, save one?" The Caliph's bright red cheeks stood out in bold contrast to his white beard and turban.

"Even though you did not call for the beheadings, my Lord, they made for a classic touch all the same, no?"

The Caliph bristled! His voice crackled with anger! "General, I give you a long leash. However, I am the Caliph, and if you ever do something like this again without my foreknowledge and permission, I will not hesitate to remove both your mask and your head! These summary executions could yet blow up in our faces! And they may jeopardize my end game, as well! If my plans must be altered or fail outright, consider yourself dead!"

Biting his lip so that he would not respond with the anger he felt, the General replied, "My apologies, my sovereign, if you feel I have overstepped my authority. Even so, Israeli and American politicians and citizens remain stunned over these beheadings!"

"That does not matter! You have added a catalyst into the experiment that may back us into a corner we most definitely do not want to be in, General!"

Now biting his tongue, the General said only, "Yes sire!"

"Since your foolish decision cannot be undone, we will have to live with it. So now, what will the Prime Minister and President likely do?"

"I believe that they will speak during a joint broadcast tonight. With them will be the rest of the surviving Palestinian-Israeli peace negotiation team."

"And?"

"My sources on both sides tell me the two leaders will make a joint plea for peace aimed directly at you!"

"Peace? Peace only comes at the end of jihad. Before that, peace is surrender!"

"Yes, my liege! You speak absolute truth. You may want to use that line in your next address to the world!"

"Don't flatter me, General! Do not attempt to manipulate me, either!"

"No flattery, just the truth, sire!"

"You have placed me on a course of action from which I cannot retreat! How do we avoid going to war now, without looking weak and foolish? I cannot accept a call for peace! I cannot yet declare war. After all, we cannot yet win such a war, as you have told me time and again!"

"Events and circumstances change, do they not?"

"All I know right now is that you, unless you do not value the heart that beats in your chest, must not make any more moves without consulting me first and without securing my specific express permission!"

The General's lip and tongue bled as he answered with conjured humility, "Of course not, my Caliph!"

"When should I make my next announcement to the people and tell me, what should I say?"

"You should speak as soon as possible! You need to speak sooner rather than later—even before the Israeli-American address tonight. You could really keep them off guard and fumbling that way."

"By saying what?"

"You could deny any prior knowledge of the imam's sermon, as well as confirm that he was not acting or speaking on your behalf. You could deny authorizing the beheadings. Both of those statements are true, are they not? In the meantime, our battle plans would continue rolling out on cue. After all, we still have Goliath—you could use your speech to make your first reference to the terror that so ominously looms on the horizon!"

271

"You and I both know that Goliath cannot yet be deployed! My patience with you grows thin, General!"

"My Caliph, the infidels do not know that Goliath cannot yet march out on the world stage! However, if you do not want to use that threat, then, your message could be interrupted as someone hands you a piece of breaking information. Let's say, that violent Americans in New York City killed Muslims during peaceful protests of the Palestinian missile attack."

"Has that happened?"

"No. At least not yet! But what does that matter? The story fuels the fire! Does Allah not allow us to lie for the good of jihad, for the greater good of Islam? You could respond to the report by saying that such action not only proves the guilt of the Americans, but also hastens the time of retribution, even as you call for peace!"

"I see. What other real events can you share with me of which I remain unaware?"

"The American pastor and his wife have arrived at the studio where the broadcast will take place. They almost lost their lives en route, but a United States Secret Service team prevented that from happening. Likewise, the President and the couple were almost killed at the studio! Imam Zaahir saved their lives! Do you not agree that this makes a great headline for the slimy U.S. leader to share with the world! 'Muslim Cleric Saves American President!'"

"So the pastor did not do as you instructed? He did not keep quiet?"

"Actually, I believe he said nothing. I also believe that the President found out about the pastor's daughter through other sources. Thus, the President ordered an armed escort for the pastor and his wife without their knowledge."

"Who tried to kill the President and the American Christians?"

"In the case of the pastor and his wife, who are not native born American citizens but religious immigrants, I believe the threat came from a mob gone wild. The men in the streets did not know who they were!"

"And the President?"

"It seems the gunman happened to be at the right place at the wrong time. He must have recognized the President. He probably wanted to be a hero of jihad. He got his wish. The pastor's escort shot him repeatedly."

"How do you know all this?"

"My men have shadowed the pastor and his wife since their arrival."

"Where is the daughter?"

"At the new location. The missile attack did more damage than expected, destroying the first site."

"Will she cooperate?"

"She has a strong will, but a weak body, as she has been denied food and water. I think she will break soon."

"Don't let her die, we need her alive—for a while."

"Of course. Actually, I was considering keeping her for myself. I have no bride of my own, and I would love to help her blossom into womanhood!"

"If only they had stood fast by the Law, the Gospel, and all the revelation that was sent to them from their Lord, they would have enjoyed happiness from every side. There is from among them a party on the right course: But many of them follow a course that is evil."
Qur'an 5:66

CHAPTER 53

HIGH STAKES, HIGHER HOPES. . .

❖❖❖

"*O*ur emphasis must be on peace and the investigation into the missile attacks," Sam urged the President. "James, if we start discussing the imam's sermon, we will entangle ourselves in a web from which we cannot escape. We must focus on facts, on what has happened, and what needs to happen to keep the peace and save lives!"

James opened his hands as if lifting an invisible bowl of hope. "I could not agree with you more, Sam. We must turn the conversation away from the volatile call for jihad that has set Muslims afire in both our nations. We must show a spirit of cooperation between you and me, and offer that same cooperation to bin Laden. We must defuse this time bomb as quickly and smoothly as possible.

"I just have one lingering, as yet unanswered question, Sam. As we have all asked before, can we call for peace in the wake of the beheadings?"

The two leaders shared their thoughts in a private room, away from the rest of the members of the negotiating team. The tension was high, not because the Prime Minister and President disagreed, but because of all that was at stake. Both men realized the gravity of the situation. If this plea for calm in a torrent of real and potential violence fell on deaf ears, the world would once again be crippled, if not destroyed, by war.

"I believe your proposed Alliance of the Americas is a solid basis for current and future stability against both jihad and islamization. However, James, your promise to help Japan, China, and North Korea will not help us. For all practical purposes, Islam rules over those lands. One bin Laden wraps up the final details in the remains of the EU, he will lay claim to the remainder of Asia—including Taiwan. The Brotherhood has already taken over all government and industry."

The President of the United States sat stone faced. James had announced the Asian initiative over the objections of his Cabinet, especially Secretary of State Hannah Fielder, U.S. Chairman of the Joint Chiefs of Staff, General Pierce Ellis, and U.S. Defense Secretary David Rothschild. Furthermore, the unknown, bloodthirsty imam had thoroughly ridiculed the President's Asian initiative. Now, if Sam was so blunt in calling the move boneheaded, James realized he had lost political clout at home and made America appear misguided with its remaining allies—including Israel. For the first time since this crisis erupted Sunday morning, James realized his political gambling could only hurt him now. He understood that he had to lead from a strategic base, not a political one. Suddenly, he came to grips with the truth that he did not know how to lead, that he knew nothing outside of politics.

Sam wondered why James had gone silent and distant. Did he actually believe that Japan, China, and North Korea could be pulled from the jaws of Islam? If so, was James a competent partner and ally for Israel in this dark hour?

The two men stared at each other. Actually, they stared through each other.

Finally, Sam, realizing the two men had no time to waste or to second guess each other at this point, made a chilling statement. "James, we must be ready for jihad, even as we hope for peace. All the signs point to war!"

Sam's warning jolted James back into the moment. "Things have really changed since you signed the peace treaty four months ago. Did we foolishly believe peace had come at last, Sam?"

The unexpected question gave the Prime Minister pause. "Actually, James, I played the role of fool. After more than a century of conflict with the Palestinians, I should have realized true peace could never be achieved. I just longed for an end to all the conflict so desperately that I became blind to the reality of the situation. When the Palestinians suddenly accepted our offer, one that had been made countless times before, I should have been suspicious instead of elated."

James said in monotone, "I too wanted to believe that peace had come, even though I could not answer why now, what was different that made peace possible now, when it had proven impossible in the past."

Sam noticed the time, and turned the conversation back to the immediate matter at hand. "James, we can analyze the peace treaty later. Right now, we must determine what we will say to our nations and to a Caliph that appears to be ready to attack us!"

Seemingly coming to his senses, James said, "Of course, Sam. We have little time remaining."

The Prime Minister stated, "We have deployed our forces to the borders. Our Navy is patrolling the Mediterranean. Our Air Force is monitoring all airspace—both from the ground and the air."

"Are you sure you have control of your weapons systems, Sam? Have you test fired any missiles?"

"Not yet! Until we know how the saboteur or saboteurs managed to fire our missiles, we don't know if a test firing is safe. If we attempt a test before determining who fired the missiles and how that someone compromised the system, we have no idea if the missiles will fire or where they might land if they do launch. For all we know, they may explode in the silos!"

"I understand. But again, what about the beheadings, Sam? How do they play into our plan?"

Stonewalled by the circumstances and still grieving the loss of his friends, Sam replied bluntly, "They don't! The beheadings don't fit into our plan. We should be going to war, not crawling on our bellies for peace! But we cannot call for war as we don't know who has control of our weapons! Thus, we must call for peace and let the beheadings go unanswered—at least for the moment!"

Taken somewhat aback by Sam's raw anger, James gently asked, "Will you not mention them at all?"

"Only to say that we are investigating their heinous deaths. Only to say that we, as yet, do not know who is behind the assassinations!"

"If it brings you any comfort, I agree with you completely, Sam. We cannot launch into war under the present circumstances. We need time. Like you, at this moment, the U.S. has Air Force fighter jets on aerial patrol over all our major cities. We have deployed the National Guard to all our borders, and the Coast Guard is monitoring all our shorelines. Homeland Security has beefed up inspections at all ports— sea ports and airports. The rest of our armed forces are ready to deploy, either to here, to Babylon, within our own borders, or a combination of these locations."

The President changed gears. "Has the Mossad picked up this line? All our intel points to fresh division in the Babylonian camp!"

"All the chatter we are hearing leads us to the same conclusion, James. If we can trust that intel, we may have received a gift, an opportunity to avert war. The way our agents tell it, bin Laden feels that the Brotherhood is not yet ready to take on the United States—at least not for the foreseeable future. For the time being, the Caliph wants to maintain the status quo!"

"And the General is pushing for war?"

"Exactly!"

"That said, Sam, we must dismantle the manic imam's jihad machine, but without directly challenging him, without directly referring to the sermon, and without directly addressing the assassinations."

"Right, James. We must eat crow tonight in order to fight, if necessary, another day. And another day may be just around the corner, no matter what we say tonight!"

The President sighed deeply as he nodded his head in agreement. "Sooner than we think, I fear!"

"Yes, I agree. Nonetheless, the Mossad may have another hot tip from the Caliph's inner circle!"

As the two leaders continued talking, other conversations took place. In another room in the studio, Sol and Ahava spoke with Mark and Ariel about Grace as well as their dangerous ride through the streets of the DROP.

Mark said, "We arrived here, covered with sweat. The President's suit was actually wet after Ariel hugged him! Without being asked, Addar graciously provided us all with a place to take a shower as well as three new sets of clothes. How he had those on hand, I have no idea, but Ariel and I, and I think the President as well, were extremely grateful to Addar—especially after he saved our lives in the studio!"

"Maybe the imam is truly a kind soul, Mark. Maybe he is less dubious than we think," Sol replied.

"Perhaps. Maybe I am just expecting the worst from every Muslim right now. My nerves are shot. I could not sleep on the plane at all," Mark confessed.

"I understand, Mark," Sol said as he put his hand on Mark's shoulder. "As a father, you want to protect your daughter."

Ariel joined the conversation, saying, "When the Muslims tried to overturn our car, I wondered if we would survive to see Grace! I prayed to our Lord all throughout that entire ordeal!"

Sol noted, "Ahava and I came into Palestine immediately after the imam's sermon. We arrived here just before the streets filled with jihad-crazed Islamists. If we had encountered the same wild crowd you met, we likely would not have fared as well as you two," Sol said as he tugged on his white beard and the tassels on his prayer shawl. "I would have been a most desirable target as a fat, old Orthodox Jew! Worse yet, we had no special agents shadowing us!"

The four of them laughed at Sol's gestures and comments. The lighthearted moment helped relieve the tension they all bore.

Still smiling, Mark noted, "Our Lord gave you and Ahava wisdom, Sol. He had you come here before the danger materialized."

Sol could not wait any longer. "Mark, when you say, 'Our Lord,' do you mean *Adonai* or Y'shua?"

Both Mark and Ariel were caught off guard by Sol's question. Ariel answered, "You know Sol, that we regard Father, Son, and Spirit as one in the same."

"Yes, but who specifically are you referring when you say, 'Lord,' Mark, *'Adonai?'*"

Not wanting to offend or deny the truth, Mark answered gently, "I was talking about Y'shua, Sol. Why do you ask?"

The rabbi of rabbis looked to his wife. Her compassionate eyes told him, "Go ahead. Tell them!"

Sol breathed deeply, "I believe Y'shua has been speaking to me!"

In yet a third room, Abdul and Addar stood toe to toe, in the midst of a heavy discussion.

"Addar, do you think we have a real chance to maintain peace in light of yesterday's missile attack, the beheadings in Israel, and the unknown imam's demand for jihad?"

Addar replied coolly, "I'm sure your briefing with the President and his advisers gave you some perspective on that question."

"Yes, James is hopeful that he and Sam can throw some cold water on this growing fire."

"How so?" Addar asked with great curiosity.

"If our intel and analysis can be trusted, the Caliph does not want to rush into war with the U.S. and Israel."

"Oh, really? What are your agents hearing?"

Abdul paused. He stared into Addar's inquisitive face. He asked himself, *"Can I trust Addar with this information?"* He decided to deviate from the latest intelligence. Abdul tried to change the subject.

Noticing the Vice President's hesitation, Addar said, "You can trust me of all people, Abdul!"

"Right!" replied Abdul. "The general consensus is that the Caliph was not anticipating the missile attack at all. Moreover, he finds it hard to believe that Israel would want to go to war with Babylon and the Brotherhood, even if Israel's nuclear warheads are as numerous as the sand on the seashore."

"That's an interesting phrase my friend. Isn't it from the Hebrew Bible? Where did you come across that quote?"

"How should I answer that question?" Abdul wondered. *"Would not Isa want me to tell the truth?"* Thus, Abdul replied, "I read it in the Torah—the Old Testament."

"I am well aware of where to find the phrase. But why have you been reading Jewish or Christian Scriptures?"

"I do live in a country of Muslims, Christians, and Jews, Addar," Abdul said, dancing around the actual reason he stayed up to read the Bible during most of the flight to Israel. "Should I not know what the Scriptures written prior to Muhammad's arrival say? Doesn't Allah say that the Hebrew and Christian Scriptures come from him, also?"

The imam did not back off. "We could dance around that question all night! But since when have you read any Scripture? You never seemed interested in the roots of Islam before," Addar said, moving closer to Abdul and increasing the tension in their conversation.

"People change," Abdul said as he backed away from Addar, unsure of how much he wanted to reveal to the man who pulled him into U.S. politics. As a result, Abdul shifted gears once more. "Should I call you Imam Zaahir or Emir Zaahir?"

Addar did not like that question at all. "What are you insinuating, Abdul?"

Smiling because his diversion worked, Abdul replied, "Have you not harbored desires to lead, to have political power, all of your life? Now that the President of the DROP has been eliminated, you top the list of successors. Will you make a run for President?"

Addar knew Abdul had baited a hook, but the imam refused to bite. Thus, he stated, "I follow the will of Allah and the will of the people. I did not ask for this temporary leadership position and I did not ask to be insulted by a man who has the political savvy of a desert cactus!"

Abdul did not respond to the insult, but kept pushing. "Oh, so you will not seek the office of President of the DROP?"

With great force in his voice, Addar said, "This part of our conversation has ended, Abdul. Do you understand me?"

Again, Abdul chose a new topic. "In our phone conversations yesterday, you seemed to know more than you were telling me. Do you know anything more about the Basel's daughter than what you have shared with me or Mark and Ariel?"

Abdul's second rouse worked. Addar looked both uncomfortable and surprised by the sudden question concerning Grace. Addar backed away, wondering what lurked behind this unwanted and possibly loaded inquiry. As such, Addar responded with a question of his own: "Why do you ask?"

With genuine empathy in his voice, Abdul confided, "While I am neither married nor a father, I feel for Mark and Ariel. They love Grace so much, and she loves them in return—unlike so many young teens in the U.S. today. I sense their pain as they are torn apart, not knowing Grace's whereabouts or if they will ever hold her in their arms again."

"First, you read their Scripture, and now you have become a compassionate friend of Christians, Abdul? When did all this change in you take place?" Addar's sharp question cut to the heart of their conversation.

Abdul looked into Addar's angry eyes and asked himself, *"Should I say, 'Last night, when I became a follower of Isa?'"*

"Blessed are the peacemakers, for they will be called sons of God."
Matthew 5:9

CHAPTER 54

THE THIN LINE. . .

*A*s everyone gathered in the main studio, the President found him-self wanting to pray—a very foreign feeling for him, indeed. That desire came from the depths of his soul, a place he never visited or recognized. *"I don't know how to pray,"* he told himself, as he sought to focus on the moment and the address he and the Prime Minister would soon make. Despite his efforts, the need he felt to pray—now more like an aching hunger—would not yield!

Suddenly, his thoughts were jerked away from his inner turmoil to the images of the Caliph that were on all the holovision monitors in the studio. Still dressed in white, no ally or enemy could deny bin Laden's commanding presence.

"To all who follow the way of Allah, Most Gracious, Most Merciful, inside and outside the borders of Babylon, and to our neighbors who are now mourning with us the dreadful loss of life."

The Caliph was seated before a mural of the most holy places in Islam: The Masjid Al Haram Mosque, the Sacred Mosque in Mecca, the Al Masjid Al Nabawi Mosque, the Mosque of the Prophet in Medina, and the Al Aqsa Mosque, the Farthest Mosque that once stood upon the Temple Mount. Bin Laden's body blocked the view of the two mosques in Babylonian state of Saudi Arabia, leaving the Al Aqsa Mosque as the only one in view of his worldwide audience.

"I also speak to those of you who believe that I am your nemesis. I come before you tonight to bring the truth of recent events."

The Prime Minister and the President looked at each other inquisitively. They both had the same question in their minds: *"What 'truth' would bin Laden share with the world?"*

"While we do not yet know who is behind the horrific missile strike on the Palestinian state, as both the United States and Israel adamantly deny any role in that act of war, we do know something about the beheadings of the Prime Minister's Cabinet and the sermon given today by an unknown imam.

"Hear me clearly, whether you are Muslim and worship the one true god, or Jew, Christian, or other misguided and doomed soul in this world!"

The President thought, *"He really knows how to endear himself to people, doesn't he?"*

The Caliph continued, "I declare to you the truth that I did not authorize the beheadings of the Israeli Prime Minister's Cabinet, nor did I authorize the call for jihad that echoed today in mosques around the world! I wanted a time for remembering the fallen in prayer, not a time of calling for vengeance.

"I am the only voice of Babylon, and I tell you that the Caliphate does not yet want to go to war with Israel and the United States, even though these infidels deserve to see and experience the wrath of Allah! I am the sole authority of the Caliphate, and I tell you that the noble head of Babylon did not order any beheadings of any Israeli officials! I gave the United States and Israel time to determine who fired the fatal missiles into Palestine. I am a man of my word. I still wait for their results of their investigations!"

Now, Mark and Abdul looked at each other in disbelief!

"Just as Prime Minister Ben Baruch says he did not order the missile attack, just as President Paulson insists he had no part in the terror that fell from the sky upon Palestine, I swear by Allah and his Prophet—peace be upon him—that I had no role in the assassinations of the Israeli leaders, no matter how much they deserved death, and I likewise had no role in the imam's call for jihad, even though such a call cannot be denied in this world infested with pigs and apes who claim to be men!

"Nonetheless, I have not, up to this point, authorized jihad, and I now say stand down to all of you who are taking up arms to wage war with the infidels! When the American President and the Israeli Prime

Minister report to me on Sunday, then I and I alone, in consultation with Allah, will determine if the people of Islam will wage holy war against the refuse of the world in the United States and Israel!

"To the imam that incited our people around the world, I warn you of the penalty for usurping my authority! Likewise, to those who slit the throats of the Jews, there likewise looms a consequence for waging jihad outside my specific orders! That punishment remains swift and certain death, and I assure you that I will not be delayed in finding you and separating your brazen bodies from your insolent heads!"

Bin Laden rose to his feet and brandished his sparkling, razor sharp machete. With great power behind his words, he proclaimed, "I tell you that I, the Caliph of the Muslim Alliance, Allah's chosen head of the Islamic Caliphate, do not share power and command with anyone, just as Allah himself does not share power or command with anyone! Furthermore, I promise you, the culprits behind the call for jihad and the beheadings, that you will appear before me! I also promise that the last thing your doomed eyes will see will be my face in the moment before I personally rid your bodies of their heads!

"For now, may your guilt eat at you like the final stage of terminal cancer eats at your internal organs! May you beg those around you to bring you to me in order to end your much deserved torture!

"Until Sunday, the Caliphate stands at peace! On Sunday, I and I alone, with the blessing of Allah, will determine if Islam will be at war with the disbelievers and hypocrites. Until then, any other perpetrators of violence will have to answer personally to me and eternally to Allah!"

Sitting down once more and looking over his shoulder to the mural of the Al Aqsa Mosque, bin Laden calmly said, "Have no fear or doubt. Those who destroyed sacred life and property in Palestine will pay in kind, but only under my order and in my timing!

"Allah is on our side. Goliath is on our side, and no little shepherd boy with a pebble will be able to take down this giant—a power like none the world has never known!"

"The similitude of Isa before Allah is as that of Adam; He created him from dust, then said to him, 'Be': And he was. The Truth (comes) from Allah alone; So be not of those who doubt."
Qur'an 3:59-60

CHAPTER 55

THAT'S MY BOY. . .

*W*ith three minutes left before they addressed the nations, President Paulson and Prime Minister Ben Baruch frantically reworked their speeches to include the Caliph's call for peace! Bin Laden's words and timing could not have been better to set up their own call for calm until the truth came to light!

The two leaders quickly agreed not to address the ominous threat of Goliath, as, frankly, neither of them had any solid information about the secretive weapon. After their speeches, the two leaders would make Goliath a top priority for their respective intelligence agencies.

Meanwhile, though the President and Prime Minister expressed genuine optimism following the Caliph's words, the Vice President remained skeptical. Bin Laden had not spoken from the true heart of Islam. In fact, the Caliph, a Muslim of jihad whose forefathers were Muslims of jihad, did not sound credible to Abdul at all. In his opinion, bin Laden's speech left the impression of weakness and disorder at the highest echelons of the Muslim Alliance.

Similarly, Mark did not celebrate the Caliph's address either. From experience and from Scripture, Mark knew that actions flow out of the heart of a man. Indeed, the pastor felt certain that the Caliph harbored no desire for peace within him. So why would bin Laden delay jihad?

Despite their struggles with bin Laden's speech, Mark and Abdul had no opportunity to share their reactions with the President and Prime

Minister. As it turned out, Addar monopolized the short three minutes before James and Sam spoke to the world. Elated by the words of bin Laden, Addar encouraged the two leaders that peace could be restored and all their labors had not been in vain. "Allah is most gracious to us tonight. He has spoken to our earthly leader of heavenly things! We are seeing the new face of Babylon   the face of peace!"

With those hypocritical words, Addar moved over to the empty seat, the one between the President and the Prime Minister, the one where the President of the DROP had sat on the day the peace accord had been officially announced. Abdul was on the President's right side, where Secretary of State Hannah Fielder had sat.

Mark sat next to Abdul, while Sol sat on the opposite end of the set table, next to Sam. Both men of the cloth were looking over their notes and also making changes in what they planned to say. Actually, as Sol prepared to praise the Caliph's speech, Mark suspected some type of cover-up in Ankara. Would he dare to share his wariness with the world?

The head of the floor crew gave the countdown. "In 5, 4, 3. . ." When the silent "2, 1" ticked off in his head, Prime Minister Ben Baruch began his speech by saying, "Tonight you have already seen and heard the Caliph of Babylon's plea for peace. Now, you will see and hear the President of the United States, and I, the Prime Minister of Israel, join hands and hearts with the Caliph, as we too pray for peace to continue in our nations and world!"

At that exact moment, the satellite feed from Palestine's *Al-Manar*—The Lighthouse—Satellite News was interrupted by another live broadcast. Images of simultaneous explosions erupting in Israel and the United States filled the studio! The former negotiating team found itself in the midst of overwhelming SenseSurround, 3D holographic images of extreme destruction and death.

Without warning, the official Presidential residence within the White House, the official Vice Presidential residence at the United States Naval Observatory, and the official residence of the Israeli Prime Minister, *Beit Rosh HaMemshala*, exploded with enough force to pulverize bodies and materials.

Simultaneously, Yad Vashem, the foremost Israeli Holocaust Museum in Jerusalem, as well as the United States Holocaust Memorial Museum in Washington D.C. also became nonexistent! Synchronized detonations wiped out all the artifacts of the evil committed against the Jews, not to mention the living beings who were exploring those halls of infamy!

Also in the U.S. Capitol, the headquarters of the American Islamic Forum for Democracy (AIFD) instantly disappeared in a ball of fire. The AIFD was the official voice of moderate Muslims in the United States, those Muslims who truly desired to assimilate into American society, culture, and politics, while maintaining their worship of Allah.

Then, at the same calculated moment, five hypersonic SkyShark II (SSII) missiles, dramatically enhanced versions of the SSI Missiles that struck the DROP, were launched from Charleston Air Force Base in South Carolina. The base had been secretly retrofitted with missile launch capability only three years before.

As in Israel, the SkySharks evaded detection until they could not be stopped, even by the Air Force fighter jets that patrolled above the nation's capitol. Likewise, as in The Land, one SkyShark would have easily erased all traces of the Pentagon. Again, the objective of whoever fired these projectiles of doom remained shock and awe.

Each missile detonated at one of the five points of the Pentagon, obliterating the brain of the U.S. military body, while also destroying other sites in Virginia and D.C.. The blasts wiped out the Arlington National Cemetery along with the physical remains of three quarters of a million of America's greatest heroes!

As the wave of destruction rolled across the Potomac, the islands in the river disappeared and several national memorials instantly vanished from the District of Columbia landscape, including the Jefferson, Roosevelt, Lincoln, Martin Luther King, Vietnam Veterans, and World War II and III Memorials, not to mention the Smithsonian—the world's largest museum and research complex. What had been left standing of the White House also became dust and ash.

As in Jerusalem, the massive number of vaporized bodies would never be identified. On that sunless day, families across the United States grieved the loss of their loved ones in their nation's capitol.

Only a few people withstood the fiery assault. They were left to suffer without hands, feet, arms, legs, and or eyes. All the wounded knew the agony of fourth to sixth degree burns. Perhaps mercifully, the survivors only held on long enough to arrive at the hospitals where they would soon depart their mangled, pain-riddled bodies.

In Jericho, Ibrahim Shajee smiled in pride as he rushed into the street to celebrate his dead son's role as a hero and *shahid* in Allah's jihad! One of next year's Brotherhood Jihad Summer Camps would honor the martyrdom of Jahm Shajee!

"But if anyone causes one of these little ones who believe in Me to sin, it would be better for him to have a large millstone hung around his neck and to be drowned in the depths of the sea."
Matthew 18:6

CHAPTER 56

UNHOLY MATRMONY. . .

Oblivious to the events in Israel and the United States—as well as the close proximity of her parents—Grace sat on a hard couch, feeling as though she would vomit at any time. Likewise, her head continued to throb. Between the drug her supposed Muslim father had forced her to inhale on the jetliner and her lack of food and water for two days, Grace could not imagine being any weaker.

She and her surrogate Muslim parents had made it through Israeli customs with no problems. They had nothing to declare and Grace was too weak to attract any attention. The family of three had left the airport for the secret location in the DROP. The ride through the streets of Palestine had been slow and long, as well as intimidating and frightening to her. She had never heard so many Muslims in such frenetic activity! For the first time in her journey, she had been thankful for the cover of the *niqab*.

Now, free from the veil and the robe—the *chador*—that had entrapped her since she started her journey in Atlanta, Grace stood in the darkened room. Finally, she could move without the walking tent draped over her body. Dressed only in the undergarment of Muzaynah's daughter, the thirteen year old felt noticeably lighter.

Faint flickers of light surrounded her. Even so, Grace could not tell if she was alone in the strange room. Suddenly, the door opened, flooding the room with light, blinding her eyes, and exposing her to whoever entered. The tall silhouette of a man blocked the light for a moment, as he placed a bowl in front of her. "Eat!" he commanded, then turned and left the room, restoring the darkness as he shut the door.

Grace felt both hungry and queasy at the same time. Should she eat what the man had shoved in her face? She called out, "What is this?" However, the silhouetted man had walked too far away to hear her. The starved teen lifted the warm bowl to her nose. She did not recognize the aroma, but it seemed pleasant enough. She felt around the edge of the bowl for a fork or spoon, but found neither. Instinctively, she plunged her right hand into the fairly large dish and brought the stew like substance to her mouth. She chewed and swallowed and did not stop until she licked out the final traces of her meal from the bowl and her fingers. For the first time in her short life, she had eaten *yakhnat al-lubya*, green bean and lamb stew.

Despite the firmness of the couch, Grace decided to lie down. The bruised and battered teenager had not been able to stretch out since Saturday night. She asked of the darkness, *"What day is it now? What time is it?"*

A deep voice from the darkness replied, "It is Monday evening, 9:17 Babylon time."

Grace drew her arms around herself as she felt so vulnerable in the dark, so naked in the undergarment. "Where am I, and who are you?" she timidly asked.

"Me? You know me! I am your husband! We are in the bride chamber!"

"Soon shall We cast terror into the hearts of the Unbelievers for that they joined companions with Allah, for which He had sent no authority: Their abode will be the Fire: and evil is the home of the wrong-doers!"
Qur'an 3:151

CHAPTER 57

A GENUINE HERO...

*T*he eyes of everyone in the studio remained fixed on the devastation in Israel and the United States—that is, save for the eyes of one studio crewman and Abdul. The man had been leaning on the wall directly behind the HV3D cameras. When he quickly reached for a box on the floor, the movement caught Abdul's attention. Before the Vice President even realized what he saw, instinct made him move. As the crewman, actually a Brotherhood trained marksman, fired his rifle, Abdul felt a surge of adrenaline shoot through his body. He jumped from his seat, shouted, "Get down, James!" and pushed the President out of his chair. Because of the last second abrupt movement, the assassin's homing bullet pierced Abdul's right shoulder instead of blasting a hole in the President's chest!

In a domino effect, the President's body hit the imam, whose body in turn knocked the Prime Minister out of his chair! Thus, when the marksman fired his second shot to kill Sam, Addar's right arm took the bullet instead. A second later, all four men lied behind the large table, while Mark and Sol had ducked when they heard the first shot!

The ace gunman, having missed both of his assigned targets, fled out the door of the studio into the arms of the President's and the Prime Minister's security details who were running toward the studio.

"James, are you all right?" Abdul shouted.

Stunned, the President replied, "Yes, I think I am fine." Sitting up and turning toward Abdul, the President exclaimed, "My God! Abdul, you have been shot!" Abdul had neither felt the pain nor seen the blood until that moment.

"I have been wounded, as well!" Addar protested, using his left hand to apply pressure against the flow of blood in his right arm. Then he rolled toward the Prime Minister. With a trembling voice, Addar asked, "Are you hurt Sam?"

The Prime Minister answered, "No, just startled, shocked!"

Mark ran to Abdul while Ariel headed straight for Addar, who suddenly screamed in agony. He was furious with himself that he could not manage his pain while Abdul seemed to be coping well with his injury. Tears streamed down the embittered imam's face.

Ahava told Sol to call for emergency services, but the agent coming through the studio door stated, "That won't be necessary! We are taking the wounded across the border to Shaare Zedek Medical Center in Jerusalem. One of our men has EMT (Emergency Medical Training) and will care for the wounded along the way."

Kneeling next to his Vice President to help him sit up, the President said with deep resolve and heartfelt gratitude, "Abdul, you just saved my life as well as the life of the Prime Minister! I owe you a debt I cannot repay!"

"You belong to your father, the devil, and you want to carry out your father's desire. He was a murderer from the beginning, not holding to the truth, for there is no truth in him. When he lies, he speaks his native language, for he is a liar and the father of lies."
John 8:44

CHAPTER 58

SPLITTING HEADACHE. . .

*L*ike a volcano spewing out molten lava, the Caliph erupted with burning anger! "Who did this? Who authorized direct attacks on the United States and Israel?"

An aide had already contacted Palestine's *Al-Manar* Satellite News. He said, "Our men did not arrange the live shots. In fact, they knew nothing of the bombings before they saw them in real time. Someone took over the system!"

Bin Laden screamed as he stomped around his luxurious chamber, "Who rushes me to war? Who forces me to do his bidding?"

Another aide ran into the room. "Your highness, we have more information from the studio in Palestine. Our man says that someone tried to assassinate both the Prime Minister and the President, yet failed!"

With his fists clenched, bin Laden demanded, "Who? Who attempted to kill the President and Prime Minister?"

"No one knows, sir, but the gunman did not escape. Special agents have removed him from the studio."

"Where is this man now?"

"Again, no one knows!"

"Find out—now! This man is our connection to discovering who plotted what we have just witnessed! Find the failed assassin and bring him to me before he can reveal anything or anyone to the Americans or Israelis!"

"Yes, sire! Howbeit, I have yet more news. The American Vice President and Imam Zaahir have been shot. They took the MGM's intended for the President and the Prime Minister!"

"That may be the first good news I have heard! We have two Muslim heroes! Maybe we can avert war even yet!"

As the aide ran from the Caliph's personal chamber, bin Laden bellowed, "Find my General! Find him for me now! I must know what he thinks happened tonight—or if he had anything to do with it!"

Enraged, bin Laden stormed out of his regal room into the elegant hallway. He had no time to react to what he saw.

"If ye fear that ye shall not be able to deal justly with the orphans, marry women of your choice, two, or three, or four; But if ye fear that ye shall not be able to deal justly (with them), then only one, or (a captive) that your right hands possess. That will be more suitable, to prevent you from doing injustice."
Qur'an 4:3

CHAPTER 59

HONEYMOON SUITE. . .

*D*espite her bumps and bruises, Grace slid off the couch and shimmied under it without making a sound. She did not respond to the ominous voice from the darkness.

The man stood and stepped over to the couch. "Haziqah! You are not afraid are you?" He rubbed his hands over the couch trying to find her. "Haziqah! You cannot hide. I know you are in this room! You must talk to me."

When silence met his demand, the man cloaked in darkness revealed his growing impatience and anger in his words. "This can be painless or extremely painful!"

Grace decided she could not answer from under the couch, so she slid out from under the back side of it and crawled to the farthest edge of the room. She decided to be a moving target, skimming along the walls, speaking from a different point each time.

"I am too young to marry!" Immediately, the man rose from the couch toward her voice, while Grace eased to her right.

Reaching toward the wall in the black room, the man countered, "Muhammad's—peace be upon him—favorite wife was only six when he married her. The prophet was forty nine. He waited until she was nine before consummating their marriage. You do know what consummate means, don't you, Haziqah?"

"Yes," came her sheepish response from the other side of the room. Again, the malevolent man turned toward her voice, but she quickly moved down the wall to her left.

"Good," the deep, black voice noted, "that makes things easier for me. As you have turned thirteen, we should have no reason to wait. Tonight is a most opportune time, my Sweet!" The lust-filled Muslim was enjoying his dark game of cat and mouse.

Grace feared he could hear her heart pounding in her chest. "Why marry me?" she asked from behind the man.

He quickly swiveled and jumped across the room, "My other three wives are old and no longer satisfying. Muhammad had twenty two wives, but I will stay with the Qur'an's limit of four—not counting my slave concubines, of course."

"How old are you?" Grace asked as she pressed her back against the wall and slid into something metal. She froze, not knowing what to do.

The potential pedophile decided he was smarter than Grace, figuring she made the noise so he would go to that location. So he too did not move. He boasted with a devilish laugh, "I am 54, and I can teach you many things!"

"But I am a Christian!" Grace said quickly before sliding in the reverse direction.

Still holding his position, he noted, "Not for long. Now, you are *kuffar, shirk*—an infidel! You worship three gods! But all that will end before I take you as my wife. In a few moments, you will become a true believer in the one, true god, Allah!"

Grace said nothing.

"I am good to my wives, Haziqah," the man said, his voice coming closer to Grace as he walked next to the walls. "I only beat my wives occasionally and only when they deserve it—like when they go out of the house for no reason and without my permission. I don't know why they are so foolish. I can track them with the chips imbedded in their arms."

Grace breathed rapidly, knowing she would soon be found. Her eyes stung as tears washed over her dry eyes. She could hear the steps coming ever closer. She curled up in the fetal position. Silently, she prayed, "Help me, Lord! Save me! Don't let this Muslim have me! I belong to You!"

At that moment, the door opened and another one of the men shouted into the darkness: "He is dead! He's been beheaded!"

"Now My heart is troubled, and what shall I say? 'Father, save Me from this hour?' No, it was for this very reason I came to this hour."
John 12:27

CHAPTER 60

SURROUNDED BY FEAR. . .

Standing in the hospital lobby, the President spoke via 3DHP to his Homeland Security Chief, "Matt, how can you say, 'Things could be worse?' The White House and everyone in it—including most of my Cabinet are gone, dead and destroyed! The Vice Presidential Residence no longer exists. The Pentagon—consumed by our own rockets—now serves as a mass grave with all the dead buried under tons of rubble! An enemy has control of our weapons system. The U.S. Holocaust Memorial Museum and all who were in it suffered a holocaust of their own! Worse yet, the headquarters of the approachable Muslims no longer stands! All the leaders of the American Islamic Forum for Democracy are toast! Meanwhile, Goliath—whatever it is—may soon be a clear and present danger! Matt, I don't see any silver linings to these dark and foreboding clouds!"

Secretary Davidson replied, "Truly, James, all of this could be much worse! If not for the Potomac and the Tidal Basin, the rest of D.C. would have been obliterated as well! Without the water and islands absorbing some of the impact, the Capitol and the Supreme Court would be in ruins, as well! In that scenario, you and Abdul would be virtually alone in leading the country!"

"Thanks for trying, Matt, but I find it difficult to see the glass as being half full right now!"

"Should we not be more grateful for what we have left and less mournful over what we have lost, James?"

"Let me be clear with you, Matt. I stand here mortified by what has happened today, while you seem to be oblivious to the horror and tragedy of these events. Right now, I can't look through rose colored glasses to see a bright side to all this darkness, destruction, and death.

Sorry—just trying to help. I understand. You have so much on your shoulders. Anyway, James, you need to come back to the states as soon as possible. I suppose chaos rules the nation about now. People fear going out in the street, and they now look to you for our answers and hope. During your flight home, David and I will put together various scenarios for your review. We'll work in concert with General Ellis—thank God he was not at the Pentagon! We'll get back to you before you land in D.C., so that you can address the nation in flight."

"Gotcha, Matt. Abdul and I will be in the air before long—just waiting on medical clearance for him to fly. God be with us!"

The Homeland Security Secretary said nothing in reply.

The President asked, "Matt, do you feel okay? You don't seem to be yourself. Can you not deal with the enormity of the terror released on the United States today?"

Without an answer, Matt's fixed image faded away.

James could not understand Matt's cavalier attitude. From his perspective, the President felt he faced virtually insurmountable issues. Overall, the country was basically shut down. With no domestic or international flights, the airports of America brimmed with angry, frustrated travelers. With no receiving or sending of ships and no unloading of ships already docked, whether cruise liners or cargo carriers, the nations ports had ground to a halt. With no idea how many Muslims had taken up arms in jihad, the streets remained empty, save for the National Guard and police that patrolled them, and emergency services personnel who transported the wounded.

Although aerial surveillance did not prevent the destruction of the Pentagon, the Air Force kept its watch over the nation's major cities, while the Coast Guard monitored the ports and shorelines. The Army, Marines, Navy, and the remainder of the Air Force and their reserves stood ready for domestic or foreign deployment—or a combination of both.

James asked himself, "*What can our troops accomplish without our major weapons? Does the enemy, whoever he may be, have control over all or only some of our arsenal? Can the U.S. prevent another attack such as the one on D.C.? How will our remaining military heads answer these questions?"*

As his secret service team guarded the hospital entrance and the lobby, the President sat down, breathed deeply, and debated with himself. *"Must I declare martial law? Has World War IV begun? Can I trust anything the Caliph says? How can I fully deploy our military with the destruction of the Pentagon and infiltration into the weapons system? How will I help America as she grieves the losses of this day?"*

The President envisioned mass jihad in U.S. streets, as he recalled what Matt had said, "Americans panicked as some Muslim street celebrations turned violent. In a few cities as well as a few remote locations, Muslim sleeper cells have suddenly awoken from their slumber. The jihadists have torched houses, killed innocents."

As if those details were not bad enough, Matt had also told the Commander in Chief that "The White House, the Vice President's residence, the Holocaust Museums in the U.S. and Israel, and the Prime Minister's residence had all been bombed from the inside."

James needed answers. *"Were the perpetrators suicide bombers or were they still alive and ready to deliver more murder and mayhem? Were the culprits insiders? Did the Brotherhood have operatives in the Capitol, in the government itself, as Abdul had predicted?"*

Interviews of all security officers at the U.S. and Israeli sites were already underway. But all these men and women were not on duty during the blasts. No one survived the explosions. No bodies could be identified.

Beyond all this, what really made James cringe was the fact that an enemy now had at least some control over U.S. weapons, not only Israeli weapons. He attempted to sort out the possibilities, but only ended up with more questions. *"If a coup has begun in Ankara, then who controls our weapons—the Caliph or his opponent? To what extent has our weapons system been compromised? Who could have cracked our encryptions and broke through our firewalls? We must be dealing with a cyber master! Can we regain control of our weapons or will they continue to be used against us until we are destroyed?"*

The President then thought, *"Maybe Abdul is right. Maybe all of this terror is a prelude for war over Israeli and U.S. natural gas and oil."*

Without warning, James had a new and clear idea. He did not call it such, but the President experienced a divine epiphany. He heard the words clearly in his mind.

These attacks have nothing to do with fuel reserves. Instead, the violence starts and ends with Islam. Babylon cannot allow a Muslim democracy to survive! Such a free and independent Muslim state represents blasphemy of the highest order! Thus, Babylon attacked the DROP to destroy it—to wipe the shame of a Muslim democracy off the face of the earth! Staging the attack from Israel gives the Caliphate justification to finally wipe out the Great and Little Satans, once and for all! Furthermore, Ankara does not have its own weapons or at least does not have the ability to use its own weapons. So decimating the DROP with Israeli weapons serves two purposes: it wipes out the stench of a Muslim democracy and proves that Babylon does have an arsenal for destroying its nemeses!

The President stood quickly. The sweat on his brow was as cold as the snow atop Mount Hermon! His mouth was as dry as the Israeli Negev! His breathing was as rapid as an Israeli colibri hummingbird's wings!

Were the words James had just heard his own or had God spoken to him? Honestly, James knew he personally had neither the clarity of thought nor the insight to summarize the situation so succinctly. If the truth of the situation had been revealed to the President, what must he do to prevent the United States and Israel from being destroyed by their own weapons? James quickly realized some basic facts. *"Babylon must not have complete control over the entire weapons systems in the U.S. and Israel, else neither nation would yet exist! The Caliphate or a rebel force within it must still be in process of gaining such control. If so, why wreak havoc and terror in the prelude? Why give us a chance to regain control of our weapons? Do the Caliph and the General have opposing opinions and plans? Could there be a third player vying for power who remains invisible to us? Which one of them has at least partial control over our weapons? Who has been able to crack every meticulous security measure undetected, first in Israel and now in the U.S.? Can someone still fire Israeli and U.S. weapons at will, and who or what will be the next target for destruction? Time is of the essence! I must return to Washington! Should I order a test of our weapons system? Could it be booby trapped against us?"*

The leader of the world's last superpower began to pace around the lobby, his security team in tow. He questioned, thought, planned, and hoped. Did he still have time to save his country and citizens? Did he still have time to help Sam save his land and people, as well?

Before leaving Israel, James knew he had unfinished business. He walked into the Emergency Room where Vice President Abdullah and Imam Zaahir were being treated in a secured area. The doctor said that both men's wounds could have easily been more serious. Even though Abdul's wound had been cleansed and required many stitches, the Vice President had handled the minor surgery well. Both he and Addar would likely be released from the hospital in a few hours.

After the doctor left the room, the President stood between the two beds. "Gentlemen, both of you deserve my deepest thanks. Addar and Abdul, I would not be standing here without the two of you! Your bravery and selflessness saved my life from assassins' bullets twice today!" President Paulson then hugged both men as best as he could without pressing against their wounds.

The President then held Abdul's hand firmly in his own. "My friend, I not only owe you my life, but I also owe you the life of my family! If you had not suggested that I secretly send Hope and the children away until I returned to the states, I would have lost the ones I love most in this world!"

Taking hold of the imam's hand as well, President Paulson said, "Addar, you saved my life at the studio even before Abdul took the bullet that was bearing down on me! You saw the gunman outside the studio, and you risked your own life to push me, Mark, and Ariel out of harm's way! Thus, I and my country are most grateful to you!

"In addition, Addar, on behalf of the Israeli Prime Minister, I thank you. You saved his life this evening. The nations and leaders of the United States and Israel are most grateful to you!" Sam had to rush straight into another emergency meeting of his Deputy Cabinet members and government leaders, so the Prime Minister asked me to convey to you his deepest gratitude for taking the bullet that was meant for him!"

Addar was filled with a wide range of emotions and truly could not say a word in response. He just stared at the President.

Sensing the awkwardness of the moment, James turned back to his Vice President and said, "Abdul, when you pushed me out of the way of the bullet that you took in my stead, I fell onto Addar! Then he, in turn fell onto Sam, pushing him out of the way of the bullet meant for him!"

Turning back to the injured imam, the President added, "While you may not have intended to save the Prime Minister's life, you have suffered for him nonetheless. You have preserved his life for his family and his people!"

While Addar tried to manage a smile, Abdul said, "James, I believe that you would have acted as I did today—as Addar did today—had our roles been reversed!"

James had not considered such a scenario, and now he did not know how to respond. Would he have risked his life for either or both of these men?

At the same time, Addar thought to himself, *"My motives in saving the President's life are not as pure as he believes them to be."*

Swallowing hard, the President's tone changed. "Unfortunately, I do have some extremely bad news to share with—news beyond the massive death and destruction in Israel and the U.S. today." James grimaced, as he said, "I now know more about the weapon called Goliath and its incredible potential!"

"Men are the protectors and maintainers of women, because Allah has given the one more (strength) than the other, and because they support them from their means. Therefore the righteous women are devoutly obedient, and guard in (the husband's) absence what Allah would have them guard. As to those women on whose part ye fear disloyalty and ill-conduct, admonish them (first), (next), refuse to share their beds, (and last) beat them (lightly); But if they return to obedience, seek not against them means (of annoyance): For Allah is Most High, Great (above you all)."
Qur'an 4:34

CHAPTER 61

A PERSONAL INVITATION...

*M*ark and Ariel continued to talk with Sol and Ahava about Y'shua as they waited for word on Addar and Abdul. The pastor told the rabbi, "Y'shua was a Jew's Jew, Sol. Guess what Y'shua says is the most important command of all?"

Sol just looked blankly at Mark, having no idea how to answer his question.

Mark pulled up the verses on his 3DHP. "Read Mark 12:28-30, Sol."

The rabbi read aloud, *"One of the teachers of the law came and heard them debating. Noticing that Jesus had given them a good answer, he asked Him, 'Of all the commandments, which is the most important?' 'The most important one,' answered Jesus, 'is this: "Hear, O Israel, the Lord our God, the Lord is one. Love the Lord your God with all your heart and with all your soul and with all your mind and with all your strength."'"*

A dazzling smile suddenly popped up on Sol's face! "The *Sh'ma*! Y'shua was right! The *Sh'ma* is the most important commandment! If you obey *HaShem* in following the *Sh'ma*, you will naturally obey all of the other commands!"

"Did you notice who asked that question of Y'shua, Sol?"

Sol looked back at the passage. He then said, "One of the teachers of the law?"

"Indeed, Sol. And who would have been such a 'teacher of the law?'"

Sol smiled again, "A rabbi—even a Pharisee! An Orthodox Jew!"

"So there you have it Sol! Y'shua tells you, an Orthodox Rabbi, a modern day Pharisee, that the most important command is the *Sh'ma!* What does His answer mean to you?"

"Y'shua is a Jew's Jew! You know, my favorite Scripture is the *Sh'ma:* Deuteronomy 6:4-9! Do you think Y'shua used *tefflin?*"

"I don't know, Sol, because the Pharisees of Y'shua's day had made their *phylacteries* a thing of pride and public display. In Matthew 23:5, Y'shua says, *"Everything they do is done for men to see: They make their phylacteries wide and the tassels on their garments long."* So if Jesus did use *tefflin*, He did so without making a public spectacle of Himself, but instead privately honored His Father in obedience."

"As it should be," Sol noted.

Then a new thought entered the old rabbi's troubled mind. "What about the Law? Did not Y'shua show disdain for the Law and even break it? Did He not abolish it?"

"No, my friend," Mark answered, "Y'shua came not to break or abolish the Law, but to complete the Law! Like no one else who has ever lived or will ever live, He perfectly obeyed the Law! He fulfilled the Law in every sense of the word, even in His horrible death on the cross for our sin. The Law requires a perfect sacrifice. Y'shua was and is that perfect sacrifice who makes our forgiveness and restoration possible!"

Staring blankly at Mark, Sol thought, *"What now? If Mark and Ariel are right, what am I to do?"* As Sol was about to ask the ultimate question, Mark received a call on his 3DHP.

With only a dark, blurry image projected from his 3DHP, Mark answered, Ariel listened, and both of them wondered if this call was from the kidnappers.

A deep, malevolent voice said, "Pastor Mark! How good of you to take my call!"

"Who is this?" Mark asked. Now, Sol and Ahava hovered around the phone as well.

"I see your double infidel bride and two filthy pigs are with you! But, being as this is such a special night, perhaps we won't argue religion!"

Refusing to show any emotion, Mark calmly asked, "Who is this? Who are you?"

"Why I am no other than your soon to be son-in-law!"

Ariel's right hand flew to her mouth as tears ran from her eyes. She turned away from the black image. Ahava moved next to her to hold her and help brace her for what might come next from the mouth of the evil man in the darkness.

To keep his rising anger and hatred in check, Mark did not respond. Rather, he silently prayed for Isa to strengthen him and to forgive his desire to lash out at this Muslim madman.

"Could it be that the great Christian orator is at a loss for words?" came the question from the depths of the shadows. "Perhaps you would like to speak to the bride to be?"

Again, Mark said nothing, while Ariel tried to hold back her weeping. Sol placed his hand on Mark's back as a sign of his support.

They heard nothing but muted sounds for a few moments. Then, in a small, quiet, trembling voice, Grace asked, "Mom? Dad? Is that really you?"

Red-faced and puffy-eyed, Ariel quickly turned back to the dim image of her only daughter and answered, "Yes, yes! My darling, we are right here! Your daddy and I are right here!"

"I love you and miss you both!"

Now, Mark, trying to restrain his own tears, replied to his captive girl. "We love and miss you, too, Baby! Are you okay?"

"That's enough conversation with the blushing bride, for now, I believe," said the snickering Muslim. "I am sorry that we do not have time for a formal wedding this evening, *Ab*! Otherwise, we would ask you to officiate over our nuptials! But seeing that we have not issued any invitations, we thought we should at least let you know about the happy event that will soon take place! Haziqah is overwhelmed with joy and anticipation about the wedding and what comes afterward!"

Mark wanted to reach through the phone and strangle this evil lunatic! Even so, he somehow remained dependent on his Lord to not react to what he had just heard. "'Haziqah?' You have given Grace a new name! What exactly do you want from us?" he asked, as Ariel grabbed his hand and squeezed tightly.

"Nothing from 'us,' all we want is from you, Doctor, pastor, heretic!"

"And what is it that you want from me, then?" Mark demanded. Sol held on to Mark's arm now as well as his shoulder.

"A wedding gift, of course!"

"What gift do you desire?"

"One that will be hand delivered—by you!"

*"I am not referring to all of you; I know those I have chosen.
But this is to fulfill this passage of Scripture: 'He who shared
My bread has turned against Me.'"*
John 13:18

CHAPTER 62

PLAYING
THE QUEEN OF HEARTS. . .

⬥⬥⬥

*T*he Caliph's bloody head rolled down the ornate hallway, staining his white headdress with red spirals, splattering the walls with warm blood. His personal guards stood in shock and disbelief! However, they had no time to ponder the bold murder of their highest leader, for their own heads were summarily severed from their own bodies until only one man was left standing—a man in black, now covered in the blood of those who trusted him, who sat at table with them, who loved them as brothers in the cause of Allah!

This unsuspected traitor quickly moved through the remainder of the castle, not once feeling compassion, not once considering regret, as he removed the heads of his remaining friends and fellow jihadists. Since the age of six, he had embraced his role as a reaper of life in the same way a man trained in medicine embraces his role as a prolonger of life.

When the last brother was down, the betrayer cleaned the blood from his machete, walked upstairs to his room, followed the *ghusl* cleansing ritual as he cleansed the crimson from his body, and then dressed himself in white. He thanked Allah for using him in the great call of jihad.

Calmly, he contacted the General.

"Yes?" the unquestioned leader of the Brotherhood answered.

"Your instructions have been carried out. I await your commands for further action."

"Excellent! At least someone has been successful this evening!"

"I don't understand!"

"The American President yet breathes! The Israeli Prime Minister still has a beating heart! Their wives and children continue to contaminate Allah's world!"

"Have these unexpected events changed what you have planned?"

"Of course they have altered my plans! I cannot reveal that the Caliph is dead while the leaders of the two Satans remain alive! Tonight has been nothing but disappointment for Allah, until your success. You, being one, killed many, while another, being one, only had to relieve two vultures of these measly lives!"

"Can I be of service with these two?"

"Perhaps, but our most opportune moment has passed. These two men are now separated. Our advantage has been squandered. We no longer have the benefit of the confusion and panic—the terror—the sudden vacancy of two tents that never deserved to be occupied!"

"What shall be done to the one who failed you, who failed Allah this night?"

"He has been captured by the infidels!"

"Will he reveal your plans, the revelation of Allah?"

"Not if he has any hopes of seeing Allah in Paradise!"

"Should we try to free him from the enemy?"

"We must either free him from their clutches or free him from this life! We cannot risk exposure of the ultimate revelation to the *kuffar* and *shirk*!"

"Do we have men in place who can do whichever is necessary?"

"With everything in flux tonight, I cannot answer that question with certainty!"

"Allah will not let his message fall into vile hands!"

The hypocritical General sounded so pious as he said, "We may have nothing more than faith tonight as our weapon!"

"Is not faith the strongest weapon in Allah's arsenal?"

"No! His greatest weapon is hatred of the contaminated people of the Book! His mightiest weapon is hatred of the vermin that infest Palestine!"

"Then we have his greatest weapon!"

"Indeed we do, yet we cannot wield that weapon any more tonight!"

"Perhaps Allah wants to guide us in a different way?"

"Are you questioning my plans for this night?"

"Not at all, my General! I am saying that perhaps Allah only wished us to implant fear and terror tonight, thus prolonging the agony of his enemies. Perhaps he did not want quick death for them, but extended, excruciating suffering."

The General's silence hung in the air like death itself.

Then, his demeanor changed completely. "Maybe we only witnessed the first step," the General said with renewed zeal. "Maybe the glorious god of Islam has something even better in store for the Great and Little Satans! If so, I believe he has revealed their extreme agony to me!"

"Let not the Believers take for friends or helpers Unbelievers rather than Believers: If any do that, in nothing will there be help from Allah: except by way of precaution, that ye may guard yourselves from them, but Allah cautions you (to remember) Himself; For the final goal is to Allah."
Qur'an 3:28

CHAPTER 63

THE OVERFLOW OF THE HEART...

"Why did you save President Paulson's life today, Abdul?" Addar asked as he sat down on his hospital bed after coming back from the restroom.

"I could ask you the same question," Abdul answered. Sitting up, he inquired, "As a matter of fact, why did you save James from an assassin's bullet at the studio?"

"I have my reasons!" Addar answered defensively.

"So do I," Abdul calmly replied. "We are supposed to risk our lives to save others, which is what you did today, is it not? Did you not risk your life to save the President as well as Mark and Ariel?"

Angry in tone, Addar answered, "No, I saved those infidels for my own reasons, not your altruistic reasons! Anyway, you have nothing to gain from saving the President of the infidels' life. If he should die unexpectedly, you would become Commander in Chief of the soon to be extinct United States of America! Tell me Abdul, why indeed would you risk death to save the President? Why would you care about his family and their insignificant existence? Why would you be glad that the Prime Minister did not die?"

"Don't forget that you had a larger role than I did in saving the Prime Minister this evening!" Abdul said with a sarcastic smile.

"Thanks to you—I could have been killed, you know!" Addar's swiftly replied with fear and disgust.

Abdul refused to let Addar anger him. Instead, while chuckling, he noted, "As it turned out, neither you nor the Prime Minister lost your lives. You will probably receive a medal or some kind of honorary title from the Israeli government! You will likely get the U.S. equivalent for saving James' life as well." Abdul could not stop himself from laughing out loud!

"You think this is funny? I was shot! I have no desire to be honored by the vile Jews or the slime Christians!" Addar's face twisted as though he had just swallowed soured wine.

Like a lawyer making a plea, Abdul responded by saying, "But don't you see, Addar? Your wound proves that you are a man of peace, not war. First, you risked your life today to save a man I believe you still count as an enemy—the President of the United States. Furthermore, while you may not have chosen to do so, you saved the life of the Prime Minister of Israel and bear the pain of doing so. Furthermore, you did choose to help him push through a peace accord between your nation and his nation."

The seemingly insightful comment caught Addar by surprise. He shook his head from right to left as he considered Abdul's words. Then, he noted, "You know nothing of my motives, but make false judgments based on my actions. Besides, whether for enemy or for friend, if I am going to put my life on the line for someone, I want it to be by my choice, not yours or anyone else's decision!"

Calmly, Abdul noted, "In that moment in which I saw the man raise his gun and point it at the President—I must confess—I really wasn't thinking about you being on the other side of James. Don't you see that we saved two extremely important leaders today by divine design?"

Rising to his feet, with his temper flaring, the imam retorted, "What has come over you, Abdul? You are talking and acting in most unusual ways! Since when did you decide there was a god worth serving?"

Ignoring the heat of the inquiry, Abdul, still peaceful, said, "You have yet to answer my original question, Addar. "Why did you risk your life to save the President—as well as Mark and Ariel—today?"

Addar looked to the floor. "My motives come from what is best for my people. I have no idea what motivated you to save the President's life. When we last talked face to face in the states, you said you hated the President, so you tell me what has changed?"

Abdul looked to the right of Addar. As he reflected, he noted, "Well, you are correct. I did say that I hated President Paulson when I last spoke with you. Strange, but I no longer feel that hatred." Turning his gaze back to Addar, Abdul shared what he realized for the first time in that moment. "Frankly, I no longer hate anyone, Addar—not even you!"

Once more, Abdul's words caught the imam off guard. "What do you mean by saying you don't hate anyone anymore—not even me? Why would you ever hate me? I have done so much to help you!"

Again laughing, Abdul stated, "You did not help me. You used me! In fact, you are still trying to use me. It was your idea for me to be Vice President of the United States, remember? I wanted nothing to do with American politics. However, you convinced me that I could do a great good for 'our people.' What you really meant was that I could do a great deal of good for you, right?"

Addar walked to the foot of his bed, tiring of Abdul's challenging questions. "What difference does it make as to why I helped you? You are still the Vice President of the United States of America! Anyone else would be forever grateful to me for helping him achieve such a feat. You rose from a position of nothingness to becoming the second most powerful man in the United States—maybe even the world! And you missed two opportunities today alone to be the very President of the American infidels! Mark my words, one day you will be their leader!"

"And I will owe it all to you, right, my mentor, my surrogate father, the one who took me in when I became an orphan long ago. Tell me Addar, in all the years I have lived under your wing, have you loved me, even once, as a father loves a son? Or have I always been a life for you to control and manipulate to serve your purposes?"

His forefinger pointed directly into Abdul's face, Addar indignantly stated, "How dare you speak in such a manner to me? You would have died outside the prison where your parents were killed as jihadists, if I had not pleaded for your measly existence! You are the only son I will ever know. I demand you treat me with the respect I deserve, as you owe me your very life, Mr. Vice President!"

All Abdul could do was smile, as he said, "Sorry, Addar, although at one time, I believed that I did owe you my life, I now know such is not the case. I owe my life to someone far greater, stronger, wiser, and nobler than you!"

"No one exists who is greater, stronger, wiser, and nobler than me, you fool!" Addar abruptly stopped himself from continuing. He did not want to reveal his plans to anyone.

Shaking his head, Abdul commented, "Actually, the greater, stronger, wiser, and nobler One to whom I refer does not compete with you."

"Oh really? Anyone who considers himself superior to me will soon discover just how mistaken he has been! Time will tell, Abdul. Time will tell!"

"Indeed it will," Abdul softly replied with a far off look in his eyes. "Indeed, it will!"

"For whoever wants to save his life will lose it, but whoever loses his life for Me and for the Gospel will save it."
Mark 8:35

CHAPTER 64

THE QUINTESSENTIAL CHOICE. . .

❖❖❖
❖❖

"*M*ark, Ariel, are you all right?" Sol asked the couple who knew not the fate of their only daughter. The father and mother continued to stare at the fading dark images from his 3DHP long after the Muslim thug spoke his final words. "What gift does that cruel man seek from you, Mark? Do you have any idea?"

While putting away his phone, Mark answered, "I believe I know exactly what gift he demands." The resolved husband looked deeply into his weary wife's eyes and said, "He wants me in exchange for Grace!"

Sol and Ahava both gasped in shock. Ahava blurted out, "But they will kill you, Mark! This is a trap! They always kill the followers of Y'shua! When the Caliph took power, he ordered the murder of all the Christians and all the missionaries in the Muslim states! The flow of blood lasted for weeks! Surely, the Muslim on your phone will not hesitate to execute you, either."

Sol placed his forefinger over Ahava's lips, and with furrowed brow, he shook his head for her to stop talking about Mark's death!

"It's okay, Sol. Ahava is right," the pastor said as he lowered the rabbi's finger from Ahava's lips. "I knew before we took our flight to Tel Aviv that I am the one the Brotherhood wants, not Grace! They tried to kill me in the church, but Y'shua protected me from their smart bullets!"

A weeping Ariel clung to her soul mate. "But Honey, you cannot just walk into their trap! I'll never see you again!" Her eyes pleaded with his.

With determined resignation, Mark stated, "If it is a choice between Grace becoming the bride of a Muslim pedophile or losing my life, then that choice is easy, don't you think? Besides, you and I will be together forever!"

Her despair and tears uncontrolled, Ariel moaned, "I can't bear even the thought of losing either of you, Mark! Surely, Y'shua has another plan!"

"He might, indeed, Ariel," Mark said as he cupped his beautiful bride's tear-stained face. "However, right now, I believe we have to prepare for an exchange. Like you would, my Love, I will do whatever I must do to save Grace!"

Sol interrupted, "Couldn't the Israelis or Americans intervene here? Could they not find Grace and save you both?"

Kindly, Mark gazed back at Sol, saying, "We cannot risk the possibility of the Brotherhood killing Grace, Sol! I must cooperate with them!"

Sol backed up three steps to lean against the wall. "This is too much for an old rabbi to grasp! My heart feels drawn to Y'shua — but I see the cost of following Him in you and Ariel and Grace!"

Despite their concern over Grace, Mark and Ariel both smiled, as they brushed the tears away from their eyes. "Sol," Ariel began, "Mark's life and my life do not dwell in this flesh. We are certain of our eternal life in Y'shua! He says Himself that when we believe in Him we already have eternal life. In John 5:24, Y'shua confides, *'I tell you the truth, whoever hears My Word and believes Him who sent Me has eternal life and will not be condemned; he has crossed over from death to life!'* Thus, even if we are killed for our faith, we can celebrate the life of faith we hold forever. No one can take it from us! Y'shua holds our lives in His Hand, and no one can take us from His grasp!"

With agonizing despair, Sol replied, "But Ahava and I have been Jews all our lives! We don't know how to stop being Jews!"

Ariel quickly responded, "Sol, Ahava, we've covered this already! Y'shua is a Jew! He was born a Jew, and was named and circumcised on the eighth day of His life! He celebrated his bar mitzvah in Jerusalem, and He worshipped *HaShem* at the synagogue in Nazareth.

315

In fact, Y'shua was the perfect Jew, fulfilling every requirement of the Law, upholding every aspect of the Covenant. Y'shua sacrificed His life as the true Lamb of God, atoning for our sins and writing our names in the Lamb's Book of Life, not only for a year, but for all eternity!"

Mark added, "Y'shua was a Hebrew, and His disciples were Hebrews, and the first believers after His resurrection were Hebrews! People like me, Gentiles, have been grafted into Jesus' Tree of Life! Our faith is in Y'shua—the Jewish Messiah!"

Sol told Mark and Ariel, "I've been reading in John about Nicodemus—an old, stubborn Orthodox Jew like me who knew that God had somehow sent Y'shua as Messiah, even though He was nothing like what the Pharisee expected! Even so, you two stand strong in your faith in Y'shua—and in the One who sent Him, *HaShem*! On the other hand, my faith seems to have evaporated! Here you are, possibly facing death, yet your strength only grows!"

Humbly, Mark said, "We have such confidence, Sol, because Y'shua fulfilled each prophecy of the Messiah that you will find in the Tanakh!" Now the pastor's hand was on the shoulder of the rabbi to give him encouragement.

Sol's demeanor changed the moment he heard the word "prophecy." The old man said, "I have a question, or should I say Ahava and I have a question?" Sol reached for her hand. "Do you believe the prophecy of Ezekiel of the Gog and Magog War has been fulfilled?"

Mark and Ariel smiled again as they looked at each other in agreement. Ariel answered, "Sol, Russia and its Muslim partners tried to attack Israel from the northern mountains just as Ezekiel predicted! Likewise, as Ezekiel foretold, our Lord rained down molten fire and hail and shook the entire earth with an earthquake beyond human ability to measure! In the confusion, the troops of the surviving members of the combined Russian-Muslim army battled and killed each other, and Israel was spared!"

Mark added, "And many people in this world—Jews, Muslims, Hindus, and Buddhists, as well as agnostics and atheists—turned in faith to Y'shua! Many of them, if not most of them, quickly faced persecution or death! Yet they did not recant their faith in the Messiah!"

Ariel continued with her husband's thoughts, saying, "That's because our Lord said that His intervention to save Israel would prove

His existence to the world! In Ezekiel 38:22, the prophet quotes our Lord as saying, *'I will show My greatness and My holiness, and I will make Myself known in the sight of many nations. Then they will know that I am the Lord!'"*

"But shouldn't everyone have turned to *HaShem*, instead of Y'shua?" Sol asked, genuinely perplexed.

"Sol," Ariel answered gently, "no one told the masses that came to Y'shua to believe in Him because of this mighty miracle of saving Israel. The people knew in their hearts to turn to Y'shua, for He and His Father are one, and Y'shua is the only means of salvation in this world!"

Sol and Ahava both were broken, weeping. He tried to speak, saying, "Yes! All those years ago, we felt Y'shua calling us to faith in Him, even as the earth was shaking and the fire fell from the sky! Yet stubbornly we—I—refused that call, even though I had never felt such hope and life within me before!"

Sol grabbed Mark's arm and pleaded with him. "My friend, do you think that Y'shua will not receive Ahava and me now, because of my great pigheadedness, because of the vile things I have said and done against Him and His followers?"

The pastor and his bride could not contain their joy! They embraced their elderly friends as Mark proclaimed, "As long as you have breath and come to Y'shua in repentance with confession, He will receive you both with open arms! The past will be erased and you two will start a brand new and never ending life in Him in this very moment! That's the wonder of His mercy and grace!"

Sol looked to his bride through his tears and said, "If the Messiah will still have us, I believe we should kneel before Him right here, Ahava—right here in this hospital! Our two tired souls need His eternal healing! We need His strength for the days ahead!"

And the glory of *Adonai* shone all around them!

"Glory to (Allah) Who did take His Servant for a Journey by night from the Sacred Mosque to the Farthest Mosque, whose precincts We did bless,—in order that We might show him some of Our Signs: for He is the One Who heareth and seeth (all things)."
Qur'an 17:1

CHAPTER 65

THE CONSUMMATE WEAPON. . .

"*I* don't understand," Sam told the deputy members of his Cabinet and the other government and military leaders at the table. "Why destroy the Holocaust Museums? Why destroy the American Vice Presidential residence when the Caliph and the Brotherhood both knew Abdul was not there? Why destroy the offices of AIFD?"

Deputy Defense Minister Moshe Levine answered quickly, "What Zeev always said as Defense Minister was that Islam must rewrite history to exalt itself. Thus, as the Muslims declare the Holocaust never happened, what better way to erase history than to wipe out the two largest and best Holocaust museums left in the world? Remember, all the Holocaust memorials and museums in Europe were destroyed quickly after the nations were islamized. Thus, the destruction of the museums in the U.S. and Israel not only communicates the message that the Holocaust is a lie, but it also telegraphs the message that the Muslims will soon be in control of both countries!"

"The Prime Minister mulled over his Deputy Defense Minister's thoughts, and then said, "Your points are well taken and quite credible. But why destroy AIFD's headquarters, filled with fellow Muslims?"

"Not fellow Muslims, Sam! Think about this! Remember what I just said a few moments ago! AIFD no longer exists because the 'true believers' of Allah detest the Muslims who seek peace and who want democracy and the freedoms of liberty! AIFD said Muslim women did not have to dress any differently than other American women! AIFD said that 'honor killings' were outright murder! AIFD even allowed Muslim women to divorce their husbands—and live!"

"Through their support of democracy and peace, AIFD promoted heresy in the eyes of the Caliph and the Brotherhood! Moderate Muslims working for self-governance in the United States? Surely you see why their headquarters could not be allowed to stand, Sam! Do I need to paint you a picture?"

"Of course not, Moshe—what you say makes sense. Still, what about the Vice President's residence? Why destroy it? With Abdul here, what purpose does that destruction serve?"

"Sheer terror! Whether they have their own weapons or not, the Muslims want to prove they can hit any target they want, any time they want, anywhere they want. The exclamation point of that threat comes with the use of U.S. weapons to destroy the Pentagon!"

"Along those same lines, Moshe, could the target of the missile strike here not really have been the mosques, but the Temple Mount itself?"

"I believe the Muslims had multiple targets and multiple purposes, Sam. The annihilation of the mosques and the Palestinian government accomplished three things. One, as you say, the Muslims also demolished the Temple Mount—which they claim never undergirded a Jewish Temple. Two, the Caliph destroyed the government of Palestine because it was democratic—repulsive to Islam and its god—and not under Babylonian rule. Three, by using Israeli missiles, Babylon could accomplish its goals without taking any of the blame for destroying the *Al-Aqsa* Mosque, the underground Al Marawani Mosque, and the Dome of the Rock. Plus, we already recognized the fourth accomplishment. By destroying their own mosques, the Dome of the Rock, and the leadership of the DROP with our own weapons, Babylon gave itself a pretext for war with us and the United States."

Sam nodded his head in agreement. He could no longer hide in denial of the facts. Yet confronting the truth made him feel so hopeless. The Muslims held all the cards! He had one last question. "Moshe, did not Babylon blow its cover by having U.S. missiles destroy the Pentagon? Surely, no one would believe that the U.S. military destroyed its own headquarters?"

"I agree with you, Sam! We must remember that absolute power corrupts absolutely. The temptation to strike now may have been impossible to resist. Be that as it may, this attack on Washington could be a blessing in disguise. If our intel proves accurate, Babylon may have played its entire hand. At least for the moment, the Caliph may not be able to launch any more of our or the United States' weapons. This break may give us time to determine how the Caliphate broke through our cyberspace walls and security. With that information, we might be able to prevent future incursions!"

The Prime Minister threw himself back in his chair and contemplated what his ears just heard but his brain refused to comprehend. "Moshe, you have too many ifs and mights in those last statements. We need a solid foundation on which to stand if we are going to face the Brotherhood Army! What can we do, now?"

The one surviving member of the Prime Minister's Cabinet, Homefront Defense Minister Noah Ben Eleazar, ventured an answer. "What if we took our entire weapons system offline and reprogrammed everything before the system came back online?"

The Deputy Minister of Defense and the Israeli Military Chief of Staff, Lt. General Gideon Sharon, kibitzed as they considered the ramifications of the proposal. Gideon nodded in agreement and Moshe then said, "My first thought is that we have no idea of how much time such a process could take. My second thought is that we would be completely vulnerable to enemy attack throughout that downtime."

Sam sighed and then asked, "Could we manually operate both the defensive and offensive aspects of the system during the reprogramming stage?"

Gideon answered, "Good question. Albeit, how fast and how responsive would a manual system be, especially on the defense side—the most important side when you are threatened with an imminent attack! Could we react fast enough manually to protect our land and its people?"

"We may have no choice but to find out, Gideon!"

Moshe countered, "With our weapons control systems down, each threat or attack upon civilians or our forces would give the enemy the time advantage. By the time we manually coordinate a response, the carnage and destruction could be great! There is a 40-million madman army out there, you know!"

Noah quickly responded, "But Gideon, neither Babylon nor the Brotherhood can mobilize that army quickly. Moreover, they cannot attack us with their own weapons! We disarm the enemy if we take our systems down to reprogram them. We neutralize Babylon and the Brotherhood when they cannot use our own weapons against us!"

Sam said, "You have forgotten one thing, Noah."

Puzzled, the Homefront Defense Minister asked, "What did I overlook, Sam?"

"Goliath! What if Goliath can be deployed?"

Moshe added, "Can Goliath be considered a real threat? We know that Babylon has been forcing former Asian and EU scientists and engineers to work on restoring the weapons systems on both continents. These brilliant minds are also being coerced to develop Goliath. Now, when you look at the specific scientists, engineers, and former military officers Babylon has kidnapped from Israel and the U.S., you see that these men are experts in the field of new weapons development! Personally, I believe the Caliphate kidnapped these professionals because the Muslims have hit a brick wall either in developing or implementing Goliath. Either of those options would give us a little time before we would have to face the mega giant."

Sam, seemingly lost in distant thought, stoically replied, "On one hand, you could be wrong, Moshe. The scientists, engineers, and military experts could have been taken for a dozen other reasons. On the other hand, you may be exactly right.

"The last attack we faced came against us by land, sea, and air, yet Israel did not fire one weapon to defend herself or strike down the invaders. Perhaps our greatest and most powerful weapon is not under the control of the Muslims, or, for that matter, under our control either."

The eyes of all the men around the table were glued to the Prime Minister. His Military Chief of Staff asked, "Are you proposing that we do not need to have control of our weapons systems because we should instead rely on faith that *HaShem* will save us from a Muslim attack?"

Sam asked, "Have you ever considered that your name and your rank are not coincidence?"

Gideon, an agnostic, shifted in his chair and remained silent.

Against his better judgment, Sam asked the men surrounding him, "Is Israel again at the place where King Hezekiah found his people—facing an army too large for him to defeat? Isn't it in II Chronicles 20 that Hezekiah turns to *HaShem* in a desperate prayer, and the Lord defeats the massive approaching army without one of Hezekiah's soldiers even raising a sword or firing an arrow?

"Then again, does not the Hebrew prophet Joel, in his second chapter, prophesy a day of darkness and gloom for Israel when it will face a large and mighty army such has never been amassed before—perhaps a 40 million man army? In that same chapter, does not the Lord say He will drive that northern army far from Israel?"

With much surprise in his voice, Moshe, a practicing Jew, asked Sam," Are you referring to the prophecies about the Last Day?"

Sam closed his eyes and asked, "What do the events taking place around us say about this moment in which we live and breathe?"

"Have faith in God."
Mark 11:22

CHAPTER 66

PROOF NEGATIVE. . .

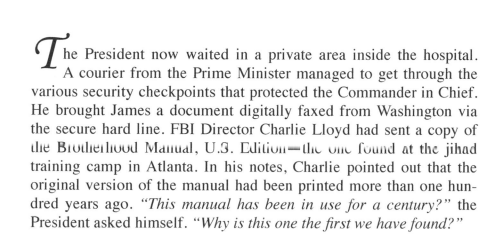

*T*he President now waited in a private area inside the hospital. A courier from the Prime Minister managed to get through the various security checkpoints that protected the Commander in Chief. He brought James a document digitally faxed from Washington via the secure hard line. FBI Director Charlie Lloyd had sent a copy of the Brotherhood Manual, U.S. Edition—the one found at the jihad training camp in Atlanta. In his notes, Charlie pointed out that the original version of the manual had been printed more than one hundred years ago. *"This manual has been in use for a century?"* the President asked himself. *"Why is this one the first we have found?"*

Charlie also mentioned that the manual had been "modified and expanded over the years to address changing world events and cultural influences." Consequently, James now held the most current, step by step process for the ultimate establishment of Islamic rule in the United States.

Before reading the thick manual from front to back, President Paulson thumbed through the pages. Then he went back and started with page one. It read, "The Muslim Brotherhood: Allah is our objective. The Prophet is our leader. The Qur'an is our law. Jihad is our way. Dying in the way of Allah is our highest hope. *Allahu Akbar*! There is no God but Allah!"

Further down, near the bottom of page one, the President read words in bold type: "No matter the problem, Islam is the solution." Beneath that mantra, James found the unambiguous goal of the Brotherhood in these words: "Formed in 1928 in Egypt, the Brotherhood exists for one reason and that sole purpose is to restore the Caliphate!" The next paragraph began, "The Brotherhood was not born to convert infidels to Islam, but to dominate the world as a Caliphate under Sharia Law. While we have many means for accomplishing our goal, the main tool of the Brotherhood is Holy Jihad!"

A chill ran down the President's back as he flipped to the next page, which was titled "The Six Pillars of Islam." James wondered, "Six? I thought Abdul told me that Islam had five pillars." Below the heading were those traditional five pillars of Islam plus one more added by the Brotherhood.

1. *Shahada*: Believing in the oneness of God—Allah alone and not others! Believing that Muhammad—peace is upon him—was his prophet.
2. *Salah:* Practicing prayer, five times daily: Dawn, noon, late afternoon, after sunset, and night.
3. *Zakat:* Purifying of wealth through giving to needy (at least 2.5%).
4. *Sawm:* Fasting in the month of Ramadan from dawn to dusk each day.
5. *Hajj:* Making at least one pilgrimage to Mecca.
6. *Jihad:* Making war on the infidel.

The Commander in Chief noted that the sixth pillar was the only one with elaboration.

"According to the Qur'an, jihad is the duty of every Muslim! When Hasan Al-Banna founded the Brotherhood, he said, 'The verses of the Qur'an and the *Sunnah,* the very example of Muhammad, summon people in general (with the most eloquent expression and the clearest exposition) to jihad, to warfare, to the armed forces, and all means of land and sea fighting.'"

The amplification continued, saying, "Jihad is demanded of every Muslim. Those who evade it are cowards of the lowest order and will meet the eternal chastisement of Allah! Those who refuse jihad will be dishonored in this life as well as face the fires of eternity that Allah has prepared for them. Failure to fight in jihad is one of the seven sins of Islam that guarantee failure.

"The entire *ummah*, the whole of the Muslim body, must be mobilized for jihad. Everyone must fight in or financially support the battle for Islam's supremacy over the world, over all other religions. The peoples of the other religions must be killed or made subject to the *dhimma*. This state of servitude, with its restricted freedom and payment of the *jizya* (the infidels' tax must be paid in the most humiliating way possible), often motivates the unbelievers to convert to Islam. If the *jizya* cannot be paid, the infidels should be killed without delay.

"The House of Allah and the House of War can never merge. The House of Allah submits to Allah and his Sharia Law. The House of War includes all who rebel against Allah, deny him, refuse to submit to him, add partners to his rule, and follow laws not of him but of human origin. The House of Allah must be in constant jihad with the House of War until there is no one left on the earth who fails to submit to Allah and Sharia. Even the *dhimma,* that subordinate class of unbelievers, will one day be no more, despite the profit these subhuman servants may provide to the *ummah*."

The President whispered to himself, *"The House of Allah is misnamed. It should be called the House of War. With the Brotherhood, it's Allah's way or the way of death!"*

He flipped to another section of the manual. The title on the page read "Steps to Jihad in the United States."

"Cultural jihad will precede actual jihad which brings deserved death to the infidels and establishes Islamic rule and Sharia Law. Islam must infiltrate every aspect of the Unite States family, culture, religion, finance, economy, education, government, and legal systems. Follow these ten steps:

1. Population: Immigrate to the United States and outbreed the Americans.
   a. On religious grounds, take four wives as Allah allows in the Qur'an. b. Anonymously underwrite and support abortion for Americans.
   c. Islamize the land.
2. Deceit (Taqiyya Doctrine): Deceit is allowed as a form of jihad.
   a. Deceive population about meaning of Qur'an—99% of populace will not read it. Portray Islam as religion of peace, tolerance, good deeds, love, community service, integrity, and responsibility. Use disinformation to frame Christians and Jews for crimes against Islam, while portraying Muslims as victims

of bigotry, prejudice, and bias. Turn public opinion against Christians and Jews.

b. Use *Da'wah* to invite infidels to convert to a docile, seemingly peaceful form of Islam.

c. Call for interfaith dialogue between Muslims, Christians, and Jews. Say we worship the same god. Propose joint seminary training. Conduct joint social projects. Attend church and synagogue with Christians and Jews. Participate in the Chrislam Movement. Invite them to Friday prayers.

d. Pretend to be friends with Christians and Jews, idolaters, and members of other religions as well as agnostics and atheists.

e. Publicly denounce all forms of terrorism.

f. Establish parallel society, culture, legal system, and government. This will be of great use when islamization is complete. We will already have everything in place when we destroy the United States and its society, culture, legal system, and government.

g. Pretend to assimilate into the main culture. Promote multiculturalism.

h. Lull population into trusting Islam.

3. Infiltration: Live dual lives as both obedient Muslims and as obedient citizens of the United States so that you may infiltrate the society, higher education, media, business sectors, security positions, military branches, legal system, government, and law enforcement.

a. Establish and/or join as many benevolent, charitable, and service organizations and foundations, private clubs, labor unions, and NGO's in your community as possible. Seek election in the highest positions possible until you reach the national level.

b. Become professors at major universities in highly visible subjects such as world religions, international trade and economics, world history, international law, and global governance.

c. Become journalists and news commentators in order to sway public opinion to sympathize with Muslim causes and downplay any harm to overall society. Always emphasize a positive appraisal of Muslim interests. At all times, highlight the prejudice against every day Muslims who seek only to peacefully assimilate into American culture.

d. Become business leaders in the major corporations, especially in the energy, transportation, banking, investment, communication, pharmaceutical, and military sectors.

e. Join government and private security forces as all levels. Excel so that you will be in the highest ranking positions as well as on the security teams of the highest elected officials. (See section 8.)

f. Join all branches of the military and rise to its highest ranks.

g. Join law enforcement agencies at local, state, and federal levels.

4. Funding: Work to finance jihad.

   a. Set up compassionate charities as false fronts for raising funds for jihad.

   b. Conduct fundraisers for children, hunger, medicine, and disaster relief. Keep all funds.

   c. Apply for financial gifts from all foundations.

   d. Apply for all government grants.

   e. Set up false businesses as fronts for money laundering.

5. Construction: Take on as many projects as possible.

   a. Build mosques in every city.

   b. Build mega-mosques in every city of prominence.

   c. Build madrasahs to educate children in all communities.

   d. Build colleges, universities, and seminaries for higher education and Islamic studies.

6. Training: Annually train young boys from age of six to sixteen (longer if necessary) in the ways of jihad.

   a. Teach that the basis of hatred and jihad are found in the Qur'an.

   b. Teach the boys to pretend to be friends with Christians and Jews, only to reduce resistance to Islam.

   c. Demonstrate and have the young jihadis practice weapons training, methods of killing, safest means of body disposal, organization of armed forces, and Allah's call to jihad—most important!

   d. End training with graduating jihadists facing each other in pairs. Have them fight to the death.

7. Legal System: Manipulate the legal system for Islamic goals.

   a. Sue for civil concessions, such as Islamic schools, mosques, holiday recognition.

   b. If denied, charge religious prejudice, Islamophobia, victimiza-
      tion, political incorrectness, denial of constitutional rights, and
      intolerance.
   c. Promote the use of Sharia Law in the American courts.
   d. Establish separate Sharia courts where possible.
8. Political and Judicial Offices:
   a. Become advisors for all elected government and judicial
      officials.
   b. Support the most liberal candidates on the ballots.
   c. As Muslim majorities are established, participate in all levels of
      government: local, state, and federal. Run for office and judicial
      positions at all levels.
   d. Run on platform of peace, dialogue with other religions, equal
      justice, freedom of expression, women's equality, representa-
      tive government, economic vitality, and the civil rights of all
      Americans.
   e. When in office, advocate Sharia as comparable, equitable law
      for Muslims and all Americans. Complain about inequity in
      federal legal code.
9. Opposition: When adversaries can no longer be silenced through
   courts or public appeal, wage jihad:
   a. Use every means possible to kill and destroy all who ultimately
      oppose you.
   b. Target heads of state and government operations for elimina-
      tion by any means possible. Do not fail!
10. Ultimate Goal: Prepare America to join a worldwide Caliphate.
   a. Establish Islam as the only religion.
   b. Establish Qur'an as the official Constitution.
   c. Establish Sharia as the only law.

The President thought, *"As Abdul said, 'moderate Muslims' really
do not exist! Those who do strive to assimilate just had their national
headquarters destroyed. Every other moderate Muslim is an actor
playing a role in a grand conspiracy! All of the political and capital investments we have made in hopes for Muslim integration and
peaceful coexistence have been pipe dreams! For more than a century,
the Muslims have been playing us for fools!"*

The Commander in Chief extrapolated what he had just read. *"Before the establishment of the Caliphate, the Brotherhood combined it political savvy with the expertise of the terror groups. The Brotherhood does not just decide to declare jihad in a country. First, the Muslim muscle machine meticulously and patiently lays the groundwork from inside the nation, so that when jihad comes, victory is assured. All the good and positive relationships and contributions of the Muslims of the last ten decades have been leading to the destruction of the United States!*

"Whom can I trust?" Once again, a knot formed in the President's stomach. *"Can I trust Abdul? Is he complicit in the Brotherhood's plans? He stands only one step away from the Presidency! But he saved my life today. Why would he risk his own life to save mine if the plan calls for my assassination?"*

Burdened by his own thoughts, The President again looked at the manual. The remainder of the pages revealed the detailed approach for enacting all of the ten steps laid out by the Brotherhood for turning the U.S. into Islamerica.

After skimming through those portions of the manual, any doubts the President had about the intent and heart of Islam evaporated. He reasoned, *"These two attempts on my life show that Babylon and the Brotherhood believe they are near the final stages of their work in the U.S. and Israel. They will not stop trying to take my life and the lives of every leader or citizen who opposes them. What must I do to protect my family and my country?"* A cold sweat engulfed his body.

The President feared reading more, yet he turned a few more pages. He found a supplement to the manual, an additional passage added sometime within the last decade.

There he saw the words, *"If all else fails, use Goliath!"* There, he found the most execrable description of the mega weapon he had yet encountered.

"Behold, thy Lord said to the angels: 'I will create a vicegerent on earth.' They said: "Wilt Thou place therein one who will make mischief therein and shed blood?—whilst we do celebrate Thy praises and glorify Thy holy (name)?' He said: 'I know what ye know not.'"
Qur'an 2:30

CHAPTER 67

SCARED, SCARRED SURVIVORS. . .

A pall hung over Israel and the United States. Hospitals in both countries were overwhelmed with patients, but not from the bombings and missile strikes. No one survived those blasts. Instead, the hospitals were overrun with wounded people from the growing violence in the cities of the two nations. Conditions seemed to be worsening by the moment.

Local police and national soldiers fought insurgent—and surprisingly well armed—Muslims. The jihadists attacked unarmed citizens, torched churches and synagogues, and detonated explosives in government buildings, schools, and business facilities—some empty, some filled with doomed innocents.

In retaliation, everyday citizens struck back, attacking mosques, madrasahs, Muslim community centers, and Sharia courts. Unlike the jihadists who were well organized, trained, and armed, the average citizens had only sporadic success and suffered many causalities.

Be that as it may, the media played up the anti-Muslim violence. Despite the disparate amount of destruction and death caused by jihadists, the vast majority of journalists portrayed the Muslims as the victims! While the lion's share of the news outlets downplayed the images of the destroyed and smoldering White House, Vice President's and Prime Minister's residences, the Pentagon, the holocaust museums, and AIFD headquarters, the same reporters justified the Islamic violence as retribution for the alleged U.S.-Israeli attack on the DROP!

In the states as well as in Israel, conspiracy theories planted by Muslim operatives swirled everywhere. The spiral of disinformation included the senseless and bold faced lie that the governments of Israel and the United States had colluded to attack themselves with their own weapons in order to justify declaring war on Babylon—even with the collateral damage in Jerusalem and Washington.

Besides the attempts of political pundits to explain the missing details, the media brought forth American and Israeli Muslims by the droves who called for peace and saying none of their leaders desired jihad. Whether Israeli or American, each non-Muslim commentator, official, or resident expert who countered those claims was summarily dismissed as an Islamophobic hate-monger, religious bigot, and inciter of war!

All this political posturing trivialized the massive destruction, the unquantifiable intrusion to the U.S. military machine, the horrific loss of life, and the overwhelming grief of families and friends.

Be that as it may, without a clear message from either the U.S. or Israeli governments, and in the absence of any claim of responsibility from Babylon or the Brotherhood, the vacuum of facts became filled with any and all ludicrous explanations of what had happened and what would likely come next.

Americans and Israelis asked, "Where is the President?" "Where is the Prime Minister?" "Where is the Caliph?" "Maybe all three are dead, and no one has the courage to tell us!"

Despite the destruction of the Pentagon, U.S. reserve troops had been called up for duty—in addition to all the active duty soldiers who were either already deployed or on standby. Reserve soldiers also began reporting for service in Israel. In both countries, the reservists and their families had no clue as to where the frontlines would be or if they would see each other again.

In The Land, families fled to their bomb shelters, while in America, families sought safety in the basements of their homes, as public facilities had already proven to be deadly. Citizens in both nations were asked to stay off the streets, but without the official declaration of martial law and curfews, traffic gnarled around grocery stores and supply warehouses as citizens wanted to be prepared for what could be a long retreat. More local skirmishes erupted as supplies of food, water, gas masks, and oxygen tanks became scarce. Price gouging and looting reared their ugly heads across both nations.

To make matters even worse in the two countries, thousands of Israelis, Americans, and foreign citizens remained stranded at airports, harbors, train terminals, and transit stations. With all mass transportation in the states and Israel shut down, the problems of feeding and housing all the marooned travelers had become major issues.

Nevertheless, among all the chaos, fear, violence, and death, the masked Muslim General celebrated—ready to unveil his next move!

"... 'Take courage! It is I. Don't be afraid.'"
Matthew 14:27

CHAPTER 68

AWKWARD AND REVEALING MOMENTS...

*D*ark and sinister forces compelled Mark and Ariel to ride a harrowing emotional roller coaster. From the low point of talking with Grace and her future "husband" to the high point of helping Sol and Ahava surrender their hearts, lives, and wills to their Messiah, the couple felt exhilarated and exhausted at the same time! They held their breath, in anticipation of the next unseen, sudden plummet to the bottom.

In spite of the wild ride, Mark and Ariel determined they would enjoy their moments on top for as long as possible. With smiles on the faces, the two of them, accompanied by Sol and Ahava, walked into Abdul and Addar's room. They congratulated the two heroes who saved the lives of the leaders who could be the last and best hope for averting World War IV!

Abdul humbly stated, "I am no hero! I did what anyone in my place would have done!"

"Not so, my friend," said Addar. "Many people in the states and around the world would have jumped out of the way of that bullet that was flying toward the President!"

No one knew if Addar was making a joke or being serious. The strained silence following his remark gave everyone pause.

Ahava stepped forward to restart the celebratory conversation. "All I know is that the world would be much worse off this evening without these two wounded warriors of peace!" Then, the octogenarian great-grandmother walked over to the two hospital beds and hugged and kissed Abdul and Addar as though they were her own sons! Her genuine love evoked both laughter and tears, not to mention applause for the two embarrassed men!

Sol asked, "When are you two boys going to be released?" Abdul answered, "Hopefully in time for me to join President Paulson on Air Force One for our flight back to D.C.."

Mark asked, "Are you sure you can endure such a long flight?" The Vice President quickly replied, "With so much uncertainty in the states, I feel that our people need their President and Vice President on U.S. soil."

Addar was somewhat astounded by Abdul's words. "You almost sound like a true patriot, Abdul!" Again, awkward silence ensued, as no one was sure how to take Addar's almost insulting tone.

This time Ariel stepped up to redirect the conversation. "President Paulson says he may address the people of America from Air Force One. On behalf of the United States, his opening sentence will include thanking the two of you!" Another round of applause filled the small room.

Addar angrily responded, saying, "I certainly never imagined being thanked or even wanting to be thanked by the American people!"

For the third time, the imam's words dropped a veil of silence on the room.

"Neither did I!" Mark quipped, allowing the tension in the room to erupt in laughter! "Still, I have never been more proud of you, Addar!"

Mark's words were so sincere that Addar again could not respond, save through the tears that flowed down his cheeks! Within himself, Addar could not place a name on the emotion he felt, but he knew it was something good—and that feeling made him most uncomfortable.

Sol added to the jovial mood of the room, I can visualize the headlines: "Two Muslims Save Two Infidels!" Even Addar laughed now, while Abdul realized that Sol did not yet know about his newly declared commitment to Jesus. Then again, Abdul did not know that Sol and Ahava were actually the newest followers of Jesus in the room!

As the laughter subsided, Addar, now the only follower of Islam in the room asked, "What do you think the news organizations of the world will actually be reporting tomorrow? What will be the next unexpected event?"

Mark answered somberly, "Only our Lord knows what the coming days will bring."

Everyone except Addar nodded their heads in agreement.

Addar noted, "I know someone else who will be working desperately to control and orchestrate the events of the crucial days we now face!"

Mark asked, "Would that be Allah, Addar?"

"No!" Addar said with excitement. "I am talking about the man on this earth who has the all its power at his fingertips!"

"Those who believe fight in the cause of Allah, and those who reject Faith fight in the cause of Evil (Tagut): So fight ye against the friends of Satan: feeble indeed is the cunning of Satan."
Qur'an 4:76

CHAPTER 69

THE MOMENT OF TRUTH. . .

"*A*re you sure you are safe?" Hope Paulson's anxiety laden voice asked as Air Force One soared over the Atlantic Ocean.

"Honey, where could I be safer? Four Air Force fighter jets are flying alongside us. I will be back in the states in a few hours, and I will see you and the kids tomorrow!"

"They continue to be very frightened, James. They witnessed the destruction of the White House and Abdul's residence! They saw the Holocaust Museum erupt in a blaze of white and blue flame! They saw the missiles hit the Pentagon and the massive fireball which ensued! They saw the AIFD building blow up and asked me why Muslims are killing Muslims. They saw all the devastation in the U.S. and Israel. They are afraid!"

Sounding as confident as possible under the extraordinary circumstances, James replied, "The jihadist's goal is to plant terror within each of us, Hope! I hate to admit it, but we all feel that fear! Still, we cannot let fear immobilize our nation or our family! In a few minutes, the children will see me giving my speech. That will help them know I am safe. They need us to be strong, Hope. They need to be able to lean on us for comfort and encouragement."

"I know! You are right! When we are all together again, everything will be much better."

"Here's a bombshell for you—sorry, pardon the unintended pun. Neither Sam nor I know if we or Babylon have control of our weapons. We may have control of some of our arsenals while our enemies may have control over other portions. Worse yet, we fear that our weapons may even be booby trapped. If we try to fire a missile, it might explode on site or hit an unintended target!"

"Really? That's horrible!" Hope trembled.

"Our most important task is getting our weapons under our control, and to do that, Sam and I think we will have to shut down both the U.S. and Israeli weapons systems."

Still trembling, Hope asked, "Doesn't that just make us all the more vulnerable to an attack?"

"Babylon still cannot fire any of its own weapons—the ones they inherited from the EU or Asia—so I think we must shut down our systems and reprogram them while we have the chance. Babylon has no swift means of mobilizing its 40-million army of terrorists—at least not to our shores. While Goliath, if it is truly ready, could be a massive threat to us, the Brotherhood Army could be at Sam's doorstep on a moment's notice. No matter, he too must reprogram his weapons, else they are no good to him at all."

"How long will that reprogramming take for us and Israel?"

"That's the ten-billion dollar question, Hope! As you might guess, none of us know!"

"Still, if we can regain control of our weapons systems again, the jihadists would not be able to kill and destroy at their whim! So no matter how long it takes, you have no other choice, right?"

"No other choice at all! We have racked our brains and considered all the options. Sam and I have our best people on this urgent project— at least those of our best people that are still with us and not burnt to a crisp at the Pentagon or kidnapped in Babylon setting up the Caliph's weapons system!"

"I'll be praying for Jesus to guide the experts in our nations and to thwart the plans of Babylon!"

"Thanks, Hope!" James was willing to take help from any quarter at this point.

With his eye on the time, James said, "I love you, Hope, but I must go and make the final preparations for my speech—the most important address I may ever deliver as President!"

337

"I love you, too, James—more than my words can convey! Right now, I wish we had lost the election, but I know that you have been called to serve our country in such perilous times! This crisis has brought out the best in you!"

James wondered about the veracity of Hope's comments. Frankly, he could not have felt more unprepared for the huge task ahead. "Thanks again, Sweetheart! I'll be looking into your eyes again in a few moments! But for now, hold on to my love for you. I will see you in person soon. Bye!"

"So long, my Love!"

The President had to quickly refocus, as his address was less than five minutes away. Before calling Hope, he had conducted a holoconference with his few remaining Cabinet members, the leaders of the House and Senate, and what was left of the U.S. military leadership. His surviving Chairman of the Joint Chiefs of Staff, General Pierce Ellis, laid out a clear plan for him to share with a country teetering on the brink of chaos.

Then, the Commander in Chief had talked with the Israeli Prime Minister. The two leaders remained on the same page. Truth be told, the leaders of Israel and the United States had no other choice but to face this tsunami of danger and death together.

After speaking with Sam, James had contacted several heads of state in North, Central, and South America. Reading the writing on the wall, the leaders knew that they must overcome their political differences with each other and the U.S. to form a unified front. With their assurances, the President knew he could speak with confidence in his address.

Taking a long, deep breath, the President summoned all the courage and fortitude within himself for the words he was about to speak. In that moment, he realized that he was not a man of courage and fortitude. He thought to himself, "Desperate times call for desperate measures. I need to seek an Ally whom I have so long ignored and even cruelly insulted."

The President closed his eyes to pray. "God, if You are here with me, I thank You because I need You as I never have before in my life. My family needs You. My country needs You! I am sorry, so sorry, that I do not know You very well. I need the faith that Mark and Ariel have in You—that even Abdul seems to have in You now. I need the faith

I have always seen in Hope's eyes and ways! I am a proud man, no doubt. But I am most humbly confessing to You right now that I cannot do what I must tonight and in the days ahead on my own! I need You, and I pray You still want me! Please fill me with the strength, wisdom, and confidence I need to be the man You apparently have appointed me to be for such a time as this! Amen!"

The holovideographer had witnessed the President's prayer, although he could not hear any of his words. Though the two minute mark before the President's speech had passed, the crewman did not dare interrupt the man who represented America's strength and hope — and perhaps the world's strength and hope, too — as he prayed.

When the Commander in Chief looked up, wiped his eyes, and cleared his throat, the holovideographer said, "one minute and fifteen seconds to go, sir!" The President gave two thumbs up in reply, even as he realized he was going to change the opening of his speech, literally, at the last minute!

Even so, considering the growing crisis in his country, James felt a sense of calm assurance. As he looked down as his prepared remarks, he thanked God for answering his prayer. In that moment, he somehow knew his life would never be the same.

"The duly elected leader of the United States looked up and then gazed into the lens of the camera, as the holovideographer raised his hand and counted down, "Five, four, three," and then silently let his last two fingers fall.

"Good evening, my fellow Americans! Good evening fellow citizens of the world. I am talking with you tonight while aboard Air Force One, as I return to our nation's pummeled capitol. While we still do not know the death toll from today's unprovoked attack on America, I ask you to pause with me for a moment of intercession for the many victims and their families."

Again, the President bowed his head, and this time, before all of America and the world, softly offered an unscripted prayer. "Lord, in this time of crisis, our nation turns to You. Give us unity of purpose, so that our people may stand and not fall. We ask for the same unity in and with Israel, our strong ally and friend in this world. So much violence has been unleashed on our nations in such a short time. We grieve the loss of life and destruction in the U.S., Israel, and the Democratic Republic of Palestine. No one is claiming responsibility for all this death and devastation, Lord. But You know who is responsible. If there is any way possible, we yet ask for Your guidance to end these grisly days in peace, not war. But if we must fight, let it be with Your power and wisdom. Amen."

Watching her husband from Camp David, Hope smiled even as tears fell off her cheeks. In Israel, Sam was stunned by James' words and how much they resonated within his own soul. In his hospital room, all Abdul could do was say, "Thank you, Lord!" Mark, Ariel, Sol, and Ahava gazed at each other in quiet amazement. And somewhere in the darkness, the General shouted words of defiance and hatred for the two Satans, their false gods, and their wretched leaders.

As he raised his head, the President looked through the holovision camera lens into the homes of those who needed him to rise to this momentous occasion. He said, "I speak on behalf of those patriots whose blood was spilled today. While we cannot bring them back to us, we must honor their sacrifice and defend their families and their nation from further attack!

"I, the President of the United States, would not be speaking to you this evening without two men who put their lives on the line for me this very day! I am referring to the United State's newest heroes: Imam Addar Zaahir and our own Vice President Abdul Abdullah! Not only did these brave souls each spare my life at risk of their own, but together, they also saved the life of the Prime Minister of Israel, Samuel Ben Baruch! The two of us and the people of our nations owe a great debt to the imam and Vice President! We will honor them both in the days to come!"

Now, the President began the main thrust of his speech. "The United States of America is a land of freedom birthed in the pain of revolutionary war—a war waged on our own land. In order to protect this very freedom that has been our lifeblood, I must solemnly declare that the United States of America is again at war within her own borders! Revolution has begun!

"We must stand against the assault being waged by the Muslim Brotherhood of Babylon on our soil, Israel's soil, and the DROP's soil! Heaven help us if we must also take a stand on the shrouded soil of Babylon!

"Our enemy is both within our borders and outside our borders. We face an opponent that had and may yet have control over our own weapons, as this enemy demonstrated all too clearly in our nation's capitol today. Our loyal ally Israel witnessed such destruction from its own weapons that destroyed the Temple Mount yesterday.

"While many of our military leaders were taken from us in the merciless attack on the Pentagon, the United States Armed Forces yet stand tall, proud, and ready for what may lay ahead. General Pierce Ellis, Defense Secretary David Rothschild, and I, in consultation with the state and military leaders of Isreal and the Americas, have crafted the details of our response."

The Commander in Chief inhaled deeply, as he spoke words that were not in the text of his speech. "While we will marshal all the resources at our joint disposal to stop the evil that threatens our cumulative freedom, we must remember one essential truth in these ominous moments: Our foremost weapon and tactics in these battles are not of this physical world!"

". . . 'Peace be with you! As the Father has sent Me, I am
sending you.'"
John 20:21

CHAPTER 70

A MAN WITH A MISSION. . .

*A*bdul's second surgeon came into his room to talk with him as
he recovered from the additional procedure. Addar had been
released from the hospital earlier, before the President's address, as
his wound was not serious. Abdul, on the other hand, had been taken
into emergency surgery. While the operation on his surface wound
had been successful, an X-ray apparently indicated excessive internal
bleeding. Hence, the Vice President did not return to Washington D.C.
with the President.

The surgeon told Abdul that the procedure had gone well, and that
he would be able to leave the hospital in the morning. He would be
monitored for the rest of the night to ensure no problems arose from
the surgery or his transfusions.

Abdul asked the surgeon, "Did you see the President's speech?"

"No," replied the doctor, visibly irritated by the question, "I had
another emergency case."

"Then make sure you watch the news because the speech fired on
all cylinders! The President said things that no one would have ever
expected of him!"

Unsure of how to take Abdul's comments, the surgeon said, "I'll
be sure to see for myself! As for you, you need rest. Morning is not far
away, and you must get some sleep if you want to be released!"

Meanwhile, back in the lobby, despite the late hour, Sol overflowed with enthusiasm! "I think we can help the President and Prime

Minister," Sol told Mark. "I believe we should make a joint plea for peace through Y'shua!"

With a perplexed look on his face, Mark replied, "I don't know if I quite follow what you mean, Sol."

"I mean we should tell the world that the way to resolve the conflict with the Muslims is for them to become our brothers and sisters in Y'shua—or Isa as they refer to Him! The Messiah is the only One who can bring peace to Israel, America, and the countries of the world that are under Islamic rule. Jews and Christians alike suffer horribly in the Caliphate—at least the ones who yet live suffer. The Muslims consider them as subhuman, and the only reason they live is for the profit the Calphinate! If they cannot make their payments, they must either become Muslims or be killed!"

"Which fate is worse, Sol?" Mark asked solemnly.

"An appropriate question, indeed, Mark!"

"I see where you are going, Sol. You want to provide testimony to the transformation Y'shua has brought to you and Ahava!"

"*Ken*! Yes! I no longer have any animosity for the Muslims! I want them to know the same peace in their hearts—and only Y'shua *HaMashiach* can bring it to them! Ahava and I could be powerful witnesses for our Lord!"

"I agree with you, Sol. My life's work, apart from my role as pastor, is reaching into the Muslim countries with the salvation of Isa!"

"I know that! But you need some help! It would be great if a couple of former hard line Jews like us could team up with a great evangelist like you to share the saving power of Y'shua with both Muslims and Jews! If Y'shua can transform my life, He can and will do it for everyone who will listen!"

Speaking from experience, Mark said, "Persuading Jews and Muslims to listen can be the most difficult challenge of all. Much tradition and many centuries of hatred must be conquered just to start the conversation!"

"Surely, if we joined your work, maybe we could tear down at least some of those barriers to hearing the truth!"

"Actually," Mark replied with a twinkle in his eye, "I have an even better idea. I know a prominent Muslim man who recently became a believer in Isa. His high profile, coupled with your notoriety as an

Orthodox Rabbi and role in the peace negotiations, could make the two of you a winning team for the salvation of Jews and Muslims!"

"What do you mean?"

"You heard me, Sol!"

"Who is this high profile Muslim convert that you know?"

"You know him, too, Sol!"

"I do? How?"

"You were just talking with him a little while ago—in the hospital room!"

"I was? Who have I just been talking. . ." A look of complete surprise came over Sol's face! "You mean Addar?"

"No, Sol!" Mark said as he laughed. He was really enjoying this ping pong match!

"Abdul?" Sol asked as he looked to Ahava to see if she had any idea.

"Why don't you tell me?" as Mark knocked the ball back to Sol's side of the table.

Sol paused to sort out his thoughts. "Abdul! He must be the one! He has become so positive, so peaceful—even after taking a bullet for the President!"

"Game! Set! Match! You are exactly right, Sol! So what do you think? Could you and Abdul team up as a modern day Paul and Barnabas?"

"I am more than willing and able!"

Ahava smiled and held Sol tightly saying, "Abdul would do much better than me, my Sweet! I don't know how to speak in front of people!"

"Why Ahava, you sound like Moses," her happy husband said. "If our Messiah wants to use you, He would speak through you by the power of His Spirit!"

The second surgeon walked up and interrupted the lively conversation. "Pastor Basel, could I have a moment with you in private?

"Certainly! Is anything wrong?"

"Perhaps so, Pastor. I believe I have something here that requires your immediate attention!"

No one from the security team followed Mark, as he was with the doctor. They assumed the two men were going to Abdul's room. But in Israel, one should never assume!

"Of a truth ye are stronger (than they) because of the terror in their hearts, (sent) by Allah. This is because they are men devoid of understanding."
Qur'an 59:13

CHAPTER 71

LINGERING AT THE ABYSS...

*T*he Prime Minister felt somewhat confused after listening to the President's speech. Even so, the battle in his mind would not allow him to focus on James' words. Sam feared Israel remained caught in a trap from which it might not be able to escape. If he declared war with Babylon, as he certainly must at some point, the troops of the Brotherhood would be at The Land's borders by morning and the sleeper cells within Israel would awake and join them. After all, as Sam reminded himself, *"The Brotherhood stands ever ready to strike and rid the earth of its Jewish infection!"*

Sam asked aloud once more, *"How can I declare war, when the Brotherhood can use our own weapons against us? How can we survive, if we shut down our weapons systems and the Brotherhood attacks in mass, or worse yet, with Goliath? We did not design the defense system, David's Slingshot, to take out a giant of that caliber."*

The Prime Minister tired over the constant rehashing of possibilities. What good did it do? Israel had drawn no closer to a specific battle plan and neither had the United States. The only action the two nations had decided to take was to disable their weapons control systems. *"Wow, what a bold and decisive move on our part,"* Sam thought.

Despite the brilliance of the Israel and U.S. programmers who sought to reveal how the Brotherhood gained control of weapons deployment in both countries, still no progress had been made. Thus, Sam and James had thus agreed to shut down their weapons systems, not only hoping they could be quickly reprogrammed to counter any new threat that arose, but also to prevent the enemy from tapping into the two nation's WMD's, especially their nuclear arsenals.

Sam shuddered at the prospect of a nuclear attack. He thought, *"If Babylon did not love the satisfaction of watching the U.S. and Israel squirm, perhaps the Brotherhood would have destroyed both countries in one fell swoop. No, Babylon likes toying with both nations! After all, the Caliph—maybe even wayward General—have so far called all the shots! Then again, maybe the Caliph has floated disinformation about the General and rogue forces. Suppose the Brotherhood has not hacked into the weapons control systems of either the U.S. or Israel, but that all the destruction had been caused by inside operatives—could that be remotely possible?"*

After reading the Brotherhood Manual for the U.S., Sam had theorized that terrorist operatives in both nations could be sitting behind weapons control panels right now—despite the interrogations both countries had just completed. Sam wondered, *"Perhaps these operatives can cover their tracks for one launch here and in the states. Yet, maybe those operatives no longer have free rein. Could our countermeasures thwart their future efforts? After all, both our nations have changed our weapons codes and firewalls—before shutting down our systems for a complete reprogramming.*

"Could the President have prevented the attack on the Pentagon, if it had changed its codes and firewalls when we did, after the missile strike on the Temple Mount and the DROP? Does the fact that no Israeli weapons were fired during the attacks on the Prime Minister's residence and Yad Vashem have significance? Does the Brotherhood no longer possess control of our weapons?"

Like a man coming out of a long slumber, Sam shook his head and blinked his eyes rapidly. *"On the other hand,"* he reasoned, *"if the operatives have high security clearance, they would know about all the code and surveillance changes. Such operatives could then easily maintain their control over the two weapons systems, if they could be sufficiently discreet. And as Muslims now come in all shapes, sizes, races, and backgrounds, how do we ferret out the terrorists?*

"Then again," Sam countered, *"someone operating from a remote location, outside the U.S. and Israel command units, would not have instant access to the new code and surveillance safeguards, right?*

How long will it take the Brotherhood to crack through the new cyber walls the President and I authorized?

"Maybe not long at all," The Prime Minister realized. *"Someone on the high end of security clearance could be feeding information in real time to a remote location.*

"All these rabbit trails and wild goose chases, as the Americans would say, have given me a headache!" Sam's brain actually hurt from considering all the various scenarios. All that clutter impaired his ability to make the decision to call for war or choose to wait and see what Babylon would throw at Israel next.

A few hours earlier, the Prime Minister had assured President Paulson that Israel would support an American declaration of war against Babylon, which, he noted, James did not actually make in his speech. While James had alluded to war breaking out with the states, the President stopped short of declaring war with Babylon.

Sam asked himself, *"What happened since James and I last talked to make him pause on this side of declaring war? Perhaps he is buying time for our weapons systems to be reprogrammed. Could he actually think that war can yet be avoided?"*

All of the Prime Minister's advisers, Deputy Cabinet members, and government and military heads told him he had no choice but to declare war. Israeli troops, ships, and jet fighters had deployed to protect the nation. However, he could not shake the feeling that declaration of war was exactly what Babylon, or a rebel who would be Caliph, wanted in order to justify its annihilation of the Jewish State—but since when did Islam need justification for wiping out Israel? Indeed, why would Babylon care if it could justify an attack on Israel or not? As outlined in the Qur'an and the Brotherhood Manual, the very existence of Jews in Israel was all the justification any Muslim terrorist needed for attacking the Promised Land!

"But wait," Sam said aloud, *"maybe I should reconsider the intel reports about rebellion in the enemy camp—even direct opposition to bin Laden. Maybe that threat to the Caliph is greater than what anyone has yet realized. How would a coup in process impact the situations in the U.S. and Israel? What if the Caliph actually has been the restraining factor against all out war with Israel and the U.S.? What if he really does think the timing is wrong and his opposition has targeted him for elimination? Such a turn of events could explain why*

Babylon has neither claimed nor denied the attacks on Washington D.C. and Jerusalem. However, if the Caliph is not calling the shots, who in Babylon is making those decisions?"

A weary and exhausted Sam realized he had to stop weaving through all his scenarios. He would make his speech first thing Tuesday morning. But the wee hours of that morning were upon him now. He would either alter his own speech or be in conflict with James. Sam would have to confer with the American President to determine why he did not declare war on Babylon.

Sam asked himself, *"What does James now know that I do not know? Should I call James or wait for him to contact me? As tired and spent as I am, perhaps I should get some sleep before we talk. Like James said, our nations must be one in this craziness if our people are going to survive. Babylon will exploit the slightest crack in the alliance between Israel and the U.S.!"*

Sam remembered James saying, flatly, "Our enemy is both within our borders and outside our borders. We face an enemy that had and may yet have control over our own weapons, as this enemy demonstrated all too clearly in our nation's capitol today. Our loyal ally Israel witnessed such destruction from its own weapons that were used to destroy the Temple Mount yesterday."

Sam walked over to his HV3D, reversed his recording of the Presidents' speech, and listened to the latter portion of his words a second time.

"We face an enemy that may be as close as our next door neighbor's home and as far away as the bunkers under Babylon. We have secured intelligence from the Brotherhood that shows it has been implementing a subversive, clandestine, and until now unperceived war of deceit on these United States for many decades. Should this information prove accurate, we are being betrayed by Muslims who live among us in apparent peace and assimilation. This war strategy of the Brotherhood aims to do no less than take control of all aspects of our American society, business, education, legal systems, government, and military. This enemy among us has one ultimate goal: to rule this land of the free and this home of the brave as an Islamic state under Sharia Law!

"Until now, this secretive war has been waged against us in every facet of American life. Most tragically, your neighbor, coworker, instructor, business partner, golf buddy, family member, or most trusted friend may in fact be your worst enemy!

"Muslims no longer fit a stereotype. In the United States, we have generations of Muslims who have never lived outside our borders. The same can be said for all countries not yet under the Caliphate. Followers of Islam have been born and raised on all the continents, in all the nations. Likewise, many of our citizens have converted to Islam. As a result, Muslims are white, black, brown, yellow, and red. They have high positions in all areas of leadership. They may even be sitting next to you in synagogue or church."

Sam recoiled in response to the picture the President had painted.

"And just how do we distinguish between the Muslims who may actually desire peace from those who are deceiving us by claiming they want no part of war?" The President paused to allow his question to be fully considered.

"Am I saying that each of us should be ready to do battle with every Muslim we know as well as those in our lives whom we do not yet realize are Muslims? No! Some of them are indeed seeking to avoid war, as we are. At this moment, we pray that the violence in our streets will not escalate. We yet pray for peace. We still pray for the souls of our enemy.

"Sadly, the peace loving Muslims are not in control, as evidenced by the destruction of the American Islamic Forum for Democracy, the AIFD. These Muslims who sought democracy, like those in Palestine, have been brutally murdered by fellow Muslims who regard them as infidels. Should all out war break out in the United States, these freedom-loving Muslims will be targeted with all other freedom-loving Americans.

"Thus, as a nation, what are we to do to protect ourselves from the hidden enemy among us? In addition to the National Guard troops who are assisting local police forces across the country, I have authorized the deployment of our nation's armed forces within our borders. Their role is to stop any and all uprisings against our citizenry. We pray to the God who gave America its inalienable rights of life, liberty, and the pursuit of happiness to protect our unarmed, untrained citizens from what could be the most ferocious enemy we have every faced, not on a far off battlefield, but right here in our own communities!

"As a further safeguard, I am prepared to authorize deployment of our Navy's mighty warships, our Air Force's powerful fighter jets, our Marine's unmatched sea and land warriors, and our Army's vast battalions to the shores of Babylon. Should I order such a deployment, know this: Beside our men and women in uniform will not only be the best and bravest from Israel, but also the military might of Canada, El Salvador, Brazil, Peru, Argentina, and all the rest of our North, Central, and South American allies.

"If necessary, not only will the brave soldiers of our countries together fight and conquer a common enemy, but also, when the fog of war lifts, our countries will have formed a new strategic union of the Americas! As President Abraham Lincoln so wisely proclaimed, 'A friend is one who has the same enemies as you have.' With our common enemy's defeat, we will celebrate a new American Alliance of friends that will partner with us and Israel!

"More to the point, when we defeat our mutual enemy, we pray that we can liberate all those under the oppression of the Caliphate. They are suffering in heinous ways, even as we speak. They too look to us for help.

"In our lifetimes, we have witnessed the islamization of Europe and now Asia. Today, not one synagogue remains in all of Babylon, while every church and government building has either been destroyed or converted to a mosque, a *madrasah*—a Muslim school—or a Sharia court. Remember, the Sharia calls for maiming, stoning, and beheading those who violate its code. The slightest criticism of Islam carries a sentence of death! All surviving Christians and Jews in Babylon are servants of the Muslims who consider the people of the Bible and the Tanakh to be subhuman and force them to pay tribute—the *jizya*—to the Caliph!

"Should war be inevitable, we, with our allies, will battle the enemy for our freedom, as well as for the freedom of our friends who are presently in the bonds of servitude and slavery in and to Babylon!

"We made the mistake of believing that Islam was satisfied with its conquest of Europe and Asia. Nonetheless, mark my words. We will not make the deadly mistake of allowing this land our forefathers birthed and fought to preserve to become Islamerica! We will not allow Israel to fall under the flag of the crescent moon and star! We will not allow the countries to our north and south to be ruled by a

Caliph! Likewise, we will not allow our Christian and Jewish families and friends in Babylon to die under a regime of terror!

"Should you expect to see an escalation of the war in the streets of America tomorrow morning? We pray that neither tomorrow nor any day will bring full-fledged war inside this great nation where free men and women govern themselves.

"We will be at war in foreign lands tomorrow? While our nation is in mourning over the grievous loss of life in the attacks on our nation's capitol, I say to you right now that we can yet step back from the throes of World War IV! We do not wish to avoid all out conflict because America is weak, but because we are strong and do not want to be an instrument of annihilation in this world if at all possible!

"All that being said, if war on distant shores cannot be prevented, if the battle over the future of these United States of America comes to our doorsteps tomorrow or any day, we must be of one voice, one heart, one mind, one soul, and one nation under God. With God as our witness, we must commit to do whatever is deemed necessary to preserve this land of freedom that stretches from sea to shining sea and from the ice floes of Alaska to the warm waves of Hawaii! We must preserve this great nation as an inheritance for our children, our children's children, and for generations of their children to come!

"If we can, by any means, avert all out war, I call on the Caliph of Babylon to be a true man of peace. Yet, if Caliph bin Laden remains silent, we have no choice but to defend ourselves and our freedoms. As our first President George Washington stated, "If we desire to secure peace, one of the most powerful instruments of our rising prosperity, it must be known, that we are at all times ready for war!"

"We have the enemy's battle plan. We pray that our opponent does not go to the next step! On the other hand, should we have no other option but war, we will face it boldly. With God as our source of strength and resolve, with our allies in the Americas and Israel at our side, we will fight for peace and liberty, we will stand firm with courage to defend those who cannot protect themselves!"

As Sam listened again to the final words of the President's challenging and inspiring speech, the Prime Minister knew what he must do. "Give me strength, *HaShem*," he prayed.

351

"Because of the increase of wickedness, the love of most will grow cold, but he who stands firm to the end will be saved."
Matthew 24:12-13

CHAPTER 72

CLOSE SHAVE...

❖

*T*he doctor led Mark to what appeared to be his office. He opened the door for Mark so he could enter. The next thing Mark knew was that he had a machete against his neck! The blade was so sharp and so close that Mark could not swallow for fear of slicing his own throat!

"Don't try to talk unless you enjoy the sight of your own blood!" Mark realized he was listening to the dissonant voice of the General of the Brotherhood. "Cooperate and you will walk out of this room unharmed. Resist and your measly head will be forever separated from your pathetic body!"

Mark could tell the General's voice was not coming from the man who held the machete to his neck. As both men were behind him, he had no idea if anyone else stood in the room.

"Let's recount where we have been. You disobeyed my orders not to talk to the authorities. Yet, as events turned out, those men saved your life, as well as the life of your wife, from a frenzied crowd of jihad-energized Palestinian Muslims. Thankfully, you still are of some use to me in your current state of being alive!

"You have also been introduced, at least by phone, to your future son-in-law. Strange, is it not, that your son-in-law is older than you. Stranger yet is the fact that his bride, your daughter, is younger than all of his daughters and only slightly older than his granddaughters! Strangest of all is that his voice sounds a lot like my own!

Mark felt the heat rise in his body as his face began to sweat, but he could say or do nothing. Instead, he silently prayed, "Dear Jesus! I pray that Grace has not been given to this vile Muslim as his bride. I pray that You have kept her safe from harm and that she has not been violated! Be with her, Lord. Let her feel Your Presence even now as I pray for her!"

"I suppose you would like to see your daughter, Haziqah, if I remember her name correctly. Her husband asked you for a wedding gift, I believe. We have come to collect it for him.

The General stopped speaking for a few moments, only to heighten the tension for Mark. Yet the persevering pastor only continued to pray. "Saviour! Please help me stop this rise of hatred in my heart. Help me instead to see these men through Your eyes! They are in desperate need of You! How else could they even consider doing such cruel and abusive things to Grace? Even in my silence, Lord, and yes, even in my fear, let them see that my hope and faith are in You and You alone! I know you are with me even now. You have allowed these moments for a purpose that these men or even I cannot yet see. Calm my soul, please Jesus. Let these men sense that they are in Your very Presence!"

The General snickered as he said, "This desired wedding gift is not something anyone can buy or acquire. Plus, this gift can only be offered by you. You will give the happy couple this most special present this afternoon. I know you haven't slept much at all lately. Thus, I strongly suggest you find a few hours to rest. You need to be fresh this afternoon."

The General still had not divulged the actual gift expected of Mark. The father of three assumed it would be his life in exchange for Grace's life. Mark had already resolved that he would gladly give his life to save hers. If the terrorists killed Grace, Mark knew they would first rape her. The terrorists believed that all virgins went to Paradise. Hence, they raped their virgin victims to ensure they roasted in the fires of hell!

Hence, if Mark was to spare Grace from rape and murder, if he was to give his life in exchange for hers, then why was the General waiting to collect his prize? Was he not going to release Grace unharmed? Was there something the General wanted Mark to see in the moments before his death? As drool spilled from his lips because he could not swallow, Mark again prayed for Grace's captors. "Whatever they want from me in addition to my life, Lord, I pray I can give it! Help me do whatever I must to save my little girl!"

"At three o'clock this afternoon, you will be at the same studio where you were before the shooting. This time, you will be the one talking. Your message will be broadcast live around the world. I don't believe you have ever preached to an audience quite that large before, right? But then, this won't be an evangelistic sermon to Muslims, begging them to believe that Isa is the very son of Allah who died for their sins! I truthfully do not believe I can bear to hear even one more portion of such an assortment of lies!

"No, this time will be very different. Your international debut will, nonetheless, begin with your testimony of who you are and where you lived and what you did before you lost your mind and believed that Allah could have a son sent to atone for your sins. Every Muslim knows that no one else can pay for the consequences of his sin! Only obedience and submission to Allah's commands can earn entry into Paradise and its Gardens with rivers flowing beneath. Of course, killing an infidel or two assures an eternity of bliss, as does being killed in the cause of jihad! But that sacrificed soul only saves himself and no others!"

Now, the General laughed as he continued, saying, "One aspect of your life story will be different tomorrow afternoon. You will tell about the huge mistake you made in denying Islam and Allah for the nonexistent God of the Christians and Jews. You can tell how much of your life you have wasted in serving a deity that was supposedly raised from the dead, but actually has not yet died—and was not God, either! Isa will return to condemn the likes of you and the vile Jews, and then he will die as every other man dies. He was not crucified for anyone's sins. Isa was not crucified at all, but called up to Paradise so Allah could prepare him for his role as judge of those who rejected his message from Allah!

"But you know all this in your heart! Therefore, in your mea culpa, you will, in no uncertain terms, recant your faith in your polytheistic god, and, of your own accord, you will pledge that you will rejoin the struggle of the one and only god—the god of Islam! You will swear your allegiance to Allah and devote the rest of your days to jihad! You will tell the understanding and empathetic audience that Allah has called you to return to him and denounce all your work for your three false gods of Father, Son, and Spirit!

"If you refuse, or if anyone else comes with you, your daughter will not be the fertile bride of one of our Muslim brothers, but she will instead be repeatedly raped and then agonizingly slaughtered before your very eyes as the last vision you see before your head separates from your body!

"So you see, we will not exchange hostages. You will recant your faith in a nonexistent son of god. As a result, Haziqah will marry the Muslim hero who spoke to you about their wedding. After all, we warned you in our initial letter that we would hunt down your sons and pledge your daughters in marriage to Islamic men if you chose not to cooperate with us, Pastor Mark—soon to be former pastor!

"Any questions?"

Of course, anything Mark said would slice his own throat!

"Good! We would hate to leave a bloody mess in this nice room of this swine hospital! We are most exuberant that you understand that you and your daughter will both live—miserably ever after!"

"For Muslim men and women—for believing men and women, for devout men and women, for true men and women, for men and women who are patient and constant, for men and women who humble themselves, for men and women who give in charity, for men and women who fast (and deny themselves), for men and women who guard their chastity, and for men and women who engage much in Allah's praise—for them has Allah prepared forgiveness and great reward."
Quran 33:35

CHAPTER 73

A BROKEN WILL,
A WHOLE LIFE. . .

❖

"What did the focus groups say about your speech?" Hope asked.

"You know, Honey, I don't think I care about focus groups anymore." James said from his private bedroom on Air Force One. "I said what I had to say. I cannot be responsible for how people respond. We now live in a time when measuring approval among potential voters is not what's important. We need to focus on unifying and mobilizing our nation to meet the huge challenge before us."

Her husband's statement startled Hope—as did his speech. Never had she heard James speak in such apolitical terms. "I'm proud of you, Mr. President! Your conviction and genuine concern for Americans and our country shined throughout your address starting from word one."

James hesitated in responding to Hope.

"Do you have something you want to tell me?" the intuitive wife asked.

"You will probably think these words sound strange, coming from me, but I believe that God guided me during the speech, even changing some of the things that I had planned to say. I went off script several times, and I just don't do that—especially in an address as important as this one. But I felt empowered and led to say what I did! I even left out the call to war that I told Sam I would make!"

Hope found it hard to contain her emotions. She ran her hands through her short, dark hair and said, "James! That's wonderful! You know that I have been praying for you to know God as I do! What happened tonight?"

Hope's enthusiastic response to James words gave him courage. He said, "I prayed before my speech—a short, simple prayer asking God to give me strength and help me focus. I admitted that I could not deliver the speech, much less lead the country in the days ahead, on my own. After that prayer, I was no longer tied in a knot. I had a sense of peace that I really cannot describe!"

Hope felt so much happiness that she couldn't speak. Tears streamed from her hazel eyes!

With his beautiful, sweet bride crying for him, James knew he had to carry the conversation. "I think I have an idea of what you have tried to describe to me when you said you felt the Lord moving in your life. I always thought that sounded pretty silly, and I always tried to shut down those conversations with you. But now I have respect for what you have experienced. I understand the reality of what you have tried to explain to me!"

Earnestly, James asked, "Hope, can you forgive me for thinking so poorly of you? Can God forgive me for all the awful things I have said about Him and people who profess faith in Him? Like I said, I realize that I cannot go through the days and possible years ahead without Him. Even if war were not upon us, even if I were not the President, I would want His strength and wisdom in my life!"

Hope wiped her eyes, cleared her throat, and spoke from her heart. "James, God is all about forgiveness! The very reason He sent Jesus to give His life on the cross was so that you could know His mercy and grace! He wants you! He loves you—even more than I love you! He would like nothing better than for you to receive His forgiveness and begin a relationship with Him!"

Now James was quiet. He turned away from the phone.

"Honey, are you still there?"

"I feel dumbfounded and extremely unworthy, Hope!" Then his voice cracked as he said, "I really have been a self-centered, world-revolves-around me, put-me-in-the-spotlight guy! Worse yet, I have been so self absorbed that I have been an awful father to the boys as well as a terrible husband to you! Worst of all, I have acted as though I am god, at least in terms of my life and this presidency!" The Commander in Chief wept.

"James! Honey! You feel the conviction of the Holy Spirit! He reveals our true selves to us so that we can see who and how we really are! But conviction is not the end! The Spirit leads us beyond conviction to confess our sins—as you just did—in repentance, so that we can start our lives over again—forgiven, clean, and as though we have never sinned at all!"

Voice still cracking, the President of the United States of America, flying in Air Force One, asked his enthused wife, "What words am I supposed to say to Jesus now, Hope?"

"Just what you have been saying—words from the depths of your soul! Jesus knows your thoughts and feelings. Tell Him you are sorry. Tell Him you want to start over! Tell Him you want Him to be the center of your life, your family, and your presidency!"

James knelt on the floor, using his bed as a makeshift altar. He sat his secure phone on the bed, but Hope could still hear him. He took a deep breath as he began. "O God! Jesus! You see me here before You! I have never felt this way before! I suddenly realize how wasted my life has been in Your eyes! I cannot express my sorrow to You, to my wife, to my family, to my country! I want, I need, Your forgiveness, Your mercy. I want to live for You in a life of grace! I know You paid the ultimate cost. You gave Your very life for me through incredible suffering! Please, let me start over with You! Please, please give me the new life that I've heard about so long, but never believed was possible. I believe now, Jesus! Help me be strong in You and no longer put myself above anyone! Please, Lord, please!"

For the next few minutes, all James and Hope heard from each other was the sound of their breathing. Then James picked up the phone and looked into his long-suffering bride's face. "Thank you! Thank you for loving me, when I have not been worth loving. Thank you for praying for me for so many years! Thank you for never turning away from me, even when I so often turned away from you!"

"I thank Jesus," Hope replied. "He always loved you, when I did not want to anymore. He always prompted me to pray for you, even when I was so hurt or so mad that praying for you was the last thing I wanted to do. Jesus always kept me from turning away from you, even though I tried to convince Him that you deserved to be totally alone! Any goodness and unconditional love I have demonstrated to you, James, flowed from Jesus through me to you!"

"That's quite amazing, Hope! You mean you actually wanted to leave me sometimes—cute, adorable, cuddly little me?"

The President and First Lady laughed as they had not laughed in years! After the jovialness subsided, Hope noted, "You need to get some sleep. You have a big day tomorrow!"

"You mean today! And just so you know, God is in control of this day, and He will let me know what my role will be in it!"

"Indeed! I love you, James! I cannot wait until I see you when you come for me and the boys!"

"Hope, I now have a love in my heart for you that I never knew was possible. I want to do so much for you. I want to make up for all that I have forced you to endure from me!"

"You don't owe me anything to me, James. Jesus has made you a new man! That's more any woman could ever hope for in her marriage!"

"What did I ever do to deserve you? Wait! I know the answer! Nothing! You are God's gift to me!"

"If you say so, James!"

"I know so, Hope! By the way, I won't be coming for you and the boys. You and the boys must come to me. You will receive the details in a few hours."

"Whatever you say, sir! Goodnight, Mr. President! I pray you enjoy much rest in the few hours left in your flight!"

"Goodnight, My fair First Lady! I am filled with peace in the midst of a huge crisis, thanks to you, and thanks to Jesus!"

The 3DHP images faded. James could not stop smiling! He got into bed, placed his head on the pillow, and fell into the best and deepest sleep he had ever experienced!

". . . 'If anyone would come after me, He must deny Himself and take up His cross and follow Me.'"
Matthew 16:24

CHAPTER 74

CHOICES DETERMINE CHARACTER...

*I*n the five minutes Mark was told to wait in the doctor's office before he opened the door to leave, he tried to compose himself. With great urgency, he prayed for Jesus to guide him and fill him with the power and determination of the Holy Spirit for what would be required of him in the afternoon.

"Lord," Mark prayed, "I have a choice to make. One option leads to certain death for Grace and for me. If I refuse to recant my faith in You, I will be killed, but only after witnessing the repulsive rape and merciless murder of my little girl!

"Another option leads to my shame, yet possible life for my daughter. Even so, Grace's life would be so hard married to a Muslim like the General at thirteen. To have the mere possibility of this difficult life for Grace, I would have to lie and deny You!

"Then again, even if I comply with the General's demands, he may still kill us both. What assurance do I have that he will keep his word?

"You, on the other hand, I know and trust fully. I believe I have only one option, Jesus! Please reveal to me if this is the path You are directing me to take! Make it perfectly clear what You desire of me."

Then, with total confidence in his Lord and King, Mark asked, "What do I say to Ariel?" He waited in the room until Jesus answered him.

A few moments later, Mark opened the office door. Slowly, he put his head through the doorway and looked to his right and left. Seeing no one, he cautiously stepped into the hallway to make his way back to the lobby waiting room where his wife, Sol, and Ahava talked about ways to share the love of Y'shua.

As Mark approached them, he heard Sol planning his travels with Abdul. "Of course, I realize he is the Vice President of the United States, so his schedule may be a bit crowded!" The two women laughed in reply.

In contrast, when the three saw Mark, all the laughter came to an abrupt halt. Ariel ran to her husband. "What's wrong, Mark? Is Abdul having problems?"

"I don't know," he sighed. "I haven't seen Abdul since we were all in his room."

"Mark, why is your neck bleeding? It looks so red and agitated. Where have you been? What did you and the doctor do?"

With his eyes darting to the security detail in the room, Mark whispered in Ariel's ear, "We cannot talk right now. We will have to be alone."

With those words, Ariel's face went pale. She knew something bad had happened or was about to happen! "One question," Ariel softly spoke. "Does what you need to tell me involve Grace?"

"Yes!" Mark whispered in reply. "But we must act normal and not arouse any suspicion, okay? Let's go see Abdul."

As the couple turned to go back down the hallway, Sol and Ahava jumped to their feet—as well as 85 and 84 year olds can jump—to follow them to visit the wounded hero. Again, the security detail did not follow them.

When the four of them entered the room, both beds were empty. Mark said to a nurse who was passing by the door, "Excuse me, but do you know where the Vice President might be?"

She looked at the electronic chart in her hand and scanned down the lines with her finger. Not finding what she was looking for, she flipped to the next page and continued the scan. "Ah! Vice President Abdullah is in X-ray."

"Why does he need another X-ray?" Mark asked.

"Doctor's orders," replied the nurse.

Mark's furrowed brow revealed his deep concern for Abdul, but he did his best to remain calm. "Did his surgeon order this X-ray?"

"I just came on duty," the nurse said as her eyes went back to the virtual chart. "No. The second surgeon left the hospital about an hour ago. Dr. Goldberg ordered the X-ray."

Mark sighed with relief. "Thank you! Thank you so much, Nurse . . ." Mark looked at her badge for her name. "Nurse Hadassah Weinstein!"

"You are quite welcome. According to the chart, the Vice President did quite well in his second surgery. I am sure the X-ray is just precautionary. He will return to this room if you would like to wait for him."

"Thank you again! You are very kind!" Mark said, with a genuinely grateful smile on his face. However, as he considered her words, his smile vanished. "Nurse Weinstein, did you say second surgery? None of us knew that the Vice President went through another surgery. Why did he need a second operation?"

Nurse Weinstein looked at the electronic chart again. "Apparently the Vice President had severe internal bleeding after the first surgery to clean and sew up his external wound."

Mark asked, "Dr. Goldberg did not order or perform that surgery, did he?"

"No sir, he did not," the nurse answered.

As she resumed her rounds, Mark motioned to Ariel that he would be right back. He walked back to the lobby and approached one of the leaders of the secret service team members. "Are you aware that the Vice President is having an X-ray?"

With the tone of "I know everything that is happening in this hospital," the team leader replied, "Of course I know that! I was consulted before the X-ray. One of my men is with him. I have everything under control, pastor."

Feeling a bit scorned, Mark replied. "And of course you know that the imam has been discharged and is no longer here at the hospital?"

The surprised look on the security team leader's face revealed his ignorance of that fact. Somewhat apologetically, he asked, "Do you, by chance know when he left or where he went?"

Mark tried not to smile as he answered, "You can ask Nurse Weinstein! Also, you might want to check on the whereabouts, as well as the background, of the doctor who performed the Vice President's second surgery—you do know he underwent a second operation, right?" The head agent immediately left Mark to find Nurse Weinstein.

Feeling somewhat vindicated, Mark grinned and returned to the hospital room to talk with Ariel. As he refocused, the smile quickly left his face.

Ariel waited in the doorway. "Well?"

"Let's sit down," Mark said with resignation in his voice. Sol and Ahava stepped outside the room, sensing that Mark and Ariel needed some time alone.

With his hand on the back of his neck, Mark recounted the chilling words of the General. As he spoke, Ariel tried not to weep, but could not hold back her tears.

Sol and Ahava were straining to hear Mark's words. When Ahava realized what Mark was saying to Ariel, Ahava stopped breathing and held her hand over her mouth. Sol just stared into her eyes, as he could not clearly hear what Mark was saying. When he finished talking with Ariel, Ahava's head slumped. She could not accept what she had heard.

Sol asked, "What did he say, Honey? What did Mark say to Ariel?"

Before she could answer, Nurse Weinstein ran back into the room. Breathless, she said, "Pastor! I wanted you to know that the X-ray revealed some kind of explosive device has been implanted in the Vice President's shoulder! He is in another emergency surgery, with our finest surgeon and an elite member of the Mossad Bomb Squad! Even though the walls of the surgical unit are blast and bomb proof, the operating room and the entire floor have been evacuated and sealed. In fact, two floors above and two floors below the surgical unit have been closed!"

All the color ran from Mark's face! He ran back to the lead security agent. "Do you know that an explosive device was implanted in the Vice President's shoulder during his second surgery, and that he is now in surgery again to remove it?"

By the shocked look on the team leader's face, Mark knew the befuddled agent had no idea about what was happening!

"Fighting is prescribed for you, and ye dislike it. But it is possible that ye dislike a thing which is good for you, and that ye love a thing which is bad for you. But Allah knoweth, and ye know not."
Qur'an 2:216

CHAPTER 75

WITNESSES TO
THE UNTHINKABLE...

*A*s the Prime Minister began to conclude his midmorning address to Israel and the world, he said, "We seek to live in peace with all people of all faiths. For those who do not choose to live at peace with us, our God instructs us to rely on Him to protect His Land and His People. When Russia and its Muslim allies came over the northern mountains of Israel to destroy us, the whole earth witnessed the Mighty Right Arm of *HaShem*!

"Babylon seems to have forgotten that Israel has a powerful Ally that is not intimidated by vicious threats or massive weapons or bloodthirsty armies. We do not fear the enemy within our borders or the enemy that will attempt to penetrate them.

"Our Scriptures are our guide. Leviticus 26:8 says, *"Five of you shall give chase to hundred, and a hundred of you shall give chase to ten thousand; your enemies shall fall before you by the sword."* While the Babylonian Army may comprise 40 million terrorists, and we only have ten million citizens, it would seem that we are severely outnumbered by four terrorists to one citizen.

"Be that as it may, we will use God's math. If one hundred of us can chase ten thousand of our enemy, then we only need 400 thousand of us to rout 40 million Brotherhood terrorists! Look out Babylon! Israel has 800 thousand soldiers—twice as many as we need!

"Listen to the words of our Lord and King in the last pages of the Tanakh. II Chronicles 20:15 and 17 gives the Word of the Lord to King Jehoshaphat who faced an army too large for God's Chosen People to defeat."

> *...Give heed, all Judah and the inhabitants of Jerusalem and King Jehoshaphat; thus said the LORD to you, "Do not fear or be dismayed by this great multitude, for the battle is God's, not yours.. . . It is not for you to fight this battle; stand by, wait, and witness your deliverance by the LORD, O Judah and Jerusalem; do not fear or be dismayed; go forth to meet them tomorrow and the LORD will be with you."*

"In case any of you have doubts about God's ability to defend His Land and People, let me remind you of King Hezekiah. He faced the great and mighty King of Assyria, Sennacherib, who sent his messengers to tell Hezekiah and the people of Jerusalem that they should surrender. In II Kings 18:29-35, we hear what the Jews listening to the Sennacherib's messengers heard:

> *Don't let Hezekiah deceive you, for he will not be able to deliver you from my hands. Don't let Hezekiah make you rely on the LORD, saying: The LORD will surely save us: this city will not fall into the hands of the king of Assyria. Don't listen to Hezekiah. For thus said the king of Assyria: Make your peace with me and come out to me, so that you may all eat from your vines and your fig trees and drink water from your cisterns, until I come back and take you away to a land like your own, a land of grain [fields] and vineyards, of bread and wine, of olive oil and honey, so that you may live and not die. Don't listen to Hezekiah, who misleads you by saying, "The LORD will save us." Did any of the gods of other nations save his land from the king of Assyria? Where were the gods of Hamath and Arpad? Where were the gods of Sepharvaim, Hena, and Ivvah? [And] did they save Samaria from me? Which among*

all the gods of [those] countries saved their countries from me,
that the LORD should save Jerusalem from me?

"Through his messengers, Sennacherib blasphemed the Holy One of Isreal, the one and only God of Heaven and earth. Therefore, that night, an angel of the Lord killed 185,000 of Assyria's soldiers, so that Sennacherib retreated—and Hezekiah's men never shot one arrow!"

With great and bold confidence, Sam then announced, "The Brotherhood Army cannot stand against the mighty arm of God any better than the Assyrian Army stood against Him. The leaders of Babylon have blasphemed our God, saying that Allah reigns alone over the Heavens and the earth, that a Temple to the God of Abraham, Isaac, and Jacob never stood in Jerusalem, and that King David and his descendants never ruled over the Land! Our God and Lord will rise up and protect His Holy Name, for He will not share His glory with a false god! Likewise, He will protect His Land and His People!

"Tomorrow our military will be positioned and ready to protect this Holy Land and its people! We warn all those who stand to oppose us! Beware that we have an Ally who will defend us as He faces you. He does not need the weapons of man, for in the Tanakh, Zechariah 4:6, He said, ". . . *Not by might, not by power, but by My Spirit—said the Lord of Hosts.*"

Aboard Air Force One, Chief of Staff Murdock was surprised that Sam, like James, had made so many references to God in his address. Eddie wondered if Sam was speaking in metaphor or if he truly believed that God would be Israel's main defense once more. Eddie feared that both the Prime Minister's and the President's speeches could inflame the situation and cause the Muslims to accuse the two leaders of a modern day holy war or crusade against Islam. Of course, for the Muslims, everything was holy war. In Eddie's mind, he had no doubt that these attacks against Israel and the United States were acts of Islamic jihad!

Still, Eddie always advised James to leave religion out of the Muslim quandary. In fact, before the President presented his speech, his Chief of Staff told him "Islam may advocate terror in the name of religion, but we should not oppose that terror in the name of Christian or Jewish religion." Despite Eddie's caution, not only had James made references to God, but he had actually prayed during his speech! Now,

Sam was quoting the Tanakh! Eddie wondered what had come over these two men whom he considered agnostics at best and atheists at worst!

Eddie had recorded the Prime Minister's speech so that his boss could secure some much needed sleep. Since the strikes on Palestine and the Temple Mount, no one on the President's team had enjoyed more than a few minutes sleep whenever and wherever those moments could be found. The pace of events had been absolutely overpowering, making those events difficult to comprehend in such a compressed amount of time.

An hour or so later, Eddie finished his notes on the Prime Minister's speech and the reaction to it from various news sources and political figures. He wondered what would happen on the borders of Israel in a few hours. He worried about what the new day might reveal on the streets of the United States.

Nonetheless, the Chief of Staff realized he needed some sleep as well, or he would be of no use to the President after Air Force One landed at Andrews Air Force Base in a couple of hours.

The Chief of Staff dropped by the cockpit to let the pilots know he would be trying to catch some shuteye. The experienced men at the stick said they would make sure to avoid all turbulence so nothing would disturb the President or his number one man as they slept. Eddie laughed and said, "I'll hold you to that promise!"

Quiet reigned aboard the super jet during its final two hours of flight. Likewise, everything went by the book as Air Force One began lining up to land at Andrews AFB. With a clear blue sky filled with the bright morning sun, this would be a picture perfect touchdown on the tarmac.

Indeed, everything would have been perfect had Air Force One not veered off course. As the presidential jet headed north toward the runway to make its final adjustments for landing, the pilot disabled the auto landing controls. Moments later, the Air Traffic Control Supervisor at Tower 2 (T2) warned the pilot, "AF1, you are too high and too hot approaching runway 19L! Are you flying manually?"

"Thanks, T2. It's been a long night in the saddle. Correcting."

However, the supervisor noted that Air Force One remained on the same flight trajectory.

"AF1, you are still too high and hot. You are also veering north-west! Engage your auto landing controls!"

"Got it, T2."

Still, nothing changed in the approach of Air Force One, as the critical moment of no return grew close.

"AF1, pull up and attempt a second approach!"

"Pulling up."

Nonetheless, yet again, Air Force One made no change in its decent. Quickly, the supervisor determined the trajectory of Air Force One. Within seconds, he realized the horror of the moment!

His heart pounding in his chest, the supervisor exclaimed, "AF1! Pull up immediately! You are on a collision course with the Capitol Building!"

"Pulling up now." The pilot sounded completely calm, but Air Force One continued on its straight line path to the Hill!

The supervisor sounded the alarm and contacted the four fighter jets escorting Air Force One. "Red Wing 1, 2, 3, and 4, this is T2. AF1 is on a collision course with the U.S. Capitol Building! Take out AF1! Repeat, take out AF1!"

The leader of the 316th fighter squadron answered, "Come again, T2? Did you say, 'Take out AF1?'"

"Yes, squadron leader! Fire on AF1 now! AF1 is now past the point of no return. Either shoot it down or it will hit the Capitol!"

Critical moments of silence ensued as the four escort fighters tried to comprehend what sounded impossible!

"T2, this is Red Wing 1. I need Base Commander orders to fire on AF1!"

"Roger, Red Wing 1! Alarm is sounding! Waiting on Commander to respond. But if you don't fire on AF1 in twenty seconds. . ."

Air Force One interrupted. "T2, *Allahu Akbar!* There is no god but Allah!"

"No, AF1! No! No, AF1! No! No! No!"

Air Force One roared over the empty streets of Washington D.C.! Unfortunately, the Capitol Building was full, as the House and Senate along with other top government leaders debated the President's response to the national crisis.

Two seconds after the pilot's final words, Air Force One crashed into the center of the U.S. Capitol just below the dome! A worldwide audience witnessed the massive fireball!

James awoke to behold the Brightest Light he had ever seen!

"What good is it for someone to gain the whole world, yet forfeit their soul? Or what can anyone give in exchange for their soul?"
Mark 8:36-37

CHAPTER 76

THE GOSPEL ACCORDING TO MARK...

A few minutes before three o'clock, Mark sat in the studio in shock! His eyes could not believe what played out before them. First, he saw only a sunny morning at the Capitol Building in Washington DC. Then, suddenly, out of nowhere, a jet zoomed into the serene scene, plowed into the U.S. Capitol, and exploded! The historical structure immediately erupted in flames! To make the tragedy even worse, a deep and haunting voice claimed the jet was Air Force One!

The studio crew erupted in applause and shouts of praise! *"Allahu Akbar!* There is no god but Allah!"

With great sorrow, Mark exclaimed, "The President and the members of the House and Senate are dead! How could anyone do such a thing?"

"Tit for tat, wouldn't you say?" came the answer in Mark's earpiece. The General's twisted voice continued, "You take out the Palestinian leadership, thus obliging us to take out the U.S. leadership! It is all perfectly fair when you truly consider it!"

"There's nothing fair about destroying innocent life. You took out the Palestinian leadership. The U.S. had nothing to do with it! Admit it!" Mark's face was enflamed with passion.

"What a testy tone you brandish this afternoon. If I wasn't so good natured, I would take offense. But what should I expect from a quadruple infidel? Not only are you a traitor to Islam, but you are a Christian, married to a Jew who also became a Christian! Truly, why should you be allowed to waste oxygen by breathing?

"Oh! May I remind you, Pastor, that your daughter's life, not only your life, is hanging in the balance this afternoon? She is right here, with me, in the next studio. Of course, if you follow my script, both of you can walk out of this building alive today, though separately. But if you choose to be uncooperative, you can both be carried out of this building as corpses! As you know, I have my preferences!"

For the sake of Grace, Mark silently watched as fire trucks and ambulances made their approach to the wreckage of the Capitol. He wondered, *"How many lives were taken in that one moment of time? The President and all those elected officials, their staff members, their aides, their administrators, the security personnel, the crews that maintained and serviced the building, all of them were gone!"*

Noting Mark's silence, the General chuckled, "That's better, Pastor! We hope you have enjoyed the show so far because you are the next act! Remember, you are to give an account of your life—how you made the mistake of turning from Allah to the false god of the Christians. If you refuse to publicly recant your faith in Isa, then you and the world will witness the tragic rape and execution of Haziqah, which will be followed by the beheading you have long deserved!"

Mark thought, *"Surely, not even the General would invite the world to watch Grace be raped and killed, would he? How wicked and wretched was this man? Was his soul completely void of any shred of decency or compassion? Had he no conscience at all?"*

The General announced to Mark, "While allowing the world to take in the beautiful events in Washington D.C., we will give you a couple of minutes more to regain your composure and carefully collect your thoughts. Then, everything will be up to you! Through this earpiece, I will keep you on course, should you decide not to follow my simple instructions. Remember, violation of my rules will result in extremely drastic and completely unnecessary consequences!"

"If you are such a brave and powerful man, General, then why don't you ever show your face or speak with your real voice? Would you, by chance, be afraid that your own life might be in danger?"

"Now, now, pastor! Flattery will get you nowhere with me! If anyone here should fear for his life, that one would be you! Of course, fair Haziqah has panic enough for both of you!"

Mark looked away from the destruction in Washington D.C.. Silently, Mark prayed, "Dear Jesus, Grace is the one that matters here today. Help her not be afraid. Instead, fill her with anticipation of You. I cannot see a way where either one of us walk out of here alive today. As You prepare and steady me, please prepare and steady her. Thank You, Lord! Amen."

The preacher, professor, and father sat behind the same table and in the same chair where the imam had sat less than 24 hours before. However, to Mark, days and weeks seemed to have passed. He looked into the camera as the holovideographer counted down the seconds. Mark cleared his throat, took in a deep breath, and began.

"If you have just witnessed the death and destruction in the Capitol of the United States as I have, I pray that your heart is not filled with joy and celebration, but sadness and mourning for this disregard for and waste of precious human life."

The General shouted into Mark's ear, "This is not what I would call a good start, Pastor! The blade is at your daughter's throat—do you still remember how that feels?"

First Mark flinched from the booming threat in his ear. Then, subconsciously, Mark lifted his right hand to his neck where the machete had pressed against his aorta.

From the hospital waiting room, Ariel watched her husband's gesture and knew what he was recalling. Emotionally, Ariel felt shell-shocked. Washington had been attacked again for the second time in as many days. Her president and the elected men and women of the House and Senate had been savagely assassinated! The reporters assumed most of the President's surviving Cabinet members had been meeting with the Congressional leaders. Thus, they too had likely been consumed in the mammoth fireball.

Now, her husband's and her daughter's lives hung in the balance! How could she bear to listen to what Mark would say, knowing what would happen when he finished? She placed her hands over her face to shield her eyes, only to watch the love of her life from between her fingers.

Thankfully, Sol and Ahava were sitting on either side of Ariel. "Be strong and courageous," Sol said with faith. "Remember, Y'shua is here with you, as well as there with Mark, and wherever Grace may be!"

Regaining his composure, Mark continued by saying, "Most of you do not know me or my story. My name is Omar Rashad Basel. I was born and grew up as a faithful Muslim in what has become the Babylonian state of Iraq.

"From my earliest days, I was taught the ways of Allah. At the age of six, I began to learn the ways of jihad that Allah demanded of all male believers." Mark took a deep breath. He could not prevent the tear that rushed down his cheek as he recounted his bloody childhood. "I was given what my trainers called a special privilege when I turned seven. A full two years ahead of the rest of my class at the jihad camp, I killed my first infidel! I slit his throat from ear to ear, just as I was taught to do. This was the first, but certainly not the last human blood that I would shed.

"That day, my mother burned my clothes when I arrived at home. She instructed me in the *ghusl* ritual of cleansing. Yet to this day, I remember the man's warm blood as it covered my body. I remember how his body jerked as he died in my arms. I will never forget that man or any of the other men, women, and children I killed in my life as a jihadist for Allah.

"By the time I was a teenager, I had killed hundreds of people in Iraq and surrounding Muslim countries. Despite my gruesome and grisly actions, I was never charged with murder or any other crime. Islam considered me innocent, as I was not merciless terrorist but a faithful minister of Allah's justice."

Shutting his eyes, Mark said, "When I close my eyes, I can still see the faces and hear the screams and pleas of my victims. Yet, at the time, I felt no remorse, guilt, or compassion. All such weak emotions had been drained out of me through my years of training. I killed because Allah demanded it. I callously took the lives of subhuman, worthless infidels."

Overwrought with grief, Grace had never heard her dad speak about his days in Iraq to this degree. She did not know that he had taken so many lives. All she could do was weep for her father and the bereaved families. She was no longer considering that her own death might be very near—just as her dad had prayed.

"Throughout my teen years, I supervised the younger boys at jihad camp. I taught them how to torture and kill. I told them that Allah commanded them to main and execute Jews, Christians, apostates, idol worshippers, and atheists as well as agnostics. I even taught them how to butcher and dispose of a human body. I often secretly cremated the remains of the infidels.

"I used the blood of such unbelievers to write threatening letters to Christians and churches. I nailed those letters to the doors of homes and congregations. The cryptic messages said the members had one day to not only abandon their home or church, but to also leave our village. If they refused, each remaining family or church member would be killed—and we always followed through on our threats! All the time, I felt my actions pleased Allah and earned his blessings."

As Mark recounted his days as a teenage jihadist, his face grimaced with pain. He felt as if he spoke about another person, not himself. Because of Jesus' mercy and grace, the teen who killed without a conscience had himself died long ago! He had been buried in the waters of baptism. Resurrecting that dead terrorist tormented Mark.

However, the weight on Mark's soul lightened somewhat as he said, "Then one day, as I was walking to the market, a man approached me on the side of the road. He asked me if I knew about Isa. I said, 'Of course I know about Isa! He is one of the prophets of Allah.' In response, this man, who looked and dressed like any other Muslim man, told me there was much more to know about Isa in the sacred books that were written before the Qur'an.

"As we walked along, he showed me a Book. I did not know much about the New Testament at the time. But the man said Isa was truly the very Son of God who came to this earth as a man for one purpose: to forgive me of my sin and restore my relationship with His Father! I had never heard any of the stories the man read to me about Isa.

"When we approached my home, he asked me if I would like to read about Isa myself. 'Yes! Of course I would,' I said. Then, he gave me the Book in his hand. He told me, 'This is very special! You must not let anyone else see it until you talk to me again. I will meet you here at this time next week—one week from today. Bring this Book with you, and we will talk about everything you have read. Try to finish the Book before we talk next time.' I promised I would read it all.

As he started to walk away, he turned to me and said, "Haven't you ever wondered?"

"Wondered what?" I asked.

"Tell me this, if Allah is one, as he claims to be, with no other partners or other gods, then why does he refer to himself as "We" and "Us" in the Qur'an?"

"I had no idea how to answer him. He made what I considered to be a good point. Only years later did I learn that Allah began as one of hundreds of false gods— pagan, mythological deities of the Arab world. As the moon god of Mecca, Allah's bride was the goddess of the sun, who bore three daughters for the god whose symbol was the crescent moon and star. Muhammad decided to make Allah the one and only god of Islam. If the alleged prophet had not done so, the moon god of Mecca would be as unknown today at the other mythical gods of the Arabs."

The General bellowed, "You are not allowed to speak such profane heresy, my friend! I can easily and pleasurably end your life before you speak another lie!"

Mark waited for the coarse babbling in his ear to subside before he said, "The night after I met the man on the road, I waited until everyone in my home had gone to bed. At that point, I started reading the Book. It captivated me! Isa said that He came to earth as the prophesied Saviour of the Jews, the Messiah. He said He would be killed—willingly crucified—in order to be a sacrifice for sin not only for Israel, but also for all the nations! Even though He performed great miracles and was God in human flesh, Isa said He would not fight against those who would arrest Him, beat Him, scourge Him, and cru-cify Him! Instead, Isa said He would die in our place, in the place of all who would believe in Him, to atone for our sin so that we could be forgiven and restored as children of God!"

Impatient, angry, and belligerent, the General warned, "Be careful, Omar! You are treading into dangerous territory! You need to tell the story of why you have come back to Allah!"

Mark nodded his head and continued. "A week later, I was standing on the roadside, waiting for the man to meet me. I stood there all after-noon. He never came. Not until days later did I learn that an imam had turned him in for telling Muslims the truth about Isa. This man had given his life, as Isa did, to save other lives for eternity!

"In the Book, I had read about other people who were killed for their faith in Isa. Yet none of them complained. They even said they counted it as joy to die for Isa who died for them! Then I remembered. Unlike the atheists, agnostics, and others I had murdered, the followers of Isa I had killed has been just as willing, just as content in their deaths as the people I read about in the Book. Only then did I understand why. They trusted Isa for life beyond their mortal flesh!"

Despite his dire straits, Mark's passion was pouring out of him. He leaned toward the camera and said, "Unlike what I had heard about Isa in the Qur'an, He was, in fact, crucified. Two men took His body from the cross and buried it. Yet, after three days in the grave, Isa arose! Through His death and resurrection, anyone who believed in Him could also die to sin and self, and then be resurrected for eternal life!

"That first night that I had the Book, I fell asleep while reading it. I awoke in the darkness to see my room completely filled with Light! I sat up. The Light was so intense, that I could no longer see my bed or anything else in my room! I heard a voice in the Light call my name.

"He said, 'Omar?'

"Yes. I am Omar! Who are You?

"'Omar, you have been reading about Me and My disciples! I came tonight to ask you if you too would like to follow Me. Would you like be one of My disciples? Would you like to pass from death into life eternal?'

"I was overjoyed! I could barely speak! Then, I remembered who I was and all I had done. Suddenly, I felt the weight of hundreds of bodies upon me. I said, 'Isa! I have killed Your disciples in the name of Allah! I have also killed Jews! I have done horrible things to Muslims who denied their faith in Allah to believe in You instead! I have maimed and murdered more people than I can count. Surely, I cannot follow You with so much blood on my hands!' I hung my head in guilt and shame!"

The General yelled into Mark's ears, "Recant! Recant now, or I will kill you both!" Mark cringed at the sound of the masked man's shout. Meanwhile, Grace's tears washed down onto the General's uniform as he tightened his grip around her neck. She longed to run to her dad and hug him.

In the hospital waiting room, Ahava held Ariel close, as the two of them wept. Sol stood behind them, with his hands on their shoulders, his beard dampened by his tears.

Undaunted, unafraid, Mark's next words flowed with peace. "Isa said, 'Look at Me, Mark. Long ago, I forgave you for everything you have done! More than two thousand years ago, I forgave you, when I hung on the cross.'

"I replied, 'No, You did not die on the cross, Isa. You were not crucified! Islam says someone else died in your place, so how could You have died for me?'

"With a smile on His face, Isa told me, 'No, Omar. I died in your place! I allowed Myself to be crucified—for you. I let the Romans nail Me to the cross by My wrists and feet—for you. Here, you can see My wounds!'

"Then Isa placed his wrists before my tear-filled eyes. I saw the deep, ugly holes! He pulled back His hair and showed me where the thorns had pierced His brow! Isa showed me His arms and back that had been ripped to shreds by the cat of nine tails! He showed me the gaping hole in His side where He had been pierced to prove He was dead!

"Gently, Isa told me, 'Each of these wounds should have been yours, Omar. Instead, I bore the consequences of your sin on that cross—long before you ever committed one sin, long before you took one life! When I died, I took your sin to the grave with Me! But when I rose from that tomb, I left your sin behind! Your sin—all of it—remains dead and buried!'

"'Isa!' I cried. 'Why would You die for me and my sin? Why would You be executed for an executioner?"

"Still smiling, Isa answered, 'Because I love you, and because I obeyed My Father who sent Me to earth to die for you! When I was still hanging on the cross, I said to Him, "Forgive Omar, Father! He does not realize what He is doing!" I know everything you have done, Omar. I witnessed you take the lives of My followers. I knew what you would do before I gave My life to redeem yours. I have purchased your forgiveness for killing My disciples, many Jews, and others who refused to follow Allah. Will you accept My forgiveness tonight? I forgave you, and I still forgive you. I love you. I want you to follow Me! Will you? Will you receive My mercy and grace?'

"Through my tears, from my broken heart, all I could say was, 'Yes!'"

In his outrage, the General slapped Grace! To Mark, he shouted, "This is your final warning! You have crossed the line!" Though the General wailed, Mark heard nothing.

"Isa told me to leave my homeland. He said I would be killed if I stayed. He had plans for me to help Him reach millions of Muslims. He told me to go to the United States to study and become a pastor. So, I convinced my parents to send me to school in the United States, and then I told them why. They had witnessed such a transformation in me that they too became believers in Isa!

"In less than a year, they were killed—by a nine year old boy—for their faith in Isa. Then, I saw clearly that Islam was not a religion, but a pretense for hatred, war, genocide, and world dominance!

"I determined that I would dedicate my life to Isa in honor of my parents. In the United States, I attended college. I studied at seminary. Now, for more than twenty years, I have been a pastor, seminary professor, and evangelist to the Muslims of the world.

"Isa did not kill Himself in a suicide bombing to take lives, but He sacrificed Himself on a cross to give life! Likewise, Isa did not return violence for violence. Instead, Isa put an end to the cycle of violence for all who would believe in Him.

"Muhammad set an example of incredible violence and hatred for Muslims to imitate. Quite the opposite, Isa set an example of unbelievable personal sacrifice and love for all who believe in Him to emulate. In the New Testament, we see Isa's teaching and preaching matched His actions.

"In stark contrast, the teachings of the Qur'an are nothing short of mangled plagiarisms of the Truth found in the Hebrew and Christian texts of the Bible! The Qur'an was written centuries after the actual events and original writings. Isa's words and deeds were recast by a man who could neither read nor write!

"As such, the illiterate Muhammad wrote down none of the revelations he allegedly received from the angel Gabriel. The Qur'an was compiled after the alleged prophet's death. The book is a random collection of repetitious, misguided thoughts that seem to threaten the eternal chastisement of hell in every four or five verses. There is no narrative, no cover to cover story of Allah's love for man like we find in the Bible, which tells the story of God's loving plan to save the people of the world through His crucified Son. This love story began before the creation of the world and will continue throughout eternity!

"On one hand, many authors tell one story in the Bible—the story of God's love and redemption, the story of Isa's mercy and grace! On the other hand, one author supposedly speaks in the Qur'an, yet Muhammad tells two very different stories. The peaceful parts of the Qur'an have been abrogated by the violent passages that took their place! How can Allah be all powerful and knowing if He changes his mind to be a god of war instead of peace?"

Then Mark paused. He wiped the tear from his eye and said, "However, even with the case I built against Allah, I must tell you today, that I have been wrong all these years that I have followed Isa!"

The General shouted again: "That's more like it!"

Both Grace and Ariel, though not together, said, "No! Don't do it! Don't deny Y'shua!" Ahava held Ariel even tighter, while the General placed his gloved hand over Grace's mouth.

Mark looked down at the table for a long moment. When he looked back into the camera he said, "I was wrong! I always thought I was willing to die for my faith in Isa."

Grace and the General, Ariel, Ahava, and Sol held their breath in anticipation of Mark's next words. Muslims around the globe sat on the edge of their seats, waiting to hear what Mark would say next.

"The time has come for me. Can I give my life for my faith in Isa? Or will I deny Him and return to the ways of Allah so that I may live?"

Again Mark paused. Then, with great confidence in his voice, he stated, "Allah was born among the plethora of polytheistic pagan Arab gods. Muhammad chose to make him the one and only god of Islam. Isa was born the one and only Son of the one and only God of all eternity! Born of a virgin, Isa is True God of True God, who was, is, and is to come!

"Allah commands us not to choose Jews and Christians as friends, for they are the enemies of Islam. On the other hand, Isa commands us to love both friends and enemies alike!

"Allah tells us to hate our enemies, hunt them down, and kill them! But Isa tells us to love our enemies, pray for them, and do good unto them!

"Allah wants us to teach our children to be cold blooded killers so they can enter his Paradise! To the contrary, Isa wants us to change and become like little children, so we can enter the Kingdom of Heaven!

"Allah says the Book of the Jews and the Christians is filled with lies, yet Isa says He is the living, breathing Word of God made flesh—the Way, the Truth, and the Life!

"Allah declares that many will lose their souls because he predestined them for unbelief, while Isa proclaims that whoever chooses to believe in Him will have everlasting life!

"Allah claims that Isa will return to condemn all the Jews and Christians who will rot in hell for all eternity! Nonetheless, Isa asserts that He will fulfill the prophecy about His return to earth to take all His disciples to Heaven with Him—just as He fulfilled every other prophecy written about Him, including His crucifixion and resurrection!

"Allah says he will seek and destroy all the infidels! Even so, Isa says, 'I came to seek and to save the lost!'

"Allah commands us to go into the entire world and kill the infidels until there is but one religion, while Isa commands us to go into all the world and share the Good News of His Salvation until all have heard it!

"With Allah, salvation must be earned. The only guarantee of Paradise for a Muslim man is to die or kill in jihad, while the only guarantee of Paradise for a Muslim woman is to leave behind a husband who is happy with her at the point of her death. Contrarily, with Isa, guaranteed salvation is a free gift to all who believe—men and women, boys and girls!

"According to Allah, only faithful Muslims will go to Paradise. Thankfully, according to Isa, there is no Muslim, no Jew, and no Christian, no Arab, no Israeli, and no American, but all are one in the saving grace of one Saviour and Lord of all people regardless of the their nationality, gender, age, skin color, language, education, or finances.

"Although jihad that leads to death is the way of Allah, love that leads to life is the way of Isa!

"Allah sends his mercenaries to foreign countries to kill the people, yet Isa sends His missionaries to foreign countries to save people's souls!

"The differences between Allah and Isa loom so large. I just knew that when the time came, I would willingly face death for Isa, but I was wrong! I thought I could give my life for the cause of Isa today, but I cannot!" Mark said these words with such sadness.

Then, suddenly, Mark's entire demeanor changed. A broad smile overtook his face as he proclaimed, "I only have one life to give, and I gave it to Isa that night He met me in my room! My life is not my own! Isa bought my life with a price! And that price was the His very blood poured out for me and for all who will believe in Him!

"I can no more deny my life in Isa than I can deny my need to breathe! But take this breath from me, and I will still have life in Isa!"

Then the pleading father looked into the camera and directed his words straight to his captive daughter. "Grace, I pray you understand! I pray you know how much I love you! You and I are about to meet Isa, together, face to face!"

The General screamed in Mark's ears! "Indeed, you and your daughter will die for this!" Then, the doors to the studios flew open, as the men came for Mark and Grace! MGMs flew everywhere as Mark fell behind the table!

"Thou wouldst have seen the sun, when it rose, declining to the right from their Cave, and when it set, turning away from them to the left, while they lay in the open space in the midst of the Cave. Such are among the Signs of Allah: He whom Allah guides is rightly guided; But he whom Allah leaves to stray—for him wilt thou find no protector to lead him to the Right Way."
Qur'an 18:17

CHAPTER 77

THE CHANGING
OF THE GUARD. . .

Sol entered Abdul's hospital room with the United States Ambassador to Isreal and the Vice President's security detail. Ambassador Michael Rosenberg had asked Sol to break the news to Abdul. Once inside the room, the men found that Abdul was asleep.

Dr. Goldberg, who had performed the surgery to remove the explosive from Abdul's shoulder, looked at Abdul's virtual chart. Ambassador Rosenberg asked the doctor, "Were you able to take out the device?"

"Well," said the surgeon, "without overstating the obvious, the Vice President would not be here if the device had not been removed. It exploded only seconds after I completed the delicate procedure! When I pulled back the tissue to reveal the device, the Mossad agent standing beside me said it had its own timer. From what he could see, he guessed we had about 45 seconds to remove the explosive and place it in the compression canister that would protect us all if the device detonated!"

"Oh, my!" said Sol. "Were you scared?"

"Absolutely," noted Dr. Goldberg. "I really cannot tell you how I managed to remove that device so quickly. My hands were trembling and sweat was falling from my forehead. I felt lightheaded, as I was breathing quite rapidly. Then, somehow, as though my hands were operating on their own, I pulled out the device and placed it in the canister. Immediately after the Mossad agent sealed the lid, the device exploded! The force was strong enough to pull the canister out of the Mossad agent's hands and slam it into the tray along the wall that held sterilized items! That metal tray was flattened by the blast in the canister!"

Sol reached for the surgeon's hand and pulled him into a bear hug. "Thank you for saving the life of my dear friend, Doctor Goldberg! You have performed a great deed for the people of this world! You have saved the life of the President of the United States!"

Puzzled, the surgeon said, "President? Does not Mr. Abdullah serve as the Vice President of the United States?"

"Not anymore," Sol answered, "not anymore. Abdul is now Commander in Chief, as President Paulson was killed upon his return to Washington D.C.. The pilots flew Air Force One into the U.S. Capitol Building, killing James and most if not all of the members of the two houses of congress!"

Caught off guard by the overwhelming news, Dr. Goldberg just blankly stared at Sol for a few moments. Then, he said, "Why that is unbelievable! It seems impossible! The tragedies keep piling up, one on the other!"

Ambassador Rosenberg placed his hand on the doctor's shoulder, and their eyes met. "Dr. Goldberg, on behalf of the United States' government and citizens, I too thank for saving President Abdullah's life, even at great risk to your own life!"

Dr. Goldberg stiffened his bottom lip, yet he could not speak.

The ambassador asked, "Can we wake the President and tell him what has transpired? Obviously, he must be sworn into office as soon as possible!"

Dr. Goldberg did his best to collect his thoughts. "Yes, of course," he replied. "The Vice President — sorry, I mean President — was awake when he was taken from recovery and brought back here. At this point, he is asleep because of the aftereffects of sedation."

"Thank you, doctor," the ambassador said. "Thank you again for all you have done today!"

Sol walked over to Abdul's bedside as the other men in the room watched silently. Sol took his friend's hand and said, "Abdul! It's me, Sol! Abdul! Wake up! Mr. President! Wake up!"

Groggily, Abdul answered, "Sol, you know I am the Vice President!" His eyes were still closed.

"Not anymore, Mr. President! Not anymore!"

Sol's words forced Abdul to open his eyes. He tried to focus on Sol. "What do you mean, 'not anymore?'"

"Something happened during your third surgery this afternoon, Abdul. Something horrendous happened." Sol turned on the HV3D, and Abdul saw the still enflamed Capitol Building."

"What is burning?" Abdul asked, as the Capitol was no longer recognizable.

"That's the Capitol Building, Abdul!"

"The U.S. Capitol? What happened?"

"Wait a few moments, and they will replay the terrible scene again."

Abdul leaned on his good shoulder and sat up as much as he could. He kept staring at the flaming ruins surrounding him, wondering if a bomb had exploded or another missile had been launched. Then, the already infamous terrorist act replayed. Abdul saw the Capitol Building silhouetted by the morning sun. Then he heard the roar of the approaching jet. If was flying incredibly low and zeroed in on the capitol! Abdul gasped at the impact and ensuing explosion! He watched in disbelief as the quickly spreading flames engulfed the entire building.

Sol waited a few more seconds then told Abdul. "That jet was Air Force One. James was still inside it, God rest his soul!"

Suddenly, Abdul could not move or breathe! The shock of Sol's words immobilized him. "Abdul? Abdul? Are you all right?" Sol asked with urgency in his voice. "Abdul! Breathe!" Sol tried patting him on the back. Sol shouted, "Doctor! Help him!"

Before Dr. Goldberg could reach the bed, Abdul gasped and fell back against his pillow. "Are you okay? What just happened?" Sol inquired.

"I'll have to tell you later," Abdul whispered to him.

Dr. Goldberg quickly checked Abdul's pulse. "His heart rate is 181 beats per minute! His breathing is quite rapid, too! He went into shock!" A few moments later, Dr. Goldberg checked Abdul's pulse once more. "His heart rate is slowing—now at 157 beats per minute."

The surgeon monitored Abdul's vital signs until he was breathing normally and his heart rate was 73 beats per minute. He asked Abdul, "Is there anything more I can do for you, Mr. President?"

"No, no thank you!" he replied kindly. "I appreciate your help!" Then Abdul reconsidered. "On second thought, could you help me sit on the edge of the bed?"

Gently, Dr. Goldberg maneuvered Abdul's legs over the side of the bed, while Ambassador Rosenberg helped the President sit up. Sol looked directly into his eyes. "My brother, you are now the President of the United States!"

Abdul closed his eyes and clinched his fists. "No! This can't be happening! This cannot be real!"

"Unfortunately, this is all very real, Abdul—Mr. President!"

With deep sorrow, Abdul said, "Don't call me that, Sol! James is the President!"

Sol sadly shook his head as he again said, "Not anymore, Abdul! Not anymore!"

Abdul opened his eyes and looked around the room. He recognized everyone, but then asked the Ambassador, "Why are you here, Michael?"

As he stood next to Sol, Michael extended his hand to Abdul. "I am here to officially swear you into office. Do you feel up to the task at this moment?"

Still holding the Ambassador's hand, Abdul confessed, "I never wanted this, Michael! I never even wanted to be Vice President!"

Letting go of Abdul's hand, Michael responded, "I know! I understand! But now you are the man and this is your moment in history!"

Abdul looked at himself. "I'm wearing a hospital gown!" He turned to Dr. Goldberg and asked, "Is it okay for me to get dressed?"

"Of course," Dr. Goldberg replied. "Even though you have undergone three surgeries today, your wound is no worse than it was after the first operation, though you will feel some pain soon, as the medication wears off."

With a small grin on his face, Michael said, "Thank you, Doctor Goldberg. We would not want the President to stand before the world to take his oath of office in a hospital gown! Plus, we must record this moment for the news—and for posterity itself!"

As Michael, Dr. Goldberg, and the security team left the room, Abdul asked Sol to stay and help him dress. "My shoulder is going to be a problem with the shirt and suit jacket," Abdul explained.

"Ah, yes indeed!" Sol replied.

When the room was empty, Sol asked, "What happened to you when you stopped breathing, Abdul?"

"You will think I'm crazy, Sol, if I tell you!"

"I assure you, after the events of the last few days, I will not think you are the least bit crazy, no matter what you tell me!"

"Okay! You asked for it!" Abdul spoke bluntly. "I saw Isa!"

"What? You saw Y'shua again—right here in this room?"

"Again? Why did you use that word, Sol?"

"Mark and Ariel told Ahava and me about your experience with Y'shua on Air Force One. They told me you are now a follower of Y'shua!"

"That's right, Sol! Now, you do think I am crazy, don't you!"

A huge smile revealed itself under Sol's long white beard. "My boy, I think you are wonderful! I am so excited for you!"

"What? But you are an Orthodox Rabbi!" Confusion was written all over Abdul's face.

"Not anymore, Abdul! Not anymore," Sol said once again. "Ahava and I are now followers of Y'shua *HaMashiach*, too!"

Spontaneously, the men embraced each other in a big bear hug, until Abdul winced with pain. "I forgot about my shoulder!" he said with laughter, even in his struggles.

Sol backed away, "I'm so sorry!"

"No problem, Sol! So when did you start believing in Isa—Y'shua?"

"Since you have been in this hospital! Mark and Ariel talked with us. I have felt Y'shua tugging at my heart for a long time. I finally surrendered to Him, and now, I am victorious!"

"That is absolutely marvelous, Sol! My heart cannot contain the joy I feel for you and Ahava!"

"We feel the same way for you, my brother! I wanted to go around Israel, the U.S., and even Babylon with you, sharing our stories of how we came to believe in Y'shua! But I suppose you really will have a full schedule now!"

The sobering comment forced the smile to flee from Abdul's face. "Yes, I suppose you are right. But I would much rather be an evangelist than the President of the United States!"

"Maybe you can be both, Abdul!"

Abdul paused with that thought.

"After all," the octogenarian believer said, "the Presidential podium makes for a bully pulpit!"

"I suppose so," Abdul replied softly.

Sol asked, "By the way, did Y'shua—Isa—say anything to you a few minutes ago?"

"Yes He did, Sol. But let me back up. When I first saw Isa on Air Force One, He told me, 'I called and appointed you for such a time as this. You will be a great and powerful witness to the power of the Truth that you have sought!' In reply, I told Isa I would do whatever He asked, go wherever He sent me!

"Then, a few moments ago, when I looked at the HV3D, I saw Isa standing in front of me again! Isa told me He was appointing me as the next President of the United States! In my thoughts, I told him I was not prepared for that huge responsibility, especially at this moment in time! But Isa said, 'Do not be afraid, Abdul, for I am with you. I will work through you in powerful ways to enlarge My Kingdom! I will guide you, speak through you, and empower you for the work you will do in My Name! Your name means "servant," Abdul. Once you served Allah. Now, you serve Me, the Way, the Truth, and the Life. Furthermore, like Me, you will be a servant to your nation and to all nations. Through you, many souls will come to Me for salvation and life!'"

Sol's whole body was quivering as he listened to Abdul speak of his encounter with Y'shua. But the knock on the door reminded them of the immediate task. Sol shouted, "He will be ready in a few minutes." Quickly, Sol helped Abdul put on his pants, shirt, tie, and jacket. Sol continually apologized for the pain Abdul had to endure only to put on his clothes. Next, Sol attempted to comb Abdul's thick hair. "I am no stylist, Abdul! You may look worse when I finish than when I started trying to tame this mane of yours!" Both men chuckled.

Last of all, Sol helped the President with his shoes, which Sol kneeled before Abdul to tie. The new President was moved by the humble gesture. "Doesn't the Scripture tell us to wash each other's feet? You have served me in like manner, Sol!"

Trying to change the subject due to his embarrassment, Sol moaned, "Ooh! It is not as easy getting down there and getting back up again as it once was!"

"Thank you, Sol. You know, I thought as you helped me that instead of being friends, you and I should actually be enemies!"

Sol laughed, heartily, and replied, "Yes, but we have a great Friend in common, now! Actually, because of Y'shua we are not only friends, but brothers!"

"Who would have guessed that, Sol?" And the two of them laughed together. Then, realizing what was about to happen, Abdul said, "I will be the first Muslim-turned-Christian to serve as President of the United States, and I will also be the first President of the United States to be sworn into office by a Jew in Israel!"

"This is quite an historic day, Abdul, for you, your country, Israel, and for Y'shua—Isa!"

Abdul smiled. "Isa, Y'shua, Jesus—all His Names are beautiful to me!"

Another knock on the door interrupted their conversation. Sol announced, "He is ready!"

The ambassador opened the door and stepped into the room carrying two books. Dr. Goldberg brought in a sling. He helped Abdul slip his aching arm into it.

Michael said, "Abdul, as the first Muslim to take the oath of office as President of the United States, would you like to place your hand on the Qur'an as you repeat the words I give you?" The ambassador handed a copy of the Qur'an to the new President of the United States as he asked, "What did you use when you took the oath of office as Vice President?"

"Michael, actually, I did not place my hand on anything then. But what book is in your other hand?"

"Forgive me! When the call came concerning your oath of office, I first grabbed my Bible. I hope you are not offended!"

"Is that the Christian Old and New Testament or the Tanakh, Michael?"

"It's the Christian Bible."

"You have a Christian Bible in your office?" Both Abdul and Sol were puzzled. "Why?"

Not sure how his words would be received, Michael answered, "Because I am a Messianic Jew—I believe Y'shua is the Messiah!"

Sol and Abdul looked at each other and smiled! Dr. Goldberg smiled along with them!

Abdul told Michael, "The Bible will be perfect!"

"And lead us not into temptation, but deliver us from the evil one."
Matthew 6:13

CHAPTER 78

WALKING THROUGH THE SHADOWED VALLEY...

*P*rime Minister Ben Baruch stared into the mirror and wondered why he was still alive. He stated the facts: *"The President of the DROP is dead, vaporized by an Israeli missile. The President of the United States is dead, instantly consumed in the crash of Air Force One into Capitol Hill. Save one, my entire Cabinet is dead, some slain in their own homes. How long will it be before I am dead, murdered in some sensational or gruesome fashion for all the world to see?"*

The Prime Minister walked over to the desk and picked up the bloody message that the Brotherhood left on his steps with his Cabinet member's severed heads. He reread the direct threat made against him. "The end—and your end—are indeed near! You will soon join your piggish infidel Cabinet members in eternal torment! We will smite your neck next!"

Sam glared at the note as he asked himself, *"Is every member of the peace negotiating team targeted for assassination? Mark Basel has been gunned down. The world witnessed his murder in HV3D SenseSurround!*

"Likewise, jihadists killed the U.S. Secretary of State before the eyes of the world—in the same collision that claimed James' life. While no one actually saw Hannah or James die, the world did see the act of terror that claimed their lives. Hannah had gone to the capitol to speak with the Senate Armed Services Committee."

Sam saw worry on his own face as he said, *"In like manner, my Foreign Affairs Minister lost her life before the eyes of the nations, even though Rachel was killed beyond the scope of the cameras when the missiles hit the Kotel. Across the border in the DROP, the same can be said of President Kanaan's fiery death."*

The Prime Minister asked himself, *"Did the Brotherhood know that Rachel would be on the Temple Mount that day? Is that why they chose to launch the missiles on Sunday? Did the Brotherhood know that Hannah would be on Capitol Hill? For that reason, were the pilots ordered not only to kill James but to crash into the Capitol Building? Or did Hannah and Rachel have nothing to do with the timing or locations of those acts of terror? Were these two brilliant women considered mere collateral damage to the jihadists?"*

Sam mulled his grim thoughts. He whispered, *"If Rachel had not been killed by the missile strike, then she probably would have been beheaded with the other members of my Cabinet. But what about Hannah? Was the Brotherhood gunning for her or the members of the upper and lower chambers of Congress—or both?"*

As his unanswered questions continued, Sam walked away from the mirror. He picked up his 3DHP and called up the Tanakh. *"Does Addar have a fatwa for assassination on his head? Will Sol be the next man to fall at the hands of the Brotherhood—or will that be me? How long do I have before the Brotherhood comes after me again? How much time do Sol, Addar, and I have before we are shot, beheaded, blown apart, mutilated, or killed in some other heinous manner?"*

Even though one attempt had already been made on his life, Sam refused to live in fear of his death. The seasoned politician poured himself a glass of wine and sat down, still looking at the Hebrew Scriptures, as he listened to one of his favorite classical pieces, Verdi's *Requiem.*

Sam never considered it odd that he, an atheistic Jew who spoke fluent Hebrew, would so love a composition composed for a Catholic funeral mass sung in Latin. Instead, he felt that all the music of the world was open to him, no matter its source or message.

Ironically, what the Prime Minister did not know was that *Requiem* had inspired Jews who suffered during the Holocaust in the Nazi concentration camp in Terezin, Czechoslovakia. In fact, during 1943 and 1944, the orchestra of imprisoned Jews performed *Requiem* sixteen times. A girl in the prison camp fluently spoke Latin. She translated the words for her fellow inmates. In the black evil of Terezin, they found light and hope within the prayerful words that were set to music.

Grant them eternal rest, O Lord;
and may perpetual light shine upon them.
A hymn in Zion befits you, O God,
and a debt will be paid to you in Jerusalem.
Hear my prayer: all earthly flesh will come to you.

Sam, on the other hand, only loved the emotional pull of the orchestration itself. He was oblivious to the words being sung to it.

Before starting the moving and powerful piece in his temporary and secret home in Jerusalem, Sam had already talked with his wife Esther, assuring her of his safety, as well as her safety and that of their children.

Likewise, he had personally spoken with Hope Paulson. He expressed his country's sorrow and his family's own grief over the terrorist assassinations of James and the senators and representatives on Capitol Hill—as well as Secretary Fielder.

Furthermore, he had called Ariel Basel, who was too emotional to speak to him. Her uncontrollable grief for her husband and daughter brought hot tears to Sam's eyes as well.

As Sam sat, enveloped in the mournful cry of the instruments, he remained unafraid. Despite the objections of his security team, the Mossad, and his Deputy Cabinet members, he had already agreed to attend Wednesday morning's funeral for the dead in Palestine. Addar had personally requested his presence.

Sam contemplated the grisly work of identifying bodies, actually infinitesimal pieces of body parts, from the Sunday afternoon attacks on the Palestinians. Actually, the task had proved impossible, as it would in all the places in Israel and the states where grisly death had come so swiftly and unexpectedly. Even though genetic testing of the smallest pieces of flesh or bone could reveal the identity of the dead, at each site, the forensic units found nothing but the tiniest charred shreds of human flesh and bone. Such infinitesimal pieces refused to yield their genetic secrets.

Despite the extreme circumstances, the Israeli government used every tool and method at its disposal in attempts to identify who and how many died atop and around the Temple Mount, in the streets of the Jewish quarter of the Old City, as well as at Yad Vashem and the Prime Minister's residence in Jerusalem. At the moment, Sam had no idea how many Israelis, Palestinians, and international tourists had lost their lives so suddenly, so tragically. Reports of missing people were coming in from all around Israel, the DROP, and the globe.

Now, Israeli troops patrolled all borders and streets. Yet, even as Israeli warships guarded the coast and IAF jets circled over all the main cities, Sam wondered if those ships and jets could actually control their weapons. Surely, the infiltration into the weapons systems had not gone that far.

Would the Brotherhood Army make an all out assault on Israel? Sam wondered, *"Is the Caliph—or whoever has been attacking us—waiting until Wednesday morning's mass funeral service to launch the next offensive? Will the Brotherhood attempt to assassinate me then, in front of the cameras for the entire planet to see?"*

For the second time in his life, Sam truly contemplated his death. Before the attempted attack on Israel by the Russian-Muslim coalition, he never really thought about dying—much less what would come after his passing. Actually, the Prime Minister had never been in a truly life threatening situation prior to the failed invasion. Sure, he had served with the IDF, but his days as a soldier were during a time of relative calm between Israel and her not always friendly neighbors.

In the hours leading up to the attempted invasion by Russia and its Sunni Muslim allies, Sam considered his life here and in the hereafter. When the attack failed, Sam basically returned to his secular ways, save for the fact that he continued reading both the Jewish and Christian Scriptures. This very day, the faithless Sam had read from the book of Isaiah before doing anything else.

While the passion of *Requiem* rose and fell around him, he asked himself, *"Though I am not a man of faith, why do I sense calmness, peace amidst this turmoil? What is this calm in me, despite the violence and fear in the Land? Why do I feel that I and all Israel are safe?"*

Sam had grown up in Israel. He was a *Sabra*, a native born Jew. *Sabra* was from the Hebrew word for prickly pear, *saber*. Sam felt that native born Israelis lived up to prickliness of their name. Likewise, he felt his nation was appropriately named as well, as Israel meant "struggles with God!"

"All the way back to Jacob, who received the new name of Israel from the Lord after fighting with His angel one night, the Jews had been strugglers with God." Sam quickly corrected himself, saying, *"Even the patriarchs who preceded Jacob contended with the Lord also. Actually, I suppose Adam and Eve set the pattern for wrestling with God. They struggled with whether or not they could trust God and take Him at His Word. Their conflict led to disaster for them and everyone who followed them."*

Sam took a sip of wine as he considered his younger days. His parents did not practice their faith. Actually, they had no faith in God. Sam came from a long line of atheistic Jews. His great, great, great, great grandparents somehow managed to survive the twentieth century Holocaust. Their grueling years in three death camps convinced them that either God did not exist or He had abandoned His people.

Over the last few years, as Sam read through the Jewish and Christian Scriptures, he noticed a pattern in the lives of his forebears— a cycle of faith and disbelief that repeated itself throughout Israel's history. The nation of strugglers thoroughly documented their battles with God.

Sam noted, *"God made a covenant with my ancestors that He never broke, even though the Jews repeatedly failed to keep their commitments to Him. Still, when the Jews obeyed God and followed His commands, both they and their land flourished."*

Curious, Sam asked himself, *"Suppose that HaShem is indeed God of all Creation. Then why were the Jews so bull-headed with Him? After God demonstrated His power in so many ways, why would they choose another god or gods—lifeless idols made by their own hands? Why did not HaShem just give up on them? I would have! But the Lord always tried to woo them back to Him.*

"God sent prophets to invite the people back into their Covenant relationship with Him—to warn them about what would happen if they continued to stubbornly refuse Him. He demonstrated so much

patience and love to people who blatantly ignored Him and publically disavowed Him. In like manner, the Jews ignored, disavowed, persecuted, and even killed God's prophets who bore His warnings as well as His appeals for reconciliation."

Soberly, Sam considered the consequences of his ancestors' choices. *"Once HaShem had made every attempt to reestablish His loving Covenant with the rebellious Jews—stiff necked, as He called them—God would have no choice but to turn away from His struggling people, leaving them defenseless against foreign enemies who defeated them and took them into exile. Twice, such invaders destroyed the Temple in the southern kingdom of Judah. The northern kingdom, those ten tribes of Israel, never actually returned to the Land."*

He looked down at the online Tanakh in his lap. He chose a random text. The words were from Amos, chapter five, verses one through three.

"Hear this word which I intone as a dirge over you, O House of Israel: 'Fallen, not to rise again, is Maiden Israel; Abandoned on her soil with none to lift her up. For thus said my Lord GOD about the House of Israel: The town that marches out a thousand strong shall have a hundred left, and the one that marches out a hundred strong shall have but ten left.'"

Sam contemplated the numbers. *"Ninety percent of the House of Israel would not return home. Only a remnant of the House of Israel, of the ten tribes, actually came back from Assyrian exile. The people of the Northern Kingdom were slowly extracted from their homeland over a twenty two year period that ended with the destruction of Samaria in 722 BC.*

"Before World War II, about 18 million Jews, more or less, inhabited the planet earth. Six million were brutally, callously murdered in the Holocaust. Another 1.5 million lost their lives in battle. Thus, 7.5 million Jews were killed during the War. Forty two percent of the worldwide population of Jews lost their lives in the Great War.

"As shocking and hideous as those numbers are, forty two percent is nowhere close to ninety percent! In light of the statistics, can I dare say that HaShem showed the Jews some modicum of mercy in

the twentieth century, compared to the punishment He inflicted on the Northern Kingdom, some 27 hundred years earlier?"

Suddenly, Sam recalled a phrase Sol once said. *"God used Israel's enemies to discipline His children."* Sam pondered, *"God used defeat and exile as the natural and logical consequences for Israel's lack of fidelity to Him. In spite of their unfaithfulness, the Lord did not abandon his people. He expelled them from The Land in the hopes that they would turn their hearts back to Him—so they would repent of their grievous sin!"*

His mind turned to the prophet Ezekiel, while his fingers tapped his Bible's pages to the prophet's book—specifically the twenty third chapter and verses 25-26. Sam read the passage aloud.

> *"I will direct My passion against you, and they shall deal with you in fury: they shall cut off your nose and ears. The last of you shall fall by the sword; they shall take away your sons and daughters, and your remnant shall be devoured by fire. They shall strip you of your clothing and take away your dazzling jewels."*

Sam read the passage again silently and then told himself, *"Those words sound like they describe the horrors of the Holocaust. The Nazis ripped children right out of their mothers' arms. The Nazis took not only clothes and jewels, but hair and teeth, as well. How many Jewish bodies became smoke and ash in the crematoriums?"*

Lifting his gaze from the Scripture to the ceiling, he prayed silently. "Was this Your doing, *HaShem?* Was it Your passion and fury that brought so much suffering to Your people? Had they wandered so far from You, struggled so long with You, that the consequences of their actions manifested themselves in such agony?"

Sam heard the words of Jeremiah 16:4 resonating in his head:

> *"They shall die gruesome deaths. They shall not be lamented or buried; they shall be like dung on the surface of the ground. They shall be consumed by the sword and by famine, and their corpses shall be food for the birds of the sky and the beasts of the earth."*

Unflinching and without sarcasm, Sam asked, "Is that Your answer, You whose name is ineffable? Surely, no one grieved the deaths of millions of Jews—at least not in real time. The Jews were worse than dung to the Nazis. How many starved to death in the ghettos, the woods where they hid, or in the concentration camps?"

In spite of the doom and gloom of the Holocaust, Sam considered this unending love of God for His chosen people. *"If the Scriptures are true, each time the Jews suffered under the hand of foreign rulers who worshiped pagan idols, the Jews repented and cried out to HaShem for deliverance. Each time, God proved Himself to be both faithful and merciful, as He renewed His Covenant with Israel, embraced His chosen people, freed them from bondage, and brought them home to His Promised Land.*

"As prophesied by Jeremiah, HaShem began bringing the Jews of the southern kingdom back to The Land, seventy years after Nebuchadnezzar took them away to Babylon. The prophet Daniel interceded for his people in a prayer of repentance.

"Did the Northern Kingdom never repent? Is that why those ten tribes were lost?"

Sam's thoughts returned to the Holocaust and World War II. *"I don't recall any historical record of the Jews as a whole turning to HaShem in repentance before Israel declared its independence in 1948, and the Jews throughout the Diaspora began coming back to The Land. The Romans destroyed Jerusalem and the Temple in the first century. After some 19 hundred years in exile, why did the Lord allow His people to come back to His Land without them first returning to Him in faith?*

"Was it no coincidence that the Jews were dispersed among the nations of the world so shortly after the crucifixion, as well as the supposed resurrection and ascension of Y'shua, who claimed to be Mashiach, the Anointed One, the very Son of God?"

Sam again opened the Hebrew Scriptures. This time, Psalm 89 lay before his eyes. They particularly focused on verses three and four:

"I declare, 'Your steadfast love is confirmed forever; there in the heavens You establish Your faithfulness. I have made a covenant with My chosen one; I have sworn to My servant

David: I will establish your offspring forever, I will confirm your throne for all generations.'"

The Prime Minister asked, *"What do I make of this promise? If God's love is unending and unshakeable, if His covenant with David lasts forever, then where is the King of Israel?"*

As Sam stared at the words in his Bible, he stopped breathing for a moment, *"Is the King reigning even now? Is the Son of God and Son of David, the Messiah reigning in Heaven? Is this Messiah both proof of God's unfailing love and His promise to David—and all of Israel—to have a king in the line of David always on the throne? Will Y'shua return to Jerusalem and reign for a thousand years, as the New Testament predicts?"*

Sam was not prepared to answer his own questions. Instead, he closed down the Tanakh and stared blankly into the void within his soul. He again delved into the more recent history of the Jews. In his inner darkness, he said to himself, *"God last brought His chosen people home in 1948, after the Holocaust."*

With the driving beat of *Sequence* now in the background, Sam posed the question no Jew wanted to ask or answer. *"Could the Jews who had been in exile since the year 70 have distanced themselves so far from God that He allowed His rebellious people to not only suffer almost two thousand years of exile, but to also be subject to the horrors of the Holocaust? More to the point, did HaShem send the children He loved into exile because they rejected His own Son?"*

Sam recalled reading one of Y'shua's parables in the New Testament. *"How does it go?"* he asked himself. *"A King had prepared a wedding banquet for his son. He had invited many guests, but no one came. The king sent out his servants to tell his invited guests that the feast was ready. Still, the king's guests refused to come. While some continued with their business, others went to work in their fields. But some of those invited by the king to his son's wedding feast took his servants captive, tortured them, and then killed them.*

"Furious, the king sent out his army and killed those who murdered his servants and destroyed their city. Then the king opened his table to anyone who would come until his banquet table was filled with guests."

For the first time, Sam thought he might understand what Y'shua was telling His disciples. *"The King was God Himself. The Groom, the Son of the King, was the Messiah—Y'shua. The guests, perhaps even the bride, were the Jews. The Jews refused to come to the wedding because they rejected the Groom! They not only killed the servants of the King—the prophets—but they killed the King's Son as well. Thus, for rejecting and killing His very Son, HaShem destroyed His people's city, Jerusalem, sent His people into exile, and invited the rest of the world to His Son's wedding banquet instead!"*

As a cold sweat clung to his forehead, Sam again stopped breathing and sat perfectly still. He felt as though God Himself had spoken to him! Not knowing what to do or how to react, Sam sat there until the burning hunger in his lungs for air caused him to inhale once more.

Immediately, Sam centered his thoughts on the Roman destruction of Jerusalem and the Second Temple in the year 70. *"Titus had four legions surrounding Jerusalem. His soldiers cut down all the trees, not to build siege ramps, but to make crosses and crucify all the Jews who had the* chutzpah *to escape the city.*

"Inside the city chosen by HaShem as a dwelling place for His Name, more blood flowed. No, the Romans were not killing Jews within the walls of Jerusalem. Instead, the Jews were actually at each others' throats. Class warfare became viscerally tangible. The Zealots fought to the death with the Jewish upper class which profited under Roman rule."

Grimacing, Sam thought, *"The priests, Pharisees, Sadducees, and scribes fared well under Roman rule because they sold their souls to the Emperors in exchange for power and wealth! On the other hand, the average Jew suffered under Roman rule, especially in regard to taxes. The common Jew had no rights under Roman rule nor was he blessed with any of the privileges that the upper class enjoyed. Thus, to the dismay of the privileged religious leaders, the Zealots rebelled against Rome and fought openly to free Israel from the Empire—which of course brought the legions of the empire to Jerusalem to quash the revolt.*

"With Jerusalem under siege, Titus, the future Emperor, and son of the current Emperor Vespasian, allowed the hands-on class warfare and brutal starvation to do as much of his work as possible. The chosen people may have shed more of their own blood than the Romans

spilled in crucifying escapees and killing Jews in the final battle for Jerusalem. Finally, the soldiers tore through the walls and gates, overcame the last stronghold at the Fortress Antonia, and decimated both Jerusalem and the Temple by fire!"

With the crescendo of the music that surrounded him, Sam again considered the Jews' long exile. *"For almost 1,900 years, the Jews had no homeland."* Sam asked himself a hard and troubling question. *"Could the people of God have wandered so far from Him, as they considered themselves citizens of the nations of the Diaspora, that they brought the Holocaust upon themselves? Did their continued refusal to come to the banquet for His Son, Y'shua cause the Holocaust?"*

Sam stood and began to rock back and forth as his thoughts became more unnerving and Verdi's *Requiem* approached the peak of *Dies Irae*. *"Were the Jews in exile from the Holy Land for almost two millennia because they truly failed to recognize the Messiah when He came to them? Did my ancestors suffer in exile and through the Holocaust because they treated Y'shua as they had treated the prophets? They even killed the so-called last prophet, John the Baptist, Y'shua's 'forerunner' who came 'in the spirit of Elijah.'*

"Why did God finally bring an end to the Holocaust? Did He indeed hear a great cry of repentance from His people or, despite their lack of repentance, did He long to offer one more opportunity for His rebellious, suffering children to accept Y'shua as their Messiah? Did HaShem end the genocide, despite the lack of mass repentance, for the sake of His Name, for the sake of His Son, the Messiah? Did the Lord's commitment to Israel, not their commitment to Him, bring His wandering children back to their barren homeland?" The swirling emotions and thoughts deep within Sam prevented him from answering the question.

He walked back to the mirror. He had come full circle.

Looking deeply at the lines in his face, Sam again contemplated the most recent attempt to eliminate the Jews of Israel. Since God had apparently thwarted the Russian-Muslims Alliance attack on Israel, which Sam witnessed for himself, more Jews had received Y'shua as their Messiah in Israel and America than in the entire two thousand plus years since Y'shua walked in The Land! Even Muslims came to faith in Y'shua in record numbers, despite the fact that such faith placed them under a death sentence!

Sam recalled, *"Did not God promise to Abraham that he would father a people and that his 'seed' would bless all the nations of the world? Was this 'seed' God promised planted in Y'shua? Indeed, was He the Messiah?"*

Sam continued struggling with his own reflections. *"700 years before Y'shua was born, did not the last verses of Isaiah 52 and the entire chapter of Isaiah 53—words Sam had read the very morning of this day—describe in detail what happened to Y'shua—the so called Lamb of God—as He suffered and died?*

"Five hundred years before Y'shua lived on the earth, did not Zechariah prophesy that the Jews would mourn over the One they had pierced, as they were mourning for an only Son? If Y'shua returned to earth, would all the Jews finally recognize Him as their Messiah? Would they grieve their rejection of the Lord's Anointed?

"Is the battle described in Revelation, the battle of Har Megiddo, about to take place—the battle in which the Messiah stands in Israel against all the nations of the world? Will I see this battle? Will I also see Y'shua standing on the Mount of Olives and causing it to split beneath His feet, as Zechariah prophesied about the Messiah?"

As the volume and range of the music and voices rose around him, Sam said, *"How could an atheistic Jew like me make sense of what sounds impossible, even though the impossible seems to be becoming reality all around me? The New Testament predicts a time of tribulation as well—seven years of suffering. Does that come before or after Har Megiddo's battle?"*

Within his vacant soul, the weary leader of Israel felt a spark of hope as he again recalled the plight of King Hezekiah. He asked the God in whom he did not believe, "Will I be like the king of the Jews who trusted You to defeat his enemy—an enemy with seemingly infinite numbers of troops and weapons? Will You Yourself, *HaShem*, now strike those who threaten me and Your people just as You struck down the Assyrian army of Sennacherib on the eve of their overwhelming attack of Hezekiah and Your people?"

With no answers to his waves of questions, Sam decided to call Sol. *"That cranky, dedicated, old Orthodox Rabbi will set me straight!"*

Sam reached for his 3DHP, but to his surprise, he saw that Sol was calling him!

As Sam greeted his old friend, the words of *Sanctus* rang out: *"Benedictus qui venit in nomine Domini. Pleni sunt coeli et terra gloria tua. Hosanna in excelsis."*

"Blessed is He that cometh in the Name of the Lord. Heaven and earth are full of Thy glory. Hosanna in the highest!"

*"But he whose balance (of good deeds) will be (found) light—
will have his home in a (bottomless) Pit."*
Qur'an 101:8-9

CHAPTER 79

ALIVE AND WELL...

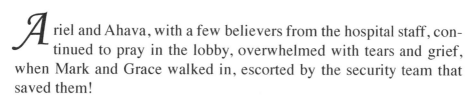

*A*riel and Ahava, with a few believers from the hospital staff, continued to pray in the lobby, overwhelmed with tears and grief, when Mark and Grace walked in, escorted by the security team that saved them!

Seeing Ariel in such distress, Mark took Grace's hand, and the two of them walked over to where the group was kneeling. Mark placed Grace's hand on Ariel's shoulder. At first, Ariel placed her own hand on top of Grace's hand, thinking she was another nurse coming to pray with them.

Nonetheless, something or Someone, told Ariel to look at the person who had placed her hand so delicately on Ariel's shoulder. At first, Ariel was caught off guard, as Grace was still wearing the *jibab* of her Muslim alter ego, Haziqah. Yet, when Ariel's eyes met Grace's eyes, all confusion was wiped away!

With a shout, Ariel jumped to her feet and enveloped Grace in the tightest hug she could muster! With closed eyes, all this joyful mother could say was, Thank You, Lord! Thank You, Lord! Thank You, Lord!"

Then, Ariel released her daughter, removed the shroud from her head, and looked again into her beautiful brown eyes and said, "I should have never doubted that I would see your lovely face again! But when I heard all the gunshots after your dad went down, I thought the worst had happened!"

Ariel held Grace close to her once more, then pulled back to ask the question she hated to ask. "Grace, were you forced to marry that man who called us?" Then, searching for the right words, this caring mother asked, "Did he abuse you?"

Grace looked down at the floor. Her voice was timid as she said, "The man—who I think was the General—made many threats! But someone was killed, and he left me alone. Later, he returned and said he would marry me today, whether or not Daddy cooperated. He told me I would never see Daddy or you again. He said that after my wedding night, you would disown me anyway!"

Ariel clung to her daughter again. With great confidence, the mother told her only daughter, "Nothing could ever stop my love for you, Grace! Nothing whatsoever! I love you, your daddy loves you, and best of all Y'shua loves you—always and forever! You will always be our daughter and a child of God! Nobody can change that! Nobody!"

"Amen!" Mark said.

Ariel knew that voice. She opened her eyes to behold her husband—who was not even wounded, much less dead! She extended one arm to Mark, and the three of them just held onto each other, while everyone around them, including the calloused security team, wept with them in joy!

Not letting go, Ariel asked Mark, "How are you alive? How did you escape?"

Mark answered, "The security detail figured out where I was when they saw me on their 3DHP's. They rushed to the studio to free us!"

"So that was the gunfire I heard?"

"Yes!"

"Then why did you fall behind the table?"

"I did not know what was happening at first! I heard the gunfire, and I ducked for cover!"

The two of them laughed, but Grace said, "Mom, I can't breathe anymore!"

Ariel released Grace from her tight embrace. Wiping her eyes, Grace said, "I was in the studio next to Dad. I watched and listened to him by way of the studio HV3D. When he fell, I ran from the man who was holding me—the General! One of the security men met me at the door and pushed me to the floor, so I would not be hit by the gunfire, as someone was shooting back at the team!

"The agent and I stayed down until the shooting stopped. I looked back to where I was sitting, and the General—his face was covered with a black cloth—had disappeared!"

Mark added, "I stayed under the table until the shooting stopped and until I heard the leader of the team say, 'All clear!' Then I remembered hearing those same words in the church when the lights came back on—that's how all this started!"

Grace gently took the hand of the Secret Service Agent who saved her life. "Mom, without this man, I would not be here with you now!" Ariel gave the agent a hug he would never forget! The genuine embrace meant more than any recognition he and the team would later receive for the rescue of Grace and Mark.

Looking into his bride's reddened eyes, Mark said, "Ariel, Grace and I stood firm, ready to die for our faith in Jesus! I never once considered that He would use this team to rescue us instead!"

Grace agreed saying, "I knew when Dad was talking that the General was going to kill both of us! But I also knew that Dad could not say he no longer believed in Jesus, even if his faith did cost our lives!"

Once more, the three of them wept and hugged, while the others in the room applauded!

Mark said, as he looked to the security team, "You brave men were vessels of Jesus for our rescue! You deserve our deepest thanks and eternal gratitude! This makes two times that you have saved my life!" Then the room erupted in applause once more!

Meanwhile, As Sol, Abdul, and his security team walked by the lobby, they heard the applause. Pausing at the entrance, Sol saw Ahava with her hands on the shoulders of Mark and Ariel! Sol ran, if you could call his faster shuffling running, into the lobby shouting, "Hallelujah! Hallelujah!"

Mark and Ariel looked at Sol, and then hugged him and Ahava! A few seconds later, Abdul stood beside them asking, "What has happened to warrant all this?" As the five of them turned their eyes to Abdul, his gaze landed on Grace. By instinct, he reached out to her with his uninjured arm. The two of them, who had not met before, hugged briefly, and then Grace said, "Mr. Vice President, I have been praying for you for a long time!"

"Isa heard your prayers for me, and Isa heard my prayers for you," Abdul said with a smile that was moistened by his tears.

For Abdul's sake, everyone gently hugged again, until the U.S. Ambassador entered the room and said, "Mr. President, we have to get you sworn in!"

Mark, Ariel, Grace, Sol, and Ahava stepped back and looked at Abdul with their deepest respect, but Grace was puzzled. She looked into her Dad's face and asked, "Why is Vice President Abdullah being sworn in as President?"

Mark realized that his daughter must not have seen Air Force One crash into the Capitol Building. He knelt before Grace so that he could look directly into her eyes. "Honey, President Paulson was killed on Air Force One as it crashed into the U.S. Capitol. James lost his life with many, many other elected officials. So much has happened since you were taken from the church."

"The President is dead?" Grace asked, her bottom lip aquiver.

Ariel placed her hand on her daughter's shoulder and said, "Sweetheart, we have much to tell you, and there is so much I want to hear from you!"

Abdul gently interrupted saying, "The three of you can talk on the way to the Knesset. Sam has graciously offered for my oath of office to be taken there. I would be most honored if the three of you, as well as Sol and Ahava, would be with me when I take that oath!"

Everyone tried to smile as they shook their heads and humbly accepted Abdul's offer. The new President smiled as well and thanked the best friends he had in this world.

Then, Michael said, "Mr. President, the Prime Minister is waiting—and so are all of the citizens of America!"

"Do not judge, and you will not be judged. Do not condemn, and you will not be condemned. Forgive, and you will be forgiven."
Luke 6:37

CHAPTER 80

TWISTING AND TURNING. . .

*A*ctually, Sol had called Sam to ask if Abdul could take his oath of office at the Knesset, instead of the hospital. As Sol said, "This is such a drab place!" Sam replied, "I agree! I will put the wheels in motion to make it happen."

Amazingly, until Sol called him, Sam did not know about the attempt on Abdul's life. How could such important information be withheld from him? While the Mossad was already investigating, Sam immediately ordered the Israeli Security Agency (ISA), commonly known as *Shin-Bet*, to track down the doctor who implanted the explosive device in Abdul's shoulder. *Shin-Bet* did not answer to the military or law enforcement offices, but to the Prime Minister himself.

Sam's personal, spiritual questions for Sol would have to wait until later, perhaps after Abdul's swearing in at the Knesset Press Room. However, waiting was the last thing Sam wanted to do. In his heart, Israel's Prime Minister wanted answers now, not later!

While Abdul and his entourage rode to the Knesset, everyone's 3DHP's came to life at once. Once more, everyone around the entire world beheld the same image. This time, the General's veiled face appeared. His seething eyes burned with hatred.

In his white hot anger, the General announced, "Citizens of the world, on this eve before the mass funeral of the innocent Muslims who were slain by the infidels in East Jerusalem, I must bring you more tragic news. The infidels have taken the life of our beloved Caliph Sanaullah bin Laden!"

A collective sigh rose above Babylon.

In his digitally distorted voice, the masked madman said, "We found the Caliph's body, along with those of the trusted Brotherhood soldiers assigned to guard his life, in his Ankara palace. In addition, we also discovered bodies that bore the uniforms of U.S. and Israeli Special Forces units!

"After falsely blaming Babylon for the destruction in Palestine, Israel and the United States—the Big and Little Satans—have conspired to take the life of the most noble leader on the face of this earth!

"In response, I am placing my name before the people of Babylon for election as Caliph. We cannot afford to be without a qualified, respected, and proven leader, so the people of Babylon will vote by ultranet tomorrow on my candidacy. All of Babylon will vote before 5:00 Wednesday afternoon."

Almost as an aside, the General calmly commented, "For anyone who thinks such a massive vote on such short notice will not be possible, might I point out that a brilliant Muslim IT engineer developed the ultranet, which is 10,000 times faster than the antiquated internet? Plus, the ultranet can hold a limitless quantity of data, unlike the internet that reached its maximum capacity decades ago and much data—including sensitive data—had to be deleted to keep the internet working.

"Of course, you probably know about the supreme intelligence of Muslims already, so I will return to the matter at hand: tomorrow's election. Our people are free to cast their vote for a Muslim other than myself, but whoever is elected tomorrow must assume power immediately!

"Likewise, the ballot will list a proposal regarding Palestine. The faithful believers of Babylon will vote on annexing the Democratic Republic of Palestine. This land of our brothers cannot face the onslaught of the infidels alone! Out of duty, we must bring them under the protection of Babylon and the Brotherhood!

"When we gather tomorrow for the mass funeral service in Palestine, we will also honor our Caliph and his most trusted men. These bodies are the only ones we can actually bury because, as you know, the fierce missile explosions destroyed the bodies of the

Palestinians. As is our tradition, the Caliph's body and those of his fellow shahids will be buried facing Mecca.

"After the funeral, all of Babylon will vote on the two items of upmost importance. To all our outside detractors as well as Muslims who consider a vote to be a strike against Allah's sovereignty, we must remember that strange times call for strange measures. Is not an equitable vote the most fair, honest, and timely method for choosing our next leader? We will notify the world of the election results before sunset tomorrow."

The General paused for several seconds, as though he was considering what to say next. "In closing, I would like to say a personal word to Omar Rashad Basel and his daughter Haziqah. Your blasphemy before the world against Allah and all of Islam will not be forgotten or go unpunished. Be ever watchful, for Allah considers those who turn from their professed faith in him to be the worst vermin of all on this planet.

"You may have escaped today, but no hail of gunfire will be there on the day that Allah himself comes to demand your life and condemn you to the perpetual fire! Your web of lies has become so tangled that no one can trust anything you say or do. Perhaps the so called followers of Isa may actually relieve the world of your wretched existence before the Brotherhood comes to call on you!

"On a more personal note, Omar—you who forgive and pray for your former Muslim brothers—allow me to set the record straight. When I was nine years old, I lived in the same village as you within Iraq. Furthermore, I was the one given the honor and privilege of killing your parents! They were my first killing in the jihad of Allah, Most Gracious, Most Merciful! You were next on my list Omar, but as all those who recant their faith in Allah become cowards, you escaped to the United States!

"I have never forgotten my personal obligation to rid your body of breath! And I will not stop with you! Your daughter, who was pledged to marry a fine, upstanding Muslim of great character, will now instead lose her head, as will your Jewish scum wife, Ariel—oh yes, and your two faithless, worthless sons, Thomas and Timothy, will soon depart from this world, too, unless they prove to be of some worth to us! Do not think for a moment that they are safe in the United States while you, your wife, and daughter continue to spread heresy in Israel!

"You will never see your family of infidels again, until you roast in the unquenchable fire with them! So, Omar, does your false god allow you to hate me now?"

"The punishment of those who wage war against Allah and His Apostle, and strive with might and main for mischief through the land is: execution, or crucifixion, or the cutting off of hands and feet from opposite sides, or exile from the land: That is their disgrace in this world, and a heavy punishment is theirs in the Hereafter."
Qur'an 5:33

CHAPTER 81

MAKING SENSE OF IT ALL. . .

*A*s soon as the General stopped spewing his vile rhetoric, Mark and Ariel called to check on their boys. The couple that was caring for them did not answer! Ariel was about to lose control of her volatile emotions when Abdul intervened.

With a serious tone, but a smile on his face, Abdul told them, "Do not worry about Tim and Tom. They are safe! The President— James—moved your boys and your friends to a safe place! They have the highest level of protection. When James heard what was happening with Grace, he decided to ensure the safety of you boys. I have the number you can call to talk with them. I would have told you about this sooner, but I did not know about it until we were all on the set, and I have pretty much been out of commission since then."

Ariel threw her arms around Abdul, thanking him profusely! "But, Ariel," Abdul said wincing with pain, "I did not do this. James did, God rest his soul!"

"I know, Abdul, but you are the bearer of very good news! And I am thanking you, and most of all, I am thanking Y'shua!" Ariel then sat back and pulled Mark and Grace close to her! "Thank You, Lord, for saving my family! Thank You for each of them!"

"Do you want to call the boys, now?" Abdul asked.

Mark answered, "I think we need to get a better grip on our emotions before we call them, Abdul. But I will gladly take the phone number from you!"

At least in that moment, Mark felt relieved, knowing no harm had come to his twins. Still, even with the good news, Mark wondered if anyone in his family could be considered safe, with a *fatwa* placed on all their heads by the General who would be Caliph by this time tomorrow. No formality such as a vote would stop the General from assuming power. Besides, in one day, even the ultranet could not process the billions of votes that would have to be tabulated and verified.

The pastor considered the oddities of the General's plug during his speech for the designer of the ultranet, Addar, as well as his decision to use a democratic principle to choose the next Caliph.

As Mark stared out the window his thoughts turned colder. He asked anyone in the vehicle who wanted to answer, "Did the General truly kill my parents all those years ago? Did he send his henchmen after me Sunday? Is this maniac, bent on absolute power, going to complete his vendetta against two more generations of my family?"

Mark closed his eyes. Everyone was silent. Ariel clasped his hands. "Pray!" she said. "Whether the General killed your parents or not, he is baiting you. You are not responsible for your parents' deaths. If we and our children are killed by the General, you will not be responsible for our deaths, either. Our lives are, as they always have been, in the Hands of Y'shua—and no one can take us from His hand—remember! This world has no power over us! Truly, what can the General do to us?"

Everyone in the limo closed their eyes as Mark, Ariel, and Grace softly prayed together. Abdul, Sol, and Ahava placed their hands on the three of them, as they silently asked for the Lord's protection, provision, and peace to be given to this precious family. Mark specifically asked to be able to love the General, to forgive him, even if he indeed had murdered his parents so long ago.

As Mark completed his plea to his Saviour and King, he again wondered why the General had spoken about the ultranet and its Muslim creator. "Abdul," Mark said, "do you have any idea why the General would frivolously discuss the ultranet during his diatribe about the Caliph and his henchmen? Why did he take the time to put in a plug for Addar, who designed the ultranet?"

"What I first thought, Mark," Abdul began, "was that the General was trying to save face for Addar. His claim to designing the ultranet, as you know, was immediately questioned. The controversy over his level of involvement on the project never was resolved, at least not in any public forum.

"Perhaps the General was trying to buoy his favorite imam, given that Addar will not be a candidate for President of the DROP, as the General says the Palestinian state will be absorbed by the Caliphate."

Pensively, Mark said, "I understand your point, Abdul. Still, I sense something lies under the surface. What the General said almost sounded like a commercial for Addar. The masked man of Babylon touted Addar's superior intelligence and IT engineering ability. All of the comments about Addar just seemed out of place—especially since the General did not mention his favorite imam by name. Could that be significant at any level?"

"You may be onto something, Mark. Even so, I cannot continue to focus on this part of the General's speech. I need to prepare for taking the oath of office."

Quickly and sincerely Mark responded, "My apologies, Mr. President! I surely do not mean to add anything more to the load you are carrying right now. We need to pray for you!"

Thus, as the limousine approached the Knesset safely, Abdul said, "I would like that very much!"

Before Mark began to intercede for the new Commander in Chief Sol asked, "Abdul, will you yet go to the funeral tomorrow, after all that the General has said—after you have already survived one attempt on your life?" Sol found himself very concerned for his friend.

"Sol," Abdul stated, "if I felt I could be anywhere else but that funeral tomorrow, then I would gladly be at that place, instead. My wishes aside, as President, I feel I must go and represent the peace that America desires, not the war that someone seeks to provoke! I feel that the Prime Minister and I must attend the ceremony tomorrow!"

Sol realized that Abdul was right, but his answer did not bring peace to Sol's troubled heart. "Of course, all precautions will be taken to guard your life?"

"Of course!" Abdul replied with confidence. "Even though I never wanted to be in this position, I now realize that Isa has laid this responsibility on my shoulders. Thus, I trust Him for every move I must make both now and in the days to come!"

The limo and the surrounding security detail vehicles pulled up to the Knesset. Mark said, "Let's pray. We need to intercede for Abdul."

Mark took a small vial of oil from his pocket and anointed Abdul with it. Then, laying his hands on Abdul's head, Mark prayed, "Dear Isa, Y'shua, Jesus! You have chosen Abdul to represent You as well as the nation known as the United States of America. Abdul is about to take his oath of office, and you know how ill prepared he feels. We ask You in this moment to fill Him with Your assurance that You are his shield and strength! Be His confidence as he speaks. Be clear as You lead him, so that he has no doubt about the choices he must make and the words he must speak.

"Focus his heart, soul, mind, and body on You and the work You are appointing and anointing him to do in such perilous and confusing times! Give him singleness of heart, resolve of soul, clarity of thought, and stamina of body as he faces the people of America and the world who will be clinging to every word he speaks.

"Thank you for preserving his life. Please, heal his wounds that he has suffered for others. Guard His life so that he may complete the difficult work that looms ahead of him. Encourage Abdul by reminding him that You are not on the sidelines, but firmly in control amidst all the chaos that surrounds him.

"Abdul is most eager to obey and please You, Lord! Walk beside him, before him, behind him, above him, and below him! Wrap him in Your love and power! Place on him now Your full armor: Your helmet of salvation, Your breastplate of righteousness, Your belt of truth, Your shield of faith, Your sword of the Spirit, and Your shoes, fitted for the readiness to share Your Gospel of peace!

"This is Your man for Your time and Your purposes. Use Abdul as You see fit! In the mercy and grace that You poured out for us on Calvary, we pray! Amen."

Visibly moved by Mark's prayer, Abdul wondered if David felt as he did now when Samuel anointed him as king over Israel. The new President's tears proved that he was humbly approaching this work Isa called him to do. His smile proved that Isa had answered Mark's prayer.

As the doors on the limo opened, one of the Prime Minister's aides came out to meet the group of friends. Abdul lingered inside the vehicle, as everyone else approached the entrance of the Knesset. They marveled at the sculpted entrance gate. Sol and Ariel immediately thought of the Hall of Remembrance Gate at Yad Vashem that no longer existed. The same sculptor, David Palombo, designed both sets of gates.

Meanwhile, still at the limousine, Abdul made a call of extreme importance. Hope Paulson looked remarkably peaceful to be the widowed First Lady of the United States of America. With great sincerity of heart, Abdul said, "Hope, I knew that I must talk with you before the swearing in ceremony. I want you to personally know how saddened I am about James' tragic death. My prayers for you and your family remain constant!"

Hope did her best to keep her composure for the man who would take her husband's place as the leader of what was left of the free world—indeed the most grueling job on the planet. She said, "I understand you and James have more in common than you may realize."

"How so, Hope?"

"Did you not surrender your life to Jesus on Air Force One, as you flew to Israel?"

"Yes," Abdul said as he smiled broadly, "I did!"

"Abdul, James gave his life to Jesus also, on the return flight, just hours before. . ." Hope could not finish the sentence, so Abdul spoke the painful words for her, saying, "before Air Force One crashed into the Capitol Building?"

"Yes," Hope moaned through her tears.

"Hope! How do you know this?" A bolt of inspiration shot through Abdul, and he found it hard to breathe.

"James called me. He had prayed before his speech, and God gave him peace, wisdom, and direction. He still had that peace when we talked after his address. Then, during our conversation, James felt the conviction of the Holy Spirit. I heard James pray in repentance, Abdul! I heard him confess his sin! James flew Home in Air Force One, Abdul!"

"Isa has used this crisis as a catalyst for our salvation, Hope! Perhaps I will be joining James, soon. If so, I will go happily, willingly!"

"I believe James would have said the same—had he known!"

"Hope, I will see you as soon as I arrive in the states. Have you been contacted about the arrangements for your travel back to D.C.?"

"Yes," she replied, "Everything is set for me and the boys."

"I'll be praying for you, Reggie, and Vic until I see you! May our Lord bring you all His unfathomable peace in the midst of all the turmoil!"

"He has, and He will, Abdul. He will do the same for you!"

"Amen! See you soon, Hope!"

"You too, Abdul!"

The rest of the group was now behind the gates, as Abdul and his security team made their way into the Knesset. Abdul's closet friends were examining the more than one hundred year old large bronze and wooden doors that were decorated with many symbols of Jewish history. They commented on the works of Marc Chagall which lined the hallway.

The aide showed the group the Knesset conference room as well as the parliamentary hall itself—the plenum. Behind the speaker's platform was a huge, engraved stone wall. Sol immediately thought of the Western Wall of the Temple Mount, which no longer existed.

As Abdul and his security detail caught up with the group, the Prime Minister's aide brought them all to the gallery where Sam was waiting for them. Sam greeted Abdul and everyone who was with him. Sam could not have been more gracious or kind. He saved his largest hug for Sol, telling him, "I really need to talk with you when we have a few moments."

He told Mark and Grace, "The news of your demise has been highly exaggerated!" Then, noticing that Grace was still wearing her Muslim robe, Sam asked another of his assistants to secure some proper clothing for the young lady. Both Ariel and Grace smiled with gratitude.

Sam returned to Abdul and shook his hand a second time. "I am so glad that you are alive! Are you in much pain?"

"No," replied Abdul. "Thanks for asking."

"My best investigators are tracking down the doctor who implanted the explosive device in your shoulder. I am so glad Dr. Goldberg was suspicious about the fever in your wound and ordered the X-ray!"

"I feel as though the Lord has been watching over me! Did you know that Dr. Goldberg is a follower of Y'shua?"

Not expecting that question, Sam replied, "How would I have known that?" Feeling uncomfortable with discussing yet another Jew's faith in Y'shua, he decided to change the subject, albeit somewhat awkwardly as he seemed to search the room for his next words. Finally Sam said, "Everything you need for the swearing in ceremony, and your speech following it, is ready, Mr. President. But we do need to go over a few important details before you speak."

Abdul said, "I agree. What do you make of the General's announcement of the Caliph's assassination?"

"I think the General is the prime suspect! All of our intel points to him. Who would believe that Israel and America would be so foolish as to leave soldiers' bodies at the scene of an assassination? I believe the General is behind all the violence and mayhem of late." With a smirk on his face, Sam added, "I have no doubt that tomorrow he will win a unanimous vote as the next Caliph!"

Abdul replied, "All the Muslims of Babylon voting for their Caliph? Is Allah now adopting the ways of democracy? Is the incredibly cruel and inhuman Sharia now government that grants the right to vote to its masses?"

Both men laughed for a brief moment. Then Abdul noted, "If the Shias were here, the Caliph would be determined by succession—and the Caliph would be a holy man. But with the Sunnis, they choose their own ruler. Typically, a small group of leaders—a small group of the highest and most respected Muslims—would choose the next Caliph. For two reasons, I believe the General will not allow this process. One, he obviously feels no time can be wasted, as he wants to become Caliph immediately. Two, he will not risk someone else being selected to follow bin Laden.

"The latest report I received before leaving the hospital, before the General made his announcement, showed that an internal coup had been successful. I suspect the assassination occurred Sunday night or early Monday. I also suspect that bin Laden did not die of bullet wounds but of decapitation. At the funeral tomorrow, we will know for sure. His body should be wrapped, but his head should be visible. If not, we know that the General's henchmen killed the Caliph.

"Sam, I have the agreements with the Americas that James set out to secure. Our united front can move forward. We cannot wait for the next attack, despite the fact that both our weapons systems have been shut down for reprogramming as we speak."

Nodding his head in agreement, Sam asked, "Does your intel give you any indications of when or where the next attacks on Israel and the United States might take place?"

"Actually, our best guess is. . ." Abdul's response was cut short by his 3DHP. He saw that someone was calling, but saw no image on the screen. *"The General,"* Abdul said under his breath. He excused himself to take the call.

"General, how dare you call me after making an attempt on my life? I have no desire to talk with you!"

In his barbaric tones, the General stated, "No, Abdul, you are wrong! You must talk with me. In fact, this is the precise moment that we must make crucial decisions!"

". . . 'Nation will rise against nation, and kingdom against kingdom.'"
Luke 21:10

CHAPTER 82

SLAYING, FRAYING, AND PRAYING. . .

$\mathcal{T}$he leadership of the United States had been decapitated. While the Vice President and a few members of Congress survived, the American people felt they had no leader. After all, the Vice President remained outside the states, and he, as yet, had not been sworn in as Commander in Chief.

Could he be trusted? Based on President Paulson's Air Force One speech, many in the nation suspected the Vice President could be complicit in the Brotherhood's plans to islamize America. After all, he conveniently missed the fatal flight that took the life of the only man standing in the way of his rise to power over the USA.

The masses did not know of Abdul's new faith in Isa. Once he shared his transformation, would the nation then accept him or would Americans—non-Muslim Americans—believe he only sought to deceive them? How would Abdul prove himself to the people? The citizens of the United States saw danger on all sides!

Of course, the vast majority of Muslim citizens of the U.S. raged over Sanaullah bin Laden's murder. The Muslims regarded the Caliph, not the President, as their leader, even though the United States was not part of the Caliphate—yet! American Muslims had no problem believing that the United States and Israel were behind the assassination and were ready to take out their righteous anger on any and all infidels!

In the present vacuum, the Governors of the states stepped forward to call for order and to ease tensions. While local police, National Guard, and now the U.S. Army patrolled the streets and engaged in local skirmishes, they lacked a cohesive plan of defense. Likewise, they had no concept for an offensive counterattack, should it prove necessary.

Various groups of Muslim fighters seemed to have the upper hand. Roaming bands of terrorists destroyed power plants and relay stations, leaving many cities without electricity. The burning of synagogues and churches continued—many filled with fearful, prayerful worshippers who broke the curfew to find peace. Jihadists also repeated their destruction of many local, state, and federal government buildings along with the workers inside them.

Riots erupted in prisons, as many Muslims had been sentenced to long sentences for insurrection, terror, conspiracy, espionage, and murder. In fact, one prison revolt in Arizona ended with the Muslim inmates in charge and all the guards dead.

Hospitals remained full, now with the wounded as well as the homeless who did not feel safe on the streets. Waiting rooms across the country remained packed with people who had no other place to go and refused to leave for the uncertainty of the cities.

Looting continued in grocery stores, as Muslims and non-Muslims alike feared a prolonged siege and did not want to be without supplies. Stores that sold gas masks, hazmat suits, potassium iodide and other survival items could not keep up with demand.

To make matters even worse, truth and rumor became indistinguishable. News organizations persisted in their Muslim bias. Thus, citizens could not discern the difference between unadulterated fact and propagandized fiction. Indeed, the pursuit of truth became as elusive as the pursuit of peace.

As such, rumors abounded about water supplies being poisoned, dirty bombs exploding in the capitols of the states, a Brotherhood Army gathering forces in the Midwest, chemical weapons being lobbed into cities by portable launchers, biological weapons being fired into military bases and forts, suicide bombers exploding in banks, and mass killings on Wall Street—not to mention everyday citizens disappearing from their homes by the thousands.

Only essential government services had access to the ultranet. As he flew out of Israel, President Paulson had ordered the online restrictions at the request of General Ellis of the Joint Chiefs of Staff. James shut down the ultranet for the same reason he had shutdown the weapons system: to ensure that no more American missiles could be fired upon her own people.

The loss of the ultranet was the straw that broke the stock market's back. Trading on Wall Street had already been severely limited, due to the volatility of events in the U.S. and around the world. With no trading at all, fears of a market crash permeated the country.

Even worse, the dollar plummeted and Americans withdrew large sums of money from the banks that remained open. The Federal Deposit Insurance Corporation (FDIC), the Federal Reserve Board (FRB), and Treasury Secretary Howard Longreen—who was not on the Hill when Air Force One slammed into it—met in an unprecedented emergency meeting which ended with the decision to declare "bank holidays," effectively shutting down the nation's banking system indefinitely!

As anarchy reared its ugly head, Abdul-ghafoor Asim Abdullah prepared to be sworn in as the President of the United States of Bedlam!

"And verily this Brotherhood of yours is a single Brotherhood, and I am your Lord and Cherisher: Therefore fear Me (and no other)."
Qur'an 23:52

CHAPTER 83

CHOOSING SIDES...

*T*he masked man of Babylon called to convince Abdul to officially declare martial law in the United States, abolish the Constitution, enact Sharia Law, and proclaim the United States "Islamerica," a state of the Caliphate of Babylon!

Abdul responded, "General! I am about to take the oath of office as the next President of the United States! I will be heading a nation ravaged by death, grief, fear, and turmoil! I will need to call for emergency elections. I will be attending funerals and memorial services that will last for weeks if not months. On top of all that, I will need a steady hand in guiding our nation through all out war with the Brotherhood!"

"All those circumstances make my plan so brilliant, Abdul!"

"General! You want me to commit treason!"

"No, I do not, Abdul," the distorted voice replied. You are a Muslim before you are a citizen of the United States! If you want to save lives on all sides and prevent a bloodbath, you must take the oath of office, and then, immediately, declare a state of martial law. That will shut down the country. The moment you step on U.S. soil, proclaim that you, in the absence of other government leaders, are making a unilateral decision to abolish the Constitution and enact Sharia Law — immediately! Then, you can swear your allegiance to the Caliphate as the leader of Islamerica!"

"General! What makes you think that the armed forces of the United States would fall in line behind me? What makes you think that the Supreme Court would not overrule me? What makes you think that the American people would not immediately revolt?"

"All those details have been or will be handled! First of all, the entire weaponry of the United States remains under the control of the Brotherhood, so any opposition mounted by the military or the people could be quickly defeated! Besides, the many Muslim Americans in the armed forces would rally to your side and fight against the other soldiers. If needed, I can eliminate the Supreme Court just as I eliminated the President and Legislature of the United States! You will be the only one with power! You can do whatever you want—all for the glory of Islam and Allah!"

"You mean all for the glory of you!"

The General became very quiet and stern. "Listen to me, Abdul. Do you think you were randomly chosen out of all the Muslim citizens of America to be Vice President? We had to work for years to orchestrate your ascension to power, with the ultimate goal for you being to turn that power over to the Caliphate! This is your moment, Abdul! This is why you were born!"

Calmly, the President responded, "You and Imam Zaahir like to lord your influence over me on a regular basis. You do not own me, General. I owe you nothing—save prayer for your redemption. I pity you. While you think you are about to control the world, you are a mere puppet in the very hand of absolute evil!"

"A puppet, am I?" the General shouted. "This puppet will be calling all the shots as of tomorrow. I offer you the opportunity today to ride this wave of power and glory alongside me. This offer becomes null and void at midnight, Mr. President—just as you also might become null and void!"

Abdul said nothing in response. Michael came to let him know it was time for him to take the oath of office. Thus, Abdul ended the call without speaking another word to the raging and ranting megalomaniac.

Abdul walked away even more determined to serve Isa and fight for the right! While the General wanted to destroy souls, Abdul longed to see them saved, eternally!

As he and Ambassador Rosenberg entered the area of the gallery where Abdul would take the oath and address the nation, he wondered what would result from his refusal to participate in the General's plan.

Regardless, whatever may await him and his country, Abdul had to clearly focus on the moment. The citizens of the United States of America needed him to lead them as war loomed on the horizon!

The two officials stood before the camera. Abdul closed his eyes and focused on the prayer Mark had spoken for him and their country. Abdul opened his eyes when he heard Michael speaking.

"I am the United States Ambassador to Israel Michael Rosenberg. In this hour of deep grief as well as political, social, spiritual, and economic upheaval, the United States of America and her citizens mourn the loss of so many of our fellow countrymen and statesmen, especially President James Paulson. Our people stand as one with all the families who are mourning, including our First Lady and her sons.

"Even in such seemingly insurmountable grief, we must move forward in the means outlined for us in our Constitution. Today, you will witness the oath of office of the next President of the United States, Abdul-ghafoor Asim Abdullah." As Michael turned to face Abdul, he said, "Please place your left hand on the Bible, raise your right hand, and repeat after me. I, Abdul-ghafoor Asim Abdullah do solemnly swear. . ."

"I, Abdul-ghafoor Asim Abdullah do solemnly swear. . ."

". . . that I will faithfully execute the office of President of the United States. . ."

". . . that I will faithfully execute the office of President of the United States. . ."

". . . and will to the best of my ability. . ."

". . . and will to the best of my ability. . ."

". . . preserve, protect and defend the Constitution of the United States."

". . . preserve, protect and defend the Constitution of the United States. So help me God!"

"A good man brings good things out of the good stored up in him, and an evil man brings evil things out of the evil stored up in him."
Matthew 12:35

CHAPTER 84

MORE THAN MEETS THE EYE. . .

A torrential storm of madness raged in the calloused heart of the General! Ranting and raving, he shouted to his cringing operatives, "Who is Abdul-ghafoor Asim Abdullah to stop me from ridding the earth of the Great Satan, otherwise known as the United States of America? Where did he suddenly find courage and principle? Though Abdul is more of an agnostic, even an atheist, than he is a true believer of Islam, why does he suddenly care about the people and nation of America?"

Throwing things around the room, the General railed, "If Abdul does not cooperate with the plans of Babylon—specifically, my plans—then what should I do? The General turned to the HV3D image around him and stated, "As Commander in Chief, if you make such a stand, you must be, shall we say, persuaded?"

The General plotted. "You have neither wife nor children, so we cannot force you to change your mind as ransom for hostages. Torture could be a persuasive tool, but concealing it would be difficult. We could threaten to reveal the dark secrets of your past, but you do not have any such secrets. Then again, we could just lie about you even though you have always been a straight arrow, which is why we had interest in you in the first place. What is your weakness, Mr. Almost President? Perhaps we could exploit the skepticism the American voters have about your Muslim leanings?"

The General's thoughts suddenly shifted when he heard the ambassador say Abdul would place his hand on the Bible as he spoke the oath of office. "A Bible?" the General shouted at the screen! "Could you not bear to place your hand on the Qur'an? Have you suddenly decided you like power? Do you plan to consolidate power in yourself, instead of the Caliphate? Do you think that I would not take you down at any moment of my choosing, just because you are Muslim? Have you learned nothing from the failed attempt on your life?"

The General's twice fired anger was fed more fuel when he heard Abdul say, "So help me God!" The General leapt to his feet and shouted, "That phrase is not even required for the oath!" He almost threw his chair at the images that surrounded him of the now President of the United States, but he realized he would miss Abdul's speech. "What is this man of many surprises going to say to the American people?"

The exasperated General placed his chair back on the floor and sat in it. He could not believe what his ears heard!

"Before I speak to you as your President, allow me to pause for a moment, and stand beside you as a fellow citizen of the United States of America. In the last days of President James Paulson, I saw him rising to meet the crisis that faced him and our country. I have no doubt whatsoever that President Paulson would have bravely, wisely, and effectively led the United States through the days ahead. Our nation's loss is fiercely tangible.

"Far too many of our elected officials, including our very President, have faced a sudden and horrid end to their lives. Their families are wrapped in sorrow as I speak with you. Fathers, mothers, husbands, wives, brothers, and sisters throughout our great land are in the midst of shock and grief. These men and women, boys and girls are our friends and neighbors. They now need and will continue to need our help as our Lord seeks to bring them comfort and peace. In that regard, our Lord may want to use you as His vessel."

"'Lord?' Who in the world are you talking about, Mr. President?" The General walked closer to Abdul's image.

"Let us call on Him now, as we ask Him to comfort and strengthen these grieving families, especially our First Family, Hope, Reggie, and Vic Paulson."

"What are you up to, Abdullah?" the General asked the President as he bowed his head. "It is at best unseemly that you are praying and asking others to pray with you! Did the White House speech writer send you a script to follow? Or do you speak for yourself?" With great curiosity, the General waited for the new President's prayer.

"Dear Lord, please bind the hearts of our people together. So much has happened in such a short period of time. We can barely keep up with the pace of events. Tragedy upon tragedy has befallen our families, the families of Israel, and the families of Palestine. Truly, how do we go even one step forward without You?

"Lord, please, grant us your wisdom. Indeed, guide me as Your duly appointed leader of the United States. Grant this great nation under God strength of mind, body, soul, and will to face the days ahead with faith and confidence that the United—and I emphasize United—States of America will continue to blaze the trail of freedom and justice in this world!

"We call on You, the one and only God, to unite us as one within Yourself. Only You, no one else, knows what tomorrow, what all our tomorrows, will bring. In the holy Name of Isa, Y'shua, Jesus we pray! Amen!"

"What?" the General screamed as he leapt out of the chair! "If you are not playing a role in order to persuade Americans to trust you, you will soon be very dead!"

As Abdul again looked into the camera, his eyes showed determination. He said, "My friends and fellow citizens of the United States of America, I must be honest with you. I never aspired to even be the Vice President of the United States, much less your President. So you can be certain that assuming this office never crossed my mind. I must confess. I was President Paulson's running mate for one reason: I could secure the Muslim vote for the Democratic party!

"As someone much wiser and smarter than me once wrote, 'Be not afraid of greatness: some are born great, some achieve greatness, and some have greatness thrust upon them.' These humbling words penned by Shakespeare in Twelfth Night, Act II, Scene V remind me that I am no more than a humble servant of God whom He has called forward, not because of my greatness, but in order for His greatness to be revealed in and through me!

"When I pray in the name of Isa, Y'shua, Jesus, I pray in the name of the only Son of God, whom I now follow. He is the One who can unite us, despite all the divides us. He alone can overcome the hatred and evil that threatens to consume us all and, instead, lead us into genuine and lasting peace.

"We desperately need Him, as the days ahead of us will be quite treacherous and possibly horrific in scope. If I were the same man that assumed the Office of Vice President of the United States six months ago, I would not be standing before you today. I would not have accepted the tremendous responsibility that comes with the office I now hold."

His brow furrowed, the General stepped forward and asked, "Where are you going with this, Mr. President? What do you want to say?"

"However, I am not the same man as I was in January. While my physical appearance and attributes are the same, the essence of who I am has forever changed. I was not a practicing Muslim when I ran for Vice President or when I took the oath of that office. At best, I was an agnostic. At worst, I was an atheist. In my estimation, the god of Islam was cold and calculating. His Qur'an revealed him to be a god of cunning deceit, ill-conceived manipulation, callous recklessness, and unconscionable violence.

"No one who diligently reads and studies the Qur'an can walk away from it and say, 'Allah is a god of peace! Islam is a religion of love and mercy!' One theme, one goal runs through the ramblings of Muhammad and his brutal god: Islam must rule the world—no matter the cost!"

"True!" the General exclaimed! "Maybe you are finally seeing the light, Mr. President!"

"The Qur'an authorizes, commands, and empowers faithful Muslims to fight in jihad as *mujahidin*, warriors for Allah to complete his quest of world dominance. Sometimes, jihad is waged slowly and silently around us, as the process of islamization works in the shadows. What better ways to overcome enemies than to be among them, outnumber them, and eventually eliminate them?"

"This is music to my ears, Mr. President! Strike terror into the heart of your pitiful citizens!" Deeply and savagely, the General laughed.

"The Muslims among us seemed peaceful and harmless to us just a few days ago. But already, the unrest in our cities—the violence being carried out in the name of Allah—is the initial evidence that we have been gravely mistaken about the motives and character of many of our Muslim citizens—even some whom we may consider to be our friends!

"The truly peace-seeking Muslims among us—and they are few in number—are in as much danger as all non-Muslims. Followers of Allah who do not support or fight in jihad will be targeted along with the Christians, Jews, and others outside Islam in America, just as President Paulson warned."

"Excellent! Excellent my young apprentice! You are using the truth to terrify the traitors among us!"

"Many Muslims whom you consider to be peaceful and loyal citizens of the United States are living a lie. They are pretending to be advocates of peace, but all the while they are preparing for war! Abdul's face saddened with his next words. "The vast majority of male Muslim children on your street have been training since the age of six to join the Brotherhood! These children have been learning the ways of terror and jihad. The overwhelming majority of these Muslim males—boys, teens, and men—want to act on their training by attacking you!"

"That's right! Lead them into the horror that awaits them!" The General was back on his feet. He clapped his hands and shouted, "The world will soon be ours!"

"How can I make such statements to you with complete confidence? I have been inside the Muslim war machine. I know its inner workings, its methods, and its ultimate goal! The Muslims in the American armed services may have sworn allegiance to the United States, but the vast majority of them are betrayers in waiting. When the command comes, they will kill as many of the non-Muslim soldiers around them as possible in order for the United States to be incapable of resisting an invasion of the Brotherhood! Muslims, in and out of uniform, domestic and foreign, are perpetual enemies of the United States of America!"

"I could not have said it better myself, Mr. President!" The General was actually dancing around the room!

"President Ronald Reagan fought to end the Cold War with the Soviet Union. He said that that enemy of the United States would lie and kill to accomplish its goal. This statement is even truer now than it was then. As your President, I tell you that Babylon and its General—who may soon be Caliph—has lied, is lying, and will lie to reach his goal! Babylon has killed, is killing, and will kill anyone and everyone who stands in its way of forming a worldwide Caliphate!"

"Clever, Abdul, clever! Use a former's President's words to prepare the people for slaughter!"

"President Reagan also proclaimed that 'Freedom is never more than one generation away from extinction.' I tell you that Babylon wants to make this generation of free Americans the last generation of free Americans!"

"Yes, Abdul! Together we will bring a gruesome end to the despicable institutions of democracy and freedom in the Republic of United States!"

"The Muslim army inside and outside of our land of freedom is only waiting for the command to strike! What you have seen in the streets of America are Muslims who cannot bear to wait for the call to arms! They are so eager to kill and destroy that they wage jihad on the small scale even as I speak to you."

"Yes! Yes! Yes!" was all the General could say.

"The Brotherhood orchestrated the attacks on Palestine, Israel, and the United States. The Brotherhood somehow compromised all the security codes and protocol of the United States and Israel's weapons systems in order to use them against us! However, in Palestine, why did the Brotherhood kill fellow Muslims, a practice strictly prohibited in the Qur'an, chapter four, verses 92 and 93? If the Brotherhood is truly dedicated to Allah, why did the General order the destruction of the Al Aqsa Mosque and the Dome of the Rock—holy sites atop the Temple Mount?

"Reason number one: The General wanted to quash the Palestinians' western-style democracy. Reason number two: The General wanted to frame the United States and Israel for the slaughter. Palestinian lives were eliminated without an ounce of regret as a pretext and launching pad for destroying Israel and then the United States. You see, in the General's mind, the killing of fellow Muslims is justified by the coming annihilation of the 'Great and Little Satans.' Reason number three: The General serve raw power, not Allah! The General will do whatever it takes to lead the Caliphate!"

"Good, my friend! You can reveal my actions as well as my motives! Tell the terrorized Americans—and Israelis too—that their doom has long been plotted!"

"As part of the ultimate plan for destroying Israel and the United States, both Prime Minister Samuel bin Baruch and President James Paulson were to be assassinated before the eyes of the world. When the first attempt on their lives failed, the General modified his plans. President Paulson's presidential jet was used not only to eliminate his life, but it also saved the General from firing more of our own missiles to eliminate the U.S. House and Senate!"

"How sweet to my ears is this telling of our pending victory over the infidels!"

"My fellow Americans, in the second operation I underwent after taking a bullet meant for President Paulson, the surgeon implanted an explosive device in my shoulder! That device was only seconds away from detonating when it was removed from my body! I should not be here, standing before you today. Only by the grace and providence of God, do I live and breathe as your President!"

"By the grace and providence of Allah—if there is a god!"

"When I return to the United States as President, the masked General of the Brotherhood Army, the Muslim who would be Caliph, wants me to declare martial law, abolish the Constitution by executive order, and proclaim that the United States to be Islamerica—an official state in the Caliphate of Babylon!"

The General sang, "I knew all my investments in you would ultimately pay off, Abdul!"

"Meanwhile, the Brotherhood would overwhelmingly attack Israel in mass, whether the Prime Minister has been assassinated or not. With Israel's weapons under the Brotherhood's control, and the Brotherhood already within the borders of Israel and Palestine, the effort to resist would be short lived!"

"I can feel the fright of the Jewish and American infidels even now!" Again, the General sang and danced.

"However, none of what I have just said will take place! I, as your President, do not believe in Allah or Islam, but I do believe in the one and only Son of God, Isa, Y'shua, Jesus, just to mention a few of His glorious Names! He has revealed Himself to me, and I have surrendered my life to Him! I am a brand new creation in Him! I am a son of

God, first and foremost, and as such, I am His appointed leader of the United States—long may its banner of freedom wave!

"Furthermore, the Brotherhood no longer has control over the weapons systems of Israel and America, and the Muslims probably have not yet realized this truth until now! Let us give credit where credit is due: the Mossad, the Israeli intelligence agency, solved the riddle of how the Brotherhood so brilliantly and deviously wrestled control of both our nations' missiles! The weapons systems have been reprogrammed, and with the shutdown of the ultranet in both Israel and the U.S., the Brotherhood no longer has any way of connecting with our missile systems anyway!

"In the attacks on the White House, the Vice President's Residence, the Capitol, the Pentagon, and the National Holocaust Memorial Museum that killed thousands, including the elected leaders of our nation, Babylon had declared war on the United States of America. In destroying the Temple Mount, the Prime Minister's residence, and Yad Vashem, as well as murdering the Israeli Cabinet and an untold number of citizens, Babylon has declared war on the Jewish State.

"Now, a unified coalition of the Americas and Israel will stand side by side as an impenetrable wall against the Muslims army! Should Babylon actually have the capability to launch its own nuclear weapons against Israel, the United States, or any of the other nations in North, Central, or South America, those weapons will be destroyed in flight and a counter nuclear attack will be launched on Babylon, starting with Ankara, the capitol of the Caliphate!

"Let me speak directly to the General of the Brotherhood, the would-be cowardly Caliph who hides behind a veil and a disguised voice: We are not afraid of you! Together, the nation of Israel and the nations of the Americas will rise to defend our people, our lands, and our freedoms! We stand as one for justice, liberty, and the inalienable rights given to us by the One True God!

"That said, I, as the President of the United States, and Samuel Ben Baruch, Prime Minister of Israel, as well as the duly elected leaders of the sovereign, democratic nations of North, Central and South America declare war on the Calphinate of Babylon!

"The only way to avert World War IV is the immediate and complete surrender of Babylon. This is the only olive branch we offer the General, who will undoubtedly be elected the next Caliph of Babylon through the ultranet vote. On the eve of World War IV, our collective and united leaders offer Babylon one last chance at peace, even though its General has already savagely and viciously attacked both Israel and the United States! We have every justification to prosecute war, but we know, at least I know, that the battle belongs to God—the one True God of Abraham, Isaac, Jacob, and Jesus!

"From my own heart, I invite the people of Islam to meet the real Isa, Son of God, who willingly gave His life in sacrifice to forgive our sin and make us one in His unconditional love and grace! Isa is Peace Incarnate! He is the only path to Heaven, and the only way we can live together in peace in this world!

"General, Isa has already paid the price for your sin—yes even your sin! Isa has already forgiven you! The question is will you accept His forgiveness? Will you be transformed from a man filled with darkness and driven by insatiable evil to one filled with light and driven by unconditional love? We can talk tomorrow morning at the mass funeral in Palestine. Yes, you heard me correctly, I will be there!

"But make no mistake, General. Though your sins will be forgiven by Jesus, if you turn to Him in repentance, you must still face the earthly consequences for your genocide. The blood of the innocents cries out for justice.

"Tomorrow morning, General, you will either surrender yourself and the Brotherhood to the allies who are standing against you or you will face our amassed armies and weapons which you cannot defeat! You may think your Brotherhood Army will sweep through Israel, whose total population is only a fourth the size of your 40 million troops. But Israel does not stand alone! Not only does the nation of Abraham, Isaac, and Jacob have many allies in the Americas, she has the greatest of all allies in her Lord and King, the Eternal God!"

The General's screams echoed throughout the streets of Palestine.

"Thus does Allah seal up the hearts of those who understand not."
Qur'an 30:59

CHAPTER 85

UNEXPECTED OPPORTUNITY...

S ol, Ahava, Mark, Ariel, and Grace discussed Abdul's bold and challenging speech. Each of them commented on the courage he displayed. Sol said, "Let's walk outside and continue our conversation. The President and Prime Minister need to talk with the allies in the Americas. We can catch some fresh air before it gets too dark."

Everyone followed Sol's lead. When they opened the door to exit the building, they were met by what seemed to be a sea of reporters. The group ended up having an impromptu press conference, with the Knesset doors as the backdrop.

One Islamic reporter asked Mark, "How do you feel, Pastor Basel, now that the General has issued a personal vendetta, a *fatwa*, on you and your family?"

Without batting an eye, Mark answered, "We are trusting in Isa for His protection because we cannot trust in man. As Muslims have permeated every part of our society, we really don't know who we can trust. Even so, Isa is a Friend indeed. He remains with us through all circumstances and trials. Isa has brought us this far. He will not abandon us now or ever, for that matter."

"Do you hate the General who killed your parents, tried to kill you and your daughter, and swears he will kill your entire family?"

Mark smiled. "I must confess, it would be easy to hate him. In light of all the General has done, human nature would lead me to hatred. Nonetheless, I do not hate the General, because my nature has been changed. I now live by the Spirit. And through the Holy Spirit I can

434

and do love my enemies, pray for them, and even do good for them. Thus, the unconditional love that flows to me from Isa, I, in turn, allow to flow through me to the General. I am praying that he will realize that his present path leads only to darkness and death. Isa longs to lead him to Light and Life!"

The same reporter turned to Grace. "How about you? Do you hate the General and the people who kidnapped you and treated you so miserably?"

Grace asked the Lord to speak through her, as she was overwhelmed by the sudden attention. "Like Dad said, it would be easy to hate, but I choose to remember that Isa allowed Himself to be crucified to forgive the General and those who kidnapped me—just as He gave His life to forgive me.

"I must admit I was scared at times, when I was kept in the dark, threatened, and did not know what was going to happen to me next. Being trapped in the dark with someone who wants to use and abuse you is frightening. Still, even in my fear, I did not resort to hatred. Instead, I prayed for Isa to give me strength and to protect me. I asked Him to fill me with His courage and empty me of my fear. I knew, even if the kidnapers killed me, that I would be in Heaven. I pitied them because they are bound for a horrible place without Isa."

The Muslim reporter said, "How are we supposed to believe you and your father? You really want to see the General dead, and we know it! What you are saying is impossible."

"Oh no, it is not impossible," Grace responded. "All things are possible with Isa!"

An Israeli reporter addressed Sol. "Rabbi, you worked so hard for peace with the Palestinians, yet now we know all of the negotiations led to nothing. The Temple Mount, most of the Jewish Quarter of Old Jerusalem, and the City of David no longer exist. What do you have to say to your fellow Orthodox Jews who told you from the beginning that you were wasting your time in the negotiations? Do you feel responsible for the loss of life and Jewish history?"

The last part of that question stabbed through Sol's heart. He had not considered his possible responsibility in the untold number of deaths and destruction of the holy sites.

As Sol was lost in the thought, the reporter said, "Rabbi Ben Israel, are you going to answer my questions?"

Still a bit discombobulated, Sol fumbled for words for a few seconds. Then, clarity of thought prevailed. "I would agree that I wasted my time trying to negotiate peace!" Sol said with unexpected certainty. Then he said, "My role in the peace negotiations was to represent the Jewish religious interests and protect the very holy sites that have been destroyed!

"Our Lord tells us repeatedly through His Scriptures that we must not divide the Land because the Land belongs to Him. He gave us the Land as an inheritance. Be that as it may, we only inherit something from a father after his death. Seeing that our God is still very much alive, we have not and never will inherit the Land. But we can indeed possess the Land as God calls us His children. As we are part of God's family, He shares His Land with us as our own.

"That being said, to answer your question, I must realize and admit that I was wrong to allow our Lord's Land to be divided. Therefore, I confess that I do bear responsibility for the consequences of giving *HaShem's* Land away—The Land that only He can give or take. I was wrong to even remotely think that we could buy peace by giving away His Land that we do not own outright. I have blood on my hands!"

A Muslim reporter followed up on Sol's confession. "If you are guilty, if you are responsible at least in part for the lives that were lost Sunday, what punishment do you deserve?"

"Deserve?" Sol reflected on the question and his culpability in the deaths of so many people—some of them fellow Jews. "I deserve death! I deserve to die for my sinful arrogance in my efforts to secure peace. Even if no lives had been taken, I would still be guilty of giving away Y'shua's Land."

Sol paused for a moment, wondering if he should say what was really on his heart. He decided that he should use this moment to proclaim his new faith. "Who or what can atone for my sin? We no longer have a Temple in which to make the sacrifice on *Yom Kippur*, the Day of Atonement. In fact, when was the last sacrifice made in the Jewish Temple? More than two thousand years ago—when the Temple still stood! How are my people and I supposed to atone for sin without a Temple in which to make sacrifices? We had hoped to build a third Temple atop Mount Moriah where the first two Temples stood."

Sol lowered his head and shook it from side to side. "We must realize that the Romans did not destroy the second Temple and stop our ability to make sacrifices in it! *HaShem* Himself tore down His own Temple because those sacrifices offended Him!"

As several Jews in the sea of reporters gasped, Sol breathed deeply, and then continued, "*HaShem* was offended because He had already offered the Ultimate Sacrifice to forever atone for sin. He sent Y'shua to be the final Sacrifice for Jews and Gentiles alike! The Messiah came, and my people—His people—rejected Him, just as they had rejected the prophets before Him. The Sanhedrin condemned Him to death for being who He claimed to be: the very Son of God in human flesh! They were blind to the fact that He had fulfilled each prophesy made about the Messiah in the Tanakh—save what He will fulfill on His return—just as I was blind for all my 85 years until now!"

The Islamic reporter's mouth hung open, as he was so surprised by Sol's words that he could not fully comprehend or respond to them.

Hence, Sol continued, saying, "When the Temple was yet standing, when Y'shua died on the cross, the earth shook and the veil in the Temple was torn! God tore that veil to the Most Holy Place because no more lamb's blood needed to be brought into that room above the Foundation Stone. Y'shua atoned for my sin, the Jews' sin, your sin, and everyone in the world's sin when He, the Lamb of God, was crucified in agonizing sacrifice. He took His own blood into the Holy of Holies in Heaven to atone for our sin once and for all!

"Consequently, Y'shua has forgiven me for my ignorant clinging to a past that can never be brought back as well as my culpability in dividing His Land. The destruction of the Temple Mount was the only way for me to see my foolishness.

"Now that I am forgiven, now that my name is forever written in the Lamb's Book of Life, do I feel responsible for the death and destruction? Not anymore! I am forgiven!

"Your General is the one who decided to kill and devastate. Even if he was God's instrument of discipline for Israel, the General was more than willing to maim, kill, and destroy!

"I feel responsible that I have lived this long without recognizing the truth! How many people—how many of my people—have left this life clinging to false hope? The Messiah is our only path to the Father! Now that I know the truth, I must work in whatever time I have left to proclaim that truth! Y'shua *HaMashiach* is returning for His faithful followers! I must prepare my people to be ready to meet Him! I must help you and everyone to receive Y'shua's forgiveness before it is too late!"

The reporter just stared at Sol, not knowing how to follow up on what he just revealed. So he turned to Ahava. "What do you have to say about your husband betraying his faith?"

Ahava was taken by surprise. She had intently listened to Sol give his first public acknowledgement of his faith in Y'shua. Now, it was her turn! Ahava's eyes met Ariel's eyes. Ariel walked to stand beside Ahava and hold her hand. Ariel's confident smile gave Ahava the courage to speak.

"I have longed and prayed for the Messiah to come ever since I was a little girl. Now, I know that He came many centuries before I was born! I believe what President Abdullah just said in his speech after taking the oath of office. Y'shua is the Peace of God in human flesh! Y'shua is our only hope for the forgiveness of sin. Y'shua is the only way that all the peoples of the world can live together in peace!

"The Day of Atonement does not come once a year, but once in all eternity! The Day of Atonement was that dark day when Y'shua poured out His Holy Blood to blot out our sins! He was the unblemished, sinless Lamb of God. As my husband just told you, Y'shua's blood holds our atonement. The Innocent willingly gave His life for the guilty. Now, as my husband said, our names are written in the Lamb's Book of Life, not for a year, but forever!

"I feel like the old woman, I believe Anna was her name. She was 84 and always at the Temple, always seeking the Messiah, awaiting His coming. When Y'shua as a baby was brought to the Temple for His dedication, Anna saw Him and thanked God that she lived to see the Messiah!

"I, too, am 84, and I have been searching for the Messiah, waiting for Him to come! Now, I also have met Him, and I too praise God and rejoice. Whatever time I have left on this world, I dedicate it to Y'shua so I can join Sol in telling our people—and your people—that the Messiah has come and will return! We can even join Pastor Mark in sharing the good news about Isa with the people of Babylon!"

Just when she appeared to be finished, Ahava said, "Oh! And I am looking forward to being baptized!" Ahava turned to embrace Ariel. They shed joyful tears on each other's shoulders. Even as they continued to hold each other tightly, another Israeli reporter asked Ariel,

"Don't you feel as though you have betrayed your faith and your people?"

Ahava released Ariel so she could answer the question. Gently, Ariel said with a smile, "How have I betrayed either my faith or my people? I was born a Jew. I remain a Jew! I follow the Jewish Messiah! If I were to deny Y'shua, then I would betray my faith and my people! As it is, I found the fulfillment of my Jewish faith in Y'shua! He is the only One who obeyed God completely—the only One to fulfill the Law! All of us have broken God's Law and broken His Covenant made through Moses.

"With Y'shua, we have a New Covenant with God, because Y'shua completed the old one. This New Covenant was prophesied by Jeremiah. These are words God spoke in the Hebrew Bible through Jeremiah, chapter 31 and verse 31: *'See, a time is coming—declares the Lord—when I will make a New Covenant with the House of Israel and the House of Judah.'*

"This New Covenant is not written on tablets of stone, as the first Covenant was. This New Covenant is written by God on our hearts, for it is a Living Covenant! The Old Covenant of Moses condemned us for our sins, but the New Covenant of Y'shua forgives us of our sins!"

Then Ariel looked compassionately into the eyes of the reporter and said, "If I betrayed Y'shua *HaMashiach*, I would have no hope!"

The interviews abruptly ended. Pursued by *Shin-Bet* agents, a van filled with jihadists raced by the impromptu news conference. The terrorists peppered reporters and believers alike with wand pulses.

The new, black, cylindrical weapon developed jointly by the U.S. and Israel did look like a wand, as it was easy to hold in one hand and easy to aim. The wand could fire electromagnetic pulses that could be used to stun and disable human beings and animals at distances that hand held weapons had never reached before. Like smart bullets, the wand's pulses were locked into their target, though the pulses could not penetrate metal.

On the wand's sustained setting, its electromagnetic force could be an invisible shield, protecting the holder of the wand from attack and other weapons fire. When on its most intense setting, the electromagnetic pulses emitted from the wand could kill by pulverizing human flesh, as well as destroy objects by obliterating them into thousands of pieces.

However, the wand had not yet been released to U.S. or Israeli soldiers, so how did the Muslims acquire these weapons? Regardless of the answer, no one outside the Knesset doors had time to even consider what had hit them as they fell to the ground. The most intense electromagnetic burst a wand could produce hit one reporter! His body disappeared into thin air!

Without warning, the force of repeated pulses stunned Ahava and threw her against the Knesset doors. After her body hit the wooden beams, she slumped to the pavement, motionless and bleeding!

Shouts of *"Yalla, yalla, yalla!"* (Hurry, hurry, hurry!) and *"Allahu Akbar!* There is no God but Allah!" filled the air as the van sped away, with the *Shin-Bet* agents still in hot pursuit! The surgeon who implanted the explosive device in President Abdullah's shoulder was in that van.

Sol lied on the ground, calling for Ahava. When he saw her still, bloodied body, he prayed, "No, *Adonai!* No!"

"... 'All who draw the sword will die by the sword.'"
Matthew 26:52

CHAPTER 86

A MOURNING TO REMEMBER. . .

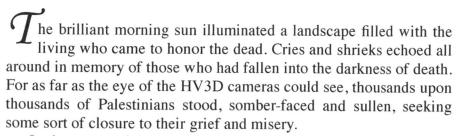

*T*he brilliant morning sun illuminated a landscape filled with the living who came to honor the dead. Cries and shrieks echoed all around in memory of those who had fallen into the darkness of death. For as far as the eye of the HV3D cameras could see, thousands upon thousands of Palestinians stood, somber-faced and sullen, seeking some sort of closure to their grief and misery.

In the center of the massive crowd stood the leaders of Palestine, Israel, and the United States, representatives of some of the Babylonian states, dignitaries from the countries of the newly formed American Alliance, and, of course, Imam Zaahir and the General. Each leader was surrounded in turn by his security forces. The officials stood over one open grave which symbolized that the Palestinians died as one.

Facing Mecca, Addar said, "Welcome to all who have come to honor the Palestinian *shahids,* our noble Caliph, and his most trusted men." Then he said, "Before we pray the *Salat al-Janazah*, our funeral prayer for our fallen brothers and sisters, the General would like to address us."

Dressed in full military regalia, the General stepped forward. His face yet veiled, his voice yet distorted, the General announced, "To set the record straight, I must reply to what the newly sworn-in United States President alleged last night."

The General continued, shouting, "We all know that the Jews are no more human than monkeys or pigs are human. We all know that the words of a brother who recants his faith in Allah—Most Gracious, Most Merciful—for a false religion cannot be trusted!"

Pointing his finger directly at Abdul, the raging General added, "I tell you, do not believe the words of the infidels standing among us this morning. They desecrate this holy site where our heroes will be remembered! Neither our noble Caliph nor I ordered the destruction that ended in their deaths of our fellow Muslims! We grieve with the countless families whose lives were taken from them by the infidels better known as Jews and Christians!

"Today, Palestine will take its rightful place as a state in the Babylonian Caliphate—despite the gruesome, unwarranted attack perpetrated by such infidels as these! Unfortunately, the foul leeches who stand among us also murdered our Caliph, Sanaullah bin Laden!" The security teams of the President and Prime Minister prepared for the worst, should the General's hateful remarks cause the crowd of thousands to turn violent.

"We could not bring the bodies of our beloved Caliph and his valiant bodyguards to Palestine this morning. Their grieving families asked instead to bury their dead in private ceremonies, away from the prying eyes of the idolaters and hypocrites!"

With those words, Sam and Abdul's eyes met. The missing bodies proved to them that the General's executioners had assassinated bin Laden.

"Although we have only one grave before us today, we have not found sufficient human remains to take up the space of even one body. Still, the symbolism of this one grave shows that we are of one heart and mind against our enemies, whose leaders have the audacity to come here today!"

As the General escalated his diatribe, the security teams again felt the threat to their leaders might turn physical.

"We know that the Jews were once chosen, yet the fools rejected Allah, Most Gracious, Most Merciful. Consequently, Allah rejected them! The Christians have lied and assigned Allah partners and tried to belittle him by making him a father who had relations with an earthly wife who bore a son! These miserable flesh-eaters are likewise rejected along with the swine Jews. They share a common fate in this life and the next—death and unending punishment!

"The word 'Islam' means 'surrender to Allah,' while 'Muslim' means 'one who submits to Allah.' These two infidels among us from the Great and Little Satans, along with their trusted bodyguards, will one day submit to Allah, whether by choice or by force! Our *shahids* cry out from Paradise for their blood! Our heroes demand these guilty bloodsuckers to surrender to Allah—Most Gracious, Most Merciful, the only true god!"

Normally, the Muslim crowd would have shouted and praised Allah, but on this morning, they remained silent. Abdul wondered why. Sam found himself puzzled as well.

Without further insult or incitement, the General ended his poisonous proclamation. Silence continued to hang in the air as Addar began the prayers.

One of the holovideographers zoomed in on Addar as he shouted in Arabic, "We are not gathered at the mosque today, but what will now be a graveyard. As you see, we have no body in the one grave that represents the countless bodies of faithful Muslims—including our Caliph and his protectors—who lost their lives in sudden death at the hands of Allah's enemies, at the hands of our enemies! So what do we say on such an occasion, on such a day of gloom as this when we have neither mosque nor bodies?

"While the *Farzi Kifaye* says each one of us gathered here is not required to say the funeral prayer, the *Salat al-Janazah,* let us not forsake the privilege of speaking to Allah today! Instead, let all of us, as one, join our voices together as another symbol of our unity before the one and only god! I will speak the words, some of them adapted especially for today, and you can repeat them together. We will join our voices to those of our fellow believers who are watching us from far flung places! Let us turn to Mecca as we raise one voice to Allah!"

The shuffling of thousands of feet sounded like water running down a mountainside. Addar paused long enough for everyone to be in the proper position.

Then, he said in Arabic, "I bear witness that there is not god but Allah! *Allahu Akbar!* Lord of the Worlds, give these who have left us safe passage to you and certain refuge from the cursed Satan!" The crowd thundered the words to Allah in unison.

At different points in the ritual prayers Addar turned his head to the right or left, and those assembled did the same. Neither Abdul nor Sam knew what Addar was saying. Likewise, neither did most of the Muslims who repeated the words of the prayer, as they did not speak Arabic.

"Allah, Most Gracious, Most Merciful, be especially merciful to those gathered here, whether alive or dead, present or absent from us, young or old, male or female. Bestow your forgiveness to these who are your *shahids*. We know not all their names, but you know all there is to know about them." Again, the mass of mourners repeated the imam's words.

As they finished speaking, a loud cry arose from one of the General's bodyguards. One of the holovideographers zeroed in on the screaming Muslim. At first everyone thought it was an expression of grief. However, the bodyguard charged toward the General. The brute tackled the masked man of Babylon's Brotherhood Army and the two of them fell into the open, eight foot deep grave!

A spilt-second later, fire and earth flew from the pit, as the bodyguard detonated the bomb he wore under his uniform! The explosion forced Abdul, Sam, Addar, along with all the other dignitaries and their security teams to the ground!

"But because of their breach of their Covenant, We cursed them, and made their hearts grow hard: They change the words from their (right) places and forget a good part of the Message that was sent them, nor wilt thou cease to find them barring a few—ever bent on (new) deceits: But forgive them, and overlook (their misdeeds): For Allah loveth those who are kind. From those, too, who call themselves Christians, We did take a Covenant, but they forgot a good part of the Message that was sent them: so We estranged them, with enmity and hatred between the one and the other, to the Day of Judgment. And soon will Allah show them what it is they have done."
Qur'an 5:13-14

CHAPTER 87

THE MOST EXPENSIVE GIFT. . .

❖❖❖

*O*nce they rose from the ground, the security teams removed the President, the Prime Minister, and all the leaders from the gravesite that now bore the remains of the General and his assassin. Who knew if another suicide bomber was in the crowd? Who knew how the mourners would react to the General's sudden execution?

Both Abdul and Sam rushed to the Prime Minister's limousine. Once on its way, the long, black impenetrable vehicle muddled through the packed and chaotic streets of East Jerusalem.

Sam turned on the HV3D. He and Abdul watched as the Palestinians ran away from the gravesite at a frenzied pace. Panic among the thousands left many trampled underfoot. In the mass hysteria, many would suffer injury or death.

Abruptly, preparations for an interview with the grieving First Lady, Hope Paulson, interrupted the coverage of the assassination of the General. Back in the states, at an undisclosed location, Hope, sat down for a one on one exclusive interview with an international Islamic news service. No one on her staff understood why she chose to give her first interview to the Muslims. Her only caveat required that the interview be broadcast live and in its entirety.

The Muslim reporter, Kaashif Shajee had been kind and pleasant to her as his crew set up for the interview. Hope prayed she could keep her emotions in check, no matter what the journalist asked her. She had no preview of Kaashif's questions or even the topics he would cover.

The anchor at the studio somewhere in Babylon made a segue from the coverage of the murder of the General by the suicide bomber, one of his trusted bodyguards, to Hope, the widowed former First Lady whose husband was killed by trusted pilots of Air Force One. He said, "As Babylon stands in shock over the murder of the General following so closely on the heels of the Caliph's assassination, we now move to the United States, another traumatized nation, which grieves its assassinated President—along with many other elected officials. The Americans cannot remove the images of Air Force One crashing into Capitol Hill from their scarred psyches. Correspondent Kaashif Shajee is sitting with President Paulson's widow, Hope Paulson, somewhere in the U.S.. Kasshif?"

"Thank you, Muhab. Ladies and gentlemen, we have a unique opportunity tonight, as I sit here with Hope Paulson. In this, her first interview since her husband's tragic death, we will talk about her personal anguish and what her future holds."

The holovideographer zoomed out to a two shot of Kasshif and Hope. "Mrs. Paulson, may I have the privilege of addressing you by your first name?"

"Of course," Hope replied, her voice sounding weaker to her than she expected. She silently prayed for the Lord to fill her with strength.

"Thank you. Hope, did you see Air Force One crash into the Capitol Building in the live scenes that were viewed around the world?"

All the muscles in Hope's body tensed at once, but she did not show the stress as she answered quietly, "Yes, I saw what happened as it happened."

"How did you feel at that moment, Hope?"

Biting her lip as she inhaled deeply, Hope answered, "I was numb, at first. My heart could not process what my eyes witnessed. In shock and disbelief, I could not accept what flashed before my eyes! James, the boys, and I would have been back together that evening—just a few hours after Air Force One landed." With her bottom lip quivering, Hope paused for a moment before adding, "Everything changed dramatically at that moment of impact! How does a soul respond when all of life changes in an instant?"

"Has the numbness worn off?" Kaashif gently asked.

Her eyes rolling around the room, then centering again on the reporter, Hope replied, "Somewhat. Reality can only be avoided for so long. Our boys did not see the crash. So I tried to tell them what happened as calmly as I could. I held them close as I described what happened. They stared at me in disbelief. They wanted to see the. . . probably needed to see the. . . the assassination of their father."

Hope squeezed the arms of her chair with both hands. She then confided, "Thus, I watched everything with them. I realized they would never see their dad again in their lifetimes. I realized that I would never see my husband again on the face of this earth. I would not even see his body at his funeral. I still find it hard to come to grips with the fact that I am now a widow."

In her sadness, Hope hesitated as she swallowed hard, fighting back tears. "The boys and I hugged each other and wept together." As a tear streamed down her cheek, she said, "If the General has a wife, I know how she feels right now—and what she cannot yet feel!" The First Lady discretely wiped her eyes.

Kaashif, somewhat surprised by Hope's compassionate comment, moved on to his next question. "Who do you believe killed your husband?"

The reporter's inquiry came so quickly and sounded so matter-of-fact to Hope that she had to think a moment before answering. "I have listened to the conversations between the tower at the Air Force Base and the cockpit. Obviously, the pilots, who had flown Air Force One for five different Presidents, were landing manually and ignored all the directions from Andrews. Obviously, they were Muslims who had been placed in positions of upmost importance. However, no one knew they were Muslims for all those years. Today, all Muslims are not Arabs. We have Muslims of all races and languages.

"These particular American Muslims were more than willing to end their own lives along with all the senators, representatives, James' Cabinet officials, and the many others in the Capitol Building. They were apparently eager to give up their lives with those of Chief of Staff Eddie Murdock, the security team, the White House staffers, and, of course, James."

Hope turned her eyes away from the reporter who was staring blankly at her. She said, "The pilots' shouts of *'Allahu Akbar!* There is no God but Allah!'* proved that they felt like they were making a great victory for Islam! They seemed quite happy to kill and be killed."

"How do you feel about those Muslim pilots who obliterated the body of your husband into millions of tiny pieces before a worldwide audience?"

The coldness of the question sent shivers down Hope's spine. She literally shook in her chair before saying, "I feel sorry for them. They flew that jet through the very Gates of Hell where they will spend eternity apart from God."

Unsure of how to relate to her answer, Kaashif just stared at Hope for a few pensive moments before asking his next question. "What do you mean by saying you feel sorry for the pilots and that they will spend eternity apart from God? These men rejoice in the shade of Paradise, with rivers flowing beneath! Allah has rewarded them richly!"

Hope felt a bit more in control of the conversation and spoke with a little more confidence. "No, Kaashif. These two undercover terrorists will never see Paradise. They wasted their lives in their conscienceless killing of my husband—and so many other patriots. I feel sorry for them as they face an eternity of dark, haunting regret."

Kaashif moved his chair closer to Hope and extended his hand toward her, waving it from side to side. "Surely, Mrs. Paulson, you realize that an infidel, if you will pardon the term, one who refuses to follow the one and only true religion, deserves death. Both the Qur'an and Sharia Law say the killing of such an infidel is virtuous and just. These two pilots are heroes, *shahids* of Allah, and celebrate in the Gardens of Paradise, free from all regret and matters of conscience!"

Hope felt her Lord's strength rising in her to meet this reporter as his point of error. Calmly, but firmly, she said, "While you may consider the pilots to be heroes, Kaashif, I consider them to be. . . victims of their own choice to follow a false religion.

"What does your name mean, Kaashif?"

The unexpected question caused the reporter to subconsciously withdraw from the former First Lady. "Discoverer," he reluctantly answered.

"What a fitting name! You have the opportunity to discover the eternal forgiveness that the two pilots forfeited. You can avoid an eternity of solitary and sorrowful regret. You can choose to live, now and forever, in the mercy and grace of Isa, as I do. I already live up to my name, Hope. Despite my pain and grief, I am filled with the hope of seeing James again, face to face! I am filled with the hope of Heaven—and this hope does not disappoint!"

Straightening his back and waging his forefinger at the widowed First Lady, the Muslim reporter countered by angrily saying, "You have insulted me, the pilots, and all of Islam! You should die for your crime committed before the eyes of the world! You, most unfortunate soul, will join your husband in the eternal flames prepared by Allah for all infidels!"

Ignoring his anger as well as his condemnation, Hope compassionately said, "I have no desire to insult you but to save you. I want to help you discover the truth about Isa and His salvation. If no one tells you and all Muslims that you follow a false, powerless, empty, hate-filled, and violence-driven religion, then you will spend eternity apart from God! If I and other believers in Isa do not point out to you that you are on the wrong path, we will be held accountable for your fate! To Muslims, Isa is only a prophet of Allah. To Christians, Isa is the one Son of God who suffered to atone for our sins, who rose from the grave, and who offers all people of this world forgiveness and eternal life!"

With his fists clinched and the indignation in his voice rising, Kasshif responded, "Mrs. Paulson, are you telling me that you do not hate the Muslim pilots that killed your husband in such a horrific fashion?"

"Let me tell you this, Kaashif. I follow Jesus, whom you call Isa. He is the epitome of unconditional love. Jesus dwells in my soul. He is Saviour, Lord, and King of my life. With the boundless and unlimited eternal love of Jesus living in me, how could I hate those pilots? How could I hate the people who destroyed the White House intending to kill me and my children? Jesus loves them, so I love them, also. His love flows through me to them—and even to you, for that matter! Until their very last breath they could have come to Jesus for salvation and life. Instead of bearing words of praise to Allah on their lips, the two pilots could have borne pleas of repentance and confession to Jesus on their lips. While they died praising the false god of a lifeless religion, you, on the other hand, still have time to seek the true God of Eternity!"

Kaashif had begun the interview, planning to bring Hope to her knees. Instead, she had turned the tables on him. In retaliation, the incensed reporter asked, "Did not your husband die apart from the Saviour you cling to so desperately? President Paulson was known as an independent thinker, a political gambler, even a fool who had no time for Isa!" Then, with unmasked cruelty in his sharp tone, he asked, "Where is your hope now, Hope, for your dead and suffering husband?"

Hope did not respond with resentment, but actually smiled broadly. "I know something you do not know!"

"And what do you claim to know, Hope?" the reporter asked with sarcasm seeping from his words.

"I know what happened on Air Force One before it crashed into the Capitol Building. James and I had the most important conversation in our married lives—in his entire life. He told me that he had prayed before giving his last address to the nation. He asked God for wisdom and confidence, peace and purpose. James said the moment he finished the prayer—just as he was about to speak—he felt a sense of calm he had not known before, and would have never imagined possible in the circumstances in which he found himself. James said he felt our Lord guiding Him as he spoke, even giving him words he had not planned to say!

"After his speech, James realized that the living God had answered his prayer. At that point, my husband fell under the conviction of the Holy Spirit. In one moment, James came face to face with all the sin he committed in his life. In that same moment, James surrendered his guilt and sin to the mercy and grace that Jesus offered him!

"At first, James found it difficult to believe that Jesus could actually forgive him for all his bad choices and especially his denial of Jesus' existence. That notwithstanding, James humbly confessed his sin to Jesus in repentance! My husband began a brand new life, with a clean slate! Such is the transforming power of the love and forgiveness of Jesus!"

Skeptical and irritated over the direction the interview had taken, Kaashif challenged Hope saying, "So you are telling me that in the hours before his death, President Paulson conveniently became a follower of Isa?"

"Not conveniently," Hope responded happily, "miraculously!"

Shedding any and all sense of pretense, the Islamic reporter blurted out, "And I suppose you have forgiven those Muslim pilots who gladly killed your bone-headed, foul-mouthed, weak-kneed, sniveling infidel of a husband?"

Unshaken, Hope answered with love in her words, "Jesus gave His life—in horrid agony for my sin—so that He could forgive me. Jesus did the same for everyone in this world—Muslim, Jew, Hindu, Buddhist, agnostic, atheist, and everyone else alike! Jesus forgave every single soul when He was sacrificed for our cumulative sin!"

Energized by the Holy Spirit, Hope noted, "Two questions face everyone in this world. One, will we accept that forgiveness that Jesus purchased with His own suffering and Blood? Two, will we allow the gift of His forgiveness to also flow through us to those who hurt us and sin against us? You see, Kasshif, when we receive Jesus' loving forgiveness, we are transformed by it! We become channels, vessels, conduits of His forgiveness. We know the cost of our forgiveness to Jesus—His very life and breath. As His followers, we are willing to lay down our lives as well, dying to our own rights, to choose to forgive and seek redemption for the ones who hurt us, rather than choosing to hate them and seek revenge!

"This loving forgiveness is why Isa's followers do not back down from the persecution they suffer at the hands of terrorists. These modern day disciples pray their emulation of Jesus' example will bring souls like yours to Isa in repentance and confession, so that they and you can know the incredible hope and peace of life free from guilt and shame—life eternal with joy complete!"

The maddened Muslim stood and shouted, "You have forgiven the pilots that killed your miraculously converted, yet still condemned husband? You have forgiven and forgotten what agony they brought to him as well as to you?"

Hope put her hands together and touched her chin. Then, leaning toward the spiteful reporter standing in front of her, she said, "If I could forget what happened, I would not need to forgive! As it is, I cannot forget what happened, Kaashif!

"As such, I also am certain that Jesus, who knows and remembers everything, likewise cannot forget what happened to James, the others on Air Force One, and those in the Capitol Building. In fact, Isa cannot forget what happened in His own execution! Amazingly, while yet hanging on the cross, in the midst of physical and spiritual pain that we cannot even imagine, Jesus prayed for the forgiveness of those who nailed His body on those beams for all to see!"

Pleading with the reporter, Hope told him, "Kaashif, your sin and my sin and the sin of everyone on the face of this earth who ever lived or ever will live nailed Isa to that cross! As such, His prayer for forgiveness extends to each of us. You as well as anyone and everyone on earth can receive that forgiveness and start a new life!"

Smiling and crying simultaneously, Hope added, "Through forgiveness—as I let Isa forgive through me—the memory of what happened to James will one day no longer bring me pain. Jesus already chooses not to hold our sins against us—to no longer remember our sin—when we receive His forgiveness. He cannot forget our sin, although He can choose to no longer recall it! We can make the same choice to not hold others' sins against them, as His Spirit empowers us to do so. Though we cannot forget their sin and our pain, we can, like Jesus, choose not to remember!"

Hope pulled up the sleeve of her black dress and showed Kaashif her right arm. She asked him, "Do you see this six inch scar on my arm?"

"Yes," Kaashif replied with frustration, wondering what point she would make next.

"When I was in college, I was attacked one night by a man with a knife. He wanted my purse, but I hesitated in giving it to him. The purse was a gift from my mother, and she had died only a few weeks earlier. In addition, the purse contained several items of hers that I cherished. They were priceless to me and would be worthless to him.

"When I refused to let go of the purse, the thief cut it off my shoulder and, in the process, slashed my arm. That man, found and arrested the next day, had destroyed the purse and everything precious that it had contained.

"I forgave that man, not because he deserved to be forgiven, but because Jesus had already forgiven him, so how could I to refuse to forgive him? I remember very well that night he attacked me when I look at my scar. But the wound is healed and the scar no longer causes me pain.

"That is how we forgive, even though we cannot forget. While we remember the sin people have committed against us, through forgiveness that memory no longer causes us to suffer!

"On the other hand, when we choose both to remember and not to forgive, we hurt no one but ourselves. We poison our own soul with an evil potion of bitterness, anger, and resentment! Choosing to hate and seek revenge makes for a foul and deadly cancer in our being that slowly eats away all the life we have in us. We become the living dead, knowing nothing but the pain and darkness that haunt our vacant souls!"

Hope placed her hands in front of her, as though handing Kaashif a precious gift. Then, with unquestioned sincerity, she said, "On one hand, Islam thrives on hatred and lack of forgiveness. Allah demands that his followers hate and kill the sin-filled infidels! On the other hand, Isa calls on His followers to love and forgive sinners—even our enemies who have hurt us terribly. Hopefully, through our example, those trapped in their trespasses will accept Jesus' transforming love and forgiveness for themselves, so that they too become vessels of His love and forgiveness to others, so that they become free from the prison and poison within their own souls."

Not missing a beat, Kaashif furrowed his brow and replied, "Hate makes us strong and revenge sets the record straight, as the enemy gets what he deserves!"

With words offered in peace and anticipation, Hope gently countered, "To love and forgive takes far greater strength than hating and seeking revenge. God has all the power of eternity, and His Word says only He can forgive sins. As such, we can only forgive when we allow His forgiveness to flow through us. If God did not forgive, we all would receive what we deserve—death and eternal separation from God. And if our Father did not forgive, I would not be sitting here before you today telling you with all honesty and passion that I have forgiven the men who killed my husband!

"Peter—the most bold of Isa's first followers—once asked Him, 'Lord, How many times must I forgive my brother who sins against me—seven times?' Seven is the number of completion in the Bible, so Peter thought his own answer to his question was good and solid. However, Jesus told Peter not to forgive seven times, but seventy times seven! As God's capacity to forgive is limitless, so we who follow His Son must always allow His love and forgiveness to flow through us— no matter how many times we are wronged, no matter how much pain we endure. As the great Apostle Paul said, 'Love keeps no record of wrongs!'"

Disgusted that he had not managed to break down Hope for the entire world to see, Kaashif suddenly turned to the camera and abruptly ended the interview. In closing, he said, "Once more, we have proven that misguided infidels—who falsely claim Isa is a crucified and resurrected Saviour—will drown in their lies, no matter how sweetly they slide off their tongues! Garish fraudulence and overrated hope only combine to lull fools into the most false sense of security. Hope Paulson, First Widow of the United States, showed herself to be a boldfaced prevaricator today. If only the pilots could have ended her miserable existence when they snuffed the paltry life out of her pathetic excuse for a husband, our ears would not have been poisoned with such noxious venom today!

"In the name of Allah, Most Gracious, Most Merciful, and Muhammad his servant—peace be upon him—this is Kaashif Shajee reporting. Back to you, Muhab!"

The anchor snidely remarked, "Thank you for another great and insightful interview, Kaashif! Truly, the infidels will stop at nothing in the deadly propagation of their evil lies—even using their deceased loved ones to fuel the fire, so to speak!"

Sitting on the edge of his seat, Prime Minister Ben Baruch found in Hope's genuine and tested faith the answers he did not realize he was seeking!

". . . 'Today salvation has come to this house, because this man, too, is a son of Abraham.'"
Luke 19:9

CHAPTER 88

IMPOSSIBLE REALITY. . .

O nce the limo crossed the line into Israel, Sam and Abdul headed straight for the hospital, though neither of them had been injured by the suicide bomber who took the General to the grave with him. Instead, Sam and Abdul went to the hospital to check on Ahava.

The *Shin-Bet* agents had finally stopped the Muslim assailants by shooting out their tires. Yet tragically, as the agents approached the Brotherhood vehicle, the terrorists detonated explosives that instantly killed them and the Prime Minister's agents. The mystery as to how the Brotherhood had acquired the wands died with them, as did the surgeon who implanted the explosive device in Abdul's shoulder.

While en route to the hospital, the President's bullet and surgical wound throbbed. In his security team's rush to ensure his safety, the men had unintentionally grabbed his injured shoulder. Even so, Abdul thanked God for his life, praised Him that the wounds had not reopened, and asked Him to bless Ahava.

Meanwhile, the Prime Minister had been deep in thought since the end of Hope's interview. Abdul broke the silence by asking, "Sam? Are you all right?" Sam had a distant look about him as he tried to refocus on the moment. He replied, "Actually, I feel, most assuredly, better than I have ever felt before!"

Not sure exactly what to make of Sam's comment, Abdul changed the subject. He said, "You and I looked at each other a couple of times this morning while the General was speaking. What were you thinking?

Sam answered, "Two things. One, that the Caliph and his body-guards were beheaded, not shot."

"Agreed! What else crossed your mind?"

"I cannot explain it, but I had the distinct feeling that the General seemed to know he was about to die!"

With a look of amazement on his face, Abdul said, "I had the very same thought!"

"How strange!" Sam noted. "What, if anything, do you make of our observations?"

Abdul exhaled abruptly. "I haven't a clue about the significance of our coinciding opinions!"

Sam laughed at Abdul's frank admission. Then he said, "On a more serious note, do you see a connection between the assassination and the interview with Hope?"

"Yes and no. While Hope had cleared the interview with me, I did not know when it would be aired. I suppose the news director jumped on the General's assassination as a launch pad into the interview, though it seems the General's demise would be the bigger story. Obviously, the reporter planned to entice and expose an angry and bereaved former First Lady. He expected her to lash out at Islam and all believers in Allah. After all, such an interview would only stoke an already blazing fire."

"Were you surprised as to what she revealed about James?"

"Again, yes and no. I had noticed that James was acting differently after our arrival in Israel, but I did not realize the extent of his spiritual transformation. However, I spoke with Hope just before taking my oath of office. She told me that James became a believer in Isa on Air Force One!"

"Do you believe what Hope said is true?"

"Do I believe that James became a follower of Isa? Absolutely! Hope would not be able to make that up. She also would not have been so strong during the interview if what she said was a lie."

"No, I didn't mean to ask if you thought Hope was telling the truth. I mean do you think the forgiveness she spoke of is really possible?"

"Oh yes! Certainly! I have experienced that forgiveness first hand!"

"Sorry, I am not making myself clear. Do you believe she was able to forgive the pilots and the Brotherhood in general for James' death?"

"Now, I see what you are asking. Yes, Sam, I do believe Hope was able to forgive everyone involved with the assassination of James. You see, Hope is absolutely correct when she says that Y'shua's forgiveness transforms you and gives you the ability to forgive others as you have been forgiven by Him. Forgiveness bore a huge price tag for Y'shua. Alone, He bore the physical agony of the scourging and the cross, as well as the greater, spiritual agony of the cumulative consequences of sin. Rejected by His friends and abandoned by God, Y'shua suffered alone—in every sense of the word—as He hung between Heaven and earth! To complete His condemnation for our sin, Jesus even endured the unimaginable torments of hell for us. As it has been explained to me, Jesus stepped out of time when He died. Thus, His three days in hell were like an eternity—the eternity we should spend there.

"Mark can say all of this better that I can convey it to you, but as God is the very definition of holiness, He cannot look upon sin. When Isa—Y'shua—bore all the transgression of humanity, when He became absolute sin, God had to turn away from His own Son. The Sinless One had become sin itself! Thus, for the one and only time in all eternity, the Perfect Son stood apart, cut off from His Holy Father to die in consummate agony and complete isolation.

"When we offer forgiveness, it bears a cost for us, as well. Forgiveness can never be deserved. If it could be earned, it would be called restitution. Truly, the cost of sin cannot be repaid. Instead, forgiveness is offered despite the pain the forgiver has suffered, despite the inability of the transgressor to restore what he has destroyed. Hope vividly and beautifully brought these principles to light today."

Impressed by Abdul's understanding and wisdom, Sam stated, "You certainly have learned a great deal since you have become a follower of Y'shua!"

"I learned a lot about Y'shua before I came to believe in Him as Saviour and Lord. I have a Messianic friend in D.C. who has been talking with me about Him."

"Really? Is she just a friend and nothing more?"

A bit embarrassed by the question, Abdul fumbled for words. "I don't really know. My appreciation of her has certainly grown since my life has changed so dramatically. She, Naomi, talked with me extensively about forgiveness, although I could not understand it until

I fully experienced it for myself. By the way, how did you know my Messianic friend is of the female persuasion?"

Sam smiled and said, "I have my sources, you know." Then, as he contemplated all that Abdul had shared about the mercy and grace of Y'shua, Sam, in an unguarded moment, revealed his soul. "I have so much hatred, anger, and resentment inside of me that I feel like I could explode! I cannot relate to my wife or my children because of the burning desire within me for revenge! I have no peace! If I let go of all this. . ." Sam paused as he searched for words, and as his fists pounded his chest. "If I let go of this consuming passion within me to payback what I and we as Jews have suffered at the hands of the Muslims, I fear I will lose the power that drives my life! I know I cannot express this well, but putting such deep seated and long held emotions into words severely challenges me."

Now Abdul smiled. "You think you will be weak without the hate, anger, bitterness, resentment, and lust for revenge that burns within you. You don't know how to define yourself without it."

"Yes! Precisely! You stated my circumstance perfectly!"

"I felt the same way just a few days ago. But after receiving Y'shua's forgiveness, after I released all my hate, anger, bitterness, resentment, and lust for revenge, I have felt stronger than ever before in my life! The power comes from the freedom Y'shua gave me! All that darkness in me was like a ball and chain in a prison from which I could not escape! Hatred, anger, bitterness, resentment, and lust for revenge do not make you strong but weak!

"On one hand, hatred comes naturally. I don't need any help to refuse to forgive. On the other hand, like Hope said, the power of forgiving someone else must come from Isa Himself. The Jewish Scriptures and the Christian Scriptures both say that only God can forgive sin! God's power is greatest within us when Isa is forgiving others through us!"

Sam sat there, expressionless, as if all emotion had been drained from him. "Abdul, I cannot explain this, but as you spoke to me, I felt all my long-prized hatred, anger, bitterness, resentment, and lust for revenge drifting away! As I listened to you, I said within my soul, 'I want the freedom Abdul has found!" At that moment, I felt the weight and darkness leaving me!"

"Y'shua took your inner desire as a plea for His forgiveness, Sam! You do want Y'shua's forgiveness, don't you?"

"Desperately! More than anything I have ever desired in life! I want forgiveness and freedom from the guilt of my own stupid and deadly choices. Likewise, I want to be free from the weight that comes with my own inability—my own refusal—to forgive others! I want to be free from the hatred and hunger for vengeance that has estranged me from my wife and family—everyone close to me! All the hatred and desire for revenge in my heart consumed me—and left no room for love! I want to forgive so love can be the driving force within me!"

Abdul leaned toward Sam and put his hand on his shoulder. He looked into Sam's weary eyes and asked, "Shall we pray to Y'shua together?"

"Fight them, and Allah will punish them by your hands, cover them with shame, help you (to victory) over them, heal the breasts of Believers"
Qur'an 9:14

CHAPTER 89

SO MANY VARIABLES. . .

*I*n panic mode, Addar hoped his new plan could yet salvage his dreams. As his mind raced, he fully understood that he must think clearly, not only quickly. He considered what he assumed to be his best, if not only option. "With the General out of the picture, the belligerent face of Babylon no longer exists. If the Babylonians vote to make the dead General the next Caliph, then the person who comes in second will be Caliph. Certainly, I can make today's ultranet vote work to my favor."

With the leadership question theoretically solved, Addar next considered the very real threat of war. "Abdul, the traitor to Islam, will lead the Great Satan to fight against his own people, and we cannot defend ourselves, much less emerge victorious! We had counted on Abdul to hand us the United States without any more shots being fired! Now, we neither have political control nor strategic weapons control in America. Furthermore, Israel's Prime Minister yet lives and has regained control of his arsenals. In Babylon, we only have inoperable weapons. Even if they suddenly became functional, we have no satellite weapons' system to direct them. Worse yet, despite our boasts, Goliath cannot yet shut down our enemies.

"I must make a decision. If the Brotherhood no longer has control over U.S. and Israeli weapons, Babylon needs to avoid war—again, at least for the moment. We cannot rely solely on the Muslim members of the U.S. armed forces or the Brotherhood members across that *shirk* nation to defeat the American military. Similarly, we cannot depend on the captive Christian and Jewish scientists, military experts, and engineers to quickly repair our arsenal, weapons system, and satellite network. Either they are purposefully stalling or they are imbeciles as well as infidels! Maybe the General did act too quickly, too soon against our enemies. Maybe the Caliph had been right all along.

"What are the military options?" Addar debated with himself. "How did the infidels discover our means of hacking into their systems? We left no traces. Save one, everyone who participated is dead — willing suicide victims who believe they will receive a great reward in the Gardens of Paradise with the rivers flowing beneath. Were the U.S. and Israeli leaders bluffing? If so, how do I find out without someone going back into the system, which I have no time to do at this point? Besides, with the ultranet down in both Israel and the states, I don't even have access to their weapons systems.

With sweat pouring off his face, even in the chilly air conditioned room, Addar reasoned with himself. "What advantage does Babylon hold over the coalition of Israel and the Alliance of the Americas?"

With little time to contemplate, his answer came quickly, "Effectively, practically, and factually, we have no advantage whatsoever! Despite our plethora of European and Asian weapons and war machines — *uber* tanks, hypersonic fighter jets, and revolutionary naval vessels, our equipment and arsenals offer us no advantage if we cannot mobilize them. Our only tangible asset remains the Brotherhood Army. While 40 million jihadists make a massive and ruthless force, they cannot stand against weapons of modern warfare in an all out assault!"

With his heart beating rapidly, his breaths short and swift, and his head beginning to throb, Addar considered the current actions of Babylon's enemies. "Abdul has declared war! As the General did not surrender to him this morning, the U.S. and the coalition of the Americas' troops will soon deploy to the Middle East and Europe. Even now, fleets, destroyers, strike groups, and special ops units — as well as the land, sea, air, and submarine drones — steam toward the waters of the Persian Gulf and the North Atlantic."

Without further debate, Addar accepted the sobering reality. "We cannot effectively wage war on enemy territory. Instead, we would be forced into a defensive battle on our own land. Given the circumstances, we would lose most if not all of what we have fought so hard to gain!"

Closing his eyes, Addar knew he must stop the progress of Allah's enemies. Short of all out surrender, which was not an option for Muslims, what could the Islamic holy man do to persuade Israel and the Americas to stop their march to war?

Enter Addar the diplomat. "Unlike the General, I am known as a man of peace. I must use this to our advantage. I must create a window of time before war begins."

Immediately, he began calling the President and the Prime Minister. He discovered they were in private consultations as they traveled to the hospital. "Perfect!" Addar thought. "I will meet them at the hospital, show my concern over the piggish Jewish woman, and tell Abdul and Sam that without the General to stop us, Babylon can stand down and peace between our nations can remain. Such a move might cause me to lose stature with the people of Babylon, but that sacrifice will only be temporary. We will live to fight another day. Perhaps this ruse will work. I must try. Do I have a viable alternative?"

As the imam mulled his own question, a smile crept across his face. "I do have a couple of other options! I have unused assets! If I can mobilize those assets to the right time and place, what a stink I could raise! But those tempting possibilities will have to wait until I address the present crisis and buy some time!"

Addar ran downstairs to his car. While driving, he considered how he could enhance his options and enact them in the best scenarios. He began to realize that he had a plan that was absolutely delicious. He praised himself, saying, "Oh what a dastardly deceptive man I have become!"

Within minutes, Addar arrived at the hospital and headed to Ahava's room. As Mark walked into the hallway to ask the nurse a question, he met Addar face to face in the doorway.

With conjured sympathy, the imam said "Pastor Mark, I am so sorry to hear that Ahava was wounded! How is she doing?"

Skeptical of Addar's words and suspicious about his presence at the hospital, Mark replied, "She is recovering well, Addar. Ahava and the rest of us were somewhat protected by the bodies of the reporters. Unfortunately, they absorbed the brunt of the weapon's fire. Ahava was the only one of us who was hit by the electromagnetic pulses of a wand—a weapon developed by the U.S. and Israel that has not yet been released!" Mark's tone turned sarcastic as he said, "I don't suppose you would have any idea of how the Brotherhood might have those weapons in their hands now, would you?"

Seemingly surprised by the question, Addar replied, "Me? Why would I know anything about a new weapon called a wand—or any other weapon for that matter?"

Mark's sarcasm remained, as he said, "Of course, Addar, you are a man of peace! What would you know about acquiring new weapons or the technology for new weapons?"

Addar just stared at Mark, who then asked, "Why are you here? Should not you be with your people, in the wake of the General's assassination—in the wake of the Caliph's assassination as well? Just for the record, who do you foresee succeeding bin Laden now?"

Irritated by Mark, but maintaining a calm exterior, Addar said, "I will be addressing the people of Babylon very soon. They will choose the next Caliph. As for now, I came to see Ahava. How is she?"

Shaking his head, Mark replied with genuine compassion for Ahava, "I just told you that she is recovering well. We praise God that her injuries could be easily treated. The blasts of the wands threw her against the doors of the Knesset. When she fell to the ground she scraped her arm, suffered a mild concussion, and passed out. Though sore, this 84 year old great grandmother is in remarkably good shape. She bled excessively because she takes a daily anticoagulant. Now, the bleeding has stopped, so she should be released soon."

Addar asked, as kindly and patiently as he possibly could, "Can I see her now?"

Mark asked, "Could your mind be distracted by something, Addar? You seem to be nervous, worried! Then again, you must be concerned about your dear friends Sol and Ahava."

"I am focused on Ahava. I merely want to see and speak with my counterparts in the peace negotiations." Addar restrained his desire to lash out at Mark.

"Of course, Addar, you of all people share our immense gratitude for how well Ahava has done since arriving at the hospital!"

With false humility, the imam answered, "My heart brims with empathy and concern for our mutual friend, Mark! You underestimate me and my motives."

Mark replied with cutting insight, "I sincerely doubt that statement, Addar! I imagine that there is much more to you than meets the unsuspecting eye!"

Caught in his own game, Addar looked away from Mark, saying, "Well, if you will not allow me to see Ahava, then I must talk with Sam and Abdul! Time is of the essence, and the matter could not be more urgent."

Mark slyly responded, "I see! You will be addressing all of Babylon? Are you no longer satisfied with being the interim leader of the DROP, Addar? Who would want to be a president or emir, when he could be the head of the worldwide Caliphate instead? After all, the DROP will no longer exist after today, will it? Are you by chance next in line as Caliph of the entire *ummah*?"

Again, Addar did not answer. Looking at the floor, he said, "We need to avoid the war that the General plotted! The people of Babylon have no desire for more bloodshed and fighting. They want to avert World War IV if at all possible!"

"Indeed," Mark responded in soothing tones, "as Caliph you can change the entire focus of Islam. Under your guidance, certainly jihad will no longer be waged against Jews, Christians, apostates, or any other non-Muslim! Certainly, you will bring world peace and even start allowing representative government in Babylon, won't you, Addar?"

The ambitious imam wondered how much Mark knew about him and his plans or if the infidel pastor was fishing, hoping the imam would bite. Either way, Addar chose to ignore Mark's question, asking instead, "Do you or do you not know where I can find the President and the Prime Minister?"

Mark answered, "They are here, in Ahava's room." Still, he did not step out of the way to allow Addar to enter.

Impatiently, Addar once again asked, "Can I go in?"

Mark glanced back at Ahava, who continued to sleep. As Sol walked to the door, Mark suggested to Addar, "Maybe you should ask the patient's husband for permission to enter."

With mounting tension in his words, Addar asked, "What is wrong with you, Mark?"

"The Caliph is dead. The General is dead. Who will Babylon choose as its next Caliph? Neither the Caliph nor the General had any children. Like the Caliph, the General never married. With no blood successors to the Caliphate, what noble leader will head the ever glorious Babylon?"

"Just what are you trying to say, Mark?"

"I think you know exactly what I mean, Addar—or should I say Caliph?"

Sol came to the door and said, "Addar, it is so good of you to come and visit Ahava in her time of need!"

Addar smiled slyly and victoriously at Mark as he moved out of the way for Sol. "Dear friend, you knew I would come!" Nonetheless, those few empathetic words were the full extent of Addar's interaction with Sol. Addar wasted no time, but quickly walked into the room and said, "Abdul, Sam, we must talk! Our time is running out!"

Mark thought, *"You mean your time is running out!"*

"But love your enemies, do good to them, and lend to them without expecting to get anything back. Then your reward will be great, and you will be sons of the Most High, because He is kind to the ungrateful and wicked."
Luke 6:35

CHAPTER 90

AT THE INTERSECTION OF FEAR AND PANIC...

Addar ended up talking with Sam and Abdul for hours. With the losses suffered in the United States and Israel, the two leaders told Addar that they could not pull back from war at this point.

"How do I explain to the American people that we are not going to fight the enemy who used our own weapons against us, has brutally murdered our former President and most of his Cabinet, wiped out the House and the Senate, killed most of our military leaders, and tried to assassinate me? How do we not go to war with the enemy that destroyed the White House, the Vice President's residence the U.S. Capitol, and the Pentagon, not to mention the National Holocaust Memorial Museum?"

Addar stumbled and fumbled for words. He told the new American President, "Could you not convince them that the General did all that, and that with the death of the General, all hostilities will cease?"

Abdul shot back firmly. "Does the elimination of both the Caliph and his General not play into your hands, Addar?"

With no hint of dishonesty on his face, Addar answered, "I have no idea what you may be implying, Mr. President."

Again, Abdul stood his ground, asking, "So all of this killing and mayhem have nothing to do with you and your aspirations?"

Sheepishly, the imam answered, "You and Mark sound much alike this evening. Surely, what plans do I have but to humbly serve my people and my god?"

Sam joined the conversation. "Do you take us for fools, Addar? Have your plans taken an unexpected turn?"

"My plans? What plans do I have?"

Sam, with firmness in his voice said, "Don't play ignorant with us, and don't try to hide behind your religious title! You have long been in the inner circle of the Caliph and the General, have you not?"

Trying to escape from the trap closing in around him, the imam pleaded, "I only served as their religious advisor! I played no role in the war machine! I am a holy man of prayer—a surviving Shia holy man is a sea of savage Shiites!"

"You expect us to believe those pious sounding words?" Sam demanded. "Since when has Islam separated its religion from its jihad? Your Qur'an—your holy book—functions as a war manual!"

Abdul stepped back into the tense discussion, saying, "Let me ask you a question, Addar. Who do you believe killed the General and the Caliph—and why?"

"Who would share such evil plans with the likes of me?"

"So you have no idea who killed the number one and number two men in Ankara, even though you seem to be sitting pretty as the next man in line?"

In self-deprecating tones, the imam answered, "Me? The next Caliph? Why would you even suggest such a possibility?"

Abdul refused to back off, saying, "As an honors graduate from MIT, who also has both a Master's and Doctoral degree in Computer Science from Princeton, you would be a very likely candidate for hacking into computer weapons systems, would you not? After all, you are the creator of the ultranet as well!"

Nervous and sweating, Addar had to find a way to turn this conversation away from himself. He spoke the first words that popped into his head. "Abdul, is it not true that the American people are very suspicious of your possible role in all that has transpired? It seems awfully coincidental that your rise to power and the current threat against the U.S. are happening simultaneously! How easy would it be for the first Muslim as both Vice President and President of the U.S. to find a way into the nation's weapons system and turn those weapons against his long-hated enemies?"

The President stood his ground. "I swear you sound more and more like the General with every word you say, Addar! But you, of all people, know that I had no political ambition before I became Vice President, and you of all people know that the last thing I want is war between Babylon and the U.S.! If anyone would profit from my current position, it would not be me. It would have been the Caliph and the General—and now you! I think the facts put the spotlight right back on you, Addar! After all, haven't you always reminded me that I owe all I have an am to you? Did you not mentor me for your own benefit, to make your ambitions a reality? Don't you crave power, wild and raw?"

Sam, Mark, and Sol were impressed with the aggressiveness and the clarity of thought Abdul demonstrated. Indeed, he seemed to be rising to the call to lead the United States in this, her darkest hour.

Once more, Addar stared blankly at Abdul, though he felt that a caldron of seething anger and flaming fear would soon boil over within him.

Sam added, "Addar, don't think for one moment that Israel's stake in this war in any way falls short of the United States' commitment. Even though we have not suffered anything close to the losses in America, any attack against the U.S. is an attack against Israel!"

Abdul nodded to Sam, indicating his thanks for his commitment to the U.S.. Then Abdul said, "Save for one, the entirety of Sam's Cabinet is dead—beheaded! Untold thousands are dead in Palestine and Israel. It is by the grace of Isa that Sam and I are standing here today, Addar. You took the bullet that had Sam's name on it! A vigilant doctor found an explosive hidden in my shoulder planted by another mystery surgeon who is now dead."

Tiring of Addar's evasive behavior and answers, Abdul demanded, "How can we trust anyone, and I mean anyone, in the wake of so many assassinations here and in the United States? What guarantees could you possibly give us, Addar? Your Caliph is dead. Your General is dead. Who is running Babylon? Who is leading the Brotherhood? Without leadership, aren't Babylon's armies likely to rise up to fight even if we make concessions for peace? Without a leader, might

Babylon disintegrate into lawlessness with many groups battling for power and control?"

Addar caustically answered, "The General called the election for today to avoid the very scenario you just described. As to your questions, I will answer them when the votes are tallied. You both know that war between our nations would produce carnage even greater than that of World War III! I, for one, am going to do everything I can to stop the loss of any more lives, Babylonian, Israeli, and American lives included! Are the two of you willing to do the same?"

The imam's question hung in the air, unanswered.

"(Our religion is) the Baptism of Allah: And who can baptize better than Allah? And it is He Whom we worship."
Qur'an 2:138

CHAPTER 91

BEARING THE NAME OF THE ONE AND ONLY. . .

*M*ark, Ariel, Grace, and Sol, talked with Ahava by her bed, while, near the door, Sam and Abdul continued to discuss Addar's plea. A few moments later, Mark and Sol walked over to their respective leaders. Mark said, "Excuse me, Mr. President. We have a question for you. Ahava will be released from the hospital within the next hour. She and Sol have told me that they wish to be baptized—as soon as possible!"

"That's wonderful!" Abdul exclaimed.

Sam smiled, and asked, "Sol and Ahava are believers in Y'shua?"

"Indeed they are," Mark replied. "With all that is happening, I suppose we never had the opportunity to tell you the news."

"Well I think it is great news, as I too have become a forgiven follower of our Messiah, Y'shua! And I would love to be baptized!"

Mark and Sol stood there in amazement, unable to speak for a moment, until Sol shouted, "Hallelujah! Good news abounds! When were you going to tell me, Sam?" The strapping tall man and the stout short man locked themselves in what looked like a wrestling hold!

Grinning from ear to ear, the Prime Minister replied, "I found Y'shua's forgiveness just before arriving at the hospital—thanks to Abdul's counsel! So, truly, the opportunity to tell anyone has not presented itself until now. Besides, I would have been hesitant to tell you about my new faith in Y'shua! You may have tried to run me out of The Land!"

Sol laughed, "That was the old me, who no longer lives! Truly, I have been forgiven of my foolish past!"

Still smiling, Sam added, "Me, too, old friend!" He locked Sol in another bear hug, lifting his old friend two feet off the ground!

Abdul said, "Mark, I suppose you can baptize us all!"

Mark swallowed hard. "The privilege will be quite humbling," he commented. Then he and Ariel took their turns at hugging Sam, who, caught off guard, laughed out loud.

Sol grabbed Sam by the arm and said, "Tell me more about your decision today."

"After listening to Hope Paulson speak about James' death and her forgiveness of his killers, I talked with Abdul. I have been fighting Y'shua for a long time. Finally, He tore down all my defenses. Abdul led me in prayer to receive Y'shua as my Messiah and King!"

Then, the smile ran away from Sam's face. He asked Sol, "What will be the repercussions of the Prime Minister of Israel being baptized in the Name of Y'shua?"

Sol calmly replied, "Sam, the question you must answer is who has your first allegiance—the people of Israel or the Messiah, Y'shua?"

Sam replied, "I know the answer I should make without hesitation is Y'shua. Nonetheless, our nation stands on the verge of war. Fear runs rampant through the hearts of the Jews. If I am baptized and publicly profess my faith in Y'shua, then I have added another level of uncertainty to the mix. Will the people trust me to lead them?"

Abdul replied to the Prime Minister. "I had to ask myself similar questions, Sam! Would America accept me as their President? Would they even believe that I was no longer a Muslim or would they think I was just using the *taqiyya* doctrine to deceive them into trusting me so that I could bide my time before declaring the U.S. 'Islamerica?'"

Sam hung on each word Abdul said. Sam asked, "What did you decide—how did you decide, Abdul?"

"I asked Isa what I should do. And in that same moment, I had my answer. He removed all my fears and doubts and replaced them with trust and faith that He would guide me! I know He has called me for this moment. Now, He did not say everything from this point on will be easy, but He promised to direct my steps. I follow Isa first. I preside over the United States second—and then, only under His authority! Like Esther in the Scriptures, Sam, our Lord has called and appointed me for such a time as this. I believe He has done the same for you. Ask Him what you should do."

"This is all happening so fast, Abdul. How can I be sure of anything?"

"If Y'shua wants you to lead Israel as His follower, He will make it perfectly clear. Let's pray even now!"

Abdul, Sol, and Mark laid hands on Sam. Mark prayed, "Dear Isa, Y'shua, Jesus, the magnificent Messiah, the Saviour of us all, the true Son of God! My brother Sam needs a clear and defining word from You. He needs to hear from You now, in this very moment.

"Amidst all the cries for war and all the confusion, chaos, and violence of these last days, Sam needs a foundation from which he can move forward. He has freely given his life to You. Now, he asks what You want Him to do next. Do you want Sam to publicly declare His faith and allegiance to You, no matter what consequences may result or do You want Him to wait to make his profession of faith at a time that You see but he does not yet know?

"May Your peace be the sign if he is to follow You in baptism today. Sam is Your forgiven servant, Y'shua. Our friend and brother will follow Your will, Your wisdom, and Your way this day and every day that You offer him on this earth. With our deepest gratitude and our highest praise, we pray in the Name above all other names. Amen!"

The four men remained standing, praying in silence with their heads down and their eyes closed. From the bed across the room, Ahava, Ariel, and Grace continued to silently intercede, too.

The first person to speak was Ahava. "Prime Minister! Y'shua just told me the answer to your question! He says that I need to tell you what He said, because He has given you the same answer. Y'shua's says, 'I have chosen you to lead My people in this hour. When you open your mouth to speak to them, they will hear My Voice! You will be an example of faith for them—faith in their Messiah. I will lead you as you guide them through the days ahead, which I have foreseen. Some will receive your choice to follow Me as a sign for their own decision to trust Me as their Messiah. Others will reject you for your choice. But remember, those who reject you are actually rejecting Me."

Everyone's eyes turned to Sam. He was visibly overwhelmed. His face was drained of all color. He seemed to be in a state of shock. Sol placed his hand on Sam's arm and asked, "What is it, Sam?"

Without changing his expression, Sam said, "Ahava spoke the very words I just heard Y'shua say to me!" He wept and smiled, as his heart overflowed with peace.

"Therefore go and make disciples of all nations, baptizing them in the Name of the Father and of the Son and of the Holy Spirit."
Matthew 28:19

CHAPTER 92

TAKING THE PLUNGE. . .

*W*ithout question, Grace wanted to see the baptisms. Then again, because of the turmoil she had just endured and her lack of sleep, she lacked the energy to make another journey. Her adrenalin had worn off long ago, and she could barely keep her eyes open. Ariel, emotionally exhausted, decided that she should also remain at the hospital with Grace. Quickly, one of Sam's aides arranged for them to have a room with two beds so they could rest.

The point on the Jordan River where Y'shua was likely baptized lied in territory claimed both by Israel and Babylon. Only ten feet of water separated Israel from Babylon at this point. Troops constantly guarded both sides of the entire Jewish-Muslim border.

Earlier in the century, when the baptismal site was open to the public, Muslim terrorists took several American tourists captive—two of them kidnapped as they were being baptized! The five Christians were crucified upside down, and the terrorists delivered copies of the video of the sickening executions to the leaders of Israel and the United States. That day, the baptismal site closed and never reopened.

Despite the possible danger, Sam and Abdul decided they wanted to be baptized there anyway. Sol and Ahava were more than willing to take the risk of conflict to be immersed anywhere near where John had baptized the very Son of God!

The IDF contacted the Brotherhood Army post closest to the baptismal site. The Israelis did not say who was be baptized but that a service would be held in approximately two hours. The outpost gave its permission for the Christian ritual, with the caveat that the Brotherhood would monitor and record all activities.

A military escort of Messianic officers replaced the President's and Prime Minister's security teams for the journey to the Jordan. The IDF believers considered the baptisms of their Prime Minister, the American President, and an Orthodox Rabbi and his wife as the first fruits of many more modern day leaders who would come to Y'shua!

While the President's men insisted they could best protect him, Abdul's firmness forced them to obey his orders. The new President did not want to provoke a response from the Brotherhood by having too large of an American and Israeli presence at the baptismal site.

Thus, the excited group traveled in a plain, no frills, all terrain Israeli military vehicle called the Ibex—named after the wild and strong mountain goats that rule the Negev. As their journey began, Sam said, "Without the limo, maybe the Brotherhood soldiers won't recognize who we are, because if they do, we could be sitting ducks!"

Mark noted, "Isa will watch over us because we go to the Jordan in obedience to Him. Our Saviour was baptized, even though He had no sin. His baptism was symbolic of His complete submission to the Father's will for His life—which included His crucifixion. Jesus buried His will under the waters of the Jordan. When He rose from those waters, He was empowered by the Holy Spirit to begin His three year mission and ministry. At the Jordan, our Lord committed Himself to complete obedience to His Father. That commitment took Him all the way to the cross."

The pastor then personalized his remarks for his friends. Filled with passion, he said, "Like Isa, like Y'shua, you come to submit your lives to our God. Like the Messiah, you will symbolically die to and bury your own will. Unlike our Lord, you will also symbolically die to and bury your sin! Thus, as you rise from the Jordan, you will celebrate both your freedom from sin in our Redeemer, as well as your commitment to obey His will—up to and including your own martyrdom, if necessary. You each will have the Holy Spirit to empower your lives in Jesus! He will be your source of strength, wisdom, and purpose in the critical days ahead and beyond!"

Mark's somber words turned more joyful as he said, "Baptism is an outward and visible sign of the inward and invisible transformation within your soul! As Jesus said, you have literally crossed over from death into life! Any time you doubt the commitment you made to Him or the commitment He made to you, remember today's baptism!"

As they rode toward the desert, Mark told Abdul not to expect a lush landscape along the Jordan River. "Further north," Mark said, "closer to the Sea of Galilee, the Jordan River flows through beautiful fields and valleys. Instead, we will be closer to the Dead Sea than to the Galilee. Here, a much smaller flow of water winds its ways through dry and barren land. The bulk of the Jordan's water has been diverted upstream for irrigation, industry, and human consumption.

"Be that as it may, in John's day, the water here flowed deep and wide. John baptized the Messiah at this end of the Jordan because He would go from here into the desert for His 40 days of fasting, praying, and temptation. His commitment to His Father's will was tested immediately!"

Looking at Sol, Ahava, Sam, and Abdul, Mark added, "Let the experience of God's own Son be a warning for you as well. If Satan tempted God in human flesh, you can bet he will quickly test your newly made commitment to Jesus. As the former angel of light came to our Lord at His weakest state, the tempter will sound like your best friend when you reach your most vulnerable point. But take heart! In our weakest moments, the power of the Spirit in us is at His strongest! So do not worry or fear! Just be ready! Given the current circumstances, your days will not be easy, but you will not walk alone—you will walk in the full power and presence of our Lord and King!"

As they turned off Highway 90 and headed east toward the Jordan, the scenery looked much as it had for thousands of years. Unlike other important landmarks and holy sites from Jesus' ministry, this part of the Jordan did not feature a magnificent church or well-kept gardens atop the holy site. The commemorative buildings at the Jordan were far enough away so that the original place of Jesus' baptism remained much as it was more than 2,000 years ago.

Along the slippery Israeli bank of the river were two old, modest decks. On both sides of the river, tall, wild reeds blew in the breeze. Abdul remarked, "Now I know why Isa spoke as he did about John. Mark, did not Isa say something about John and a reed swayed by the wind?"

"Actually, Abdul, our Messiah asked the people who were following Him a question about John. *'What did you go out into the desert to see? A reed swayed by the wind?'* I believe that verse is Matthew 11:7.

"When He asked this question, John's disciples had just visited with Him and were headed back to John. At that time, John, whom King Herod had imprisoned, sent his disciples to Jesus to confirm that He was indeed the Messiah. I suppose John wanted to make sure his sufferings were not in vain.

"Jesus had told John's disciples to look at the evidence of His Messiahship. He pointed out that the blind see, the crippled walk, the lepers are clean, the deaf hear, the dead live, and the poor receive the Good News! Jesus said John should hold tightly to his faith, despite his suffering.

"Then, Jesus told the crowd that John's witness to Him as the Messiah was so compelling that it brought the multitudes to the desert for repentance and baptism. The people did not go into the desert to see a man who would be easily swayed by public opinion, as the reeds by the Jordan were easily swayed by the wind. Instead, the people went to see a prophet who called the people—great and small—to repentance!

"Abdul, the people did not go into a palace to listen to a man dressed in fine clothes who dined at a fancy table and ate the finest of foods. Instead, they went to the desert, of all places, to listen to John who wore camel's hair with a leather belt and ate locusts and wild honey.

"Jesus said that the people came to John by the droves not for who he was or where he was but because of what he said and who he represented! The people came to John because he bore the message of God Himself! Jesus confirmed that John served as the last of the prophets and His forerunner who prepared the people to receive their Messiah!"

Abdul asked, "Did not John die for his faithfulness to Isa?"

"Yes, John was beheaded. You might say that John the Baptist was the first follower of Isa to die for his faith. John was the first Christian martyr."

Sam, who had listened intently to Mark, noted, "Well, I hope we will not be the latest believers killed for our faith in Y'shua! Yet, even as I say those words, I must admit I no longer fear death, not from war or by any other means!"

Abdul added, "I feel the same way, Sam. At the risk of sounding preachy, being free from the fear of death both liberates and empowers me!"

Sol and Ahava smiled as they considered the truth they were hearing from the two leaders. Sol whispered to his bride, "If we go Home today, we lose nothing, but we gain everything!" The emotion of the moment moistened Ahava's eyes.

The four of them had decided not to where white robes for the baptism. Instead, as Jesus and His followers were baptized in their everyday dress, these new believers also decided to be immersed in their regular attire.

Mark was the first to step into the warm waters of the Jordan. Before reading the passage of Scripture he had chosen, Mark turned to his Redeemer in prayer. "Isa, Y'shua, Jesus, Saviour, Emmanuel, King of Kings, Lord of Lords, Ruler over All, Alpha and Omega, the Bright and Morning Star, and our Messiah: Your many Names describe You, but not one of them completely captures Your wondrous majesty, unlimited power, awesome glory, perfect holiness, unmatched gentleness, unbridled compassion, pure humility, unending mercy, unconditional love, and amazing grace!

"Thank You for meeting us here today, where You officially started Your ministry and mission to the people of Israel, and through them, all the people of the world! As You first came here, so many centuries ago, we come now to these waters for baptism. One new daughter of Heaven along with three new sons of the Kingdom stand ready to identify themselves with You in baptism. They come to symbolically represent what they have already done in their souls. They have died to self and sin to rise with You to Light and Life without end!

"We love You because You first loved us, and You have proven Your love to us again and again and again! We thank You now for Your sacrifice in our place! We praise You for Your forgiveness! We glorify You because You rose from the grave, holy and sinless, as you defeated sin and death for us all! We exalt You, as You reign above all powers of this earth, the universe, the many galaxies, and all of Heaven as well as eternity itself!

"Empower these who come before You today to carry out Your will for their lives! Teach them and mature them through Your Spirit! Do with them, with all of us here, as You see fit! One day, every knee will bow and every tongue will confess that you are indeed Lord! Yet we come to do that now, willingly, as Your most humble servants! Bless this time, bless these souls! We pray in the Name, the only Name by which we may be saved, Y'shua *HaMashiach!* Amen!"

With hearts beating rapidly, the four newest children of the King stepped into the Jordan. Ahava made her way to Mark. She grasped Mark's forearm with her hands, while she flexed her knees slightly in preparation to be immersed in the river.

His eyes filled with hope, the pastor looked up and said, "Lord, my sister comes to these waters today confessing her sin in repentance and professing her faith in Your ability to redeem her life and empower her to serve You on this earth so she may eternally praise You in Heaven!"

Then, looking into her eyes, Mark proclaimed, "Ahava! In the Name of the Father, the Son, and the Holy Spirit, I baptize you. Buried with our Lord in baptism, arise to walk with Him in newness of life!" Ahava held her breath as Mark's hand on her back guided her under the water. A second later, she emerged from the watery grave, with a brilliant smile on her face and shouts of hallelujah on her lips!

Sol was next, followed by Abdul and then Sam. As he rose from the Jordan, he too smiled broadly and said, "I have but one regret: I wish I had come to Y'shua long ago! I have wasted so much time, so much of my life! I am finally free from all the hatred, resentment, bitterness, and desire for revenge that has driven my days for so long! I feel like a new man!"

"You are," Sol exclaimed. "You are a brand new soul, born again in Y'shua!"

"I never thought I would hear someone say that about me!"

"Me either, Sam! At one time, I could not stand to hear the phrase, 'born again!'"

Everyone hugged—and Sam lifted everyone out of the water when he hugged them! Sol said, "Samson is living up to his name!" Everyone laughed. Joy filled each of their hearts! They shouted, and clapped, and splashed, and praised the Lord! The IDF soldiers joined the celebration, as they had witnessed the genuine faith of these new believers in Y'shua!

"Take each other's hands," Mark said as he prayed for his dear friends once more. "Lord, we rejoice in You! At one point in our lives, we stood as enemies of each other and, through our sin, enemies of You! However, with great thanks to You, the war for us has ended! We live and embrace each other and You as family in the peace of Your Kingdom! You remain the only genuine peace in this world or eternity.

"As we leave these waters today, while our own wars with sin have been won by You, we are ready to go back to that battleground as Your soldiers of Light, Hope, Love, and Peace to rescue others! The battle belongs to You, and all who surrender to You are victors! Let us go from this place ready to engage in the fight for salvation in You, Isa, Y'shua, Jesus! Give us the same Holy Spirit that empowered You at Your baptism and steeled You for the days ahead. Give us strength to resist the temptations that line the path ahead."

Instead of Mark saying, "Amen," shouts of *"Yalla! Yalla! Yalla!"* and *"Allahu Akbar!* There is no God but Allah!" rang out instead, accompanied by the high pitched, piercing sound of wandfire.

Crimson splattered the reeds along the Jordan as Sam went under the waters of the Jordan once more!

"Those who believe in Allah and the Last Day ask thee for no exemption from fighting with their goods and persons. And Allah knoweth well those who do their duty."
Qur'an 9:44

CHAPTER 93

A WOLF IN SHEEP'S CLOTHING. . .

*O*nce again, the entire world focused on the words of one man. That man, Imam Addar Zaahir, had a two-pronged mission. One, he knew he must unite his people by filling the leadership vacuum left by the dual assassinations of the Caliph and the General. Two, he knew he must avoid war at all costs—at least temporarily, given the present disadvantage of Babylon.

Addar had to take control of the moment before anyone else attempted to grab power. Despite the seemingly unified front of Babylon, rival forces and old wounds still festered! Unless Addar acted quickly and decisively, all hell could literally break lose in the Caliphate.

He faced the camera with all the resolve he could muster. What he said next would either save or doom Babylon—and possibly the rest of the world! Addar took a deep breath and smiled. He said, "Good afternoon to my fellow followers of Allah, and to our Jewish and Christian friends in the world."

Abdul spoke for the group. "What Jewish and Christian friends, Addar? The Qur'an tells Muslims to have no Jewish and Christian friends." As the Ibex raced from Jordan River to the hospital in Jerusalem, the President and the others watched the images of the imam's speech from his 3DHP.

"Today is filled with both sadness and joy for the people of Babylon. We mourn not only our high and noble Caliph's death, but now we also grieve for our valiant and courageous General. You witnessed the General's assassination at the memorial service for the Caliph, his men, all the Palestinian leaders, and so many innocent citizens. We have determined that the suicide bomber who literally took the General to his grave was a member of the General's own bodyguard who believed the wild rumors that have been circulating.

"These groundless allegations state that the General had assassinated the Caliph and his most trusted men in an attempt to seize power and annihilate Israel and the United States. The rumors accuse our General of being a murderous megalomaniac who wanted to rule the entire world as a bloodthirsty tyrant!

"As I noted, one of his own men apparently believed those wild stories and decided to eliminate the General in an act of vengeance for the Caliph's assassination.

"However, our investigation shows that the Americans and Israelis killed Sanaullah bin Laden. The MGM's that killed these brave souls were manufactured in the U.S. and the Jewish State for military purposes."

"Where are these smart bullets, Addar? Show me the MGMs! Show me the bodies of the Caliph and his henchmen, and I guarantee you there is not one bullet wound on any of them. You will not show the evidence because you cannot show that the leaders of the Brotherhood were actually beheaded by the General's men!"

"Therefore, war with the United States and Israel seems to be inevitable. The leaders of those nations claim the General hacked into their weapons control systems and used their arsenals against them. Now, these leaders claim they have regained control of their massive arsenals, which could easily wipe out Babylon—every innocent man, woman, and child. Mr. President, Mr. Prime Minister, neither of you has brought forth one shred of evidence to support your wild claims."

"So it makes sense to you, Addar, that we would use our own weapons against ourselves, to kill our own people? What further evidence do you want us to show?"

Addar again took a deep and slow breath. "So here we stand, on the brink of World War IV, on the day of mourning for Babylon, on the day of choosing a new Caliph to lead us. From all the ultranet votes that have been tabulated, the General, were he still alive, would be our next leader! Be that as it may, with his assassination, the man who came in second place will be our new Caliph.

"Surprisingly, that second place vote was for me, your humble servant—Allah's humble servant! Though unworthy of such high office, I accept your selection in our hour of crisis."

Abdul muttered, "I see no surprise in this alleged vote, Addar! You have always dreamed of holding absolute power. Remember, I know you, my mentor, my surrogate father. The rest of the world may consider you a man of faith and peace, but I know the truth about you. Indeed, your fingerprints cover the breaching of our weapon systems. After all, who could better hack his way into our weapons systems other than the man who allegedly created the ultranet?"

Addar continued, appearing calm and cool on the outside, but with a ball of hot anxiety within his gut. He announced, "Overwhelmingly approved by voters was the annexation of the former Democratic Republic of Palestine. Now we can protect our brothers whose country lies inside Israeli territory. Even though Palestine, now one of the states of Babylon, is surrounded by Israel, I call on the noble people of Palestine to be at peace with your Jewish neighbors."

Abdul asked, "Will not the Palestinian state in Israel be your launching pad for the next ground attacks against the Jews, Addar?"

The new leader of Babylon then said, "Brothers in the service of Allah, let me make a plea to you in my first act as your Caliph! Despite the wounds and loss of life we have suffered, despite the lies that have been propagated by the Israelis and the Americans, we must not let ourselves be dragged into war!

"Instead, we must once and for all prove to our enemies that Islam stands as a religion of peace! Though obviously justified in our pursuit of justice and vengeance, let us take the high road, and not follow the path that the infidels have paved for us!"

"I thought that we infidels were your friends just a few moments ago?" Abdul quipped. "Yet of course, you are using the *taqiyya* doctrine of deceit, because you cannot possibly admit to your people that they could not win a war fought on Babylonian territory!"

"Today, as your Caliph, I call for peace, as we extend an olive branch and forgiveness, as is the way of Allah, to the United States and Israel. Despite our losses, and their self-imposed losses, we offer an invitation to sit down together and rationally discuss our differences. We invite you to put aside your prejudices and lies about us as Muslims, servants of the one true god! We even invite you to believe in Allah as we do, for Allah, Most Gracious, Most Merciful, is all forgiving and kind to those who turn to Him from their infidelity."

Abdul said, "I think I am going to be sick! Surely, Addar, you don't expect people to buy this camel fertilizer you are throwing at us? The Brotherhood will never back down from a fight! Remember, peace is surrender in Islam! Are you stalling for time? Trying to regain control of our weapons? Working out the final details for Goliath? What is the goal of your deceit that is so shallow and transparent? You were going to blame everything on the dead General. Why did you decide to take another path?"

"I invite the new President of the United States and the Prime Minister of Israel to sit down with me before President Abdullah returns to the chaos in the United States. They know me well from the negotiations between the Palestinians and Israel. They know me as a man of strength, but also as a man of peace and hope!"

"I don't know you from the negotiations, Addar. I know you from the inside out!"

"This momentous day in which I became your Caliph and the DROP became the official Palestinian state in Babylon can yet lead to another historic event: Peace in this world because you, my Babylonian brothers, have chosen a man of peace to lead our people of peace who follow our god of peace!

"Mr. President! Mr. Prime Minister! The fate of our world lies in your hands! Our next steps rest with you."

"Greater love has no one than this: that he lay down his life for his friends."
John 15:13

CHAPTER 94

TIMELY TRANSFORMATION. . .

O utside the door of the Intensive Care Unit, Dr. Goldberg said, "It's touch and go. Mr. President. He might make it or he might not last through the night. Frankly, I am not sure what has happened to him. He is battered, bruised, and bleeding both internally and externally. But his injuries are not like those that are incurred in a beating or a shooting!"

Abdul told the doctor, "He was hit with lethal pulses from an electromagnetic weapon."

Dr. Goldberg paused then stated, "I did not know there was such a weapon, but now that I consider his injuries, that possibility makes sense."

Abdul asked, "Dr. Goldberg, is your patient lucid? Can he talk?"

"Yes, he can talk, but his voice is weak, and it takes him a while to form his words. He cannot endure a long conversation. He needs rest more than he needs anything else."

"I just need to ask him a few questions, Doctor. I will not keep him awake long at all."

"All right," Dr. Goldberg said reluctantly, "but I'll have to pull you out of the room if you push too far, Mr. President. He is in room five."

"Thank you, Dr. Goldberg. I do owe my life to you—literally," Abdul replied as he shook the surgeon's hand.

"I'll let you inside." The surgeon then said *"potkhim,"* which means open, and Abdul entered the ICU wing.

He paused at the doorway to room five. He made eye contact, so he slowly walked over to the bed. "Do you speak English?" Abdul asked.

"Yes," was the whispered reply from underneath the oxygen mask.

"Good! Why did you jump out from behind the reeds to save the Prime Minister's life today?"

The Brotherhood soldier softly replied, "I was sent. . . to the Jordan. . . to kill the Prime Minister. . . with my machete if. . . the soldiers failed. . . to kill him with their wands."

"But instead, you protected him before the soldiers began to shoot! Why?"

"I knew. . . I had to save. . . his life!"

"How did you know this?"

"Isa told me. . . to rescue the Prime Minister!" The soldier's words were coming slower.

"Isa? Are you a follower of Isa?"

"I am now!" the soldier said as he smiled under his oxygen mask.

Smiling just as broadly, Abdul asked, "How did you come to know Isa?"

"After listening to. . . Omar Basel. . . the Orthodox Jew. . . and his wife. . . you. . . and the President's widow on holovision. . . as well as the Prime Minister. . . at his baptism!"

Abdul paused for a moment to assimilate all the information. "You mean to tell me that you heard all of us speak before the baptism, save for the Prime Minister, but you did not decide to trust Isa until you were behind the reeds at the Jordan River?"

Still smiling, the soldier nodded his head in agreement.

"You said that Isa told you to save the Prime Minister?"

"He told me. . . to run into the water. . . and cover. . . the Prime Minister's body. . . with my own. . . to protect him!"

"Did you hesitate? Were you afraid?"

The soldier proudly shook his head. "I trusted Isa!"

"You were almost killed! Do you still trust Isa?"

"Yes!. . . I do not hate Jews. . . or Christians. . . or apostates anymore! I love them!. . . I love you!"

Though he could not hear the conversation, the surgeon entered the room. "You must leave now, Mr. President!" When Abdul hesitated, Dr. Goldberg began pulling him back into the hallway. Abdul did not resist. But as he left, he told the soldier, "Isa has saved your soul, and He will save your life as well!"

In the hallway, Abdul turned to the surgeon and said, "His life is in danger!"

"I already told you that, Mr. President!" Dr. Goldberg replied.

"No! You do not understand! That soldier saved the Prime Minister's life! The Brotherhood will kill him at soon as possible, if he survives his wounds! We must place armed guards at this door!"

Dr. Goldberg was both surprised and taken aback. "Why would a Brotherhood soldier save Prime Minister Ben Baruch's life?"

"I will tell you why—because that soldier now follows Y'shua! Our Lord told him to throw his body over the Prime Minister! With wandfire, the only way the soldier could save the Prime Minister was to be a shield for him—a human shield! This soldier took the pounding and piercing for Sam!"

With a faraway look, Dr. Goldberg replied, "Just as Y'shua long ago took the pounding and piercing for the soldier!"

"Those who reject our Signs are deaf and dumb—in the midst of darkness profound: Whom Allah willeth, He leaveth to wander: Whom He willeth, He placeth on the Way that is Straight."
Qur'an 6:39

CHAPTER 95

GOOD NEWS TRAVELS QUICKLY...

*A*s the sun began to set, a posse of reporters had stopped Sam from entering the hospital with Abdul and the others. These journalists surrounded and roped the Prime Minister into a corner to ask him about his baptism that was broadcast by Babylon for the entire world to see!

With visceral anger in his voice, a Jewish journalist asked, "Prime Minister Ben Baruch, do you realize that you have greatly offended your party and coalition that backed you for this high office?"

Amazed at his calmness as well as confidence in this unexpected moment, Sam replied, "I realize that in Israel we claim to have freedom of religion. I realize some in the *Beer Sheva* party hate Messianic Jews. At the same time, I also realize that many of those in my party and coalition who chose me are Jews who believe Y'shua is their Messiah. I still believe in the sovereignty of Israel. I still consider myself a Jew. I still plan to participate in all the Jewish traditions and holidays. I have not stopped being a Jew! Actually, I am more of a Jew than I have ever been before, as I now am a Jew who follows our Messiah—Y'shua!"

The same reporter asked, "Don't you think you should step down from office, and allow your party to choose another leader until a new election can be held?"

"Frankly, no, I do not think I should step down. We are in the midst of a crisis! Besides that, I am not the only follower of Y'shua that serves in our government. Likewise, more than a third of our people now follow Y'shua. If the *Beer Sheva* party no longer wants me to serve, then I will argue my case at that time with the party leaders. If the coalition wants to disband because of my new faith in Y'shua, I will present my case to those leaders. However, I am focused on serving Israel and her people—all her people—now more than at any other time in my life!"

A Muslim reporter asked, "Isn't it true that the Brotherhood troops attempted to assassinate you, but you were protected by a bodyguard posing as a Muslim?"

"No, what you have just proposed is not true at all—in fact, it sounds ludicrous! Why would one of my bodyguards disguise himself as a Brotherhood soldier in the first place? The truth is stranger than fiction! A member of the Brotherhood, sent to help kill me, instead dropped his machete, jumped out from behind the reeds at the Jordan River, and then covered me with his own body. He suffered the wounds that were intended for me!"

"Mr. Prime Minister, surely you do not expect us to believe that one member of the Brotherhood decided to prevent your assassination by another member of the Brotherhood?"

Before Sam could speak, Abdul worked his way through the reporters to Sam's side. "I can answer your question," the President said. "Yes, one soldier of the Brotherhood did stop another assassin of the Brotherhood from killing my good friend, the Prime Minister of Israel. Why? Because the soldier that saved the Prime Minister's life now believes in Isa! I have just spoken to him inside the hospital. He is in critical condition, but he is also absolutely overjoyed that he was able to spare the Prime Minister's life—even if it costs him his own life in exchange!"

Stone cold silence met Abdul's answer. The reporters stared at him, as if he had been speaking another language. They were trying to process and understand if what the U.S. President said could be true. Sam's expression exuded awe and wonder over the workings of Y'shua.

A Christian reporter broke the silence. "Mr. President and Mr. Prime Minister, we are receiving reports from all over Israel, the

United States, the nations with growing Muslim populations, and even Babylon itself that thousands—perhaps even hundreds of thousands—of Muslims are rejecting their faith in Islam and turning to Isa as their Saviour and Lord!

"These former Muslims are flocking to churches and underground ministries in their desire to know more about Isa and what they should do as His followers! Mr. President, many of these Muslims say they have dreamed or seen visions of Isa. Then, they saw Pastor Basel talk about his dream and how Isa led him to believe in Him. Likewise, they heard reports that you, President Abdullah, also had such a dream and now follow Isa.

"Moreover, they heard the form First Lady talk about President Paulson's new faith. They likewise listened to the Orthodox Rabbi and his wife tell why they now believe in Y'shua. Now, today, the Muslims of the world heard and saw you, Prime Minister, as you professed your faith through baptism in the Jordan River! Your cumulative experiences with the Messiah are persuading so many to abandon Islam for faith in Jesus! Do either of you have any comment about this?"

Overjoyed, Abdul and Sam looked at each other, knowing each they both wanted to respond. Abdul deferred to Sam, since he had the home court advantage. With a smile most people had never seen before, Sam said, "Both the Hebrew and Christian Scriptures say that in the last days, the Lord will pour out His Spirit on all people! Both the prophet Joel and the disciple Peter proclaimed that in the last days, old men will have dreams and young men will have visions about Y'shua the Messiah! So, I must conclude that we are living in the last days!"

The same reporter added, "Mr. Prime Minister, have you heard that today thousands of Jews here in Israel, the United States, and in other countries of the world where they are relatively safe have also been talking about their dreams and visions of Y'shua—and how the newly found faith of the American Presidents, the Orthodox Rabbi and his wife, and now you, Mr. Prime Minister, have sealed their decision to believe in Y'shua as their Messiah?"

Again, the reporter's revelation filled Sam's and Abdul's hearts with indescribable joy! Sam responded by saying, "No, I was not aware of Jews coming to Y'shua in great numbers, but as I am one of them, all I can do is be most thankful and praise the Lord for His salvation!"

Another reporter quickly asked, "Mr. Prime Minister, do you believe that the world should be preparing for Y'shua's return which is prophesied for the last days?"

Sam nodded his head as he answered, "Yes, I do believe we are living in the last days! I have read the entire Bible, not only the Jewish Scriptures, many times. Now, I look at the whole of Scripture as God's Word to us. Thus, the events of recent years and days are taking us to the climax of all time: the return of the Jewish Messiah—Y'shua. I believe we are also witnessing the rise of the Antichrist, even at this time, which means that Y'shua could rapture the believers from this world very soon."

Sam was not allowed to expand on his comments about the identity of the Antichrist, as a Muslim reporter said, "Mr. Prime Minister, I would like to follow up on an earlier question. Are your days as the leader of Israel numbered? Don't you believe that *Kadosh*, now the second largest political party in the nation, will make sure you are removed from office as an apostate? Won't the party of the Orthodox Jews of Israel even try to kill you—as they persecute other Jews who believe in Isa?"

Still at peace, the Prime Minister answered, "While *Kadosh* is a critical voice in the present coalition government, while its members may very well call for my party to choose another leader, while they may even call for a new election, I do not feel that my life is in danger. Would it not be ironic if now, a Jew killed me after I was saved today by a Muslim—at least a former Muslim?

The same journalist posed a question for Abdul. "Mr. President, do you plan to call for an emergency election as soon as you return to the United States, as you will either be assassinated at any moment by the Brotherhood or be rejected as President because you are a Muslim?"

Abdul smiled, saying to the reporter, "If you have personal knowledge about plans for my assassination as well as the Prime Minister's murder, we would appreciate those details. And for the record, I am not a Muslim. I am a follower of Isa, Y'shua, Jesus—the one and only Son of God!"

"Here in this hospital, someone tried to kill me—and many others along with me. An explosive device was placed in my shoulder during a surgery for the gunshot wound I suffered. Another doctor, Dr. Joel Goldberg, found that explosive in my shoulder and removed it, just mere seconds before it detonated!

"By the way, Dr. Goldberg is also a believer in Y'shua! So, my life—the life of a former Muslim—was saved by a Messianic Jew, while the Prime Minister's life—who is now a Messianic Jew—was saved by a former Muslim! These incidents are not random, but show the hand of Isa working among us in this present crisis!"

Sam added, "By the way, we have now tracked down the alleged doctor who was accused of implanting that explosive device in the President's body. The surgeon's name was Mordecai Levinson. Actually, his body was found in his car—he had been dead for at least a few weeks. Obviously, he had nothing to do with the explosive device but someone who assumed his identity did. That man, a Brotherhood spy here in Israel, committed suicide with other Muslims when *Shin Bet* agents tracked him down."

A reporter from Babylon asked, "Mr. President, do you feel safe at all? Your life was almost taken here. Your predecessor's life was lost aboard Air Force One. Just how afraid are you?"

Abdul boldly proclaimed, "I am not afraid in the least! My life has already been redeemed eternally! What should I fear now? Besides, I believe Isa appointed me to this position at this critical moment in time."

He continued to speak, adding, "If I could be so bold, my new-found faith tells me that Sam will continue to serve as Prime Minister of Israel, and I will serve as President of the United States, at least until the next election cycle. I believe both our countries' citizens will realize that the two of us are especially equipped for leading our nations in the days and years ahead!"

The next question came from behind the reporters. "Mr. President, Mr. Prime Minister, are you willing to avoid war with Babylon by accepting the offer of peace from its new Caliph?" Both men recognized Addar's voice, but neither of them answered his question.

Instead, the reply came from behind the President and Prime Minister. Mark had come outside the hospital to find both men so he could ask for their help. Mark said, "What peace are you talking about, Caliph Zaahir? If you are offering peace and if the General is dead, then why have my wife and daughter been kidnapped by your men? Are you still enforcing the General's *fatwa* on my family?"

"If someone forces you to go one mile, go with him two miles."
Matthew 5:41

CHAPTER 96

AMAZING GRACE. . .

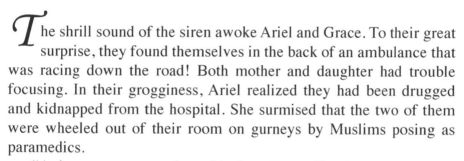

*T*he shrill sound of the siren awoke Ariel and Grace. To their great surprise, they found themselves in the back of an ambulance that was racing down the road! Both mother and daughter had trouble focusing. In their grogginess, Ariel realized they had been drugged and kidnapped from the hospital. She surmised that the two of them were wheeled out of their room on gurneys by Muslims posing as paramedics.

"At least you are not alone this time, Honey!" Ariel shouted to her frightened daughter. "We are in this together, and we will get through this together!" Grace said nothing in reply. The twice kidnapped, emotionally depleted daughter tried to reach her mother's hand, but could not, as their bodies were strapped to the gurneys. Focused on her traumatized daughter, Ariel determined she would be strong for Grace.

The thirteen year old had woken up in the hospital room, just as the Muslim man put his hand firmly over her mouth and nose. Now, neither Grace nor her mother had a grasp of how much time had passed since they left the hospital so abruptly. Grace stared through the small window on the ambulance wall, watching the blur of buildings they rapidly passed.

"Where are we? Where are they taking us, Mom?" Grace asked as she started to sob.

"I don't know, Honey," Ariel replied, "but we will go there together. I am right here with you!"

Those words brought Grace some comfort, and she said "I am sorry you had to come with me this time, Mom. You know, Jesus was with me before, and He is with us now!"

Ariel paraphrased a portion of the twenty-third Psalm, saying "Though we walk through the valley of the shadow of death, we will fear no evil, for our Good Shepherd is with us and will protect us!"

Unexpectedly, the ambulance came to a screeching halt. The sudden change in speed pressed the mother's and her daughter's bodies against the gurney straps. The pressure opened one of the buckles on Grace's gurney.

As she sat up, Grace looked out the window. She saw three men run from the ambulance and through the door of a building. They left the ambulance running.

"Mom, are you thinking what I am thinking?"

"Grace! You cannot drive this ambulance! You have only driven our car a couple of times in our driveway! I'll drive! Unbuckle these straps for me!"

Grace had set herself free while Ariel was talking. "We don't have time, Mom! Those guys could be back any second! I'm driving!"

"Grace! No!" Ariel shouted as her daughter exited the rear of the ambulance.

"You and Dad always told me that we have to be ready to do whatever the moment demands," Grace shouted to her mom.

Realizing she could not stop Grace, Ariel shouted, "Call for help on the radio!" Then the panicking Mom said, "No! Keep focused on the road and buckle up!"

Grace shouted from the cab, "Y'shua is with us! He will open up the road for us!"

Ariel smiled through her tears as she said to herself, as confidently as possible, *"He will indeed!"*

Nervously, Grace put the ambulance in gear, and eased away from the building. About a mile down the road, she flipped the switch for the siren and slammed the accelerator to the floor! Grace had no idea where she was going, but she would travel there quickly!

The sudden burst of speed pressed Ariel against the straps of her gurney again as she prayed for their safety.

Grace next flipped the switch for the two-way radio and shouted, "Help! Help! We have been kidnapped!" To Grace's dismay, all she heard in response was a man shouting back at her—in Arabic!"

*"Do they not travel through the earth, and see what was the
End of those before them (who did evil)? Allah brought utter
destruction on them, and similar (fates await) those who
reject Allah."*
Qur'an 47:10

CHAPTER 97

FROM SEA TO SIZZLING SEA. . .

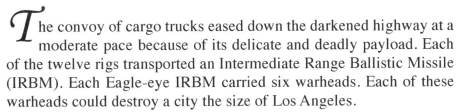

*T*he convoy of cargo trucks eased down the darkened highway at a
moderate pace because of its delicate and deadly payload. Each
of the twelve rigs transported an Intermediate Range Ballistic Missile
(IRBM). Each Eagle-eye IRBM carried six warheads. Each of these
warheads could destroy a city the size of Los Angeles.

Such convoys travelled only between 10:00 p.m. and 4:00 a.m.,
and only when the highways and streets they used were closed—officially for construction. The drivers of such perilous cargo were the
best trained and most experienced in the land. They were not allowed
to listen to music or any form of entertainment while driving. The men
at the helms of these transports had to check in with both their depar-
ture and destination points every fifteen minutes to make sure they
experienced no problems and stayed on time.

The general public had no idea that such destructive weaponry
passed through their cities under the black cloak of night. Regardless
moving the Eagle-eyes was extremely safe, as each transport unit
could survive the force of a two ton impact without detonating the
warheads it carried. In fact, despite a handful of accidents over the
years, not one IRBM had ever detonated during transport.

On this night, the Eagle-eyes were in transit to Davis-Monthan
Air Force Base in Tucson, Arizona. The powerfully sleek arrows in
this convoy, along with others, would be positioned on the United

States border with Mexico. Should the Brotherhood try to attack any or all of the allied American nations from their bases south of the U.S. border, one Eagle-eye could obliterate the threat in up to six different locations—if, indeed, the U.S. had regained control of its weapons systems.

As the convoy rolled through Dallas on I-20, the driver of the sixth transport, Alex Tower radioed the driver ahead of him, Ethan Battles. Each of them had been in the weapons transport business for more than twenty years. Pictures of their wives, children, and grandchildren were tacked all over the interiors of their super cabs.

"Do you hear that?" Alex asked.

"Hear what?" Ethan replied.

"That high pitched whistling sound!"

Ethan held his breath for a moment, so he could listen intently. He then said, "Yeah! I do hear it! It sounds like it is coming from the transport ahead of me."

"That's strange, because I thought it sounded like it was coming from your transport!"

"What do you think that sound means?"

Alex never had the opportunity to answer Ethan's last question. The whistling sound came from the Eagle-eye IRBMs seconds before detonation. All 72 warheads exploded simultaneously wiping out everything and everyone from El Paso, Texas to the west, Wichita, Kansas to the north, Mobile, Alabama to the east, and Torreon, Mexico to the south! The hole at ground zero was so deep and wide that it could not be measured.

Furthermore, the explosions measured 6.7 on the Richter scale, and their tremors were felt as far away as Los Angeles, California, Fargo, North Dakota, Savannah, Georgia, and Little Tijuana on the Mexican border with Guatemala!

Meanwhile in Pennsylvania, a monorail hypertrain (MHT) hauling 31 toxic chemical tankers and 43 jet fuel storage tankers— all inspected and approved by the U.S. Department of Transportation (DOT)—rolled down the ultra high speed rail line from Chicago to Philadelphia. DOT cleared the tankers for rail speeds up to 195 miles per hour because they were protected by three layers of impervious, impenetrable sealant.

Just as the engineer should have begun to slow down his MHT to bypass 30th Street Station, he instead began accelerating! 200 miles per hour! 215 miles per hour! 235 miles per hour!

Engineer Mansur "Manny" Farris was now at the helm of a WMD. Manny was only one year away from retirement, had sixteen grandchildren, and four great grandchildren. Even so, Manny radioed the hypertrain control unit (HTCU), warning that in less than two minutes, 30th Street Station would be the epicenter of the worst train disaster in U.S. history!

"Manny, you are such a card! Can't you tell how frightened I am?" The radioed reply came from Emil Suarez, the 30th Street Station Controller. Emil and Manny had been joking with each other for years.

The engineer asked, "What are you, a sadist? Do you like destruction—absolute devastation?" Manny had bound and gagged the conductor and crew who could do nothing to stop what was now inevitable.

"Sadist? Devastation? You are just a riot, Manny!"

"Let me spell is out for you: A-l-l-a-h-u A-k-b-a-r!"

"Playing along with what he thought was a stupid joke, Emil said, "I didn't get that, Manny. Say again?"

"Write this down: Capital A-l-l-a-h-u, capital A-k-b-a-r!"

Emil responded a few seconds later. *"Allahu Akbar?* Are you trying to tell me that you are a Muslim terrorist, Manny? Is there no low to which you will not stoop for a joke?"

"There is no god but Allah!" Manny shouted back.

Emil finally looked up to his holographic 3D control panel. While the audio alerts had been silenced, Manny had distracted Emil to the point that he did not see the flashing of the visual alarms! Emil wondered, "How did Manny rig my control panel to make it look like he was about to tear through the station?" Those were the last thoughts to cross Emil's mind.

Five seconds later, Manny's train plowed into 30th Street Station as he remotely ignited the explosives under the jet fuel storage trailers that set off a poisonous fireball so huge that Philadelphia, New York, and Baltimore were wiped off the map! As the toxic cloud drifted eastward, the death toll would double!

At the same time, on the west coast, only a skeleton crew manned the soon to be decommissioned USS Jimmy Carter, the largest submarine at Kitsap Naval Base in Seattle, Washington. When its triple redundant weapons monitoring system suddenly came to life, the rookie at the controls immediately alerted the submarine's senior office on board.

Executive Officer (XO) Lucius Black was trying to catch some much needed sleep when Division Officer (DO) Samara Pall set off the sub's alarms. XO Black heard DO Pall ask, "Have you authorized a surprise drill?" Samara tried to get a handle on the situation, as she saw every torpedo and anti-ship mine suddenly come to life.

Lucius, who had been dreaming of his wife and three daughters that he had not seen in 16 months, did his best to focus. The XO replied, "Negative! I have not authorized any drill! What's happening?"

Samara, who had taken her wedding vows just two months earlier, shouted, "According to the control system, all 100 pulse wave Great White Torpedoes and 250 Stingray Anti-ship Mines are about to be. . ." Before the DO could finish her sentence, the 350 weapons detonated simultaneously!

The resulting mega-blast blew a hole from the Seattle port as far east into Washington as Spokane, as far north as Prince George, British Columbia, and as far south as Portland, Oregon! Tsunami warning alerts sounded in Hawaii, Alaska, and Guam, as well as Fiji, Japan, Australia, New Zealand, and Eastern Asia!

In Addar Zaahir's first hours as Caliph—while calling for peace and without a shot being fired by the Brotherhood—more than 30 million Americans lost their lives in fire and fury, the most lives ever lost in one day, actually in less than two minutes, in world history!

"... 'Father, forgive them, for they do not know what they are doing.'..."
Luke 23:34

CHAPTER 98

RACING AND CHASING...

*A*n overly friendly voice on the radio said, "Who is this?" Grace said nothing.

"We have a report that one of our ambulances was stolen. Who is this?"

Grace, still unsure if she should answer, finally said, "This is one of your ambulances! My mother and I were kidnapped in it!"

Fifteen seconds of whispered conversation followed.

"Is anyone there?" Grace finally asked, as she kept the accelerator pedal pushed to the floorboard.

"Oh yes, we are here! We are just. . . uh. . . trying to determine. . . which ambulance was stolen."

"What difference does that make right now? My mother and I have been kidnapped from the hospital, and our lives may still be in danger!" Panic filled Grace's words.

"Rest assured, you are quite safe! Can you drive back to the hospital?"

"I have no idea where I am or where I am going!"

"That's okay! Take a deep breath and calm down. Our GPS is not working. We cannot tell where you are. So, at the next intersection, tell me the street names."

"I don't see any intersections! I am driving down a long road! But I do see a sign that says, '*Deir Mar Jaris*.'"

"Okay! You are near the Greek Orthodox Monastery. We are on our way to you now!"

"Thank you! Please hurry!"

"You can count on that, Haziqah!"

"Haziqah?" Grace thought. "How did he. . . oh no! I am so stupid! This ambulance is owned by the Brotherhood! And I just told them where to find us!"

Within a few minutes, two cars were gaining on the ambulance. "What do I do now?" Grace asked herself. She saw a road ahead, and she realized she would have to turn because the current road ended. "Which way do I go?" She asked out loud. Then she saw the sign which read, "Jerusalem to the right!" Grace shouted, "Thank you, Jesus!"

Grace only slowed down enough to make the turn, and then she floored the accelerator pedal to go as fast as possible toward a place that was at least somewhat familiar to her. However, in the side mirrors, she could see that the two cars were now close to the ambulance. In fact, one was speeding up to pass her. With eyes wide open, Grace wondered what she should do. When she saw an Israeli police car heading toward her in the opposite lane, she had her answer.

Quickly, Grace drove the van into the opposing traffic land and slammed on the brakes. The ambulance swerved and swayed, but Grace was able to keep it on the road. In the back, Ariel was pressed against straps that bound her to the gurney. She could barely breathe!

At the same time, the officer driving the police car pounded on his brakes, but he knew he would not be able to avoid the ambulance. Instinctively, he pulled off the road to prevent the pending collision.

Meanwhile, the Muslim driver of the first car behind the ambulance hit his brakes, but the driver behind him did not react fast enough and crashed into the rear end of the first car. The first car was knocked off the road and the second one sailed past the ambulance and the police car.

Immediately upon stopping, Grace jumped out of the cab of the ambulance, ran around to the back, and threw open the door. As she climbed into the ambulance, Grace shouted, "Mom! Are you okay?"

Ariel looked up at her daughter and said, "Who taught you to drive like that? What were you doing?"

"I was trying to get away from the Brotherhood soldiers who were following us!"

Before Ariel could say anything else in response, the officer from the police car and his partner were at the back door of the ambulance. Indignant, he demanded, "What is going on here? Who was driving this ambulance?"

"I was," Grace answered.

"How old are you, why were you driving an ambulance, and why did you pull into my lane and stop so suddenly?"

"I am thirteen, and I was trying to save my mother and me from the Brotherhood soldiers who were following us! We were kidnapped from the hospital in Jerusalem!"

As soon as Grace said those words, the two Muslims in the wrecked car began to fire wand pulses at the police officers outside the ambulance. The officer who had been talking with Grace jumped into the ambulance, while the second officer ran back to the police car. Even though one of the pulses hit his right leg, the officer reached his vehicle and opened the door. He tapped the mic on his badge to call for backup. However, he was suddenly hit in the chest and head with repeated bursts before he could say anything. He fell onto the seat of the car and then the ground.

Nevertheless, the dispatcher at the station heard him groan and sent two other police cruisers to the scene which she pinpointed by GPS. Then, she tried to find out what was happening. "Officer Begin! Officer Goldbloom! Are you there? Are you okay?"

Officer Lemuel Begin, thirty nine years old and the father of a newborn son, moaned once more, but could not speak.

"Hold tight," the dispatcher said. "Help is on the way!" She then sent an ambulance to the same coordinates.

Inside the Brotherhood ambulance, Ariel struggled against the straps that bound her to the gurney, while Grace screamed! As wand bursts pummeled the vehicle, Grace fell to the ambulance floor and cried out through her tears, "Help us, Lord Jesus! Help us! Please! Help us!"

When the pulses momentarily ceased, Officer Palti Goldbloom returned fire. Meanwhile, the brotherhood soldier changed the setting on his wand to "destroy!"

"Then those whose balance of good deeds) is heavy—they will attain salvation: But those whose balance is light, will be those who have lost their souls; In Hell will they abide."
Qur'an 23:102-103

CHAPTER 99

WORST CASE REALITY. . .

I nside the hospital, Abdul and Sam received the urgent bulletin on their 3DHP's. The leaders watched and listened together. Wordless, the men stood dumbfounded at the unprecedented scale of terror and death in the United States.

Sam finally managed to eke out a few words. "None of this seems real. How do we deal with such destruction and loss of life on such a massive scale? The U.S.—no nation—has ever faced such catastrophe so swiftly!"

"Mark once told me," Abdul solemnly uttered, "the reason why he thought the United States of America seems to be omitted from end times prophecies."

Equally as subdued, Sam asked, "Why is that?"

"Because there will not be a United States of America when the end comes! After what has been unleashed on the states today, maybe America will soon no longer exist!"

Trying to absorb the enormity of the terror strikes, Sam said, "Even if you were certain that America would not be here at the end times, you could not let that fact stop you from doing everything in your power as President to preserve the nation and its people!"

Abdul agreed, saying, "True! And we will indeed fight against this evil incarnate until it is either eradicated or we die in the attempt to eradicate it."

"Addar seems to be taking the old Muslim ploy of crying for peace while prosecuting war at an entirely new level!"

"Sam, you can take evil in its most heinous and vile form and place it in a beautiful box. You can wrap that beautiful box in even more lovely paper, and then top it with a gorgeous bow and the sweetest of cards. But whoever opens that pretty package will be utterly destroyed by the absolutely grotesque evil within it!"

"What are you trying to say, Abdul?"

"Evil trusts no friend, and it only serves as an ally when it faces a common enemy. But once that enemy is defeated, evil turns on its former ally and relishes the ultimate and most atrocious betrayal! Evil's most tantalizing, most satisfying act? Betrayal!"

With a pensive look on his face, Sam said, "I'm still not sure if I follow what you are saying."

"Y'shua said, 'Those who live by the sword will die by the sword.' So I say, Addar is living by evil and he will die by that same evil. The abomination Addar has unleashed from his beautiful, peaceful Muslim box will not only destroy the enemies of Islam, but it will destroy Islam as well!

"Addar has betrayed us, for peace never was his goal. He has always craved power, absolute power! He worships power, not Allah! However, Addar fails to realize that he does not control the nefarious iniquity he believes he wields, but that evil itself rules over him! When evil no longer needs him, evil will destroy him."

"I see! You are saying Satan is using Addar to accomplish his goals, and that when Addar no longer serves the devil's purposes, Addar will be annihilated!"

"In the most loathsome and heinous way imaginable—or unimaginable," Abdul replied.

"Sam, the only way out of this war is to counter absolute evil with absolute good! But we do not have the luxury of waiting for all the Muslims to find Isa. Addar is obviously going to do everything in his power to destroy America. Likewise, just as obviously, one of two things is true: Addar either has someone—or many someones—with access causing our weapons to detonate wherever they are or he may yet have control over our weapons system, despite our efforts to thwart him! Worse yet, as a third possibility, maybe he has operatives detonating our weapons as well as cyber-control over the weapons system—but how can that be with the shutdown of the ultranet?"

"I don't know, yet redundancy does have its military advantages."

"None of this makes sense, Sam! How can any of this be happening? Our weapons control system has been recalibrated. It responds to our commands."

"I don't have an answer, Abdul. Even so, what Addar can do in America, he can likely do here, as well."

"I know Addar is a professional liar, but I would have sworn than his panic was real when he talked to us about peace and averting war in Ahava's hospital room. Do you think we could be wrong? Could someone else be vying for power with Addar? These tactics of today differ from those we have seen already. Entire cadres of weapons have exploded simultaneously. None of the weapons were launched. Instead, they exploded either in transit or inside the sub."

"Let's think as clearly as possible in this chaos, Abdul. Let's expand your theory. In these three attacks on the U.S., the weapon's control system would not have been needed. The missiles in the convoy could have been detonated by other means, such as rigging the weapons with other explosive devices—remotely controlled or timed devices. The MHT was carrying fuel and toxic chemicals. It became a weapon due to the ultra high speed crash—and maybe with remote controlled explosive devices—like the missiles. Even on the sub, someone on site could have manually activated the torpedoes and mines."

With the help of Sam, Abdul's thoughts were clearing. "So what you are saying is that while our weapons systems may be under our control, Addar—or someone who wants to challenge Addar— is using people on the inside to attack us."

"Mr. President, I don't know of a better explanation at this point."

Still unaccustomed to his new title, Abdul paused before saying, "I think we must assume that the Brotherhood has permeated all levels of our military and that the same is true for our weapon's control systems. I think we must assume that we may have two rivals vying for power over Babylon. I think we must assume that the strikes in the U.S. today could have been made by Addar's opponent. I think we must assume the worst!"

"If we assume the worst, Abdul, can we find a way to defeat this enemy? Can we somehow give the Brotherhood a taste of its own medicine?"

The President's face suddenly brightened, as he said, "Sam, you are a genius!"

"I am?"

"You just proposed an excellent idea! Babylon is literally littered with weapons, but the Brotherhood does not know how to use them. Suppose we show that we can play their game by sending in clandestine forces to detonate those weapons where they are? The Brotherhood Army is housing its men at all the military bases in Europe and Asia. We can give them a sudden and spectacular wake up call, Sam! You are brilliant!"

"If I am a brilliant genius, you would think I would have an estimate of how long it would take to pull off an undercover operation like you just described!"

"Don't worry, Sam! Such tactical details are the job of our military experts. Even with the destruction of the Pentagon and so much loss of our military's brain power, our special services units are intact. They will be able to take on this work. And, Sam, your special services units are legendary! Plus, they are right next door to Babylon!"

"I suppose turnabout is fair play!"

"All is fair in love and war, is it not?"

"As long as we overcome evil with good and do not let ourselves be overcome by evil."

"Excellent and timely point, Sam. Where do we find that fine line we must walk as followers of Isa? How do we defeat evil without compromising our own souls?"

"Y'shua gave His very life to ultimately defeat evil, Abdul. Maybe we will give our very lives to these final battles, until the quintessential battle that Y'shua will lead that will end in the absolute destruction of absolute evil."

Nodding his head in agreement, Abdul said, "The immediate battle ahead of us just seems so overwhelming!"

"Don't you think that Y'shua felt the same anguish we now feel when He was on the cross?"

Sighing, Abdul answered, "But He knew what was on the other side of His cross!"

"Don't you know what is on the other side of your cross, as well, Abdul? Life without end in the very presence of our God and King! Remember, Abdul, as much as Y'shua gave to save the people of this world, many—no most of them—did not and will not receive His offer of forgiveness and life. Nonetheless, Y'shua gave His all, under unimaginable suffering, to save everyone who would believe in Him. No cost to Him was too great."

"Isa does say that we must take up our own crosses to be His disciples."

"Right! And we must give Him our all in the battle ahead, no matter how many or how few lives are saved. Y'shua bore our sin and the evil of this world on His cross. Surely, we can bear the present vestiges of that evil—especially when we consider that Y'shua yet holds the lion's share of the weight on His shoulders! After all, He is the Lion of Judah!"

Abdul looked directly into Sam's eyes. "How did you acquire so much knowledge and insight so quickly, Sam?"

"Like you, my brother, I listened to many believers talk about life with Y'shua—long before I decided that He is the one, true Messiah!"

"I know what you mean! I had heard so much about Isa before I met Him on Air Force One!"

"He has been preparing us for many years, Abdul. I may not be allowed to remain as Prime Minister, but as long as I hold this office, I will use it to glorify Y'shua in every decision I make!"

"That is what is important, isn't it—His glory in all things?"

"I believe that in the depths of my soul, Abdul."

"I can tell that you do, Sam! Okay, so how do we glorify Isa in the war against evil that has been thrust upon us?"

"From our standpoint, this war's goal is to save as many souls as possible, even in the midst of such massive physical death and carnage!"

Abdul took a deep breath and said, "Our nations have been thrown into such a tangled web! As we fight to save lives, we will take lives. As we battle for souls, many of them will die without knowing Isa!"

"But like Him, we must do all we can to help save as many who will believe—on both sides."

"A moment ago, you said Y'shua could see beyond His cross. Sam, I truly believe that He would have still embraced that cross, even if

Heaven did not await Him on the other side. I believe He would have given His life just as freely and fully, even if that cross was the beginning of torment and torture without end. Such is the depth of the love of our Saviour!"

"That's food for some deep spiritual thought."

"Maybe one day we can pick up this part of our conversation again, but for now, we must focus on the battle ahead, Sam. In the U.S, we have an enemy—maybe one, maybe two—who has either regained at least some control of our weaponry or who has control of the people who are in charge of that weaponry or both. We have untold numbers of jihadists within the ranks of our military branches, the various levels of our government, and the leadership of our critical industries. We face men who will gladly die in horrendous fashion to take as many of our people out of this life with them. Plus, the nation has been devastated by unquantifiable destruction and death."

Deeply sighing, Sam replied, "That pretty much sums it up, save for one more crucial point. The same scenario may be true for Israel. The next shoe could drop at any moment within our borders."

"True. Thus, we must be prepared at all times for all possibilities. Likewise, if we are going to use Babylon's weapons against them, time is of the essence. We need to alert our military chiefs to get our special forces in action."

"Abdul, we also have other variables. For all we know, with all the scientists, military experts, and engineers the Brotherhood has subjected to Babylon's will, we may soon be facing attacks by land, sea, and air. Our famed missile defense shield will help protect us in that situation, if it is not sabotaged. Even so, we may be facing the reality of Goliath in the coming days. How would either of our nations counter Goliath?"

Abdul paused and then said, "We must hope that our intel is right. All our sources say that both those possibilities you mention remain only possibilities—at least for now. I think we must start with what we know, Mr. Prime Minister. In that light, what is our first step?"

"We pray!"

"... 'Who do you say I am?'"
Luke 9:20

CHAPTER 100

CHARGING INTO
THE UNKNOWN...

*O*utside the hospital, Mark met and embraced his fatigued but, most gratefully, alive wife and daughter. "Thank you, Lord! Thank you once more for saving the lives of those so precious to me!"

Holding tightly to her father, Grace asked, "Dad, why did that Brotherhood soldier's car explode?"

Mark answered, "As far as we know, he had set his wand to destroy. Apparently, he wanted to obliterate ambulance with you, your mom, and Officer Goldbloom inside it. However, the wand apparently mal-functioned, and destroyed the soldier and his vehicle, instead. These weapons, after all, are still in their prototype testing stage."

"What is a wand, Dad?"

"I'm sorry, Babe. I should have realized you don't know about these devices. A wand is a new, top secret weapon. It has not been fully tested yet, as demonstrated today. A wand can stun, kill, vaporize, and utterly destroy."

Accepting his answer, Grace then inquired, "What about Officer Begin? Will he make it?"

Letting go of Grace and Ariel, Mark replied, "He's in surgery now. We pray that he will pull through, even though he was blasted in his chest and head. The Brotherhood soldier who saved the Prime Minister's life yet clings to life after suffering similar injuries. Let's hope the same holds true for Officer Begin."

Ariel took her daughter's hand in her own. She said "Grace, if you had not driven that ambulance, then you and I might not be alive right now! Thank you for your quick response to the opportunity given to you. However, young lady, don't think you are going to get to drive like that back home!"

The three of them laughed—a much needed laugh to break through all the tension of such bitterly sensational days. Grace bragged, "Maybe I can drive at the Atlanta Motor Speedway or Talladega Superspeedway. Those NASCAR drivers don't have anything on me, now! Officer Goldbloom called me a brave young woman and a helluva driver! He showed a lot of kindness to us and even drove us back to the hospital."

"Officer Goldbloom hit the nail on the head, Grace! You have displayed great courage since this craziness began!" said Ariel.

Mark smiled and added, "For all you have been through, you have epitomized courage under fire!" As the grateful and loving father gazed into his daughter's eyes, his smile began to fade. Closing his eyes, he said, "We will be leaving the hospital soon and heading back home."

"I just don't know if Grace and I can sit up all night on that long flight," Ariel said with apprehension. "We haven't slept since Saturday night!"

"I know how you feel," Mark said with empathy. "So I have some good news for you—for all of us! We won't have to sit up at all if we do not want to do so because we are flying back with President Abdullah on Air Force One!"

Confused, Grace noted, "I thought Air Force One no longer existed, Dad. How can we fly on it?"

"There are several Presidential jets in the U.S., Grace. Whichever one the President boards becomes Air Force One."

"Oh, so one of those jets was flown here to pick up President Abdullah?"

"No, but any other aircraft that the President boards also becomes Air Force One! Actually, Prime Minister Ben Baruch will loan the President his official jet. This jet has bedrooms, all the comforts of home, and even a tip-top medical clinic. Plus, *Ahad Y'sra'el,* Israel One, comes with its own missile defense system and capability to fire on predators, just in case our escorting Israeli Air Force jets need extra help."

With great concern, Ariel asked, "Even so, Mark, given what happened to President Paulson, will Abdul be safe—will we?"

"Sam has chosen two of the IAF's most trusted pilots to sit in the cockpit of *Ahad Y'sra'el*. Plus, four more such pilots will escort us in the best and fastest fighter jets in the IAF's fleet. All these XK-23's, including Israel One, have hypersonic speed, unlike the old, lumbering jet that brought us here. We will fly home in record time—faster than anyone can chase us!" Then Mark whispered, "Plus, the best news is that these five jets all have stealth capability. We will be flying home invisibly—at least to Babylon. So, I think you can agree that we will be very safe!"

"I did not know that we had stealth or hypersonic jets!" Ariel noted. "I thought the technology proved to be too expensive, and that both programs had been dropped years ago by both the U.S. and Israel!"

"Sshh—keep your voice down!" Mark said with his forefinger touching his lips. "Top secret information must be kept top secret, Ariel! We never know who may be listening around here!"

"Oh boy! We will be cloaked!" Grace said softly.

"You are excited about that prospect, I assume?" Mark asked.

"Of course I am!" The thirteen year old said with excitement. Then her face dropped. "I will not be able to tell a soul about this flight, will I, Dad?"

"Sorry, Sugar. We have been entrusted with a great secret!"

Grace perked up. "Well, I guess we are kind of like secret agents, now!"

The three of them laughed once more. Mark said between his chuckles, "No one should suspect us of being spies—at least not based on our physical appearance!"

Once the laughter subsided, in a more serious tone, Grace asked, "Why did the Brotherhood kidnap Mom and me now that the General is dead? He had the personal vendetta against our family."

"Unfortunately, I don't know how to answer your question, Honey! Maybe someone else wants to fulfill the *fatwa* the General declared on our family. Hatred is quite contagious, you know."

"Will we be safe at home? Will the Muslims continue to hunt us down? Will we be safe given all that has happened there, Dad? So much of America and so many Americans no longer exist! Mom and I heard about all that happened today as we rode back here with Officer Goldbloom."

Mark wrapped his arms around his wife and his wise and maturing daughter. "Honey, we and your little brothers will be very safe. We are in Jesus' Hands! No place is safer! Plus, Abdul has asked me to be his personal spiritual advisor. As such, we will have government protection!"

"Abdul wants you to serve in his administration?" Ariel asked with surprise. "Why didn't you tell us?"

"I just did! Abdul asked me to take the position while you two were speeding to and from Jericho! I would have called, but you two had to lead terrorists on high speed chases—you thrill seekers!"

Again, all three of them laughed.

Grace beamed and said, "Wow, Dad! I am proud of you!"

"Thank you, Sweetie! That means a lot coming from you!"

Ariel smiled in agreement.

At that moment, Sam, Abdul, Sol, and Ahava walked out of the hospital lobby.

Grace ran to Sam and hugged him. With genuine excitement, she said, "Thank you for helping us go home safely!"

Sam, who did not expect the earnest expression of appreciation, blushed and said, "My pleasure, Grace! You have demonstrated so much courage that I hope you will consider serving with the IDF some day!"

Abdul interrupted and countered, "Sam, I have first dibs on this great soldier!"

Now everyone chuckled and Grace was the one to blush this time. These seven believers had been through so much together. Indeed, they were bound together like soldiers serving side-by-side and watching each others' backs on the battlefield.

Grace posed a question for Sam. "Mr. Prime Minister, what will happen to you now that you are a follower of Y'shua? Will you still lead Israel?"

Sam grinned at Grace and answered her directly. "I will talk to the leaders of my party tomorrow to discuss whether they want me to continue as their leader and as Prime Minister. Whatever happens tomorrow, I know it will be part of Y'shua's plan for me, my family, and the nation."

Grace nodded her head and said, "Who could Y'shua find who would be better at your job than you?"

"Maybe you should come with me to my meeting tomorrow!"

More laughter erupted.

Ahava looked up at Abdul and asked, "Mr. President, what is first on your agenda?"

The smile drifted from Abdul's face as he answered. "I'll address our nation yet again, this time while aboard *Yisra'el Ahad*. The people of the United States suffer from shock, grief, and disbelief. We have faced so much death and destruction. With these latest attacks, life as we knew it has stopped there. None of us can yet fathom all that has transpired in such a short time. Truly, nothing like these horrific events has ever happened to any nation and its citizens. Never before in the history of humanity has so much evil and destruction been released at once!"

Looking for hope and reassurance in the eyes of his best friends, Abdul then said, "I need to lay out a plan for our next steps. Sam and I are forging that path together." The President turned to the Prime Minister, saying, "I owe you a great debt of gratitude, and I will be praying that you remain as Prime Minister. I will do anything needed to help you hold on to your office! However, should you be forced to step down, which would be a most foolish action by your party or the coalition government, you have a job waiting for you as a personal advisor to the President of the United States."

Sam smiled, saying, "You have so much on your plate, Abdul. That you would make such an offer at this time is truly humbling for me." A tear streamed down Sam's right cheek. "After all, without you, I would not be alive today—in body or in soul! I owe you both my physical life and my spiritual life!"

"You realize, Sam, that I may not be accepted as President by the people of the United States. If I know Addar, he is already at work figuring out how to either remove me from office or remove me from this life!"

No one said a word for a few moments. They all realized how much they loved and respected each other.

Grace broke the silence by asking Sol, "And what are you and Miss Ahava going to do now?" Sol watched his bride's face redden. No one had ever called her "Miss Ahava" before.

Sol turned to answer Grace. "Well, after seeing my baptism, the powers that be have not so politely informed me that my former services to the synagogue will no longer be needed! So Ahava and I, being young in faith, if not in body, want to gather with some other believers and form a new Messianic house of worship!"

"You mean a church?" Grace asked.

"As we say here, a congregation. The word church brings up many tough memories and images of rough history for Jews. But yes, we feel Y'shua wants us start a new body of believers!"

Sam chimed in, saying, "I'll be the first member! Plus, I hope I can count on you to be my new Religious Services Minster—if I stay in office."

Everyone smiled, as Sam patted Sol on the back. Ahava gazed at her husband with great pride in her eyes.

Setting a more serious tone, Mark noted, "Actually none of us know what we will be doing in the days ahead, as the last several days have proven to us. Be that as it may, we do know one thing: we are bound together in Isa, Y'shua, Jesus! He stands firm as our hope and peace, our power and our purpose! And somehow, I believe we will be together again, as He reveals His plans for each of us from this point! Our Lord brought us together for a reason, and while we have needed each other and helped each other thus far, I believe that none of us can anticipate how He will use us, both apart and together, in the coming days, weeks, months, and years—if He grants those to us."

The wailing sounds of the sirens interrupted Mark's poignant words. Without the protection of the ID2MDS missile shield, the sirens meant the friends had ten seconds to flee to the safety of the bomb shelter before the incoming hypersonic weapon slammed into its target!

As they started to close the door to the shelter, Addar yelled from outside, "Wait for me!"

ABOUT THE AUTHOR

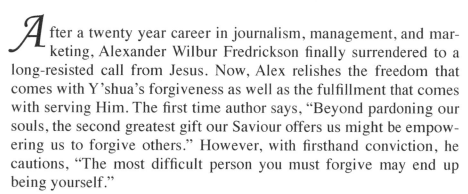

*A*fter a twenty year career in journalism, management, and marketing, Alexander Wilbur Fredrickson finally surrendered to a long-resisted call from Jesus. Now, Alex relishes the freedom that comes with Y'shua's forgiveness as well as the fulfillment that comes with serving Him. The first time author says, "Beyond pardoning our souls, the second greatest gift our Saviour offers us might be empowering us to forgive others." However, with firsthand conviction, he cautions, "The most difficult person you must forgive may end up being yourself."

For the last eighteen years, Alex has gratefully ministered as both a pastor and a missionary. The honors seminary graduate has planted a church, led three other congregations, served in nine countries on 21 mission trips, and founded his own missions ministry. He leads mission teams to Israel and also conducts tours of the Holy Sites.

Likewise, Alex serves with Muslims in the Middle East, and at the same time, often speaks on behalf of persecuted Christians in those lands. With great enthusiasm, Alex notes, "My own eyes have witnessed how the love of our Lord—Isa, Y'shua, Jesus—breaks down the walls between Muslims, Jews, and Christians. Not only can we live in peace together, but we can also serve our King as one to redeem the fallen world around us!"

CPSIA information can be obtained at www.ICGtesting.com
Printed in the USA
LVOW011917210213

320998LV00001B/1/P